The Tower

Book One of the
Gulf Coast Tarot Mystery series

Irene McGarvie

The Tower

Book One of the
Gulf Coast Tarot Mystery series

Irene McGarvie

Nixon-Carre Ltd.
Toronto, ON

Library and Archives Canada Cataloguing in Publication

McGarvie, Irene, 1957-
     The tower / Irene McGarvie.

(Book one of the Gulf Coast tarot mystery series)
ISBN 978-1-926826-34-9

     I. Title. II. Series: McGarvie, Irene, 1957- . Gulf Coast tarot mystery series ; bk. 1.

PS8625.G385T68 2013   C813'.6   C2013-900167-0

Published by:
Nixon-Carre Ltd.
Toronto, Ontario, Canada

www.nixon-carre.com

Distributed by Ingram

Disclaimer:
This book is a work of fiction. Names, characters, places and incidents either are the product of the author's imagination or are used fictitiously, and any resemblance to actual persons living or dead, events, or locales is entirely coincidental.

General Notice:
Any product names used in this book are for identification purposes only and may be registered trademarks, or trade names of their respective owners. The author, Irene McGarvie, and the publisher, Nixon-Carre Ltd. disclaim any and all rights in those marks.

Printed and bound in the USA

Thanks

I would like to thank the many people who have been instrumental in helping me complete this book:

My friend and fellow ukulele addict Charlene Matyjakowski, who read and re-read the manuscript for me and who became almost as obsessed with the characters as I am. For the record, this Mrs. Matyjakowski does not have pink flamingos on her lawn but I'm working on her.

My friend Sue Rogge who gave me the benefit of her understanding of the Tarot, and double checked my interpretations of the Tarot readings in this book.

The friends who nagged me mercilessly to hurry up and complete it, Chantal Patenaude, Sharon Whyte, Sharon Russell, Maryann Steiner, and Jackie Avis.

The folks at the Pinellas County Sheriff's Department who helped me get the procedural details right. I'm not naming any of you so that you won't be embarrassed if I've messed up anything, but you know who you are.

The great guy at the Erie County Medical Examiner's office who was kind enough to spend time discussing the intricacies of decomposing bodies and autopsy procedures. I'm not naming you either so you won't be embarrassed if I've messed up any of the details, but you know who you are.

My brother Bill, who was instrumental in convincing me that I really can write fiction.

My apologies to my brother Alan who is a lawyer, and is one of the sweetest men I know. He is definitely NOT the model for any of the sleazy, wife-swapping lawyers in this book.

The friends who enjoy spending time reading about and discussing murder and sex. I love you guys. What a bunch of demented perverts we are. (Hey Megan, I haven't forgotten you, you're in this category.)

Finally, I'd like to thank all of my friends and their dysfunctional families and sociopathic relatives who have given me enough inspirational material to keep me writing for the rest of my life.

Irene McGarvie
Florida, 2013

Chapter 1

The body of the first woman washed up on the shore of Lake Erie at dawn. A fisherman discovered it as he was preparing to launch his small boat for what would probably be the last nice day of fishing for the season. The body was tangled up with rope, and in such a state of decomposition, that at first he didn't know what he was looking at; he thought some garbage or a large fish had washed up. It wasn't until he got closer that he understood what he was seeing.

When the report of the discovery of the body came out on the news, the killer was disturbed that it had surfaced so quickly. That was not part of the plan. He had expected that it would take months, if ever, for any evidence to surface, and by then he would be long gone. The intense media coverage the first few days after the discovery almost caused him to abort his plans, but as time went on and no additional evidence surfaced he began to relax, and when no police came around questioning him, his confidence returned. His façade was perfect, no one suspected him of anything. Just a few more loose ends to tie up, the plan would still work. Everything was still on schedule, and he was determined to be much more careful in the future.

With any luck the next one would never be found.

The Tarot cards were laid out face down in formation on the table between the two women. The dark haired woman began turning over the cards to expose the pictures.

Puzzled, the two women studied the cards laid down on the table in front of them.

This doesn't look very good, they both thought.

1

The teacher's voice broke into their thoughts.

"Okay class, let's pack it up early today. That snow out there is looking nasty. Be sure to write down the cards so that you can analyze the spread carefully this week at home. See if you agree with your partner's analysis," said the teacher.

"Excuse me, Helen, before we go could you just take a look at what Myrosia and I have here? It looks pretty disturbing to me, but maybe I've gotten it wrong..."

The drive out to the lake house had been treacherous. It was snowing heavily, with blowing snow forming huge drifts across the roads. The Skyway was closed so she had to take the longer route down Ohio Street to Fuhrman Blvd. then out to Route 5. What normally would have been a fifteen minute drive took more than an hour. So, although the class had ended well before nine, it was after ten p.m. when Myrosia pulled up to the curving, snow covered driveway of the stately lake front home. The snow plow had just been by and had deposited a large mound of snow at the end of the driveway.

Damn, Buffalo, New York. in January. Thank god for 4-wheel drive, she thought as she forced her Mercedes SUV through the pile of snow into the driveway.

The house itself was not visible from the road, but as she turned the bend on the long driveway the house came into view.

The grounds were lit up by the yard lights, and a few of the interior lights had gone on with a timer, but she could tell from one glance at the house that no one was home.

Working late again, she thought. I spend so much time alone in this house I might as well be single. He's always out with clients.

The automatic door rumbled open and, as she pulled into the enormous heated garage, she noticed with surprise that not only was her husband's Cadillac Escalade missing from its usual parking spot, but his summer car, the blue Porsche 911, was missing from its spot as well. Her sporty little Mini Cooper convertible was still sitting in its winter parking spot.

That's odd, she thought. The Porsche was there this morning when I left, and Dave never mentioned that he was taking it anywhere.

She felt a momentary rush of alarm. Had it been stolen? But then she realized that the little burglar alarm light was flashing green. Everything was fine. He must have taken it in for servicing.

Pulling off her winter boots in the vestibule, she noticed that the small signed Picasso drawing was missing from its prominent spot near the door.

"Oh my god, we've been robbed!" she cried out as she realized that all the paintings were missing from the walls.

She froze in panic. Could the burglars still be in the house? No, that was impossible. There were no tracks in the snow. Her SUV had been the only vehicle in or out since the snow storm began a few hours earlier. The fear and panic eased off, only to be followed by feelings of anger at being violated.

The phone was in her hand and she was already punching the speed dial to reach her husband's cell phone as she surveyed what was missing. Everything of any real value was gone! All the paintings, the sculptures, and even the Provasi furniture that they had bought in Italy were all gone. The furniture in the family room was still there, but that wasn't worth much. Those were just some of the original pieces of furniture from early in their marriage and the kids had pretty much worn them out over the years. She had been planning to replace all of it before their daughter's wedding in June.

She felt a twinge of relief when she saw that the dining room table that had belonged to her mother was still there. It wasn't worth much, but it held great sentimental value for her, memories of Sunday dinners with the family back when her father and her brother were still alive. The china cabinet was still sitting there, and a quick glance reassured her that all of her mother's china was still in its place.

She got her husband's voice mail. "Dave, I've got to speak to you right away. Call me right back! I just got home and we've had a burglary. We've been robbed! Everything's gone! Everything! I'm not sure what to do. I guess I should call the police. I wish you were here to help me with this."

Confused, her eyes caught on the burglar alarm sensor on the wall. Still flashing green, how was that possible? Had she reset it when she came in? No. Then why hadn't it gone off when the burglary happened?

Useless piece of crap! What a waste of money. Wait till I get my hands on those crooks that own that security company. We've been paying them for years for nothing, she thought.

"I'm gonna sue you!" she shouted in impotent rage at the flashing green light on the burglar alarm.

She knew it was an idle threat. All her years being married to a lawyer and working at a prestigious law firm had convinced her that the only ones who really win in a lawsuit are the lawyers.

She walked into her husband's main floor study. It was empty. Even the file cabinets were gone. All that was left were some worthless paperback books lying in piles on the floor.

This must have been some operation, she thought in amazement. With two men and a moving van it would have taken them all day. They must have known our schedule. She shivered at the thought of someone watching their movements and taking the time to know their schedules well enough to know when the house would be empty.

She could see the marks left in the cream colored carpet by the dolly used to move the heavy oak file cabinets.

I could understand someone taking the file cabinets. They were expensive and impossible to trace, but why would someone want the files, she thought.

She punched the speed dial again and got the familiar voice mail. "Dave, where the hell are you? Have you got your phone turned off? I need to speak to you right away. It's worse than I thought. Even the files in your office are gone!" Her voice raised in pitch as her frustration at not being able to reach him increased.

Finally, she punched in the speed dial to get the office answering service.

"Hello, this is Myrosia Walker. Would you please page Mr. Walker and tell him to call home immediately. It's an emergency," she said in the most professional tone she could muster under the circumstances.

"I'm sorry Mrs. Walker. Mr. Walker left specific instructions that he was not to be disturbed this evening."

"What do you mean he is not to be disturbed? I'm his wife and this is an emergency!" she replied.

Furious, she hung up the phone. That answering service had to go. What kind of incompetents were they hiring to represent the firm? She made a mental note to start looking into finding a new service.

What should she do? She didn't know if she should call the police before she spoke to Dave. She wasn't accustomed to being unable to consult with him over something this important. They had been married for almost 24 years and working together in his law office for the last 15 years. He was such a control freak; he insisted that she consult with him on everything. He hated when she tried to make any decisions on her own. He wouldn't even let her choose paint colors for the guest room without checking with him.

Why couldn't she reach him? He lived with his phone on his hip. He never turned it off, and he checked for emails and text messages continually. He was always staring at that thing, so why couldn't she reach him?

She tried texting him. "Call me, emergency, robbery."

As she waited for him to call her back, she wandered around the main floor surveying what was missing when it suddenly struck her as odd that the thieves had been so neat and careful. Nothing was broken, and the place hadn't been ransacked.

She called her husband's best friend and business partner, who was one of the other lawyers in the office, and got him on his cell phone.

"Hi Bob, it's Myrosia. Sorry to call you so late, but is Dave with you?" she asked.

"No, he's not. I haven't seen him since I left the office at noon. Is there anything I can help you with?" he replied.

"Didn't he have a dinner meeting with you and Peter and the guys from the McKinley Group?" she asked.

"No, I was in court all afternoon and I've been home here alone all evening. I don't know what he's working on, but I'm sure he'll be home shortly. He probably just got slowed down by the snow."

"Yes, I'm sure you're right," she replied uncertainly, thinking back to their conversation at the breakfast table when he had told her about his evening plans. "But I just got home and we've had a major robbery at the house, and I can't reach Dave to ask him what to do."

The lawyer in Bob suddenly kicked in.

"Myrosia, you might be in danger, they could still be in the house with you. I think you should go out to your car and call the police."

"No, no, there's no one here. There were no tracks in the snow when I came in. This must have happened hours ago. But everything's gone," she replied.

"What do you mean 'everything's gone?'" he asked.

"I mean everything. The place is practically empty. Just the old furniture is left… All the art, everything from Dave's study, even the file cabinets."

"Have you called the police?" he asked.

"No, I was trying to reach Dave to see what I should do."

"Let me take care of it. I'll call someone I know over at the Sheriff's office and report it. I'll call you back. In the meantime just relax, and don't clean anything up or touch anything. Why don't you just sit down and have a drink, and I'll call Peter and Keith and see if I can track Dave down for you," he said.

"Yes, okay, thanks. I could use a drink right now."

Peter Donovan and Keith MacKenzie were the other two partners in her husband's law firm. The four of them had been friends since law school and had decided to go into business together a few years after graduation. The arrangement had worked well. They each maintained their own independent specialties within the practice while sharing overhead expenses. It gave them the appearance of a large firm and the prestige that went with it without the years of drudgery that most lawyers have to endure before being made partner.

Hanging up the phone, she went to the big wine fridge in the kitchen. Empty.

As she ran down the basement stairs to get a bottle of wine

from the wine cellar she noticed that the exercise equipment and all the weights were gone.

How odd, she thought, what kind of thieves would go to the trouble of stealing free weights?

All the wine was missing from the wine cellar.

As she was standing there, staring at the empty room that this morning had held hundreds of bottles of wine, the phone in her hand rang.

Oh finally, she thought, Bob must have gotten a hold of him.

"Myrosia, it's me." said Bob. "I haven't been able to track down Dave, but I called my friend at the Sheriff's office and they're sending someone right over."

"Bob, even the wine is gone. All of it, and Dave's exercise equipment, the weights and everything," she said.

Just then a terrible thought struck her. "Were the contents of the safe okay?"

"Oh my god, I haven't looked upstairs. Let me call you back."

She ran upstairs. It was the same up there. All the cheap pieces of art were left on the walls, but the expensive items were gone. The expensive pieces of furniture were gone, and only the older pieces remained. She ran into the bedroom. The closet doors were wide open. The shoe rack was pulled away from the wall. The safe that was hidden behind it was open... and empty!

It wasn't until then that she noticed that one side of their enormous walk-in closet was empty. All of his clothes were gone.

She backed out of the closet, sat down on his side of the bed and pulled open his bedside table. Empty.

She jumped up and frantically pulled open all the drawers in the dressers. Her things all seemed to be in place, but his were gone.

A piece of paper sitting on her pillow caught her attention. She sat down on the bed and began to read:

Myrosia,
This isn't working for me. I've found someone else.
I'll be in touch in a few days.
Dave

7

She sat there in shock, too stunned to recognize any emotion. They'd had breakfast together this morning. Everything had seemed fine. He never let on that there was anything bothering him. They each had taken their own vehicles to the office because she was going to her Tarot class that night and he said he had a dinner meeting with some clients who were putting together a big real estate deal. Everything seemed fine when he left for the courthouse shortly after noon. He had even called her at the office in the middle of the afternoon. He had left her with a ton of work on her desk and she worked her way through it methodically until it was time to meet her friend Joanna and catch a bite of dinner before their class.

Looking around, she realized that this wasn't a spur of the moment breakup. Dave was a meticulous planner and obviously he had been planning this for ages. How had she not seen it coming? She lay down on the bed and began to sob. The full impact of what had happened began to sink in. The tears began streaming down her face until another terrible thought hit her.

She jumped up and ran into her study and turned on her computer.

"Come on, come on," she shouted in frustration as she waited for the computer to boot up. When the computer finally came on she went straight to their bank web site. Just as she feared, the bank account was in overdraft. She checked the other bank where they had some investments. The accounts had been closed. Next she went to check the business account, but her password wouldn't work. She tried it three times, but it was no use. She could not get in.

She sobbed in frustration as she sat there pondering her next move, when her thoughts were interrupted by the doorbell.

She looked out the window and saw a Sheriff's deputy standing on the steps while another one stood a bit further back on the driveway surveying the yard. She jumped up and splashed some cold water on her face and did her best to wipe the tears from her eyes before she ran downstairs and opened the door.

"Mrs. Walker? We got a report of a burglary. May we come in?"

"Oh, uh, of course," she said as she held the door open for them.

"We got a call from Bob Williams that you've had a break-in. What seems to be missing?"

"Oh, uh, yes, I wasn't sure what to do so I called Bob right away. Bob is one of my husband's partners in their law practice. I couldn't reach my husband so I called Bob."

She paused as she tried to collect her thoughts. The two stone-faced deputies waited.

"Well, uh, when I walked in and saw that everything was gone, I thought it was a burglary, but, uh, then I found this note."

Her face flushed as she handed the note to the deputy.

The deputy read the note and handed it to his partner. There was an awkward silence as the two men surveyed what they could see of the almost empty house.

"Well, this seems to be a domestic matter and there's not much we can do about that," he paused, "but I guess we should make a report in case the matter winds up in court. Would you mind if we had a little look around?" he said as he handed back the note.

"No, please do."

"Is there any sign of forced entry? Anything vandalized?"

"Uh, no. I guess that's part of what confused me when I walked in and saw the place like this," Myrosia explained.

"We'll just take a quick look around and make sure that the building is secured for you."

A few moments later they had completed their cursory inspection. As they left one of the deputies took a look at her red eyes and flushed cheeks and said, "Is there anyone you can call to come and stay with you tonight?"

"Uh, no thank you. I'll be fine," she replied.

She watched as the police car drove out the long driveway and then picked up the phone and dialed her friend Joanna.

"Oh my god Joanna, you'll never believe what's happened," Myrosia sobbed, and proceeded to relay everything that had transpired.

"Do you want me to come out there and stay with you?" Joanna asked.

"Oh no, the roads are too dangerous, and that little tin can that you drive wouldn't make it out here tonight. I'll be fine, I'll just cry and feel sorry for myself for a little while and then I'll try to figure out what to do next. I'll call you tomorrow."

"Are you going into the office tomorrow after all this?" Joanna asked.

"That hadn't even crossed my mind; I don't know what I'm going to do. I guess maybe I should. It'd give me a chance to talk to the rest of the staff and find out what they know. It'll be interesting to see if Dave shows up there."

They hung up and next she called her daughter who was in college in Los Angeles.

"Nicki, it's Mom." She paused. "Something awful has happened. I got home about an hour ago and found a note. Your father has left me."

"Oh Mom, I really don't have time for your hysterics right now. So you and Daddy had a little fight. Big deal. I'm in the middle of exams, and I'm planning a wedding. I don't have time for this," her daughter replied.

"No, no, that's just it. We didn't have a fight. I got home and everything was gone and there was just this note saying he was leaving me," said Myrosia.

"What do you mean, 'everything's gone?'" Nicki asked.

"I mean, I am sitting on the couch in the family room and everything of value in the entire house is gone: the paintings on the walls, the big television, all the wine, everything. All gone. Even the bank accounts have been cleaned out," explained Myrosia.

"You're exaggerating. What time is it there? It must be after 11. Just get ready for bed. I'm sure Daddy will be home soon. Look, I've got to go. Leslie is coming over and we have to make some decisions about the bridesmaid's dresses. If I've got time, I'll try and call you tomorrow," said Nicki.

The phone went dead.

There was no one else to talk to. Not that talking would make any difference. She couldn't call her son Dylan. He was spending a semester studying in England, and it was the middle of the night over there. Her mother would be sound asleep in her apartment in the seniors' complex, and there was no point in waking her up and upsetting her. There would be plenty of time to tell her later. But she suspected that her mother probably wouldn't be too surprised. After all these years, she had never liked or trusted Dave.

The tears began streaming down her face. She had no idea how long she had been sitting there crying, with the phone in her hand, when the doorbell rang again. Who could that be at this time of night? she wondered.

Nervously she got up and glanced through the glass panels beside the door and saw a familiar vehicle parked in the driveway. She relaxed when she realized that the person at the door was her husband's business partner, Bob.

"I spoke to the Sheriff's deputies and they told me what happened," he said when she opened the door. "I thought I'd come out and check on you, and I figured you could probably use this." He lifted up the bottle of wine he was holding. "Or maybe even this," holding up the bottle of scotch he had in his other hand.

"I'd have sent it out by St. Bernard, but they were all busy tonight," he said.

She laughed in spite of herself, you could always count on Bob to know just exactly the right thing to do or say to lighten up any situation.

"Bob, you're a life saver. Come on in," said Myrosia.

"Just a minute, I've got some more stuff in the truck. I'll be right back," he said as he handed her the two bottles.

Before long, they were sitting in the family room in front of a roaring fire in the gas fireplace. Wine glasses filled. There were egg rolls, fried dumplings, and potato chips on the coffee table between them.

"We haven't done this since college days. It's just like old times," she said.

"Well, not quite, the booze is a lot more expensive now, and we're missing a few players," he said.

They both sat in silence staring at the flames in the fireplace as they thought about the changes that had taken place in the intervening years since college.

"Did you know that Dave was planning this?" she finally asked, breaking the silence.

He hesitated. "Well, no, not exactly. I knew that he was seeing someone, but it never occurred to me that he would just walk out on you like this."

"You knew he was seeing someone? What are you talking about? Why didn't you tell me?" she asked.

"Come on Myrosia, Dave's had one long series of women ever since college. I just assumed that you knew but chose to ignore it. I hated watching the way he treated you, but I thought the two of you had some sort of, uh, understanding," he said.

She was stunned. "An understanding? What would make you think that?" she asked.

"Well obviously you knew about his involvement with Rhyanna back in college. I remember how you reacted when you found out about that. And you knew about his assistant at the office. I just assumed that you knew, or at least suspected, about the others," he said, staring down into his drink.

"That fling he had with Rhyanna, and her suicide, well that was just dreadful. It was so tragic, but that was before we got married and he assured me that it was just a one-time mistake that he'd learned from. He vowed that once we were married he wouldn't cheat. That incident with his assistant, well, that was definitely a bad time in our lives, but when I found out about it he agreed to go to marriage counseling, and that's when I started working in the office. I really thought we had put all that behind us," she said.

They sat in silence for a few moments while she wondered how truthful her words were. Her mother never trusted Dave. Her friend Joanna couldn't stand him, and now she finds out that Bob knew all along that he had been cheating on her. Could she have really been blind to what other people could so clearly see? Had she gotten herself into this situation because she had chosen to ignore the warning signs?

"Bob, how could you of all people do this to me? Why didn't you warn me? You know how it feels to get dumped. Remember how you felt when Janice left you," she said.

Bob's wife Janice had left him a few months previously and since then he had been spending more and more time out at the lake house with Myrosia and Dave.

"I'm sorry Myrosia. I was in an awkward situation. I mean I'm friends with both of you, what could I do?" he said as he poured them each another glass. "Besides, I really thought you knew. I never thought he'd leave you. You seemed like the perfect team, both at home and at work. Let's face it, we all know that he'd never have been so successful without you."

They sat in silence again for a long time.

He kept pouring and the wine went down so easily that she never noticed that the bottle was empty and that he had started pouring scotch for her.

"Bob, he's taken everything," she finally said.

"Yes, I can see that," he said glancing around the room.

"No, I mean EVERYTHING! That bastard has cleaned out our bank accounts. He's taken everything. How could I be so stupid? Why didn't I see it coming? Especially with what I see at work every day, how could I let him do this to me?" she said.

She stood up and walked over to the mantle piece. "Look at what he left me: framed photographs of the perfect family," she said as she picked up a picture of the two of them on vacation in Hawaii.

Suddenly she screamed, "You bastard!" and threw the picture at the wall, breaking the glass.

Bob jumped up and reached out to her and she fell sobbing into his arms. With his arms around her they sat back down on the couch and talked and drank for hours.

When she woke up her head was throbbing. The snow storm was over and the sun was shining through the large expanse of glass overlooking the lake. She had a vague embarrassing recollection of kneeling in the bathroom, vomiting, while Bob held her hair back, then having him help her back to the couch. She realized that she was still lying on the couch, but now she was covered by a blanket. The empty bottles and glasses were gone from the coffee table, the broken glass was picked up, the food was gone, and there was no sign of her company from the previous night. As she made her way upstairs to the shower, the missing furniture confirmed that the events of the previous evening hadn't been a dream.

As devastating as the previous night's events had been, she knew that she couldn't allow herself to be paralyzed by self pity. She had to recover the missing money and the contents of the safe.

"Well girl," she said to herself, "take a shower, and pull yourself together. You've got a lot of work to do."

Chapter 2

Some Tylenol and two cups of coffee later, Myrosia was ready to go to the office.

The snow plows had cleared the roads, and the Skyway was open again, but still it was almost 10 am when she pulled into the underground parking lot of the building on Main Street where the law office was located. She wasn't surprised to see that Dave's car wasn't there.

Wimp, she thought. You couldn't face me.

When she stepped out of the elevator and walked into the lobby of the office it was obvious that the rest of the staff had already heard the news. Two women were leaning over the receptionist's desk whispering, but they stopped and straightened up when they saw her.

"Oh Myrosia, we just heard about you and Dave. We're so sorry," one of the women said. The other women nodded in agreement.

She wondered how they found out so quickly. Did Bob tell them? She would have thought he would have been more discrete.

"I'm surprised to see you in here today," said Cori, the receptionist, with a faint hint of a sneer.

Myrosia was struck by what a beautiful young woman the receptionist was. As always, her hair, nails, makeup and clothes all said money, obviously far more money than her job provided. For months now there had been something a little bit arrogant about her attitude and her lack of punctuality. It was like she wasn't worried about getting fired. For the first time Myrosia wondered whether Cori was Dave's new girlfriend, but no, she quickly dismissed that idea. If Cori was the other woman she wouldn't be at work today. She'd be off with Dave planning their new life with Myrosia's money.

"Well, I've got a lot of things to deal with, and what better place to start than here," she replied as she walked past them toward her office.

"Has anyone seen Dave this morning?" she asked.

"No, he hasn't come in yet. He had an appointment with one of his divorce clients but he called in to cancel that," the receptionist replied.

I'm not surprised, she thought as she went into her office and closed the door. She hung up her coat, exchanged her winter boots for some shoes and settled down at her desk.

The first matter of business was to call the bank manager.

"Hi Tony." she said when she got him on the phone. "This is Myrosia Walker. I was looking at our personal accounts and I noticed some large withdrawals yesterday. Were these withdrawals in cash or was the money transferred somewhere?"

"Yes, Dave was in yesterday afternoon and made a cash withdrawal and also made a wire transfer," he replied cautiously. "Is there a problem?"

"Oh no, no problem," She tried to make her voice sound casual. "I think Dave might have transferred those funds to the wrong account by mistake. Is it possible to have the transfer reversed? Also, can you get me the financial institution and account number that the funds were transferred to?"

"I don't think it can be reversed, but let me confirm that and call you right back. Are you at the office?" he said.

"Yes, you can reach me here," she replied.

Her next call was to their accountant.

"Steve, it's Myrosia Walker. I was just going over our finances and I was wondering if you would have a list of all of our investments and tax returns for the past few years, including my mother's investments?" she asked.

"Why do you need that? I'm sure that Dave has all that in his files," he replied.

"Yes, but his files are a bit of a mess right now. We had a temp in here who didn't work out and things are mixed up," she lied, "and I need to see them today. We are thinking about making some changes and it would be a big help if you could send me that information."

"Sure, I'll get my admin to take care of that. How many years of tax returns do you want?" he said.

"Oh, the last three years should do it," she said.

"Should I e-mail them to you at the office, or on your home e-mail?" he asked.

"Send them to both," she replied, and gave him her home e-mail address.

She hung up and thought, that was easy, obviously he hasn't heard yet.

She looked at her watch, and wondered if her friend Joanna would be able to answer her phone.

She picked up the phone and dialed.

"Hi Joanna, it's Myrosia. Is this a good time to talk?" she asked.

"Yes, my 11 o'clock didn't show up and my 12 o'clock isn't here yet, so this is a great time. I'm sitting in the stock room with my feet up," Joanna replied.

"Well, I'm at the office trying to sort out my life and I was wondering if you wanted to come over to the house tonight. I was thinking I could pick you up after work and you could stay over with me tonight, have a girl's night sleepover. I can't face being alone there tonight," Myrosia said.

"Yes, that would be great. But don't pick me up here at the shop. Pick me up at home. I want to grab a few things," Joanna replied.

"Okay, that'll work for me. I'll pick up something to take home for supper for us and then I'll pick you up at your apartment around 6:30," said Myrosia.

"So that's settled. I'll be waiting for you. But don't keep me in suspense any longer. I've gotta know. Did Dave show up at the office yet today? Did you find out who he ran off with?" asked Joanna.

"No to both questions. Right now I'm just trying to track down some money. Oh, I've gotta go. The other line is ringing. We'll talk tonight." said Myrosia.

It was the bank manager on the phone.

"Hi Myrosia, its Tony Barrucci at the bank. I'm sorry. I've

17

got some bad news. The wire transfer went through before the end of the business day yesterday and so we can't reverse it. Also, both your personal line of credit and your business line of credit are over their limits. We were about to do the automatic transfers from your accounts to cover them, but your accounts are over their limits now as well. I couldn't help but notice that your savings account has got a balance of $5 in it. Is there a problem? I know that Dave has been making some major business investments, which is why you refinanced the house back in November," he said.

"We refinanced the house in November? What you are talking about?" asked Myrosia.

"Dave made all the arrangements. You co-signed the documents. Everything was handled and witnessed through your office," he said.

"Of course Tony, it's just that we've got so much going on at the moment. It just slipped my mind. So refresh my memory. How much is the new mortgage?" asked Myrosia.

"Let me see. The property appraised at $3,900,000 and we maxed it out at close to 70% loan to value, so the new mortgage is $2,700,000. We normally wouldn't go quite that high, what with the current economic situation, but you and Dave are such good customers, and of course your parents did all their banking with us for years, so we approved it," he said.

She was momentarily stunned. This was the first she had heard anything about refinancing the mortgage. They had agreed to pay off that mortgage, not increase it. None of this made any sense. How had the appraisal come in so high? There was no way the house was worth almost $4 million in this current down market.

"How much are the payments on the new mortgage?" she asked.

The bank manager was starting to feel uncomfortable with her line of questioning.

"Myrosia, I know that Dave has been working on some big deals, and you have always been such good customers of the bank so I feel awkward asking you this, but have you and Dave gotten in over your heads?" he asked.

"Oh no, everything is fine. All this is in our files somewhere, but if you have the numbers in front of you, could you save me some time and tell me how much the payments are so I can make a note of it?" she asked.

"$14,251.59 a month," he replied.

"Which account are the payments coming out of? I don't see it on any of the statements I've got here," she said.

"The payments are coming out of the account that Dave set up for the development company," the bank manager explained.

"Can you take money out of the new account to cover the overdrafts on the lines of credit?" she asked, trying to keep the panic out of her voice.

"Let me see, uh, no, there isn't enough in there to cover it either," he replied.

Now what? Think fast. What to say to keep this guy calm? I need to buy some time to figure out what's going on.

"Oops, sorry about that Tony, it's just my files are in a bit of a mess and I don't see the documentation. Business is booming. We've got so much going on here that I've been swamped. Would you mind faxing me over copies of everything involving these transactions? Everything involving the new mortgage, the new business account, and the wire transfer. I'll transfer some money in to cover everything. Can you give me till Friday afternoon? We've been so busy. We've had some computer trouble and to top it all off we've got a new clerk in here who isn't working out too well so everything's a mess," she lied, trying to sound calm and business like.

The bank manager began to relax a bit. Obviously she had the money. It just needed to be moved from some other financial institution.

"Oh, of course Myrosia, that's no problem. I'll fax that right away. But you know, if you kept all of your investments with us, it would be much more convenient for you."

"Oh, I know Tony. I keep telling Dave that. Let me see what I can do. Don't forget to send me those faxes. Bye." she said as she hung up the phone.

She leaned over her desk with her head in her hands.

Now what, she wondered. He obviously thinks we have more

money than we do. I'll have to let him keep on thinking that for a few days until I figure out what's going on.

She got up, went to the kitchen and got two coffees, and then carried them over to the cubicle where the clerk who looked after the trust accounts desk was situated.

"Hey Stella, I see you've been hard at it all day. I made you a coffee," she placed the coffee down on the desk and casually sat down with her own coffee. "So, obviously you've heard about the situation with me and Dave."

"Oh Myrosia, I am so sorry. I was so surprised this morning when I heard," said Stella.

"Who was it that told you about my situation?" Myrosia asked.

"I heard Cori the receptionist telling some of the other girls about it out front when I got here this morning," Stella replied.

"Have you heard who he's gotten himself involved with?" Myrosia asked.

"Oh no, I was so surprised. He always seemed so devoted to you. I know he loves you. I'm sure he's just having a mid-life crisis and will come crawling back begging you to forgive him," Stella replied, unable to make eye contact.

Stella is such a lousy liar, Myrosia thought. She's also the biggest gossip in the office. Obviously she knows something, so why isn't she talking?

"I'm sure you're right, Stella. Dave and I have gone through difficult times before. I'm sure we can work this out. In the meantime, we've still got a law firm to run. I'd like to talk to you about the trust accounts. Is there any money in either of them that can be released and transferred into the business account?" Myrosia asked.

"No, I wouldn't think so. Dave went through those accounts last week and transferred everything that was due, but I'll have another look for you if you want," she said.

She opened another window on her computer and pulled up a spreadsheet showing the trust account entries.

"Here's the real estate trust account."

Myrosia walked around the desk and looked over the woman's

shoulder.

"Wow, that total looks a little low doesn't it? It's been years since it's been that low. What about the family law trust account?" asked Myrosia.

The administrator opened another window. It looked too low as well.

"Can you give me a copy of those files?" Myrosia asked.

"Well, uh, I don't know if I should. I've been given strict instructions not to allow anyone to copy this file," she replied uncertainly.

"I wouldn't want to get you in trouble. How about if you just print me out the list of the recent transactions in those accounts?" Myrosia asked.

"Oh, uh, I guess that would be okay. How far back do you want?" the administrator asked.

"Oh, for now let's go back three months," she replied.

This was the first time she had ever been grateful that the partners picked these women for their looks rather than for their intelligence.

Back at her desk, she began looking through the trust accounts. It quickly became obvious that the law office's portion of the funds from the recent transactions had been released way before the work had been completed, and even more disturbing was that thousands of dollars that was due to be released to other parties had been withdrawn from the account.

She was sitting at her desk pondering the possible implications of the missing trust account money when there was a rap on her office door. It was Keith MacKenzie, one of the partners. Although he participated in the big commercial real estate deals with the other partners, Keith primarily practiced criminal law. He was a big man with a booming voice that was particularly impressive in the court room.

"Hi Myrosia, I'm so sorry to hear about you and Dave. If there's anything you need don't hesitate to ask. You know that Jeannie and I will always be there for you," he said placing one of his big hands on her shoulder.

"Thanks Keith, I appreciate that," she replied, but wondered how much truth there was behind his words. She and his wife Jeannie had never been particularly close. She knew that Jeannie had not been happy with the decision to have Myrosia work in the office, and she suspected that she'd be pleased to have her gone. It just struck her that she had never been particularly close with any of the partners' wives.

"Well, I won't keep you. You've probably got a lot to do, and I've got to see a client over at the jail, so I'm off," he said and was gone just as quickly as he had appeared.

She swiveled her chair around to check her fax machine. The faxes had come in from the bank, so she scanned all of the documents and e-mailed the files to her personal e-mail account at home. She put a copy of the files onto a memory stick and put the stick in the inside zippered pocket of her coat. Finally she made paper copies of everything and put them in her brief case. I don't want to leave these things lying around. I know it'll all come out in court, but I'd hate to have these details get out any sooner than they have to, she thought.

Before she had a chance to begin reading the new documentation from the bank, there was another knock on the door and Bob poked his head in.

"Hey Myrosia, how are you doing? I'm kind of surprised to see you in here. I thought you'd still be sleeping it off after last night," he said.

"No, I'm fine and I've got a lot of things to do."

"Have you eaten yet? Come on down to the deli and I'll buy you a sandwich."

"Yes, that would be great. I'm starving and I've got some things I need to talk to you about," she said.

She got up and followed him out to the elevator.

When they were seated, off by themselves in the corner of the deli with their sandwiches and coffee, she spoke first.

"Bob, I know I told you last night that Dave cleaned out our personal bank accounts, and cancelled my access to the business account, but it's even worse than that. I spoke to the bank manager and he said that our accounts have gone way past the overdraft limits. I've got no access to any money, nothing at all. Not only that, Dave refinanced the house back in November and took out a mortgage of close to $3 million. I didn't know anything about it, and I don't know where the money went," she said quietly, struggling to hold back the tears.

"What has gotten into that guy? What an idiot, mortgage fraud! Do you think you could prove that you didn't know about the mortgage refinancing?" he asked

"I don't know, maybe, but regardless, the money is gone, and I've still got all the house expenses to cover. The mortgage alone is over $14,000 a month, then there's the electric bill, my car payment…" the tears started to flow again.

"Myrosia, honey, don't worry, we'll get this all straightened out." He reached across the table and patted her hand. "I know what it's like to go from having money to being completely broke. It's really stressful, way worse than never having had money. But don't worry, that money hasn't just disappeared. We'll find it, and we'll force him to give it back. In the meantime I can give you some money to carry you over." He pulled out his wallet. "All I've got on me right now is $120. Here take it. I'll get you some more money after I have a chance to get to a bank machine. Or I can write you a check. Wait, no that won't work. If you put it in your regular household bank account they'd just seize it once they find out what's happened. No, you're going to have to open another bank account somewhere," he said.

"Thank you so much Bob. I don't know what I'd do without you," she said as she took the money and put it in her wallet.

"But there's more." She lowered her voice to a whisper. "I think he's stolen money out of the trust accounts."

"No way. Dave wouldn't do anything as stupid as that."

He paused for a moment and then said, "No, there must be some mistake. There's got to be another explanation. That's a criminal offense, not to mention grounds for being disbarred." He paused again. "Look, something like this could destroy the reputation of the entire firm. Maybe we should keep this to ourselves for a few days until we know for sure what's going on," he said thoughtfully.

He clenched his fist. "What's the matter with him? Do you know if he's been gambling, or is he doing drugs? He's always been so in control. I have a hard time believing he'd be so stupid as to touch the trust account money."

"Obviously I'm the wrong person to ask. I thought I knew him. We've been together since we were kids and I didn't even realize he was cheating on me. Do you have any idea where he's gone and who he's with?" she asked.

"No, I don't know who. I suspected he was seeing someone by the way he kept having 'meetings' outside the office, but I don't know who it is this time. I always thought that he was a little too friendly with Cori at the reception desk, but he'd never leave you for her. I know for sure that he was involved with that girl Christine who used to work for us. I saw them together in his car. But that was a couple of months ago and she's left town since then. Besides, he loves money too much to run off with one of the staff." He thought for a moment. "No, It's more likely one of with his wealthy divorcee clients."

There was a moment of silence and then he asked, "Are you sure you want to find him?"

"I don't give a damn about the bastard. He and his girlfriend, whoever she is, can rot in hell as far as I'm concerned. In fact, it's probably better if I don't find him for a while. I'd probably kill him and, although it would be satisfying, I'd just be in even more trouble. No, I just want to find the money and extricate myself from this whole mess," she said.

"Well, in that case, have you talked to the girls in the office?"

"Well I tried to see what Stella knows, but for the first time ever she isn't talking," said Myrosia.

"That's odd." Bob made a puzzled expression at the thought of the notorious office gossip suddenly hesitating to discuss the latest office scandal.

"I'll try her again later, but first I'm going to see if I can trace that wire transfer, then I'm going to go through his office and see if he left any clues. I know that's probably a waste of time since he obviously thought this whole thing out pretty well, but I've got to try. After that I guess I'll try discretely talking to the rest of the staff. They already know about the break up, but I don't think they know about the money," she said.

"I wouldn't be so sure about that. They almost always know more than they let on," he said.

There was a moment of silence as they both pondered exactly how much the staff knew.

"Do you want to start divorce proceedings and go after his assets? I can help you with that if you want," he said.

"I appreciate that, but let's wait a day or so and see if I can figure out how to keep the bank happy. I'm hoping Dave'll call me and I can convince him to be reasonable. Besides, I've got to find the assets before I can go after them."

"Which vehicle is he driving, the Escalade or the Porsche? Maybe you could track down the vehicles and steal them back from him. That would piss him off, he'd be sure to call you then."

"I don't know which one he's driving. They're both gone. With all this snow I assume he's driving the Escalade. But you're right. If I managed to grab one of his precious vehicles he'd be furious, and it sure would be great to give him a taste of his own medicine," she said with a smile.

Chapter 3

Back in her office she began the process of trying to cajole some information out of the bank in Belize where the money had been transferred. No luck.

Now what should I do? She wondered.

She pulled the faxes from Tony at the bank out of her briefcase and set them on her desk and began looking for the documentation regarding the new mortgage. She found it and immediately looked at the signature page. There was Dave's signature and just below it was her signature. Well it certainly looked like hers, but she knew that she had never signed it. Who had? Maybe if she could talk to the person who witnessed her signature she could find out who was in on this with Dave. Christine Bennett, the person that Bob said he had seen Dave with back a few months ago. Well that made sense, stupid girl. Dave was obviously manipulating her. But could she be the one he was with now?

She picked up the phone and called the human resources clerk.

"Lisa, it's Myrosia. I'm looking for contact information for Christine Bennett that worked here up until a couple of months ago. Could you get it for me?" Myrosia asked.

"Well I can give you her Buffalo address and phone number, but the last I heard was that she moved back to Rochester and I don't have a forwarding address for her. We mailed her last paycheck to the address we had, but it came back undeliverable. I tried calling her, but the phone was disconnected. There wasn't anything else I could do. I figured she'd contact us when she didn't get the check but so far I haven't heard from her," said the human resources clerk.

"That's kind of odd. Who forgets to pick up their final paycheck?" said Myrosia.

26

"Not me, that's for sure. I couldn't understand it. I'd be screaming in an instant if I didn't get my paycheck. I need every penny I get just to get by. I heard she had an inheritance so I guess she isn't hurting for money," said the human resources clerk.

Disconnecting the phone Myrosia sat for a few moments pondering this new development, but it just didn't seem to make sense.

This isn't working. Maybe I should try his office, she thought.

Using her key to open the door to Dave's office she was startled to find that the office wasn't empty. One of the partners was in there looking through Dave's file cabinet. He slammed the file cabinet closed and looked up startled when the door opened.

"Oh Peter I'm sorry. I thought the door was locked. I didn't expect to see anyone in here," said Myrosia.

"Uh, well Dave called me and said he'd be away for a few weeks and asked me to handle a couple of his divorce cases while he's gone. I was just looking for some documentation," said Peter.

"Did you find what you needed? Dave usually keeps the divorce files on the other side of the cabinet," said Myrosia.

"It's okay. I'm done. I've got what I was looking for."

"So Dave called you? Did he ask you to handle our divorce for him?" asked Myrosia as she moved further into the room.

"Oh no, that subject didn't come up, uh, I'm so sorry about everything," said Peter awkwardly as he moved toward the door.

"Well next time he calls would you please tell him to call me. Obviously we have a few important matters to discuss."

Once he had gone Myrosia spent more than an hour of meticulous searching through Dave's desk and filing cabinets, but she still hadn't found any clues to where the money had gone. She made a list of the divorce cases he was currently handling and compiled a huge list of names of women whose divorces he had handled in the past, but nothing seemed to jump out at her.

He had taken his laptop with him and had changed his network password so she couldn't access his files, but maybe the network administrator could let her into his account so she could see what he had been working on.

Most of the staff had already gone for the day when she knocked on the network administrator's door. The young man had helped her a lot in the past when she was researching other matters, and she suspected that he had a bit of a crush on her, so she decided to be straight with him about what she needed.

"Jeff, I was wondering if you could do me a favor." She paused. "Obviously you've heard that Dave left me, and well, he's changed his network password so I need your help to get into his computer files."

"Yeah, I heard about that. Sure I can get you into his files," he replied.

Within moments they were looking at all of his confidential files.

"Here's his new password, hotsexsun," he said as he wrote it down on a scrap of paper and handed it to her.

"That's great Jeff. Is there any way you can copy everything that's in his files onto a memory stick for me, just in case he decides to try to delete anything?" she asked.

"Sure I can, but it's not really necessary. I have a back up of everything that he's deleted for the past six months. I set that up a while back because of that time that Peter was in here screaming that his admin had deleted everything on his hard drive by accident," he said.

"Does Dave know that you've got all this?" she asked excitedly.

"Probably not. I told all the partners, but I doubt any of them paid any attention to me when I told them. The bunch of them, their eyes just glaze over any time I try to talk to them about the computer network," he replied.

"Can you get me copies of everything he's deleted since you started this?" she asked.

"No problem. I'll do that for you right now," he replied.

"Wait a second. Will he know that someone is accessing these files?" she asked.

"No, he won't be able to tell anything. But about the copies, it's too big to go onto a memory stick for you but I can put it all onto a separate file on your laptop and then set you up with a cloud. That's just an online storage system for backup. That way you can access it from anywhere, on any machine."

"A cloud? Is that safe?" she asked.

"You mean safe from hackers? No, nothing is ever safe from hackers." He smiled. "You just got access to all his confidential files didn't you?" He paused. "But this is about as safe as you can get. Besides, most of this stuff isn't of interest to anyone else."

"I know it's late, but do you have time to set me up tonight before you leave for the day? I was hoping to have a chance to look at this at home this evening," she asked.

"Sure, no problem. Give me your laptop and I'll have it set up for you in a couple of minutes," he replied.

Sure enough, it was only a matter of minutes and the laptop was ready and Myrosia was heading down the elevator to the parking garage. She made a couple of stops to pick up some Thai food and a couple of bottles of wine before heading over to the Marine Drive apartments to pick up her friend Joanna. She couldn't find a convenient parking spot so she called Joanna from her cell phone to tell her that she was waiting for her in the no parking zone near the front door.

"Don't forget your bathing suit, so we can soak in the hot tub tonight," Myrosia said.

"Oh Myrosia, you are such a prude. It's just us girls tonight. Why do we need bathing suits?" Joanna laughed.

Myrosia was only barely paying attention to the evening news on the radio while she waited for her friend. It was the usual assortment of local crime reports, a few assaults, a botched armed robbery, and a domestic dispute that had resulted in death. But what caught her attention was a report stating that the planning department at City Hall had turned down a request for a zoning change that would have paved the way for a new housing development on a parcel of industrial land on the waterfront.

How odd that they'd turn down a zoning change request. I wonder if that was a project Dave was working on, she wondered idly, and then changed the radio to her friend's favorite oldies station when she saw Joanna coming out the front door of the building.

As Joanna climbed into the SUV she glanced into the back seat. "I see some take-out food and a couple of bottles of wine, but where's the chips and chocolate bars? We need some comfort food. Stop at the corner store up here."

"I didn't pick up any junk because I've been trying to lose a few pounds. Dave's been complaining that I've been putting on weight, and Nicki said she doesn't want to be embarrassed by me at the wedding," Myrosia replied.

"Oh, to hell with dieting, you've always been too sensitive about your body. You look fantastic. You're just 'sturdy' from good Polish peasant stock, besides, who cares what Dave thinks anyway. Just stop at the store," Joanna said.

Joanna came out of the store and placed the two bags on the floor in the back seat.

"You know," she said as she climbed back into the front seat, "if there's anything Nicki should be embarrassed about, it's the way she talks to you. That girl doesn't treat you with much respect. Could you imagine talking to either of our mothers the way she talks to you? I know I'd have gotten a smack upside my head from my mother if I even thought some of the things that Nicki says to you."

Myrosia laughed. "You've got that right. My mother might look like a sweet little old lady, but she can still wield a mean wooden spoon or a fly swatter. The staff at the seniors' residence all knows not to mess with her."

"Does your mother know what happened? Did you have a chance to talk to her today?" Joanna asked.

"No, I called her this morning to see how she's doing, but she was having a pedicure so we couldn't really talk. Besides, this isn't something I wanted to tell her over the phone. I'm pretty sure she could sense that something was wrong. She always knows these kinds of things. I've got to go and see her in person, but I've been too busy trying to come up with a plan to try and hold everything together. I'll go over and see her one day this week. I hate having to tell her about all this, but I don't think she'll be as surprised as I was, she never approved of me marrying Dave. 'Always with the big deals, who does he think he is,' she would say. The jerk was happy to use my parents' money to start the law firm and to put his real estate deals together, but he was embarrassed by them, didn't want his big shot real estate partners to know that the money came from pawn shops and junk yards. Not glamorous enough for the great David Walker," Myrosia replied sarcastically.

"Don't you mean the great Dawid Kowalczyk?" Joanna replied with a smile.

The fact that Dave had changed his name from the Polish name he was born with, Dawid Kowalczyk, to the more English sounding David Walker as soon as he was legally able to do so, was always a sore point with Myrosia's parents. They thought he was ashamed of his Polish ancestry while he claimed he did it to make it easier for potential clients to spell. Myrosia knew that both reasons were true. He hated the dumb Polack stereotype and wanted to put as much distance between himself and the alcoholic father he grew up with, and he also believed that David Walker was easier for potential clients to spell and pronounce. He had legally changed his name before graduation from college so that the framed diplomas that were displayed so prominently on his office wall would have the appropriate name.

"Yeah, the great Dawid Kowalczyk probably figured he was slumming when he married Myrosia Dabrowski, but I guess my parents' hard earned money was worth it." Myrosia gave a bitter little laugh. "But seriously, I think I've been partly to blame for the way Nicki treats me. Obviously I should've put my foot down years ago, and now it's too late. She doesn't respect me. She thinks I'm an idiot."

"Don't be so hard on yourself. You know you aren't an idiot. You're great at your job, Dave wouldn't be such a great hotshot attorney if he didn't have you doing the research for him and keeping everything organized. Besides, raising kids is hard work. You've done a good job with Dylan. I've never heard him put you down the way Nicki does. I think it's Dave's influence. Dave's always belittling you, or maybe it's just genetic, maybe Nicki got some of those jerk genes from her father," said Joanna.

"I was hoping that going away to college would help Nicki to mature a little. My mother thought it was a waste of money that she should have stayed here in Buffalo, but I was hoping that once she got out in the world a bit she would start to realize that I'm not quite as stupid as she thinks, but it doesn't seem to be working. She doesn't listen to a thing I say. Well hopefully Dave's still underestimating me too. That'll give me a better chance of getting back what he's stolen from me. Still, it's so embarrassing to get taken by surprise like this, especially with all the nasty divorce stuff I see at work every day. I keep thinking I should have seen this coming," Myrosia replied.

"But why would he be so mean as to clear out the house and bank accounts and leave you penniless in that heavily mortgaged house? If he wanted a divorce why not just split everything down the middle and just walk away and start over?" asked Joanna.

"I don't think he really cares all that much about the furniture or the art. He is just playing with my head. I think that this is all just a strategy to wear me down so I'll be more willing to settle for peanuts. Besides, he knows that the court will make him split the family assets, but that's only if I can prove what he's got. If he manages to hide things well enough and can manufacture some business losses it'll be that much less he has to split with me. But he's made a big mistake. I can't believe that after all these years together he doesn't know me well enough to know that this will only make me more determined to fight," said Myrosia.

"Great! So, have you got a plan?" Joanna asked.

"Well, I'm working on it. I can't believe all this has happened in the last 24 hours. This time last night we were on our way to our Tarot class totally oblivious to everything that was about to happen," Myrosia said.

As they drove along, Myrosia updated her friend with the disturbing information that she had learned during the day. Intent on their conversation, the two women never noticed the vehicle following them at a distance.

After dinner the two women sat sipping their wine as they soaked in the hot tub. Glass walls looking out at the lake surrounded the indoor pool, sauna, steam room, and hot tub. In the summer the glass walls slid open to allow access to an outdoor pool and then to the sandy beach of the lake beyond. In the daytime the view from the pool area was spectacular but at night you really couldn't see out.

"I've always loved this pool area. I don't really care much about the rest of the house, but this pool area was always my dream. We worked so hard to achieve all of this. It was almost completely paid off, and now my dream has turned into a nightmare and collapsed around me, just like the Tower card in the Tarot spread last night," Myrosia said. "You know, I wasn't really interested in learning the Tarot. I just signed up for the class because you kept nagging me about it. But now the more I get into it, the more amazingly accurate I find it to be. But last night, when we turned over that Tower card I was sure that there must be a mistake."

"I've always hated that card," said Joanna. "Some people are afraid of the Death card, but there's no reason to be afraid of it. It just means change and rebirth, but the Tower card means that your whole world is collapsing around you. That sure is the case for you."

"Yes, that's the best way to describe it. My whole world has collapsed. Now that I've found out that the bastard has put a huge mortgage on the house. I know I'm not going to be able to keep it, regardless of what I can salvage in a divorce settlement." Myrosia paused. "You know, I've been going through an incredible range of emotions in the last 24 hours. At first when I walked in and thought we'd been robbed, I was really scared. Then my next emotion was anger at being so violated. Then I felt grief about all the things that were gone. I felt confused about what to do when I couldn't reach Dave on the phone, but then when I found his note I was crushed, totally devastated. Heartbroken can't even describe what I was feeling. It was so humiliating when the police arrived. I really think I might have killed myself last night if Bob hadn't shown up when he did."

"You aren't still thinking about killing yourself are you?" her friend asked, startled at her revelation.

"No, now I'm mad. I want revenge. I've been fantasizing about killing Dave, and it's probably a good thing I haven't seen him yet, but I'm definitely not feeling suicidal," she replied, smiling to reassure her friend. "If I was going to kill anyone it would definitely be him, not me."

"Let's cool off in the pool for a few minutes, this heat is getting to me," Joanna suggested, and the two women climbed out of the hot tub and stepped over to the pool and eased themselves into the cool water.

Later that evening, showered and dressed in pajamas, fluffy slippers, and fleece bathrobes, the two women sat at the dining room table with their mugs of hot chocolate. Myrosia had the laptop open in front of her and was working her way through the old files, while Joanna read a new Tarot book that she had just purchased. The two women remained like that until Myrosia broke the silence.

"I am so frustrated! I'm packing it in for tonight. I'm halfway through these old files and I can't find any clues in here yet. All I've got is just one long list of women divorce clients. I don't know what else to do." Myrosia moaned as the tears began to well up.

"There's got to be something you can do. He can't just scoop up all the money and disappear and leave you here to deal with the fallout. Let's take another look at that card spread from last night. Maybe it can give us some ideas," said Joanna.

She reached into her bag and pulled out the sheet where she had written out the spread from the previous night's class. Then she laid out the cards exactly the way they had fallen.

"Let's see, the first card is the Fool. This represents you and the present situation that the cards are revealing," Joanna said. "You're embarking on a new adventure."

"Some adventure, it looks like a dangerous one. The card shows the Fool about to step off a cliff, but in this case I'm not stepping off willingly. I've been pushed," Myrosia added.

"The card covering it is the King of Wands reversed. This is something about your present situation that you don't understand, or don't know about. Well it's pretty obvious that there's a lot about your present situation that you don't understand. This card represents a man who isn't what he appears to be. It could be a man with a violent temper who expects people to worship him and treat him as if he were a god. Yeah, that sounds like Dave. 'Little Hitler.' But this could also be a man with low self esteem, and Dave never struck me as having low self esteem. If anything he thinks too highly of himself."

"I don't know about that. Dave isn't nearly as self-confident as he pretends. All the money, the cars, this house, the big deals, I've always suspected that it was his way of covering up that, deep down, he's a scared little boy from the east side of Buffalo," said Myrosia.

"Well, you know him better than I do," Joanna replied but didn't sound convinced. She thought for a moment before going on. "Card number three is the King of Pentacles reversed. This is the underlying issue. I think this is a man with money problems, who will cheat or steal to get what he wants. Hmm, that sure sounds like Dave too. Do you think these two cards could be referring to the same man, or is there more than one man involved?" Joanna paused for a moment. "Oh, my god, you don't suppose that Dave has run off with another man do you?" asked Joanna.

Myrosia laughed, "Well, anything is possible, I suppose. Obviously I never knew the real Dave, just the facade, but no, with all the cheating he's apparently done over the years I think we can safely say that Dave isn't about to switch teams. No, in fact, I'd be more inclined to think that Dave is homophobic."

"Yeah, you're probably right. That thought just jumped into my head," replied Joanna, pausing again to think before continuing. "Card four is the Queen of Swords reversed, this is in the position that represents the immediate past, something that led up to the present situation. This is a cold, cruel, aloof woman, someone who is analytical, opinionated, and tactless, a real bitch. Could that be this Christine woman that Dave was seeing?" said Joanna.

"Maybe, but it just doesn't feel right to me. She never struck me as being manipulative. She just seemed young and naïve. Could that be me that the cards are referring to? Do you think I'm a bitch? It occurred to me today that I don't have a lot of close women friends. What is it about me that keeps me from getting close to people? Do you think the Tarot cards are saying that I caused this situation because I was cold and aloof to Dave?" Myrosia asked.

"No, it couldn't mean that. You are one of the kindest people I know. Sure, you are competent and efficient, and don't put up with much crap from your staff at work, but I don't think any of this refers to you," Joanna replied.

"Talk about taking crap from the staff at work, that receptionist Cori is getting more and more arrogant. You should have seen her today, it's like she's thrilled to see this happening to me. I don't know what I've done to make her feel this way about me," said Myrosia.

"Maybe it has nothing to do with you. Maybe it has to do with Dave. You don't suppose she's his new woman?" asked Joanna.

"That thought passed through my mind too, but I don't think so. Dave loves money and prestige too much to run off with the receptionist. No, I could see him having a fling with her if he thought he wouldn't get caught, or if he could use her for some reason, but no, he's planned this out carefully. I think he thinks he is getting rid of me and 'trading up,'" said Myrosia.

"Yeah, you're probably right. Let's keep on looking at this Tarot spread. The next card is the Tower card. I hate this card! But it's in the fifth position? This is supposed to represent the best outcome. How can having your world collapse around you possibly be the best outcome? I don't know, I guess the idea would be that once the Tower, which represents your false life, is turned to rubble, and you are thrown down on the rocks below, that after a period of fear and disbelief, or pain and recovery, you can finally rebuild a new, true life. It's like as if your inner eye is suddenly opened and you can start to see. Once you destroy the lies you are left with a foundation of truth and then you can rebuild your life," said Joanna.

"But I'm too old to start over. I'm almost 45 and I've been married to the same man since college. I haven't really even dated anyone else. I don't have the time or energy to start over. I've wasted my whole life with this man," Myrosia moaned.

"Forty-five isn't very old. Besides, by the looks of things I don't think you have a choice. Let's see what the rest of the cards have to say. Card six, the immediate future, is the 3 of Swords. Well that is pretty clear. There's going to be a lot of emotional pain, suffering and tears in your immediate future. I don't think we need to be psychic to figure that out."

Joanna continued. "Card seven is the Queen of Wands. This is supposed to represent how you deal with the situation. You are a very creative woman with lots of energy who can take charge and get things done well. Yes, that definitely sounds like you.

"Card eight is the 5 of Pentacles. In this position it represents your home and work situation. I must be reading this wrong. It looks to me like homelessness and unemployment, a really destitute situation." Joanna glanced around the room and out to the pool area. "But that can't be right, how could you go from all this to homelessness? It can't mean literal homelessness. It must be symbolic. It probably just means that your husband is gone and your income will be reduced. Besides, you'll never be really homeless. If you're stuck you can always move in with me," Joanna said.

Myrosia didn't say anything, but inwardly shuddered at the thought of being forced to move in with Joanna in her tiny little apartment.

"Card nine is the 8 of Cups. In this position it represents your hopes and fears. Helen called this the divorce card. Look at it, the person is walking away from 8 spilled cups. I think this means that you are afraid that you're going to have to walk away from this luxurious life, and that you're hoping that there will be something better down the road," Joanna said.

"I think it's saying that I've been a fool living an illusion, and now all the cups are spilled and I can't pretend everything is perfect any more. I really loved Dave and I thought he loved me, when in reality I've wasted 25 years of my life on someone who wasn't worth it," Myrosia replied.

"Yeah, but it's more than that. Let's look this card up in our course notes," Joanna paused as she thumbed through her loose-leafed binder of notes. "I thought so. Here is what else Helen said about this card, 'this card is often called the divorce card, but it can also refer to a literal trip from somewhere familiar to an unknown land. It can indicate that someone has a spiritual calling that they have been avoiding but can't avoid any longer.' Do you think you might have some sort of spiritual calling?"

"A spiritual calling?" Myrosia laughed. "I don't think so. In this case I think it just means I'm getting a divorce."

"And the outcome card, card ten is the Hanged Man."

As the two women sat there at the table pondering the cards, they had no idea that they were being watched. He watched the house from the tree line near the lake shore, just as he had done so many times before. His routine was always the same. He parked at the vacant house next door whose owners had gone to their winter home in Florida. Then he trudged through the snow on the beach and positioned himself in the shadows of the trees at the property line. From this vantage point, with his binoculars, he could clearly see the two women as they moved about the main floor of the house, but they couldn't see him, and wouldn't expect to see anyone standing out there in the darkness.

That's so typical of people living in these big isolated houses on the lake, he thought. They never bother to close their curtains because they never expect anyone to be watching them.

In the daylight his footprints would be visible, but no one would be looking for them.

He stood there in the shadows watching until he saw the women heading up the stairs. When the lights in the house went out he retraced his steps back to where he had parked.

Not tonight, but soon, he thought.

Chapter 4

It was barely dawn on Wednesday morning and Myrosia was lying in bed unable to sleep. The house was silent except for occasional creaking noises as the house contracted in the bitter cold. Joanna was still sleeping soundly down the hall in the guest room.

There's got to be something I'm missing in Dave's computer files. I'm not sleeping anyway so I might as well get up and keep searching, she thought.

She got up and put on her robe and slippers and went down to the kitchen. She carried a cup of coffee and a bagel into the dining room and set it on the table where she had left her computer the previous evening. Working methodically through the files, more than an hour went by fruitlessly before she hit pay dirt. Hidden away in a folder marked 'Continuing Education Points' was a treasure trove of photographs of half naked women along with copies of emails addressed to an e-mail address that Myrosia didn't recognize.

Joanna came shuffling down the stairs. "I smell coffee."

"Forget the coffee, I've found something else that will wake you up. Take a look at this," replied Myrosia.

Joanna walked around behind her friend and her eyes widened in surprise when she saw the picture on the laptop screen.

"Ew, gross! What is that?" gasped Joanna.

"It appears that Dave had some interests I wasn't aware of."

Myrosia pulled up one file after another containing dozens of photographs of women in sexually explicit poses complete with leather bondage wear and assorted accessories including whips, chains and paddles.

The two friends studied the photographs in stunned silence.

Finally Myrosia broke the silence. "Although there are lots of pictures, it looks to me like there are only a few different women, but it's hard to tell because their faces are pretty much obscured by those leather masks and gags. It kind of looks like they're deliberately trying to conceal their identities."

"Well it's no wonder that they're covering up their faces. I sure wouldn't want any pictures of me looking like this floating around," said Joanna. "Wait! ... go back to the previous one. There, doesn't she look a bit like Bob's Williams' wife Janice?" said Joanna

"Maybe a little bit, it's hard to tell, but it can't be her. I can't imagine someone like 'The Princess' being interested in kinky stuff like that," said Myrosia.

"Maybe that was why Bob married her. I could never figure out what the attraction was on his part. He seems like such a nice guy. Why would he marry such a bitch? Anyway, you never really know what goes on in people's bedrooms. Some of the most unlikely people have the kinkiest sex lives. You wouldn't believe the stories I hear every day at the beauty salon," replied Joanna.

"I know. She always seemed so cold and standoffish, like she was too good for the rest of the partners' wives. Even the way she left Bob was so cold. Imagine texting your husband to tell him that you want a divorce. She couldn't even be bothered to tell him in person, what kind of person does something like that?" said Myrosia.

"Well, isn't that pretty much what Dave did to you? He didn't text you. He just cleaned out everything and left a note on your pillow. Same thing if you ask me," said Joanna.

"Oh my god, you're right. I guess I hadn't thought of it that way." said Myrosia.

"Well, when you've got money you can do whatever you want. Don't you wish you could just take off somewhere exotic with a new lover to get over a failed marriage? It would be a lot easier than sticking around here to deal with all of this," replied Joanna.

"Yeah I envy her being able to do that, but still, these can't be pictures of her. I mean, why would Dave have pictures like this of his best friend's wife on his computer? Besides, Janice can't stand Dave. They've been pleasant to each other for Bob's sake, but they've never really been friendly to each other, so I can't believe that she'd have had an affair with him," said Myrosia.

"But that could have all been an act to cover up what was really going on between them. Maybe she's the one that Dave took off with," replied Joanna.

"A few days ago I would have laughed if you'd said something like that to me, but now I just don't know. There's so many things that I thought I knew about Dave that I was wrong about, so I guess I really don't know anything anymore," Myrosia said.

"That reminds me. Did I tell you what I heard last week? Brenda at work told me that she had heard from one of her clients that someone has gone and bought one of those big old houses on Nottingham Terrace in the Central Park area and turned it into a swingers' club," said Joanna.

"A swingers' club?" replied Myrosia.

"Yeah, a swingers' club, you know, one of those places where couples get together to swap partners. This one is supposed to be really exclusive and they cater to all kinds of weird stuff. Apparently they have a big bondage room made up to look like a dungeon."

"I heard of those back in the 1960's and 70's, but now with AIDS and everything why on earth would someone want to get involved with something like that?" said Myrosia.

"Oh come on Myrosia, don't be so naïve, lots of married people cheat on their spouses," said Joanna.

"I'm not being naïve. I've heard just about everything dealing with the divorce clients at the office, and even before that at my parent's pawn shop. I know that people do lots of stupid things where sex is concerned. Besides, it's not like I haven't been attracted to anyone else over the years, but these days it's just not worth the risk. So how busy can a club like that possibly be?" said Myrosia.

"Very busy and very exclusive. Apparently you have to be sponsored by one of the existing members and there is a big initiation fee so that pretty much limits the membership to people who can afford the fee. I suspect that the members are a lot of professional and public figures who want to maintain their privacy. I'm surprised that you haven't heard anything about it from your rich divorce clients at the office," replied Joanna.

"When did they open? Maybe it hasn't been open long enough to be a factor in any of our clients' divorces," said Myrosia.

"I think they opened sometime in the last year, but I only just heard about it last week, so they certainly have managed to maintain their secrecy. The only reason Brenda heard about it was because one of her clients is a seamstress who repairs leather goods and someone brought in some sort of harness thing that they wanted her to repair. Brenda's client wouldn't say who brought it in, but she did say that we would die of shock if we knew who it was," said Joanna.

"Well, I don't care how many skanks Dave plays his kinky games with, and I don't care who goes to some sick sex club. At this point all I want is to get my money back and get him out of my life permanently. So let's hurry up and get ready and I'll drop you off at your apartment on my way into the office," replied Myrosia.

"Oh my god, Myrosia. You've got to get an AIDS test! With Dave running around with all these women he's put you at risk!" said Joanna.

It was early and the office was almost deserted when Myrosia got there. She didn't even stop to take off her coat. She went straight to the network administrator's tiny office. As she suspected, the young man was slouched in his chair staring at his computer monitor. He was wearing the same clothes he had on the previous day. When he looked up at her and she saw his bloodshot eyes she wondered if he had even gone home the previous night.

"Hey Jeff, what are you doing here so early? Are you sleeping here now?" she smiled at the self-conscious look on his face. "Well I'm really glad you're here. I wanted to ask you a question. I think Dave's got a hotmail account. Is there any way I can get in and read his emails?" Myrosia asked.

"What's his user name?" Jeff replied.

"Oh god it's so tacky, I'm almost embarrassed to say it, but it's 'hotbuffalolawyer'," Myrosia responded.

"Do you know his password?" asked Jeff.

"No, I found a couple of really disgusting emails that he had saved in a hidden file, but I don't know his password," said Myrosia.

"No problem. Last night after you left I was thinking about your situation and I had an idea. I spent hours monitoring the office network watching to see if he was logging in and sure enough, about midnight he logged on to look at the family law trust account spreadsheet and while he was logged in I was able to get into his computer and I installed a key logger program so now every time he logs on to the internet, no matter where he is, it sends me a copy of everything he types into his computer, including the passwords. This way I don't have to wait until he logs into the office network any more. We can see everything he's doing. I've set up an alarm on my phone that will tell me whenever he logs on. We just have to wait until the next time he logs into hotmail and we'll know his password," explained Jeff.

"Wow that's brilliant Jeff! Creepy, but brilliant. I am SO glad that you're on my side and not his," exclaimed Myrosia.

The young man blushed as she bent over to give him a kiss on the cheek.

"Oh, I had another question for you. You're quiet and don't spend a lot of time talking to the other employees, but you're really smart and I bet you hear everything that is going on around here. Do you have any idea what's up with that girl Cori? She's getting so arrogant, it's like she's not worried about losing her job. What's that all about?" asked Myrosia.

"Well, I hadn't really noticed that she was getting any more arrogant. She's always been a bitch toward me. But if you say she is, then I guess she figures she's landed herself a rich old guy and won't need the crappy receptionist job much longer," replied Jeff.

"Really? Do you have any idea who she's after?"

"I don't know. Either one of the partners or one of the clients. That'd be my bet. Why else would a girl that looks like her, a greedy gold digger, take a minimum wage receptionist job. She's chasing money, old men, and hot new cars. She's definitely not interested in guys like me," replied Jeff.

"Trust me Jeff, there are lots of girls who'd be interested in you, and you really wouldn't want a girl like Cori anyway. But what makes you say she's greedy?" asked Myrosia.

"Where to begin… Well for one thing she's cheap. She always manages to weasel out of paying for her coffee and donuts when someone goes down to the deli to pick them up. That trick is getting really old with the rest of the staff. For another thing, she gets really jealous when one of the other girls has something that's nicer than she has. She gets really bitchy then. She always wants to have the best and I suspect that she'll do almost anything to get what she wants… Also, I can't prove it but I think she is a thief too. Christine came in one day with a pin, a broach that for some reason really pissed Cori off. It wasn't anything expensive or anything, just a little pin shaped like a sports car, and she had it pinned to her coat. Christine was bragging to the other girls that she had a new boyfriend and soon she'd have a real sports car too. Later on when she went to get her coat the pin was missing. She accused Cori of stealing it but couldn't prove it. Cori complained to Keith about it. They were in his office for a long time, and later Keith came out and told Christine that she should not be making accusations like that without any proof. Christine was so upset that she ended up taking a couple of days off and Dave and Keith moved her into the office next to Dave's to keep her further away from Cori. The two women avoided each other after that, right up until Christine quit. I think that Cori's just bad news," said Jeff.

"Thanks Jeff. I vaguely remember hearing about that incident but I didn't give it much thought at the time. Now you've got me curious, and you've given me an idea about where to look for Dave's Porsche. I don't know why I didn't think of it before now. I guess I wasn't thinking clearly. I've got to go out for a while, so if anybody's looking for me, tell them I'll be back in a couple of hours," said Myrosia.

Jeff's comments about the sports car pin had reminded her about Bob's suggestion that she track down Dave's vehicles. The Porsche was his favorite. He really loved that car. If she could grab that one she'd hear from him in a hurry. It occurred to her that he regularly took it in to the dealer for servicing and detailing. It couldn't hurt to start there.

On the drive over to the Porsche dealership Myrosia pondered what her approach should be. Should she just look around casually pretending that she was interested in a new car? No, that approach wouldn't help her if the car was somewhere in the back of the service department. Maybe the direct approach would be better. What if she just went into the service department and said that she was there to pick up the car? If it was there, maybe she could bluff them into giving it to her and billing it to him. Then what would she do? She couldn't sell it. The ownership was in his name, but she could hide it somewhere and use it for leverage when he finally got in touch with her.

She parked on the side street just around the corner from the car dealership in a good spot where her SUV wouldn't be as noticeable. She sat watching the dealership for a few minutes trying to decide what to do. Finally she pulled her deck of Tarot cards out of her purse, shuffled them, closed her eyes, took a deep breath and drew two cards from the deck and placed them on the seat beside her. The cards that turned up were the Chariot and the Magician reversed.

Hmm, there's my answer, a combination of confidence and trickery. Here I go.

She put the cards back in her purse and got out of the car. She couldn't see any sign of the car so she walked straight up to the service department counter to where the service manager was just finishing up with another customer. When he was free she gave him a big smile.

"Hi Paul, is Dave's car ready? I'm here to pick it up."

"Oh hi Myrosia. That's good timing. Larry's just finished up with the interior. I'm surprised that you're here so early to pick it up. We told Dave that it probably wouldn't be ready until this evening but Larry was in early this morning and got right on it. I'll get him to bring it around for you," he said.

"I guess I must be psychic," she laughed. "Or I misunderstood Dave's instructions. Either way, here I am and my timing's perfect. How much does he owe you for the work?"

"Nothing, there's no charge. It's covered under the service package that he got with the car. Here's Larry now," he said as the car pulled into the pick up area.

As she turned to walk to the car she noticed a display of lapel pins shaped like Porsche's standing on the end of the counter.

"These are cute, when did you start selling these?"

"Oh they're not for sale, we give them away to our best customers. We've given several to Dave. Would you like one?"

"Yes, thank you," she said as she dropped the pin into her coat pocket and got into the driver's side of the car.

She drove out to the old auto wrecking company that had belonged to her father for years. The man who currently owned it was a long time employee of her father and still a close family friend. She hoped that he'd be able to help her now. She pulled up to the garage door where a group of men were busy dismantling a vehicle that had been in a car accident.

"Hi guys, is John around?" she asked.

"He's in the back," came the reply.

She walked back into a large room lined with shelving onto which were piled thousands of used auto parts. This had been her father's sanctuary for as long as she could remember, and she could still feel his presence.

A balding man wearing coveralls and work boots came out from behind one of the shelves.

"Hello Myrosia. It's nice to see you. It's been too long. I'd give you a hug but I'm covered with grease. What can I do for you?" the man asked.

"Hi John, I need your help. Dave and I are getting a divorce and for now I have his Porsche. I was wondering if you could hang onto it for me for a few days until I figure out what to do with it. Keep it safe for me somewhere where he won't be able to find it."

"You looking for a little revenge? Nothing like a woman scorned. I could put it in the crusher for you," he laughed.

She smiled. "That's tempting, but no, I don't want you to do anything to it. I just want to use it for leverage to get back some of the things that he's taken from me. It'll probably just be here for a few days, maybe a week or so," she replied.

"Well I'm sorry to hear that you're having problems, but I'm sure you know that nothing would have made your father happier than getting Dave out of your life," he said.

"Yes, I know. I wish I'd listened to him years ago. He was such a good judge of character. I wish I'd inherited more of his good sense," she said.

"Oh don't be so hard on yourself. You're a sensible woman. You're not the first woman to fall in love with a man that doesn't deserve her," he said.

"Thanks John, I didn't know who else to turn to for this."

"Dave's gonna be pretty mad when he finds out you've hidden his car. Do you think he'll try and get the police involved? Will he report it stolen?" he asked.

"No, … well I'm not certain, but I think he's got a few other reasons not to want any police involvement, but I wouldn't want you to get into any trouble so if the police show up just tell them the truth that I left the car here for safekeeping."

"The reason I'm mentioning it is that the car has an anti-theft GPS device hidden in it somewhere and if he reports it stolen they will activate the device and they'll know in minutes exactly where it is," he explained.

"I'd forgotten about that. Is there any way you can deactivate that thing?" she asked.

He hesitated, "I don't know, but I'll talk to the boys to see if they have any ideas," he replied.

"No, never mind. Forget I said that. I don't want to get you into any trouble. If anyone asks you why the car is here just say that I dinged up the bumper when I was driving it and I brought it over to you to repair so Dave wouldn't find out about it," she said.

He laughed. "That should work. I'll buff up the rear bumper, make it look like I worked on it."

"I hate to be such a bother. I know how busy you guys are, but do you think that you could get one of the boys to drive me back into town to pick up my SUV?" she asked.

"Sure, no bother at all. I was going to send Ryan out with the tow truck to do a pick up. You can ride along with him."

Back at the office she was passing the reception desk when the receptionist called out to her.

"Oh Myrosia, I'm so glad I caught you. Tony Barrucci at the bank has been calling trying to reach you. He wants you to call him right away. It must be pretty important," she said.

"If he calls again, tell him I haven't made it in yet. I'll call him once I've had a chance to settle in," replied Myrosia.

"Nobody told me that blocking collection calls from your creditors was suddenly going to be part of my job description," the younger woman replied, not even attempting to hide the look of triumph on her face.

"What did you say to me? Where do you get off thinking you can talk to me like that? Your job description is anything I say it is," said Myrosia.

"I don't think so Ms. High and Mighty. Now that Dave has dumped you, you've got no real function here. None of us have to take orders from you any more. In fact, I don't know how you even have the nerve to show up here at the office. It's not like you have any real work to do here," said the younger woman in a voice loud enough to be heard throughout the entire office.

All activity in the office seemed to come to a halt. Heads popped out of doorways and over cubicle partitions in order to hear what was going on.

"That's enough Cori. This is very inappropriate behavior. I need to speak to you privately in my office," said Myrosia.

"I don't think so, bitch. The only reason anyone put up with taking orders from you is because you were the senior partner's wife."

"That's enough Cori. Into my office, NOW!" exclaimed Myrosia.

"Look at yourself. I almost feel sorry for you, getting dumped like this at your age, but it was inevitable. Let's face it. Why would a man like Dave want to stay with an old hag like you? Everyone knows he only married you for your money."

Just then the three partners came out of Peter's office. Keith immediately took charge of the situation.

"Debbie I want you to leave what you're doing and handle the reception duties for a few minutes. Cori, come into my office right now. Bob, could you take Myrosia into your office."

In Bob's office Myrosia was shaking with fury.

"What was that all about? I've never experienced anything like that in my life! She has got to go!" Myrosia exclaimed.

"Myrosia, Keith will deal with Cori, but I'm afraid that you're the one that's going to have to go home, just till things settle down," he said.

"What? Why? I didn't do anything! I didn't start that! I'm fine. I just need a few minutes to calm down," Myrosia replied.

"No, it's not about this incident. Some other things have come up. I've just had a long meeting with Peter and Keith. It's really bad. Peter was at the squash club and heard from one of the other members that the Mayor's office is investigating allegations that Dave has attempted to blackmail members of the planning committee. Depending on what they turn up they might have to turn it over to the FBI. There is also a rumor that Dave has been bribing building inspectors on some of his development projects. Also, there's that matter of the missing trust account funds... Peter and Keith are concerned about the reputation of the firm so they think it would be best if you stay away from the office until Dave has a chance to answer these allegations," said Bob.

"This is absurd! How is this even possible? I mean, even if Dave actually did any of this how could news of it get around this fast?" She paused for a moment. "Obviously someone here in the office must be leaking information. Really, how could anyone outside of the office know about the trust account money?"

"You might be right. It's possible we've got a leak, but who would do something like that and why? The four of us partners have been friends for years. We wouldn't do something like that to each other. Besides, it'd be financial suicide for us to leak news like this. We're all worried sick about it," said Bob.

"But Bob, how can you expect me to just stay home? If I'm going to get to the bottom of this I need the office resources for my research. I need access to the databanks and the files. We need to maintain the impression that everything is fine and that it's business as usual around here. How can we do that if you and the other partners insist on kicking me out. How can you do this to me Bob? I thought we were friends," said Myrosia.

"Myrosia, I am your friend. I can't speak for Keith and Peter, but I promise that I will do everything I can to help you through this mess. Anything you need from the office I'll get for you, but as your friend I think it really is better for you if you are out of here. Some of the staff are saying that you are in on all this with Dave, that you aren't actually looking for him, but rather that you're here in the office covering up his tracks, giving him time to skip out, that you know where he is, and that you'll join up with him later when you've tied up the loose ends."

"That's insane! Who's saying that? Where would anyone get such a ridiculous idea? I'm the victim here. It's got to be that Cori who's spreading those vicious lies about me. I don't know what she's got against me, or the firm for that matter, but I'm telling you Bob, that girl has got to go," said Myrosia.

"Keith's talking to her right now, I'm sure he'll take care of it, but Myrosia, you need to pack up your things and go. You don't need to take everything. Anything you don't take now I can bring out to the house for you later. Let's just do this quietly without drawing too much attention. I'll help you load your car," said Bob.

"I can't believe you're doing this to me after all the years that we've been friends. Come on Bob, you know Dave and I better than anyone, so what do you think? You were out at the house on Monday night. Do you honestly think we set this all up?" asked Myrosia.

"Of course not! I know you couldn't be involved in any of this. I'm sure that these criminal allegations against Dave are all just a misunderstanding too, something that we can straighten out once we get a hold of Dave, but in the meantime, let me help you take your things down to your car," said Bob.

"Bob, can you give me a couple of minutes, I need to use the rest room, and then I promise I'll leave without a fuss," said Myrosia.

"Okay, I'll be in my office. Just come and get me when you're ready and I'll walk you down to your car," he said.

As soon as he left Myrosia downloaded all of the company

personnel records from the network onto her laptop, shut the computer down and packed it into her laptop bag. Then she walked down the hall toward the network administrator's cubicle. She stopped short because she could overhear what Peter was saying to the young man.

"Jeff, Myrosia will no longer be working here at the office so I need you to cancel her access to the network. Also cancel her voice mail, her parking pass, and her code key to get into the building. I need you to take care of this immediately, do you understand?"

Chapter 5

Leaving the office that day was a surreal experience for Myrosia. As she and Bob walked from her office to the front door she felt like a condemned prisoner walking to the gallows. Most of the staff seemed unable to face her and stayed hidden in their offices and cubicles. Stella, the clerk in charge of the trust accounts, came over to her with tears in her eyes to give her a hug.

"Oh Myrosia, I can't believe they're doing this to you. I want you to know that I have loved working with you all these years. No matter what happens please stay in touch. Maybe we can get together for coffee some time," said Stella.

"Thank you Stella, I'd like that. Yes, let's keep in touch," said Myrosia thinking that it was unlikely to happen.

Jeff, the network administrator, came forward to shake her hand. He clasped one hand over the other and she felt a small piece of paper which she took and surreptitiously placed in her pocket without looking at it, pretending to be reaching for a Kleenex.

"I'm sorry to see you go," he mumbled.

And then she was out the door.

As she and Bob silently took the elevator down to the parking garage it struck her how few personal belongings she was carrying away with her. They wouldn't allow her to take the files, so other than her computer there was really nothing that she wanted to take away from the place that had been her second home for so many years. Bob had filled up a box with odds and ends like her coffee cup, a few framed pictures of her kids, and a few items of clothing that she had kept in her closet at the office. Although he kept insisting that her departure was just temporary, they both knew that she was unlikely to be coming back, at least not as the wife of the senior partner.

They were almost to her SUV when her cell phone rang. She pulled her phone out of her purse to see who was calling.

"It's Dave. I've been trying to reach this jerk all week and now he's finally returning my calls. Excuse me, but I've got to take this."

"Go ahead. I'll wait for you. Take your time," Bob said.

Climbing into the front seat of her SUV, she answered the phone. "How dare you steal my car!" Dave's voice screamed out of the phone at her.

"I didn't steal it. I just put it away for safekeeping, but that's priceless coming from you considering how much you've stolen from me," she responded.

"I never stole anything from you. I just took what was mine. Who do you think earned all the money we've been living on all these years? Where do you think we got the money for the house on the lake that you wanted so badly? I earned it. You were just tagging along for the ride. I want the Porsche back now!" he shouted.

"What are you talking about? We earned all that money together, and it was my parents money that got you started, so don't give me any bullshit about it being your money. You know that the courts won't see it that way. Besides, I never wanted the lake house. That was just you wanting to show off. What about the huge mortgage you put on the house? I never agreed to that. I know all about how you got that clerk Christine to help you forge my name on the mortgage documents. What did you do with the money?" Myrosia shouted back at him.

"You're an idiot. You don't understand business. I needed that money for some deals I was working on, some big investments that you couldn't possibly understand. I don't know why I'm bothering. There's no point trying to discuss financial matters with you. I don't know why I kept you around all these years. I should have traded you in years ago. I just stayed with you because of the kids. I've found someone else, an equal, someone I don't have to be ashamed to be seen with," he said.

"You stuck around because you wanted to suck me and my parents dry. You wanted to use their money for your big deals. So who's the slut you're with now, huh? If she's got any sense she won't put up with you for long," Myrosia scoffed.

"There's no point talking to you about this. I want my car back and I want it right now! You'd better not have done anything to it. You'll give it back to me right now if you know what's good for you."

"Are you threatening me? What do you think you can do to me? Huh? After everything else, what more do you think you can do to me? I don't want your stupid car. I just wanted you to answer my damn phone calls. I want my money back and I want you out of my life. I want a divorce and I want the money you've stolen out of our bank accounts. When all this is settled you'll get your precious car back and not a minute sooner," she replied.

"There's nothing more to discuss. You're getting nothing from me. I owe you nothing. I want my car back. Don't try and fuck with me. You don't know what you're dealing with. I want my car back in the dealer's parking lot in one hour or I'm gonna send a couple of guys over to talk some sense into you," Dave shouted.

"So Dawid, the big shot, suddenly you're 'connected.' You're gonna send some thugs over to threaten me? Hey tough guy, it's time for you to remember who you're dealing with here. I'm not scared of you. You can't bully me, I know way too much about you. If you try anything with me you'll have bigger problems than loosing your precious Porsche. I'll go straight to the authorities and tell them some stories about mortgage fraud, illegal money transfers, bribing government officials, and missing trust account money," she responded trying to sound braver than she was actually feeling.

"Don't threaten me Myrosia, and don't even think about going to the authorities. Even you can't possibly be that stupid. You're getting in way over your head. I'm warning you, you've got one hour to return my car," he replied ominously and hung up the phone.

Myrosia sat in the car shaking with shock and anger as she tried to compose her thoughts. Who was this man I've had been married to all these years, she wondered.

After a few moments she realized that Bob was still leaning on the hood of his Hummer waiting for her. She rolled down her window and Bob came over to speak to her.

"Myrosia, you look really upset. I wasn't trying to listen in, but it was pretty obvious that it wasn't a very cordial conversation. I know it's a bit early, but why don't we leave your SUV here for a little while and we can go over to Mama Rossi's for a bite to eat. We can get one of their booths in the back and talk some strategy," said Bob.

"No, I can't, Dave's really mad and I've got to get out of here right now," said Myrosia the panic rising in her voice.

"What's he so mad about? You're the one who has a right to be mad, not him," said Bob.

"With everything that's happened I forgot to tell you. I found Dave's Porsche this afternoon and I put it somewhere for safekeeping. I figured I could use it for leverage to get some of the money back, and he's absolutely furious. He's not thinking logically. He just threatened me," explained Myrosia.

"Yeah I can see how that would get him worked up. He loves that Porsche like I love my old Hummer. I'd have probably gone ballistic if Janice took off with it when we split up, but then again I never tried to rip her off either," he said.

"I've got to go. My SUV is too vulnerable sitting here in this parking lot. I've got to get it out of here and put it somewhere safe. I've got to go and hide the Mini too before he can get to it," said Myrosia in a panic.

"Let me help you. I feel kind of bad since I'm the one who suggested that you steal it from him. What can I do?" he asked.

"Could you come with me? I'm frightened. Dave just threatened me. He said he was going to send a couple of guys over to 'talk some sense into me,'" she said.

"Sure, I'll come with you. I don't think you're in any real danger from him but I wouldn't want you to be alone just in case you happen to run into him. He's never hit you or anything before, right? I don't think he's gonna do anything now. He's just angry and making stupid, idle threats," said Bob.

"I hope you're right. A few days ago that's exactly what I would have thought too, but now I'm not so sure. You didn't hear him on the phone just now. He's changed. He's always been a jerk but now something is different. I don't know what he's gotten involved with."

"Do you want me to follow you in the Hummer?"

"No, come with me in my SUV. You drive. I've got to make a few phone calls," she replied.

"Okay, where too?" Bob asked as he climbed into the driver's seat and adjusted the seat to accommodate his tall frame.

"Take me out to my dad's old garage," she said.

Bob laughed. "So that's where you hid the Porsche. That makes sense."

Her first call was to John at the auto wreckers.

"John, you were right. Dave found out that I've got his Porsche and he is really angry so I've got another favor to ask you," she said over the phone.

"I hope you're not calling to tell me that you're gonna back down and give him his car back," replied John over the phone.

"Hell no, but I'd like to bring both of my cars over for safekeeping, and I was wondering if you had an old junker that I could borrow for a few days, I need to keep out of sight, just until Dave calms down and we can negotiate," she explained.

"Sure, I can do that. I've got an old Jeep here that you can use. It doesn't look very nice, but it runs great and has a decent heater in it. Will that work for you?"

"Thanks John, that'll be perfect. I'll be there in a few minutes."

Her next phone call was to Tony at the bank.

"Hi Tony, what's up? I got the message that you called. Sorry I didn't get back to you sooner, I've been busy," Myrosia said trying to sound casual and upbeat.

"Myrosia, you can cut out the act. I heard all about the situation with Dave leaving you and I've also heard about his legal troubles with this bribery business. I'm sure it's all a big misunderstanding and I hate to do this to you, but you've been a good customer for so many years that I'm giving you a heads up on this. I'm afraid the bank is going to have to take steps to protect our financial position … we're consulting with our lawyers about the situation. I tried to reach Dave this afternoon but he wasn't at the office and he hasn't returned any of the calls I've made to his cell phone. I'm sure you understand how difficult this is for me. I just can't risk having any other assets disappearing. I've got a responsibility to the bank's shareholders…" the bank manager said awkwardly.

"Yes, I understand. So exactly what is the bank planning on doing?" she asked.

"Well, your credit cards are frozen and so are your bank accounts as well as your mother's investment accounts, just until we can straighten everything out. Also, we're probably going to have to begin foreclosure proceedings on your investment properties, and your house at the lake, but that will take several months so you probably don't have to worry about that yet. Just get Dave to call me. I'm sure once I get a chance to speak to him we can straighten everything out. I'm sure this is all a big misunderstanding… I just wish you had told me the truth on Tuesday when you called me. Maybe I could have done something to help… but now my hands are tied," the bank manager said.

What bullshit, she thought. She knew perfectly well that nothing she could have said to the bank manager on Tuesday would have made any difference in her present situation, but she needed to keep him on her side for as long as possible, at least until she could get Dave to be reasonable, so she continued on pleasantly.

"Of course I understand your position Tony, and I appreciate you telling me this directly. When I hear from Dave I'll be sure to tell him to call you. But why are you freezing my mother's investment accounts?" she asked.

"It's just temporary until everything gets straightened out. Your mother guaranteed some of Dave's loans and so we've put a temporary hold onto her funds just until we see how everything shakes out," he explained.

"Have you talked to her about this yet?" she asked.

"No, not yet. I was just about to call her, but I was hoping to speak to you first," he said.

"Please don't call her yet. Give me a chance to talk to her first," she pleaded.

"I can't hold off calling her very long. She needs to know what's going on." He paused and then continued. "Myrosia, confidentially, I'm telling you this as a friend. You need to consult a good lawyer, and not one from Dave's firm. It looks like you might be looking at bankruptcy, and you might even be facing criminal charges for fraud."

This last phone call left Myrosia even more shaken than the shouting match with Dave had.

John was outside waiting for them at the wreckers when they arrived. As he had promised the Jeep was sitting out front ready for her.

"I filled it up with gas and got it running for you so you wouldn't have to drive off in a cold car," he said.

"Thanks so much John. That's so kind of you. Keep this one safe for me," Myrosia said, handing him the keys to her SUV.

"Oh the cars will be safe enough, but what about you? I hope you aren't planning on staying alone out there at the lake house."

"Well I hadn't given it much thought. I don't really know where to stay. But right now I've got to get out to the house and pick up the Mini before Dave gets to it," she said.

"Myrosia honey, cars can be replaced, but I'd never forgive myself if anything happened to you. Why don't you just come and stay with Betsy and me for a few days until Dave calms down. In the meantime give me your keys and the code to the burglar alarm and I'll send a couple of the boys with the tow truck to go get the Mini for you," John said.

"Don't worry John, I'll look after Myrosia," said Bob, coming and putting his hand on her shoulder.

"I appreciate your concern, but you are both being overly protective. I'm quite capable of taking care of myself." Myrosia bristled inwardly at what she interpreted as patronizing treatment. "Besides, it's my house and I'm not running away anywhere."

"Well have it your own way, but I'm sending the boys with the tow truck anyway so that you don't have to drive it back here tonight yourself, and take this with you," said John holding out a small black pistol.

"No John, I don't want it. I don't have a permit to carry one of these. You know how I feel about guns. Besides, if I tried to use it I'd probably just shoot myself," she said.

"I really wish you'd take it and keep it with you. I've got a bad feeling about all this," John insisted.

She left without the gun, but accompanied by two young men in the tow truck. It turned out to be a good thing that she wasn't alone because when they pulled up to the house there were two strange men attempting to open the garage door.

"It's a good thing I changed that burglar alarm code," she said to Bob as they pulled to a stop in front of the house.

"Myrosia, lock the doors and stay here in the car. I'll go and see if I can straighten this out," said Bob.

"No Bob, don't be stupid, the car isn't worth it. Let's just get out of here and call the police," said Myrosia.

But it was too late. The two young mechanics had already jumped out of the tow truck armed with a baseball bat and a tire iron and were approaching the strangers.

"What do you think you're doing? This is private property," said the one young man.

"Hey, we don't want any trouble. We were sent out here by Mr. Walker to pick up his car," replied the would-be car thief.

"Well we're here with Mrs. Walker and we aren't about to let you touch her car," said the young man with the baseball bat.

"No problem. Like I said, we aren't looking for any trouble. Obviously there's some misunderstanding. We'll just leave and check with Mr. Walker."

The two intruders got into their car and drove off.

"Thanks so much Karl. It's a good thing you were here," Myrosia said.

"Nothing to it. Those two weren't much of a threat."

"Are you going to tow the Mini?" she asked.

"No, if it's okay with you I'll just drive it back. Tommy can drive the truck and I'll drive the Mini. I've been wanting to see how these things handle. Too bad it's too damn cold to put the top down,"

"Well have fun. Try to keep it under 100." She laughed as she opened the garage door and handed him her car keys.

On the drive back to town Myrosia and Bob talked.

"I'm really glad I went with you. When you asked me to come

along I honestly didn't think you were in any real danger, but when we got out there and I saw those two guys trying to get into the house I realized that I've been underestimating Dave," said Bob.

"Well it turns out they really weren't all that tough."

"Things might have turned out very differently if you'd been alone out there," he said.

They drove in silence for a few miles.

"We need to stop at an ATM so I can get you some more money," said Bob.

"Bob you've been really kind, but I can't keep taking money from you. I've got to come up with a more permanent solution. If I could just get back some of the money from Dave until I can find another job or something," she said.

"I'm happy to help you. We've been friends for a long time. I know you'd do the same for me if the situation was reversed. Besides, where are you going to get a job? No other law office is going to touch you with all this hanging over you," he said.

"You're probably right. I guess I need to find something I can sell," she said.

"What about the vehicles? Are they tied up as security for any loans?" he asked.

"I don't know. They weren't, at least not that I was aware of. I guess I should do a title search and see if they are free and clear. But the only car that's actually in my name is the Mini, and I'd really hate to have to sell it," she replied.

"I understand your feelings, but even if it's free of liens you can't expect to be able to keep it in a bankruptcy. When Dave's activities become public knowledge there'll probably be creditors coming out of the woodwork," he said.

"Yeah, you're right, it's just a car, I'll do a title search tomorrow," she said.

They were back in town now and he hesitated before pulling into the office parking lot where he had left his Hummer. He looked at his watch.

"It's supper time and I'm starving. Let's go to Mama Rossi's for a bite to eat," he suggested.

She thought about it for a second and then said, "Sure, why not, I don't feel like it but I've got to eat something."

Over too much wine at dinner the subject of where she was going to stay came up again.

"I don't think it's safe for you to stay at the lake house tonight. What are your plans?" he asked.

"Oh I'll probably just crash on Joanna's couch for a couple of days," she replied.

"You know you're always welcome to come home with me."

"I appreciate that, but it wouldn't look very good, me staying alone with you," she said.

"Wouldn't look good to who? What do you care what people think? You'd be safe there and I could make it a lot more comfortable for you than sleeping on Joanna's couch," he said.

"You're just offering me the guest room, right?" she said, flirting with him.

He looked her straight in the eyes and smiled. "As far as I'm concerned, at my place you're welcome to any bed you want. It's your choice."

Chapter 6

On Thursday morning Myrosia woke up in the guest room of Bob's luxurious condo with a tremendous headache.

Oh my god, another hangover. This is insane, she thought. I've got to cut back on this drinking. I can't believe I almost wound up in bed with Bob.

In the shower she pondered the events of the previous evening. Is she really in danger from Dave? Is it safe for her to stay alone at the lake house? What is going on between her and Bob? Did she make the right decision staying at Bob's apartment?

In spite of her embarrassment at coming so close to sleeping with Bob she knew that she has to face him some time. So wrapping herself in a bathrobe she wandered out to the kitchen. But Bob was gone. There was a note and a set of keys lying on the kitchen island next to the coffee machine. The note said:

Myrosia
I hope you had a good sleep. The coffee is made. Help yourself to anything you can find to eat. Here's a set of keys to the apartment so you can come and go as you please. You are welcome to stay here as long as you want.
Bob

She poured herself a cup of coffee, perched herself on a breakfast stool and pulled out her cell phone.

"Hi Joanna. Is this a good time to talk?" she asked.

"My god Myrosia, I've been worried sick about you. I've been trying to call you but I just kept getting your voice mail. What's going on?"

"Sorry I didn't pick up. I had the phone turned off. Dave finally called me back yesterday and the conversation rattled me so much that I turned the phone off in case he called back."

"Why, what did he say?" Joanna asked.

"He threatened me," Myrosia replied.

"He threatened you? What do you mean he threatened you? After everything he has done to you I'm surprised it wasn't you threatening to kill him. What did he say?" Joanna asked.

"Well, among other things he threatened to take my cars and send a couple of thugs over to 'talk some sense into me.'"

"Why, what set him off?" asked Joanna.

"I haven't had a chance to tell you, but yesterday I managed to find his Porsche so I took it and hid it. I knew that'd make him mad and I knew it would force him to call me, but I guess I underestimated how angry he'd get," said Myrosia.

"Did you say he threatened to send some guys over to hurt you? He's never done or said anything like that before has he?"

"No, that's what really rattled me. He's always been a jerk. He often made me feel like he thought I was stupid, or that I didn't look as good as I used to, so I wasn't surprised to hear him say that, but he's never been violent or threatening before."

"Do you think he's serious? Do you think he's just bluffing or would he actually follow through with his threats?" Joanna asked.

"I don't know. I wouldn't have thought so before, but now I really don't know. He sure isn't behaving like the man I thought I was married to, and when I got out to the house there were these two guys trying to break into the garage."

"Wow, that must have been scary," said Joanna.

"Well not really, because Bob Williams was with me and I had a couple of the boys that John had sent from the wreckers. So Dave's guys just took off. They weren't real tough guys. I think they were just a couple of regular guys Dave sent over to pick up the car."

"So what did you do?" Joanna asked.

"Well I sent both of my cars over to John at the auto wreckers for safekeeping and he's loaned me an old clunker to drive."

"Good for you," Joanna laughed. "But what's your plan now?

What do you think Dave will do next?"

"I don't know. He sure doesn't seem to be ready to negotiate with me, so just to be safe I'm trying to stay out of his way."

"Did you stay out at the lake house by yourself last night? Why didn't you call me? I'd have stayed there with you."

"Oh right Joanna. What would the two of us do if we were in any real danger? No, I wouldn't do that to you," said Myrosia.

"Well you could have come and stayed with me."

"I know that, and I almost did, but I ended up staying at Bob's apartment," said Myrosia.

"Oh my god, you're kidding! What's going on? I've always thought he was so hot. Did you sleep with him?" asked Joanna. "Oh shit, wait a second. My first appointment is here early."

"I'll call you back later," said Myrosia.

"Hell no, don't you dare keep me in suspense. I've got to hear all about this." Joanna paused then yelled to someone in the background. "I'm on the phone. I'll just be a minute."

"Well, did you do the deed? How was he? My god, did he tie you up? Did he get you to dress up in that bondage stuff?"

"No we didn't do anything," said Myrosia indignantly. "I slept in the guest room."

"Bullshit, I know he has the hots for you. That's been obvious for years, and now you're both single, so what stopped you? I've always thought he was gorgeous. Give me five minutes alone with him and I'd have been all over him," said Joanna.

"Well actually, that's pretty much what happened. I really made a fool of myself. I came onto him and he turned me down," said Myrosia.

"What? He turned you down? That sucks. What happened?"

"Well, after the car incident out at the house, we drove back into town and I was going to call you and come over to your place but we decided to stop and have some dinner at Mama Rossi's. Well I guess I hadn't eaten anything all day and I had too much wine and I started flirting a bit and the next thing I knew I was beside him in the booth. We were kissing and I had my hand on his leg," said Myrosia, and then she paused.

"Yeah, go on. You're driving me crazy, so what happened?"

"Now don't you go blabbing about this in the beauty salon. This is just between you and me, right? I'll kill you if word of this gets around town," said Myrosia.

"No, of course this is just between us. I wouldn't say anything. If word of this gets out it won't be thanks to me. It'll probably be because someone saw you groping this guy and sucking face in the middle of a popular local restaurant. Duh Myrosia! What were you thinking?" said Joanna.

"I told you I had too much to drink, and at first I thought it was just a little harmless flirting," said Myrosia.

"Harmless flirting? I wonder what your mother would have to say about 'harmless flirting' if she heard about it?" asked Joanna.

"Oh my god, I don't even want to think about what she'd say. I've got to call her and arrange to go see her today for lunch. I haven't told her about any of this yet," said Myrosia.

"Quit changing the subject. What happened? How come you wound up sleeping in the guest room in his apartment?"

"Well this is the really embarrassing part," said Myrosia.

"What could be more embarrassing than getting loaded and groping this guy in the middle of a busy restaurant?" asked Joanna.

"Joanna, it wasn't exactly the middle of the restaurant, and it wasn't all that busy. We were in one of the more private booths at the back. I don't think anyone could see us," said Myrosia.

"Nobody but the waiters, the kitchen staff, and anyone who wandered by going to the restroom. Did I miss anyone? I don't suppose Mama Rossi was there at that time of day?" said Joanna.

"No, thank god. If she'd seen me she'd have hauled me out of that booth by my ear and gotten straight on the phone to my mother. This is ridiculous. Here I am almost 45 years old and I'm terrified of a couple of old ladies," said Myrosia.

"Yeah well everyone's afraid of your mother. So go on, get to the embarrassing part. I can't wait," said Joanna.

"Well we get back to his place and I'm all over him. I mean all over him, but the next thing I know the room is spinning and I'm on my knees puking my guts out in the toilet and he's helping hold my hair back," said Myrosia.

"Yeah I can see how that would've spoiled the mood," said Joanna.

"I'm so embarrassed. I've got to cut back on the wine. I'm really glad though that we didn't go any further. That would have really messed things up. He's like a brother to me. I don't know what I was thinking," said Myrosia.

"Brother my ass. He sure doesn't look at you like a brother would. So how were things between you this morning?"

"I haven't seen him this morning. He'd left for the office by the time I got up, but he was really sweet about it last night. I guess he was just relieved to be able to pry this horny woman off of him."

"Look, don't be so hard on yourself. You've had one hell of a week. Your husband dumps you and steals your money and you find yourself drunk and alone with a gorgeous man who is obviously attracted to you and you just wanted some reassurance that you're still a desirable woman," said Joanna.

"You don't know the half of it Joanna," said Myrosia and proceeded to put her friend up to date with the rest of the events of the previous day.

"So you're under suspicion of fraud and you can't even access the law office resources to try and track down the money?"

"Well not exactly. The network administrator, that young guy Jeff, managed to slip me a piece of paper with his phone number on it. I think I can get him to give me remote access to anything I need, but I'd hate to get him into trouble. He's such a sweet kid," said Myrosia.

"I'm coming," Joanna shouted. "Sorry Myrosia, I've got to go, they're backing up out there. I'll call you later. You'd better come and stay with me tonight, unless of course you want to finish what you started last night with Bob."

"Oh shut up. I'll talk to you later," and she hung up.

Myrosia's next call was to Jeff, the network administrator.

"Hi Jeff, sorry to call you during work hours. Can you talk right now?" asked Myrosia.

"Sure Myrosia, I'm taking the day off. After everything that went down yesterday I didn't feel like going in today so I called Keith and told him that I'd be working from home today. That just wasn't right the way they threw you out like that. I haven't decided yet for sure but I don't think I'm gonna go in tomorrow either, but it doesn't really matter much with all of the partners taking the day off."

Myrosia began to bristle at the idea of one of the staff arbitrarily deciding to take time off work when she suddenly remembered that the welfare of the firm wasn't any of her concern any more.

"Well I appreciate your loyalty, but don't go risking your job on my account," said Myrosia.

"Don't worry about me. They need me more than I need them," he said.

"Yes, you're probably right about that. I'm not sure the partners realize how important you are to keeping things running smoothly at the firm. You said that all the partners would be gone on Friday. Where are they going? Maybe I could take advantage of them being gone to go back in and snoop some more?" she said.

"I don't know where Bob is going, but Keith and Peter are going to Tampa, Florida, this weekend for the Superbowl game. They said they wouldn't be back to work until Tuesday. Even with them gone I still don't think it would be a very good idea for you to go back in there. Someone would be sure to tell them, and they made me cancel your pass key so someone would have to let you in. Besides, I can get you anything you need."

"You're right, but I'd appreciate if you keep me informed about anything that happens over there," she said.

"Sure, happy to. And if you need access to any of the databases, or any of the files, just tell me what you need and I'll be happy to get it for you. Whatever you need. I'll call you whenever I hear anything. You can call me anytime you want."

"Thanks Jeff, there's nothing I need at the moment, but I'll keep that in mind," she said.

She called her mother and set up their lunch date and was about to head out the door when her phone rang. It was Bob. She was tempted to ignore the call but knew that she would have to speak to him at some point.

"Hi Myrosia, did you have a good sleep? How's your head this morning?" asked Bob.

"Oh I think I'm going to live. It was touch and go for a while there this morning but the coffee and Tylenol seem to have kicked in," she said.

"I've got some good news for you. I did a title search on your vehicles. As you know the SUV is in Dave's name and it's leased, but the Mini is in your name and it is free and clear."

"Well that's good to know. I love that car, but it's nice to know if I get desperate I can always sell it," she replied.

"That's not the only reason I called. I was wondering if you're free for lunch?" he asked.

"No, I'm sorry. I've got a lunch date with my mother. It's time I filled her in on what's going on," she said.

"Oh that's too bad. I was hoping we'd have a chance to get together before I leave for Rochester this afternoon," he said.

"You're going away?" she asked.

"I thought I mentioned that I've got to go to Rochester, but I'll be back on the weekend. Meanwhile you're more than welcome to stay at my apartment. I've already told the concierge that you'll be staying for a few days. It's a lot safer for you than staying out at the lake house." He paused. "Besides, it was nice waking up this morning knowing you were there even if you weren't up yet."

"Bob, I appreciate everything that you've done for me, but I think it is better if I stay with Joanna," she said.

"Myrosia, don't be silly. That apartment of hers is nowhere near as secure as my condo, and the parking situation is horrible. Just stay at my place. You can park in the underground parking. I know how much you like to swim every day so you'll have the pool in the building to use. Get Joanna to come and keep you company while I'm gone," he said.

"I don't know. I'd feel really funny about being here when you're not here," she said.

"I could call and postpone the meeting if you want me to."

"Oh no, I couldn't ask you to do that," she said.

"That's too bad. I was hoping that you'd ask me to stay home.

Maybe we could have an evening without so much wine," he said laughing.

"Oh Bob, I'm so embarrassed about last night. That's twice this week you've witnessed me with my head in the toilet."

"Nothing to be embarrassed about Myrosia. It was my fault both times. I was the one pouring and I guess I should have lightened up some. I never realized you were such a cheap drunk," he said.

"Yeah well, you didn't force me to drink it. But that's not the only thing I'm embarrassed about. I'm so sorry that I threw myself at you. It must've been really uncomfortable for you being groped by a drunk woman." she said.

He laughed. "Uncomfortable? Did I seem uncomfortable? I thought you could tell how I felt."

She flushed thinking back to his physical response to her hand rubbing him.

"I'm really sorry I did that. You are such a good friend to me. You've always treated me like a sister, and then I get drunk and assault you like that," she said.

There was an awkward silence for a moment and then finally he spoke.

"Myrosia, are you really sorry about that? Isn't it obvious to you how I feel about you? We've been close friends all these years and yes, I've always kept a proper distance from you, but that's because you were the wife of my friend and business partner. Yes, I'm your friend, and you're very important to me Myrosia, but definitely not like a sister."

"Well, how come, later, when I threw myself at you again, why did you stop me? Why did you insist on putting me to bed in the guest room?" she asked.

"You have no idea how hard it was for me to stop last night. But I've waited for you for all these years, so I can wait a little longer. Obviously I wanted you badly last night, but I want to be sure that if we do finally make love it's because you want me too. Not because you've had too much to drink or because you're hurt and frightened, or because you want revenge against Dave," he said.

"I don't know what to say Bob," said Myrosia.

"Don't say anything. Just promise me that you'll be extra cautious, Dave's acting really strange. You can reach me on my cell phone any time you want to talk and I can always come back in a hurry if you need me. I don't want to pressure you though so it's probably better if I stay in Rochester for a couple of days to give you some time to think. But I really would feel better if you stayed at my place. Get Joanna to come and stay with you, okay?"

Chapter 7

Myrosia pulled into the parking lot of the seniors' residence a little before 11:00 am.

At the front desk she signed in and smiled at the receptionist. "Hi Carol, I'm meeting my mother for lunch today. Do you know if she's still up in her apartment, or is she in the dining room waiting for me?"

"Denise has gone up to get her. They should be down in a moment. Why don't you wait for her in the dining room?" replied the receptionist.

Myrosia chose a private table off to one side of the sumptuously appointed dining area where she hoped it would be possible for the two women to have some privacy to talk. She had barely gotten seated and opened the leather bound lunch menu when she saw her mother being escorted into the room on the arm of her personal attendant.

"Hi Mama, it's great to see you managing without a walker today," said Myrosia as the attendant helped the older women into her seat at the table.

"What I need walker for, nothing wrong with my legs. These people try to make me use walker cause they're afraid of lawyers, lawsuits, and insurance companies," the older woman made a hand gesture indicating that she was referring to the management of the senior's residence. "That's the problem with this country, too many lawyers, too many lawsuits," she said wagging her index finger.

"Will you be needing anything else Mrs. Dabrowski?" asked the attendant.

"No dear, you go take a break. My daughter and me are going to have a nice lunch. You go have your lunch."

"What, they think I need to be spoon fed like a baby? I can eat my

71

lunch without her hanging over me," she said under her breath, as she watched the younger woman walking away from the table.

As soon as she was sure that the attendant was out of hearing range she turned to Myrosia and said, "So, tell me what's wrong."

"Mama, I never said there was anything wrong."

"Of course something's wrong. You think a mother don't know these things. I heard something wrong in your voice the other day when you called. Then this morning when you called to ask me to eat lunch I knew it was big," she said.

"But Mama, we often get together for lunch," Myrosia protested.

"Yeah, yeah. So what is it? Is that Nicki giving you a hard time, or is it that swinia you married?" she said.

"No, it's not Nicki. It's Dave." Myrosia paused. "He's left me for another woman. I got home on Monday night and found a note saying he was leaving me."

"Thank god! Why you wait so long to tell me! I been praying to Saint Hedwig for this ever since you met that palant. We get vodka to celebrate. We toast the start of your new life. I gotta call Father Gorski and we get the annulment process started. God knows the church owes it to us after all the money your father and I have given them over the years. Pity it didn't happen back when we had a Polish Pope, it might have speeded things up. Never mind, we get the annulment even with that Nazi in charge. I wish this had happened years ago. If you had left him back when your children were babies then maybe that daughter of yours might not have turned out to be such a spoiled brat. Right after lunch I gotta call the church. I promised Saint Hedwig a statue if she arrange this for you. This is gonna cost me big, but it's worth every penny. Now with you free of him you can finally start to live your own life. It's not too late. You're still a young woman," her mother exclaimed as she started to wave the waiter over to order the vodka.

"Mama, wait. Don't be too hasty about the celebration. There's bigger problems than just Dave leaving me. He cleared out everything in the house, took all the money out of our bank accounts and investments. He's taken all our money and hidden it somewhere, probably in some offshore bank accounts that I can't access even if I could find them," said Myrosia.

"Quiet, here comes the waiter. Don't let him hear you. The staff here love to gossip. We don't want them to know our business. Just order," whispered her mother.

"I just want a salad and some coffee. My stomach is too upset to eat," said Myrosia.

"Glupi. You need to eat." She turned to the waiter. "Juan, how's the roast beef special today? Last time it was tough."

"Madam, I tried it and it was excellent. Mrs. Wong ordered it and she was pleased," the waiter replied.

"What would Mrs. Wong know about good meat? Those Chinese would eat a Labrador Retriever if you plunked it down on their plate."

"Mama, please ..." Myrosia smiled apologetically at the waiter.

"Well Juan, my daughter is embarrassed by me. Oh well, I guess you'd better give us two of the specials, and tell the kitchen not to skimp on the gravy this time."

When the waiter had gone her mother continued. "Okay, prosie, tell me more about that scum of a husband of yours. What do you mean he's taken everything out of the house?"

"I mean that when I walked into the house late on Monday evening everything of value in the house was gone. All the expensive furniture, the art, all the cash we had on hand, all the expensive wine that Dave had been collecting. I thought we'd had a robbery until I found his note. I've got absolutely no money. The bank has cancelled all my credit cards, and my line of credit. I've got nothing left and there's no money coming in. I've been working for Dave all these years and so now I don't even have a job. Yesterday the other partners told me not to come back in to work. It was so humiliating. Nobody is going to hire me. I don't know what to do," explained Myrosia.

"Well at least you still got the house. Once the divorce goes through and you tell the judge the whole story, they give you the house. You can sell it and you'll have plenty money to start over. You never needed that big zamek out there on the lake anyway. That was just that palant Dawid showing off, trying to be the big shot with all the country club snobs."

"No Mama, I don't even have the house. Dave refinanced the mortgage without telling me and now we owe more on it than the house is even worth. I can't make the payments and there's no equity left in the house. Dave has stolen it all. The bank manager says that they are going to have to start foreclosure proceedings if I can't make the payments, and they might even be looking at fraud charges regarding the refinancing because of irregularities with the appraisal," said Myrosia.

"Like I always said, all lawyers are crooks, and that one you married is one of the biggest. He deserves to go to jail for this. So much for all his big deals. He won't be such a big shot when he's in jail with all the perverts and murderers," said her mother.

"But there's more Mama. I don't know how to tell you this. I'm so ashamed, but he's even stolen your investments. Well he hasn't stolen them exactly, but somehow he managed to use them as security for one of his business deals and now the bank has frozen your money so we can't touch it. The annuity that Tata set up for you is still in place, well at least as far as I can tell anyway, and you've still got your social security, but the rest is frozen. If the bank takes your money to cover Dave's debts, I don't know how long you're even going to be able to stay living here. I'm so sorry Mama. I'm so ashamed that I didn't protect you from all of this," said Myrosia.

"How could he steal my investments? I gave you power of attorney, not him. He didn't have any right to do that," said her mother indignantly.

"I don't know how he did it. He must have forged my name on the documents and gotten someone from the office to witness it. I don't know how he did it, or who helped him, but I've got to try and find out if I've got any hope of getting the money back, or of clearing my name," explained Myrosia.

"What do you mean 'clear your name?' You're the victim, not the crook who stole the money," said her mother.

"Well a lot of people don't think so. People are saying that I am in on it with Dave, that this is all some sort of ruse to steal the money and hide it outside of the country. They're saying I know where Dave is, and that once things die down I'm going to join him somewhere," explained Myrosia.

"That's crazy," said her mother.

"That's not all. There seems to be some money missing from Dave's trust accounts at the office. The partners wanted me to leave because the authorities are investigating Dave for trying to bribe a government official and other possible fraud charges, and they don't want me to have any access to the files in the office in case I try to destroy evidence," said Myrosia.

"Some idea of loyalty they've got. I guess they've all forgotten that it was Dabrowski money that helped start that office. Where would they be without our help? I'll tell you where they'd be. They'd all be out chasing ambulances trying to find somebody to sue instead of being big shots doing their fancy real estate deals."

"Well Bob's been really kind throughout all this, but I think Peter and Keith are just afraid of losing everything they've worked for and are trying to distance themselves."

"They're all crooks. What about you? You're losing everything you worked for," her mother shook her head in disgust. "I guess maybe it's time for you to sell those things I gave you. This qualifies as an emergency."

"No Mama, Dave got those too. They were in the safe in my bedroom closet. I didn't think that he even knew they were there."

"What! I gave you those for an emergency so you'd have a little something to fall back on. Why did you put them somewhere Dawid could find them? They'd have been safer here in my mattress," her mother shook her head in exasperation.

"How many times did I told you that everything can fall apart like that," her mother snapped her fingers. "You've got to have something hidden for a rainy day. You, you've always had an easy time. No big problems, no war, no Hitler, no Stalin. You've never been hungry, you thought I was just being a paranoid, crazy old lady, but your father and I lived through terrible things that you can't even imagine, as children back in Poland during the war, and then after the Soviets took over. Everything was a struggle. Even after we came here everything was big struggle. You think it's hard for you to get a job?

Humph, you got a fancy college degree. Try getting a job when you can't even speak no English. We couldn't find no fancy office jobs. We had to do anything we could to get by. But we managed to made a good life for you and your brother with the scrap metal business and then the pawn shops. We never talked about our troubles because we didn't want to burden you with our memories. We wanted an easy life for you. We never wanted you to see the things we seen. We wanted you to have everything we didn't have, but how many times did I told you to keep a little something hidden away for a rainy day. But no. You, you just don't listen to an old lady. Well, I guess now you gonna see I was right."

"Mama that's not fair. I have always listened to you. I thought I had all the finances set up carefully, that everything was safe. I didn't have all my eggs in one basket. I thought the money was safe. I just never thought that Dave would do this to us," said Myrosia with tears beginning to well up in her eyes.

"Tut tut prosie, don't cry. Don't let these people see you cry. I don't try to upset you. I'm just worried about you. I know I need to take some of the blame. I should have done more to get rid of Dawid years ago. You just married the wrong man. I was luckier than you. Your father was a good man. He was a good husband and a good father," said her mother.

"I know Mama, I miss Tata so much. I wish he was here. I don't think Dave would even have tried this if Tata was still alive," said Myrosia.

"I miss him too," she said reaching over and patting Myrosia's hand. "But don't you worry. That scum Dawid is not going to get away with this. You're a smart girl, we'll fix him."

They sat in silence while the waiter brought out their food.

Finally her mother broke the silence.

"So, how much money you need?" she asked.

"I've got about $50 left from the money Bob Williams gave me, but that'll just barely put gas in the Jeep John loaned me. If I want to stay in the house, even if I don't try to cover the mortgage payments, I still have the electric bill and the heat and the insurance, the phone bills. Then there's the insurance on the cars and the car payment on the SUV, the health insurance, and money for Dylan and Nicki every month. It costs a fortune to keep those two in college. Well Dylan not so much, he's careful with his money, but Nicki thinks money pours out of a big invisible faucet in the sky. The only time that girl calls me is when she wants me to give her more money. You should see her credit card bills every month," said Myrosia.

"First thing you gotta do is cut off Nicki's spending. Cancel her credit cards," said her mother.

"The bank already froze them. She's really gonna scream when she finds out. I tried to call her just before I came here, but she's not answering her phone. I don't want her to have a problem if she tries to use them, I've been trying to warn her, but I swear that girl ignores my calls unless she wants something from me," said Myrosia.

"Well let her scream at her father, he's the one that did this," said her mother.

"I know, but there's still her rent out there in Los Angeles, and her car expenses. She's got almost four months left until graduation. Her tuition is all paid, but then there's the wedding. You'd think it was a royal wedding. The plans get bigger and bigger every day."

"That stupid boy she's marrying, he don't know what he's getting into. She gonna make his life hell. It's a good thing his family is rich. He's gonna need all the money he can get. Just tell her the truth. You got no money thanks to her palant of a father. It's time she got a job to teach her the value of money. What kind of job you think she gonna get with a degree in Art history? Anyway, she's Dawid's problem. Let him worry about that. So tell me something good. How's the boy doing over in England? He sends me emails and calls me from his computer, but I never hear from Nicki."

"Dylan is great. I'm sure he told you that he's living in a residence at Oxford. He likes his roommate, another visiting engineering student from Venezuela. They're working together on some sort of new solar cells. I'm so proud of him. He's living in a dorm room and he makes a little beer money doing tutoring, so he's not so expensive. He never asks for anything, and it's only for one semester then he'll be back at MIT for the Ph.D. program."

"He's a good boy, you don't got to worry about him. He's

gonna be fine, but you gotta be firm with Nicki. You gotta get some money but don't spend any of it unless you absolutely have to. Don't give Nicki any more money and don't pay any of the other bills until you don't got no choice," said her mother.

"I know Mama. I'm trying to juggle things to see what I can do without, but I still have to eat and I have to put gas in the vehicle. I need some money coming in. I borrowed some money off Bob Williams but I can't keep doing that," said Myrosia.

"Why not? Dabrowski money and your father's business connections helped start that law firm so you keep taking his money as long as he's willing to give it to you. Besides, he's sweet on you, so you take advantage of it. Men are pretty stupid when they think with the little head. You be nice to him, but not too nice, you know what I mean. He's not gonna buy the cow when he can get the milk for free. You remember that."

"Mama! I'm not going to take advantage of him. He's a nice man and he's been very kind to me. Besides, what makes you think he's interested in me like that?" said Myrosia.

"You think I'm stupid? I see the way he looks at you all these years. Besides, Mrs. Matyjakowski said she saw you driving around with him and going into his apartment building yesterday. You think I don't know what's going on? I wasn't always an old lady. I know about men. I didn't always look like this. I used to be young and beautiful like you," said her mother.

"Nothing's going on Mama," said Myrosia flushing slightly.

Her mother shook her head in disgust. "Humph, another lawyer. I tell you this country has too many lawyers. But I think maybe this one isn't so bad. We'll see."

"If I could find out where Dave put everything maybe I could get something back that I could sell," said Myrosia.

"You want something to sell? Look down at your hands. Why you still wearing those wedding rings? Sell the rings. You got any other jewelry you can sell?" asked her mother.

"Maybe a few pairs of earrings, not too much. You know I never really cared all that much about jewelry. The only reason I've got these expensive rings is because Dave wanted to impress people.

He was going to buy me some other jewelry one time, but I told him not to waste the money," said Myrosia.

"You learn from this. From now on, a man wants to buy you expensive jewelry, you let him. Your new man, he wants to give you a gift of cash you don't be proud and stupid, you take it, you understand me? And if it's jewelry he wants to give you make sure it's gold. That way you'll always have something you can pawn if you need money. You gonna lose on the spread, but at least you've got something," said her mother.

Myrosia ignored her mother's comment about a new man. "So you think I should go see Tito at the pawn shop and pawn the rings?"

"No, no, no, don't go there. He's a crook. He'd steal a blind man's cane if he thought he could make a dollar off it."

"I thought he was your friend, Mama. You sold him the business," said Myrosia.

"Not such a good friend that he wouldn't rob you if he thought he could get away with it. You should know by now that you can't trust people where money is concerned. No, these are too expensive for Tito to deal with. For these you gotta go see that Jew Goldstein, the one with the fancy jewelry stores. He sells all that real expensive jewelry. You'll get a better price from him. But we gotta come up with a good story to tell him. He can smell when someone needs money real bad and he'll take advantage of you, so you gotta make him think you still got plenty. Maybe you tell him you angry at Dawid. You found out he is cheating on you and you want revenge. Goldstein'll like that. Better still, maybe you tell him your new man is gonna buy you new rings. He'll smell a big sale and get greedy. You get a better price from him that way."

"Mama, I can't pretend that Bob and I are together. People will talk," said Myrosia.

"People are already talking. You think Mrs. Matyjakowski's gonna keep quiet?" said her mother.

"No, I suppose not. So what do you think I should do about selling the car?" Myrosia asked.

"I don't know nothing about selling new cars. Old junkers I know. About the car you better go talk to John. He'll know what to do.

He loves you like a daughter. He'll make sure you get a good price."

The waiter came back to pick up their plates.

"Would either of you ladies like some dessert and some more coffee?" he asked.

"No thank you. I think we've had ..." began Myrosia.

Her mother made a gesture of impatience toward her. "Yes Juan, send up a big tray of pastries and a pot of coffee up to my apartment. We gonna have dessert up there."

"Certainly madam," the waiter said and walked away to place the order.

Myrosia looked over at her mother in surprise.

Her mother smiled. "Well prosie, we might as well enjoy it while we can. These people don't know yet that I can't pay for all this. Come on; take me up to my apartment."

Chapter 8

It was after 2 pm when Myrosia left her mother's apartment. She sat in the Jeep waiting for it to warm up and pondered her mother's advice. She looked at her watch and decided to take a deep breath and make the call that her mother had advised her to make.

"Hi Bob, it's Myrosia. Are you still in town?" she asked when he answered his cell phone.

"Yep, I'm still at the office just finishing up a few things. I need to stop by the apartment and pick up some clothes before I leave. I'm glad you called. I was afraid that I might've scared you off with what I said to you this morning, and I'd hate to damage our friendship," he said.

"I've got to admit that I'm still feeling a little weird about my behavior last night, and I hesitated about calling you, but I really need some more help and you're the only person that can help me with this. I'm still out at the Manor. I just finished lunch with my mother. We had a really long talk and she came up with some interesting strategies for dealing with Dave, but I need your help to pull it off," she said.

"Of course I'll help. What do you want me to do?"

"Do you have time to meet me before you head out of town? I think it would be better to talk about this in person," she said.

"Sure, I'm just about ready to leave the office. How about you meet me at my apartment in about 15 minutes? I can pack and you can tell me what you need," he said.

Arriving at the apartment Myrosia used the electronic key fob Bob had given her to access the underground parking. She parked in visitor parking and took the guest elevator up to the lobby. She walked up to the concierge's desk and smiled.

"Hello, I'm Myrosia Walker, I'm staying with Bob Williams in the penthouse," she said.

"Hello Ms. Walker. My name is Charles. Mr. Williams mentioned that you would be staying with us, and he asked me to make sure that you had anything you needed," he said.

"I'm parked in the visitor parking area right now, but I was just wondering if I should move to the owner's spot next to where Bob parks his Hummer?" she asked.

Bob had already told her to park in one of his assigned parking spots which were in front of his private elevator that opened directly into his foyer. But part of Myrosia's plan involved making sure that as many people as possible knew that she was staying with Bob.

"Certainly Ms. Walker, go ahead and park in one of Mr. Williams' parking spots. If you'd like to leave me your keys you can go ahead up to the residence and I will move your vehicle for you."

"Oh no, that's fine, thank you. I can do it myself."

"If there is anything else I can do for you simply dial *9 on the residence phone and it will ring here at my desk."

"Thank you Charles," she said as she turned to take the guest elevator back down to move her car. She smiled as the elevator doors closed because she could see that the concierge and the doorman were already talking about her.

Up in the apartment she sat down on the sofa in the formal living room, curled her legs up under her and covered herself with a cashmere blanket. She looked out through the vast expanse of UV coated glass. From where she sat she could look out in one direction and see the lake, and in the other direction she could see downtown Buffalo. The view might be beautiful, but the sub-zero temperatures outside and all that January snow left her feeling chilled to the bone.

A few moments later she heard the gentle dinging sound of the elevator so she stood up and walked toward the foyer to greet him as the elevator doors opened.

"Hey Myrosia, it's great to come home and find you here to greet me," he said as he set down his briefcase and hung his overcoat in the cavernous front closet.

She couldn't help noticing how good he looked, with his blond hair starting to go a little grey at the temples and his tall muscular body. Wow, it's amazing what a nice suit can do for a man. Smarten up, get a grip on yourself. Oh well, he's used to having women drooling over him, she thought.

As if reading her mind he turned and smiled at her, then took the few steps toward her and gave her a friendly kiss on the cheek.

"Damn it's cold out there. I'm frozen. The only problem with living so close to the office is that the car heater doesn't get a chance to warm up. You look frozen too. Did you just get here? Would you like a hot chocolate? There's cups beside the espresso machine, and some Bailey's in the liquor cabinet if you want some," he grinned.

She couldn't help laughing. "Yes, a hot chocolate is exactly what I need, but no, I think I'll pass on the Bailey's. Do you want me to make you one too?" she asked.

"That'd be nice. I'm just gonna go and get changed. I'll just be a minute," he said.

A few moments later he came out of his bedroom dressed in jeans and a warm sweater.

"Do you mind if we bring these into my room to drink these? That way I can pack while you tell me your plans."

She followed him into the bedroom and sat in one of the big green leather chairs in front of the gas fireplace sipping her hot chocolate. While he packed she began telling him some of the strategy that her mother had suggested.

He listened to her in silence, and when she was finished he turned and looked at her. After what seemed like an eternity he spoke.

"Let me make sure I understand this. So you want us to pretend to be lovers so that you can get a better price when you sell your rings to the jeweler? And so that people will stop thinking that you're working with Dave to hide the money? And to make Dave jealous and angry so that he might do something stupid and reveal what he's done with the money?" he said.

"Well, uh, yes," she replied thinking how cold and manipulative it sounded when it was expressed like that.

"Well, the first two might work, but I think trying to make Dave jealous might backfire on you." He paused. "So, if I agree does it mean that we get to cuddle and smooch in public places and you get to grope me in dark corners of restaurants?" he asked with a straight face.

"Uh …" She didn't know how to respond.

He laughed. "Well I had to try, I mean what kind of lawyer would I be if I didn't try to negotiate something for myself in the deal. Of course I'll help you, it sounds like fun. When do we start?"

She thought that the laugh lines around his eyes made him even more appealing.

It was almost 4:30 when he pulled over to the curb in front of the jewelers.

Before they got out he said, "Okay here's the deal. If we're gonna make this work we've got to make it look good. I'm going to be the perfect gentleman and come around and help you down from this tank. Then we're going to kiss out here on the sidewalk so as many people as possible see us without it looking too much like we're trying to be noticed. I'm warning you. It's not going to be a brotherly kiss so try not to wince." He grinned. "Then when we go inside we're going to look at the most expensive rings he's got in the place, and I'm going to do most of the talking while you do a lot of looking adoringly into my eyes. None of the rings are going to be good enough to suit us though and at one point I'm going to have to excuse myself to take a business call. While I'm busy talking on the phone you can be looking through the catalogues and telling the jeweler how you want to sell all the jewelry that Dave gave you. So how's your acting? You ready?"

"Okay, let's do it. I think I'm as ready as I'm ever gonna be."

He walked around to her side of the Hummer and opened the door. He took her hand and helped her carefully down onto the icy sidewalk. Still partially in the shelter of the Hummer door he pulled her toward him and kissed her. It was definitely not a brotherly kiss and it definitely didn't feel like acting. When he finally let her go their eyes locked for a moment and he smiled. Then he leaned close to her again and whispered, "Academy award quality."

Holding hands they walked over to the door and he pressed the security button. She was still catching her breath as they were buzzed into the store.

In the store they were greeted by a sales clerk.

"Hello, how can I help you?" she asked.

"We're here to look at diamond rings for my lady. What have you got?" said Bob.

The sales clerk glanced out the window at the Hummer parked at the curb and then quickly evaluated the two people standing in front of her.

"Certainly sir. If you would like to come over to the diamond area I'm sure we can find something that your lady friend will love," she said gesturing toward what looked like a small reception room off to the side of the main store.

Inside the room the clerk asked, "May I take your coats? Mr. Goldstein will be right out to help you."

Almost immediately, before they even had a chance to get seated, the heavy-set jeweler appeared and held out his hand. With a big smile he said, "Ah, Mr. Williams, so nice to see you. Please sit down. It's bitterly cold out there today. Would you like a coffee to warm up?"

"Yes, coffee would be nice. I like mine with a little cream if you've got it, but Myrosia takes hers black," Bob said and the clerk immediately scurried off to get the coffee.

"How can I help you today?" asked the jeweler.

"I'm looking for a diamond ring for my lady, something unique and really spectacular, with matching wedding bands for the two of us. I'm not sure you carry the sort of thing that I'm looking for, but I thought we'd check with you because I always try to support local businesses as much as I can," Bob said.

"I appreciate your patronage. I'm sure that I can help you. As you know, if you don't see what you're looking for in the store today I can special order anything you want. I have connections with some of the best jewelry designers in the world and for the stone itself, well, I bring in the best stones directly from the cutters in Belgium, always beautiful and one of a kind, just like the lady herself," said the jeweler turning his smile toward Myrosia.

"Oh, how thoughtless of me. Let me introduce my fiancée. Myrosia this is Adam Goldstein. Adam, this is Myrosia Dabrowski-Walker," said Bob.

"Ah lovely to meet you. I know some Dabrowski's. Would you be any relation to Anna and Caspar Dabrowski?" he asked.

It was all Myrosia could do to keep from laughing out loud. You could almost see the gears turning in the jeweler's mind. It was obvious he was making the connections between her parents and Dave and Bob as business partners.

"Why yes, Anna and Caspar are my parents," she said smiling.

"I was so sorry to hear about your father's passing. He was such an important part of the Buffalo business community. How is your mother doing?" the jeweler asked.

"We both miss my father of course, but my mother is a strong woman. She is managing just fine. She sold the house and moved into one of the seniors' apartments at the Hazelton Manor so she is very comfortable," Myrosia replied.

"Well that's nice to hear," the jeweler replied.

Just as her mother had predicted, Myrosia could see that the jeweler was using this information to estimate Myrosia's value as a potential client.

"Well dear, Mr. Williams wants to get you something spectacular, something truly unique, so let me show you a few things so we can get an idea of what would take your breath away," he said.

Myrosia looked up at Bob and thought, I already know what can take my breath away, remembering the kiss outside on the sidewalk.

After a few minutes of feigning interest in the rings on display Bob excused himself to go and make a phone call while Myrosia continued to sit with the jeweler and discuss rings.

"Bob will probably be on the phone for a while. I know what lawyers are like when they get talking, so this might be a good time for you and I to discuss another matter. Bob is buying these rings for us, but I have a few small pieces of jewelry of my own that I would like to sell. My ex-husband bought me these and I was wondering if you could look at them for me and tell me what you think," she said.

She pulled the rings out of her purse and placed them on the black velvet pad between her and the jeweler.

"I would like to sell them as soon as possible. I want to get rid of everything he ever gave me. I just want them out of my sight. I know I'm so much better off with Bob. I'm so lucky to have him," she said gazing out to the showroom where Bob was standing talking on the phone.

"But I'm still so angry at Dave for everything he put me through all these years that I want to sell these right away. I don't want the energy of these things around me," she said, surprised at how real the words felt.

"I can certainly understand how you feel, and while these are certainly very valuable pieces of jewelry, you must keep in mind that you can never expect to recover what was spent on them originally, especially if you want to sell them quickly," he said pulling out his eye piece and examining the stones very closely.

"Oh I understand that. You know my parents had the pawn shops for years. I know how the business works. I just want to get rid of them and get a fair price," she said.

"How old are they? I see a certain amount of wear on the bands," he asked.

"These aren't the original ones he bought me when we first got married. He bought me these about 15 years ago once his practice had built up to where we could afford something better," she said thinking that actually Dave had bought them to appease her after the blow up 15 years previously when she found out about the affair with his assistant at the office.

"Do you know how much your ex-husband paid for these originally?" he asked.

"Oh I think it might have been somewhere around thirty thousand dollars," she said.

Actually she knew exactly how much he had paid for them but her mother had advised her to appear casual about the money. 'The rich get richer and the poor get screwed. Remember that.' was one of the pieces of advice her mother had given her earlier that afternoon.

"Well I don't know. There really isn't much of a market for something like this. They're not old enough to be vintage, and most buyers in this price range want something new... but maybe, since Mr. Williams is such a good customer and he's buying you something even lovelier to replace them ..." he paused waiting for a response from her.

She remained silent remembering another piece of her mother's advice. 'Don't talk too much during the negotiation. Let him sweat a bit.'

"Do you have the original bill of sale?" he asked.

"No, probably not after all this time, but I can probably get some sort of documentation from the insurance company, or maybe Dillmans in New York City where we bought them could give me something, if you want proof that they aren't stolen," she stiffened and her voice went cold, feigning offense.

"Oh no, no of course not, that won't be necessary under the circumstances. I've known your family for years, and Mr. Williams is a good customer. But I'm afraid that the best I could do would be $7000," he said apologetically.

Her mother's strategy had worked. Myrosia struggled to maintain her composure. Her mother had warned her that she'd be lucky to get $5000 for the rings, $500 if she had taken them to Tito at the pawn shop.

"That would be fine. Anything to get rid of them."

"Hey baby, I'm sorry to leave you alone so long. Did you find anything that you like yet?" Bob said as he came back into the room and stroked her cheek lovingly.

"No, not yet, but Mr. Goldstein has agreed to buy these old ones from me," she said.

"That's nice. I hope you're giving her a good price," he said smiling at the jeweler.

"Yes, he's been very kind. He knows I just want rid of them to make room on my fingers for the new ones," she said looking up at Bob smiling lovingly.

He smiled back at her. "Myrosia honey, I'm sorry to have to cut this short, but it's getting close to Adam's closing time and we've got dinner reservations, so maybe we could come back again next week and find you something."

"Oh, okay. I didn't realize how late it was getting. I don't want to keep you," she smiled apologetically at the jeweler.

"No, no trouble," the jeweler replied, hesitant to let them leave without making a sale.

"So how does this sale of my old jewelry work? Is it cash, or do you write me a check?" asked Myrosia.

"Oh I never keep that kind of cash on the premises. Usually I ask people to come back a few days later to pick up a check for the items that I'm purchasing from them..." he said.

"Oh well, never mind, maybe ..." Myrosia started to say when Bob cut her off.

"Come on Adam, just cut her a check and get it over with. You know we'll be back," said Bob pretending to be getting impatient.

"Of course, of course, I understand how you feel. Better to get rid of the old memories and make a whole new start. How should I make out the check?" he asked.

"Just make it out to Myrosia Walker. That's M-Y-R-O-S-I-A."

Chapter 9

Back at the apartment Myrosia was standing in front of the expanse of glass looking out at the lights of the city and Bob was bustling around preparing to leave.

"That was fun. I really enjoyed playing your fiancé. You're a great actress," he said.

"Yeah, it went really well, but I feel a little bit bad taking advantage of the old man like that," she said.

"Don't worry about him. He'll make his money on that deal. If I know Adam he'll probably double his money. He's made plenty off me over the years, and who knows maybe I'll go back and buy you something after all," he said.

She pretended not to have heard his last comment.

"Yeah, he kept mentioning what a good customer you are. But I've never noticed you wearing much jewelry. What is it that you buy from Goldstein?" she asked raising one eyebrow in mock curiosity.

She knew that even when he was younger Bob liked to surprise his lady friends with gifts and that the gifts had gotten progressively more expensive over the years as his income had risen. His ex-wife Janice was regularly seen sporting new baubles.

It was his turn to pretend that he had not heard her.

"Well I'm all set. I'd better get going. I wish I had time to stay and take you and Joanna out for dinner, but the snow is really starting to come down. Winters like this one really make me appreciate the Hummer. I can drive over anything with that tank. Too bad GM stopped making them." He turned to face her. "Are you sure you'll be okay? If you want I can still call and cancel," Bob asked hopefully.

"No I'll be fine. We'll probably just order in Chinese and watch a movie," said Myrosia.

"Oh that reminds me, I got some cash for you out of the bank machine." He reached inside his sweater and pulled a bulging envelop out of his shirt pocket. "There should be $3000 in there," he said handing it to her.

"No, that's too much ..." she began to say but he cut her off.

"Take it Myrosia. I know you got that check from the jewelry, but you might not be able to access that money for a few days, and you should have some cash on hand. Besides, you're a lot cheaper to have around than Janice was," he said ruefully.

"This is just a loan, Bob. I'll pay you back," she said.

"I'm not worried about it," he said. "Now don't forget to go first thing in the morning and open the account at the credit union. I called my buddy Greg who's the manager over there and he said he'd take care of everything, but if you have any problems just give me a call."

She walked over and put her arms around him and they kissed.

When they finally pulled apart he said, "Mmm, that was nice, but you really don't have to do that Myrosia. I'm not paying for your affection, and there's nobody watching. You don't need to put on the act here."

"Did that feel like an act?" she asked.

At that moment the phone rang saving him from having to come up with a response. It was the concierge announcing that Joanna had arrived downstairs.

"Yes Charles, please show her right up, and could you make a note for Philip and Randall that both Ms. Walker and Ms. Lubinski will be staying here until further notice. Please ensure that they get anything they need while they're here," he said into the phone.

They both moved toward the foyer when they heard the sound of the elevator.

"Thank you Charles for helping Ms. Lubinski with her luggage," he said as the concierge rolled Joanna's suitcase into the marble foyer. "I'll take it from here."

"Hello Joanna, I'm so glad that you could come and keep Myrosia company," he said leaning down to give the shorter woman a kiss on the cheek.

"Are you kidding? I wouldn't miss this for anything. I don't often get a chance to see how the other half lives," Joanna replied glancing around the enormous apartment.

Bob laughed. "I'll take this through to your room," he said heading off toward the guest bedrooms.

When he came back Myrosia was hanging Joanna's coat up in the front closet.

"Joanna, go ahead and make yourself at home. Myrosia knows where everything is, so if you can't find something just ask her. There's beer in the fridge and all kinds of other goodies in the liquor cabinet. It's shaping up to be a miserable night out there, so if there's anything else you need just order it in. There's take-out menus in the top drawer beside the fridge and the phone number of Mel's taxi is programmed into the phone. He'll be happy to deliver anything you need. Just tell him to put it on my tab," he said putting on his coat and pulling his gloves out of the pocket.

"Oh yeah, I forgot to mention that my housekeeper Maria comes in Monday, Wednesday and Friday mornings at about 9 o'clock. She won't bother you. She's got her own key and her own routine, but I'm giving you a heads-up just in case you sleep in and you get nervous hearing someone walking around out here."

"Thanks for everything Bob," Myrosia said giving him a very sisterly kiss on the cheek just before he stepped into the elevator.

When the elevator door closed and she was sure that Bob was out of earshot Joanna exclaimed. "Damn! That man is gorgeous and this place is incredible! I'll tell you Myrosia if you don't snap him up just give me a shot at him. He gives me hot flashes just looking at him," she said.

Myrosia laughed. "I know what you mean. I swear he gets better looking the older he gets."

"How old is he anyway?" asked Joanna.

"He's 45, just about the same age as us, but he sure doesn't look it," replied Myrosia.

"No, he sure doesn't. It's not fair how some men get better looking as they get older and women just get older. Did he make a deal with the devil or something? He must have a painting that's aging hidden in here somewhere. Holy shit, how many rooms does this place have? You could practically fit my apartment into that closet. Come on, show me around."

The two women wandered into all of the 4 guest bedrooms each with en-suite baths, then into the game room with the pool table and poker table.

"My god, this place is huge. Two people'd need walkie talkies just to be able to find each other in here. How big do you think this is?" Joanna asked.

"I'm not sure, maybe about 8,000 square feet but it could be more. There are only 2 apartments on the penthouse floor, each with their own private elevator. The other floors each have between 4 and 6 apartments and they share the main elevators. There's also an Olympic sized swimming pool on the fifteenth floor with a gym, sauna, and hot tub. Then there's squash and racquetball courts down in the lower basement below the parking levels. The funny thing is that, other than Bob working out in the gym every day, hardly any of the owners ever use the facilities, so if we want to use them we'd probably have them to ourselves," said Myrosia.

"Imagine having all this and not using it," said Joanna. "That was freaky having the elevator open up right into the apartment. Thank god the elevator in my building doesn't do that. Who knows what would wander in. How long has Bob had this place?"

"It must be about seven or eight years since it was built. Bob was one of the developers so that's how he was able to buy this penthouse suite. Janice used to have an apartment on a lower floor that she used as an art studio and an office. We were never particularly good friends so I was never in it and I don't know what they ended up doing with that apartment when they split up," said Myrosia.

They strolled into the 12 seat theatre room which featured a kitchenette and a powder room.

"Oh my god, I thought the theatre room at your house was fantastic, but this is incredible. I could just stay in here watching movies the whole weekend. Too bad I have to go to work. Do you think we could convince him to let us stay permanently? This place is so big he'd never even have to know we were here," Joanna said.

"We can order some Chinese food and eat in here while we watch a movie if you want," Myrosia said.

"Yeah but show me the rest of the place first."

"Aren't you getting hungry?" asked Myrosia.

"No, I'm having a great time indulging my fantasies of what it would be like to live like this. Bob must be one happy camper living here. I'm surprised that another woman didn't snap him up the minute Janice walked out. He must have to beat them off with a stick," said Joanna.

"Oh I have no doubt that there are plenty of women after him, and I'm pretty sure he's been getting his share of female companionship since Janice left, but actually I think he's kind of lonely. I don't think I've ever told you this. He hates when people talk about it, and he tries to keep it quiet, but he's a trust fund baby," said Myrosia.

Joanna looked at her questioningly so Myrosia continued.

"His great-great-grandfather made a lot of money in Zimbabwe back in colonial days. It was Rhodesia then, and I guess the company he formed has expanded into other industries quite successfully in the years since. From what I understand, the old man was pretty astute at setting up trusts for his descendents, so none of the family has really had to work for generations. It sounds fantastic, never having to work, but I'm not sure it's such a good thing. It actually makes for people who are pretty much out of touch with reality. I've met a number of them over the years and they are some really strange people. One of the things I admire about Bob is that he actually works. His mother, who controlled his trust when he was young, was so angry at him for some reason that she tied up his trust fund from the time he was a sophomore in college until he was 35. She can be a real bitch, I've met her a couple of times, but I think she did him a huge favor. It wasn't her intention of course. He went from being rich to being poor overnight and he ended up having to work his way through college. The trust would pay his tuition but not much more. That's why he went into business with Dave and the other partners. He made a lot of money on his own, so by the time the trust fund was finally released into his control he really didn't need it any more. He works hard and earns a lot of money but other than this condo and his sailboat, I really don't know what he does with his money. Even this condo I think was more Janice's dream than Bob's. So I don't doubt for a minute that he can get all the female companionship he wants, but the thing is that he can never really be sure if they're interested in him or his money. So there you have it, poor lonely rich boy, having to beat off women at every turn," said Myrosia.

"Wow, that story makes him even hotter, a self made millionaire with a trust fund. What a contradiction."

"Whatever you do don't let on that I told you this, not that it's much of a secret. Lots of people know the story."

They wandered through the rest of the apartment and when they got to the laundry room Joanna pulled open a fire door and glanced through.

"Oh, just the stairwell. I bet that doesn't get used much. I'd hate to have to climb up and down those 32 flights of stairs."

"It'd be great exercise though," said Myrosia.

"I don't need a butt of steel that badly. I keep telling myself that men like soft ones better anyway," said Joanna.

Next to the stairwell door was another locked door.

"What's in here?" Joanna asked.

"I've got no idea, it's probably just a storage room of some sort," said Myrosia.

"Maybe that leads to the dungeon, where he keeps the kinky stuff," said Joanna winking at Myrosia.

Myrosia just laughed.

"Well that's it," said Myrosia when they wandered back to the main living area. "There's a roof top terrace as well, but it's closed off this time of year. It's too dangerous, the wind up there would pick you up and blow you right across to Canada."

"What? You're not going to show me the master bedroom?"

"Come on Joanna, we don't need to go in there. That's just rude to go snooping in someone's bedroom," said Myrosia.

"So are you telling me you've never seen his bedroom?"

"Of course I have. I was just in there this afternoon."

Joanna raised one eyebrow and smirked.

"Get your mind out of the gutter Joanna! It wasn't like that. He was packing to leave and I was sitting in a chair talking to him."

"Come on show me. He told us to make ourselves at home. If he didn't want us to go in there he could have locked the door."

"Okay, but just a quick peek. Don't open any drawers or anything. Promise?" said Myrosia.

"Of course not! What do you think I am?" asked Joanna indignantly.

They walked into the enormous master bedroom with the king-sized four poster bed.

"You could try tying him up to that next time you get loaded and decide to attack him," said Joanna.

Myrosia ignored her friend's comment.

They walked into the largest bathroom Joanna had ever seen. Two gigantic glass shower stalls, his and hers sinks, a toilet area with a bidet, a make-up room, and his and hers dressing rooms.

Myrosia just shook her head. "There's a lot of wasted space in here."

Looking down at the gigantic marble Jacuzzi tub Joanna said, "You could have quite a party in here. Why the hell did Janice ever leave?"

"I keep wondering that myself," said Myrosia.

"Are they finally divorced yet?" asked Joanna.

"No, the divorce isn't final yet, it's an uncontested no-fault divorce, but they still have to wait out the time limit. Everything is settled financially though. Bob paid her off and she signed all the documents, so it's just a matter of getting it rubber stamped by the court. Dave was handling Bob's side of the divorce, and he told me that he thought Bob was being an idiot for giving her such a generous settlement. They had a pretty solid pre-nup but I guess maybe she was threatening to fight it or something, so Bob just agreed to just give her a huge chunk of change and get it over with. I think she was just being greedy, I mean the pre-nup was really generous to begin with and she was earning money of her own, so it's not like she really needed the money," said Myrosia.

"That's a different world that I know nothing about. When

Jack and I split up I took the $80 we had in the bank account, and threw his clothes out onto the lawn in the rain. There was nothing else to split up." Joanna shook her head and laughed. "But I do understand being vindictive. Do you remember what I did to Jack's truck? I drank a 12 pack of Bud and peed in a jug and then you and me drove over to his girlfriend's house where it was parked out front and poured it all over the seat. He had a hell of a time trying to get the smell out. For as long as he owned that truck he had something to remember me by every time the truck got warm."

Myrosia laughed. "Yes, and I also remember that you were afraid to leave your old Ford Pinto parked anywhere he could get at it just in case he tried to pay you back."

"Well it wouldn't have made much difference with that old car. It always stunk anyway, I swear somebody must have died in that thing," said Joanna.

Back in the kitchen they pulled out the take-out menus.

"Before we order let's just look in the pantry and see what kind of junk food he's got for the movies in case we need to order out for that too," said Myrosia.

"How decadent. I've never even considered ordering out for a bag of potato chips and a chocolate bar. I'd love to do that once just to see how it feels to be that pampered," said Joanna.

It turned out that there was everything they could possibly want lined up neatly in the pantry.

"Wow it looks like a convenience store in there. Where's the condom section?" said Joanna.

"I imagine that his housekeeper probably keeps the pantry stocked for him. Funny thing is I can't picture Bob sitting alone in this mausoleum eating junk food, so you might want to check the expiration dates on that stuff," said Myrosia.

"It's all current. What does he do, throw it out when it gets past dated?" said Joanna.

"The housekeeper probably gets to take home the old stuff. I can't imagine Bob throwing it out," said Myrosia.

"Nice job perk," said Joanna.

While they waited for the food to arrive they opened a bottle of wine.

"You know, even with all the expensive bottles of wine Bob's got in here this cheap Bella Rosa stuff is what I really love. I suspect that Bob stocks this stuff because he knows how much I like it. Dave had our wine cellar filled with expensive imported bottles and frankly none of it really impressed me. Give me a nice cheap bottle of the local stuff and I'm happy," said Myrosia.

"Yeah, the expensive stuff is wasted on me too. I can't tell the difference. Not that I've had the opportunity to drink too much expensive wine. The only time I've had it is at your house. I'm more of a beer drinker myself. I guess Myrosia we've just got peasant tastes," said Joanna.

"I guess we do, because you know, even though this place is beautifully decorated, and the furniture is the best you can buy, it just doesn't quite do it for me. It feels like a model home or a museum or something. It doesn't feel much like a home. It feels like Janice, not Bob if you know what I mean," said Myrosia.

"Bob must have given her a free hand in choosing the furnishings, unlike what Dave did with you when you were furnishing the lake house. She probably used a designer, that's why it feels so sterile," said Joanna.

"I can't believe I stayed married to that pompous jerk for so many years. You know what he said to me when we were doing the landscaping at the lake house? He said that he was hiring a landscape designer because if he left it up to me we'd have nothing but pink plastic flamingos on the lawn."

"And what's wrong with pink plastic flamingos? If I had a lawn I'd have the biggest, tackiest display you could imagine. Did you see what Mrs. Matyjakowski did with her yard for Christmas? Gigantic pink flamingos pulling Santa's sleigh, it was hilarious," said Joanna.

"Yeah, it was great. I drove my mother over to let her see the old neighborhood just before Christmas. We stopped in to see Mrs. Matyjakowski and the two of them got into the vodka reminiscing about the old days. I practically had to carry Mama out of there. Fortunately her grandson Jason stopped by and helped me get her into the SUV. What a sweet kid that Jason is. He looks a lot like his father," said Myrosia.

"Don't rub it in. I've made a lot of bad choices in my life but one of the dumbest was not marrying Feliks. Stupid, stupid, stupid. Dumping Feliks and ending up with that loser Jack. I fell for the motorcycle, the smooth talk, and the big dick, but it turned out he couldn't keep it in his pants. Every chance he got he was pulling it out with some new woman. I swear to god that man must have kept his zipper greased. Who knows how many illegitimate kids he's got running around. I ran into him just before Christmas. I almost didn't recognize him He looks like he's about a hundred years old. What a deadbeat. He still owes me years of back child support. He was making good money back then when Johnny and Chrissy were little but he was just so cheap, he did everything he could to avoid paying the child support. Now I get $50 a month out of his disability check, but at this rate it'll never get paid off," said Joanna.

"Well we all make stupid choices. Look at me spending all those years with Dave," said Myrosia.

"Well I should have listened to my mother, 'It's just as easy to love a rich man as a poor one, so just don't hang around with the poor ones,' she always said. But did I listen? Nope. She always said that Feliks was going to do well. Now he owns a big plumbing supply company and Jack's still a loser. I'm not much of a judge of men. I guess it's no wonder that Chrissy doesn't listen to me when I try to give her advice," said Joanna.

The dinner arrived and the two women carried it through to the theatre room.

"So what will it be? We've got internet movies and Bob must have thousands of DVD's and old VHS tapes in his collection. Do you want something new or do you want to watch a classic? Comedy or drama?" asked Myrosia.

"How about a romantic chick flick? Or we could do a Jane Austen movie marathon," said Joanna.

"Let me see, oh here's 'Out of Africa' with Meryl Streep and Robert Redford. I've always thought that Bob kind of reminds me of Robert Redford. I'd love to watch that again."

"Sure, the scenery in that one would be great on this big screen.

You know that part where she gets sick and it turns out that her cheating husband has given her syphilis and she has to go back to Denmark for treatment? Well that reminds me, did you get a chance to go see the doctor about an AIDS test?" asked Joanna.

"No, I've been kind of busy and I guess it slipped my mind. Besides, I feel really funny going in to see Dr. Albertson and asking him to test me for sexually transmitted diseases," said Myrosia.

"That's stupid. I'm sure he's heard it all before. Besides, it's not like you're the one who's been screwing around. But you don't have to go see your GP. Why don't you go over to the women's clinic that's upstairs above Giarrelli's Pizza and get tested. You can do it anonymously, give them a fake name and pay cash. They don't care. They give you the results the same day. It's supposed to be accurate if it's been at least 7 days since you were exposed. It has been at least 7 days since you had sex with Dave hasn't it?" asked Joanna.

"That's for sure, things haven't been too passionate in our house for a while now. I can't even remember when we last had sex, I think it was sometime during the Christmas holidays," said Myrosia.

"Hell Myrosia, if you can't remember when you had sex last that's a pretty good sign of problems in your marriage."

"I don't know. I thought we'd just gotten too busy. It's not like we never did it," said Myrosia defensively.

"Myrosia, you've got to promise me that you'll go and get tested tomorrow. There's diseases out there that we never even heard of back when Sister Charlotte was trying to scare us celibate in health class at Mount Mercy."

"So, how do you know so much about sexually transmitted diseases Joanna?" Myrosia teased.

"Hey, you know I've had more than my share of close calls. Besides, it's amazing what you learn working in a beauty salon."

Chapter 10

On Friday morning the two women were up, dressed and having coffee in the breakfast nook when the housekeeper arrived.

"Good morning Maria. We've met before. I don't know if you remember me. I'm Myrosia Walker and this is my friend Joanna Lubinski," Myrosia said rising from her chair to shake hands with the housekeeper.

"Good morning ma'am. Of course I remember you. It's nice to see you again. Mr. Williams called and told me that you were visiting. He told me to take good care of you," said Maria.

"No please call me Myrosia. Joanna and I were just heading out for the day, so we'll get out of your way and let you work," said Myrosia.

"You're not in the way. I usually do the big cleaning on Wednesdays. Do you have any clothes that you need washed? Just leave anything to be washed in the hamper in your bathroom. If something needs to be dry cleaned there are dry cleaner bags in your closet. Just leave the things in the bag next to the hamper and I will take it down to the man in the lobby and he will send it out to be cleaned," said Maria.

"Oh that's not necessary, we can take care of our own laundry." said Joanna.

"You don't have to worry, I am very careful with the clothes. I've been with Mr. Williams for eight years and there has never been a problem," said Maria.

"Oh no, of course not we didn't mean to suggest that there might be a problem. We just didn't want our presence here to add to your workload," said Myrosia.

"I'm sorry too. I didn't mean to offend you. I'm just not used to having people cleaning up after me. Although I think I could probably get used to it pretty easily. I've got to get going. I'm running late for work.

I'll call you later Myrosia," said Joanna as she put her dishes into the dishwasher and started toward the door.

The housekeeper began wiping down the counter tops although to Myrosia's eye there did not seem to be anything in need of wiping. "It's no trouble. Since Mrs. Williams moved out there hasn't been much for me to do in here. Now that Mr. Williams is living alone he really doesn't need me as much. He's just being kind keeping me on three times a week," said Maria.

"Yes, I've always found Mr. Williams to be very considerate. I'm sure he's a good boss," said Myrosia.

"Oh yes, he is very kind and generous, very easy to work for. Mrs. Williams, on the other hand ..." Maria hesitated afraid that she had gone too far.

"Oh don't worry Maria. I'm not going to repeat anything you say. I've known Bob for many years and he's always been a sweetheart. I've only known Janice since they got married and frankly I couldn't stand her. She must have been difficult to work for," said Myrosia.

"Very difficult. Nothing was ever good enough for her. She was a pig. She would make a mess just so that I would have to clean it up. And she was mean and cheap, not like Mr. Williams at all. One time she was throwing out some clothes that she didn't want. Mr. Williams said that I could take anything I wanted out of the pile. There were a few things that I was going to take for my daughter but Mrs. Williams took them and cut them up so that they would be useless. I don't know why someone would be so mean like that. Mr. and Mrs. Williams had a big fight when he found out. He saw the cut up clothes in the garbage and he was furious," she said.

"Did you also clean Janice's other apartment? The one she used for her studio," asked Myrosia.

"Humph, she called it her studio. I don't know how much art she ever made in there. She did plenty of other things in that apartment. She is one sick woman. The messes I had to clean up in that apartment you wouldn't believe. I'm just glad that she's gone. I don't know what he ever saw in her. Now maybe he'll find a woman who appreciates him," she said.

As she was heading toward the door Myrosia noticed that Bob's briefcase was still sitting on the floor where he set it down the previous night. It made her think about what Dave's reaction would have been if he had gone off to a meeting without his briefcase. He would probably have had a fit and blamed her for not reminding him. She hoped there weren't any important papers that he needed in there.

Her first stop that morning was the women's clinic for the anonymous testing. She knew she was being silly but she still felt embarrassed about having to get tested for a sexually transmitted disease and decided to give a false name. After that conversation with the housekeeper the first name that popped into her mind was Janice.

Upon registering and paying cash for the tests she was led into the examination room. The lab technician explained the procedure.

"Hi Janice, here's how it works, we're going to be taking urine tests, blood tests as well as vaginal, rectal, and throat swabs. You don't have to worry about confidentiality. We just want to make sure that women at risk have a comfortable place to get tested and treated if necessary. We don't report the information to anyone but you. We don't put names on anything, just a code number that you will use when you call in for your test results. It's 10 o'clock now so we should have your results back by about 3 o'clock this afternoon. Just call the number on this card and give the receptionist the code and she will tell you your results. Now I've got to warn you, if everything is fine, if all the tests are negative, we'll tell you that over the phone. However if there are any problems with any of the tests you will have to come back in and have a consultation with the nurse practitioner."

"Let me make sure I understand you. Are you saying that if when I call in for the results they tell me that I need to come back that it means that something showed up positive, that I've caught something?" Myrosia asked.

"No, no, not necessarily. Sometimes the lab messes things up and they need to re-do one or more of the tests. So if they tell you that we need you to come back in don't panic and assume the worst. We wouldn't want you doing anything foolish if it turns out that I just dropped your urine sample," the lab technician explained reassuringly.

Lying there a half hour later with her feet in the stirrups she pondered what kind of revenge she could take on Dave for putting her through this humiliation.

Her next stop was to the credit union to open an account. The manager himself handled everything and the whole process went smoothly. Sitting in his office filling out the paperwork he explained to her how her new account worked.

"Unfortunately Myrosia, our branch has a policy of putting a 5 business day hold on new accounts for any checks over $5000. What this means is that even though you've deposited this $7000 check and the funds are in your account, and you're getting interest on that money, you won't be able to withdraw that money until next Friday. I'm sorry for any inconvenience this might cause you," the bank manager said.

"Oh, well I guess if that's the policy I don't have much choice but to wait until next Friday," she said feeling disappointed.

"Bob was concerned that this might create a problem for you so he arranged to transfer $10,000 into your account. These are funds that you can access immediately," he explained.

She was about to tell the manager to reverse the $10,000 deposit. It was too much. She did not want to be under that kind of obligation to Bob, but then her mother's words echoed in her mind, 'Your new man, he wants to give you a gift of cash you don't be proud and stupid, you take it.' Bob really wasn't her new man, but her mother was right about a lot of things, so she decided to remain silent.

Back out in the Jeep she pulled out her cell phone to call Bob and thank him when she noticed that the ringer was turned off. She had turned it off the previous evening when she and Joanna were sitting down to watch the movie because she couldn't face any more angry phone calls from Dave. She had forgotten to turn it back on.

She turned it on and listened to her voice mails. There were half a dozen angry calls from Dave ranting about his car. She listened to them and laughed as each call got progressively more irate. There were also 4 calls from Jeff the young network administrator at the office.

I wonder what he's so eager to tell me?

She decided she should call Bob first.

"Hi Bob, it's Myrosia. I hope I'm not disturbing your meeting.

Do you have a minute to talk?" she asked.

"No problem, I'm always happy to take your calls."

"I just got finished at the credit union. You were right. They did hold the funds on my check, and thank you so much for that money. I really appreciate it. You've been so good to me. It takes a huge amount of pressure off. But honestly Bob, $10,000 is just way too generous. I promise to get that money back to you as soon as I get this mess with Dave straightened out," she said.

"Myrosia honey, I told you, I'm not worried about the money. I'm just glad I was able to help you. Besides I figured it wouldn't hurt your plan to pretend that we are an item if word got around that I was giving you money," he said.

"You think that will get around? So much for bank confidentiality," she said.

He laughed. "Don't kid yourself. Buffalo might be a city, but in a lot of ways it's a small town. News travels fast."

When she hung up her next call was to Jeff.

"Hi Jeff, it's Myrosia. Sorry I missed your calls, I didn't realize I had the ringer turned off on my phone," she said.

"I'm glad you finally called me back. I was getting really worried about you when I couldn't reach you on your cell phone. I tried calling your house a couple of times too and there was no answer there either," he said.

"I've been staying with a friend in town," she explained.

"If you're uncomfortable staying out at your house alone I'd be happy to come and stay with you," he said.

"Thanks, that's really kind of you, but it's not necessary. I'm fine I'm staying with a friend." For some reason she felt reluctant to say that she was staying at Bob's apartment although the news was bound to get back to the office before long and create quite a stir among the staff.

"It'd be no trouble. I'd love to hang out with you on the weekend," he said.

"That would be nice, but I've already got plans for the weekend," she said.

"Oh well, in that case I guess I'll take a road trip to Chicago with a couple of buddies for a Comic Convention this weekend. But if you want I can come out to your house next week to keep you company," he said.

He gave her the impression of a puppy dog eager for attention, but it felt creepy, like he wanted more than to just keep her company. He's just a kid, not much older than my son Dylan, she thought. She decided to ignore the undertone of what he was saying.

"What was it you were calling to tell me?" she asked.

"I've got some big news. How about meeting me for lunch and I can tell you all about it?" he asked.

"Oh no, I don't think that's a good idea. If anyone from the office saw us together they'd know that you're helping me. That could get you fired, and besides I've already got plans for lunch," she said.

"I don't need the job that badly. I do okay with an online business I've got going," he said.

"Yes, but, I really could use your help, and if you lost your job… Can you just tell me the big news over the phone?"

"Okay." He sounded disappointed, but after a short pause went on. "I decided to go into the office for a little while this morning even though I figured not much would be going on with all the partners away. Well it turns out I was wrong. There's plenty going on. You know that Keith and Peter are down in Tampa for the Superbowl right? Well guess who else isn't at work today? That bitch Cori didn't come in either. Word is that she went to Tampa with Keith. It seems that she's been having an affair with him for the past few months. Apparently he's the old rich guy that she's landed. So I'd bet she's the one leaking the stories in the office. She gets her inside information through good old fashioned pillow talk. When the old guy gets a hard-on he tells her everything," he said.

Myrosia tried to ignore the comment about Keith being an 'old guy.' He was the same age as her and the other partners.

"Wow, I wonder if Keith's wife Jeannie knows about this yet? The shit is really going to hit the fan when she finds out."

"Wait, there's more. When word got out that Cori had gone for the weekend with Keith, Stella started bawling at her desk. It seems that she's been fooling around with Peter for months and she's devastated that he didn't take her along for the weekend, but it seems that he took some new bimbo with him to Florida," Jeff said excitedly.

"My god, the whole place is imploding. It's a real Peyton Place in there. Peter's wife is going to be devastated too if she hears about this. And all this has been going on under my nose. I wonder how come I never noticed," said Myrosia.

"Well unlike everyone else around here, I guess you were spending your time actually working," he said.

"What time are you leaving for Chicago?" she asked.

"My buddy Josh gets off at 4 so we'll leave after that."

"That's a long drive. It must be nine or ten hours."

"No big deal, the three of us can take turns driving. We'll come back Sunday night."

"I hope the weather is good for you. You never know what the weather is gonna be like this time of year. I hope you don't run into lake effect snow, that stretch between here and Erie can be brutal," said Myrosia.

"No problem. I've got one of those new Toyota Mega Cruisers. It can drive through anything. Have you seen them? They kind of look like the old Humvee's but cooler. Maybe I can take you out for a drive sometime and show you what it can do," he said

"Wow that's an expensive vehicle," she said, but inside she was thinking what's with all these guys driving these expensive gas guzzling tanks?

"Yeah, well, like I said, I'm doing pretty good with my online business," he said proudly.

"Could I ask you another favor?" she said.

"Sure, whatever you want," he said.

"I know how good you are with online searches, and I'm not having much luck with something. Could you try and track down that girl Christine Bennett, the one that used to work at the office? She used to live in Buffalo but apparently she moved to Rochester and she didn't leave a forwarding address. I want to find her and talk to her," she said.

"I'll see what I can do. I'll call you as soon as I find anything."

When she hung up the phone she looked at her watch. Only noon! The next three hours are going to be torture. Not sure what to do next Myrosia analyzed her options. Should she go back to Bob's apartment? And do what, just sit there and worry? No, she needed to keep busy. Never having been one of the 'ladies who lunch' she wasn't accustomed to having so much free time. She thought about the other partners' wives and wondered what Jeannie MacKenzie and Penny Donovan did to pass the time. On impulse she picked up her cell phone and dialed Jeannie MacKenzie's home number.

"Hi Jeannie, this is Myrosia Walker."

"Oh hello Myrosia, this is a pleasant surprise." replied the other woman hesitantly.

Yeah right, thought Myrosia.

"I'm sure you're surprised to hear from me. It's been ages since we last spoke. I'm sure you've heard about my situation with Dave, and I was wondering if we could get together for lunch. I have some things I would like to talk to you about," said Myrosia.

"Oh yes, I was so sorry to hear that the two of you had broken up after all these years. For him to have run off with one of his clients, right under your nose, how devastating for you," said the other woman.

Bitch, thought Myrosia.

"Are you free for lunch?" asked Myrosia.

"I'd love to but I'm so sorry, I have a previous engagement. You just caught me; I was just running out the door. I'm meeting Penny for lunch at the golf club," she said.

"Great, I'll meet you there. I want to speak to Penny as well."

"Oh I don't think that will work. We've only got reservations for two and you know how busy they are on Friday afternoons."

"I don't think it'll be a problem, with Buffalo in the Superbowl I'm sure half the members are either in Tampa or on their way there. The restaurant shouldn't be too busy, I'm sure they can squeeze me in. I'll see you there," said Myrosia and hung up the phone before the other woman could protest.

This should be interesting, thought Myrosia as she drove over to the golf club.

In the restaurant lobby she gave her coat to the girl at the coat check and was greeted by the Maitre d'.

"Hello Mrs. Walker. Are you joining us for lunch today?"

"Yes, I'm meeting Penny Donovan and Jeannie MacKenzie. Are they here yet?" asked Myrosia.

"Mrs. Donovan is here and I'm sure Mrs. MacKenzie will be joining you shortly," said the Maitre d'. "I'm sorry, it seems there was a mistake with the reservations and we set you up at a table for two, but I'll rectify that immediately," he said as he led her to the table.

"That's fine. It was my mistake. It was a spur of the moment decision for the three of us to get together. You know how these things happen," said Myrosia.

Penny Donovan was surprised to see Myrosia, but quickly regained her composure.

"How nice to see you Myrosia. Are you joining us for lunch?"

"Yes, I spoke to Jeannie and arranged to meet you here. I wanted to have a chance to speak to both of you about my situation with Dave," said Myrosia.

"Peter told me all about it. I'm so sorry to hear that the two of you split up. I understand it came as a shock?" said Penny.

"Indeed it did. My entire life turned upside down on Monday night and I never saw it coming," said Myrosia.

"How awful for you," said Penny.

Myrosia could see that the woman was actually gloating.

"Here's Jeannie now. I'm sure both of you want to hear all the juicy details, so let's wait until she has a chance to sit down and I'll tell you everything,' said Myrosia.

"Myrosia I didn't see your Mercedes in the parking lot. What are you driving these days?" asked Jeannie as she sat down at the third place setting.

"I had to put it away for safekeeping to keep it out of Dave's clutches. I'm driving the old junker Jeep that's parked next to Penny's Lexus," said Myrosia as the waitress came over to take their drink orders.

The other two women were wide eyed with amazement that Myrosia would be so frank with them. The Myrosia that they had always known was much more reserved and would never have discussed such personal details with them.

"I think we need a big bottle of wine. It's my treat. Pick whatever you like," said Myrosia.

Turning toward the waitress she said, "Put everything on Dave Walker's account." All three women smiled.

Once the wine was poured Myrosia began.

"I know you've heard all the gossip, but I'm going to give you the real details as I know them so far," said Myrosia and she proceeded to tell them about what she found when she arrived home on Monday night and the events that led up to her being asked to leave the office. She carefully left out any reference to what she had just learned from Jeff.

The other two women listened spellbound.

"What I want to know from you is what you've heard. What I'm trying to do is find out what Dave has done with the money, and if I can figure out what is really going on with the bribery allegations and the missing trust fund money, that would be great too. I'd like to clear my name, get my money back, and get a divorce."

"Well from what Peter has told me Dave's been running around for years. I can't believe you didn't have any idea," said Penny.

"Keith thinks that Dave's probably been hiding money for years. With you working so closely with him in the office I don't know how you didn't see what was happening," said Jeannie.

"Obviously I've been pretty stupid. A lot of stuff has been going on in that office that I wasn't aware of," said Myrosia. "Do either of you know who Dave has been seeing lately?"

"No, I don't know who it is, but Peter said that she's one of his divorce clients and she's pretty high maintenance. That's why he stole the trust fund money," said Penny.

"Keith says that he thinks Dave's been bribing building inspectors for years. That's how he's been managing to come under budget on so many projects. Apparently everything has come to a head now because that waterfront deal has fallen apart and Dave stands to lose everything. That's why he tried to blackmail that city planning official. He says that Dave's probably out of the country with the money by now," said Jeannie.

"What about Janice and Bob? Do either of you know why she left?" asked Myrosia.

"We should be asking you about that. From what we understand they broke up because he's been having an affair with you for years," said Penny.

"No, that's not true. I've always been faithful to Dave."

"Oh really? I heard that you've moved in with Bob and that the two of you were seen looking at wedding rings. I'm sure that didn't just happen overnight. This had to have been going on for some time. Besides, you just told us that he was the first person you called when you discovered the situation on Monday night," said Penny.

"Well it's true that I did call him on Monday night, but that was because I was trying to find Dave, but I haven't moved in with him. We did look at wedding rings but it's not what you think," said Myrosia.

"Well I heard that you've been seen kissing and holding hands with him all over town," said Penny.

"That's a bit of an exaggeration. He's been very kind and supportive, but I'm definitely not the reason why he and Janice split up," said Myrosia.

"Well I heard that there were sexual problems between the two of them. But I guess we should be asking you about that," said Jeannie.

Myrosia ignored the innuendo.

"What kind of sexual problems?" asked Myrosia.

"I heard they were into some really kinky stuff and it got out of hand. I guess she decided that whatever it was he was into just wasn't something that she could tolerate any more," said Jeannie without looking up from her salad.

"Hmm, that's interesting. That reminds me of something else I wanted to ask you about. Do either of you know anything about a really high end swingers club over on Nottingham Terrace?" asked Myrosia.

"Yes, I heard something about that, but that's something else we should be asking you about. Keith told me that Dave was behind the whole thing," said Jeannie.

"What are you talking about? That's the first I've heard anything about that!" said Myrosia.

"I heard that you and Dave and Bob were all into that group sex stuff and Janice couldn't put up with it any more," said Jeannie.

"No, that is absolutely not true. I have no idea how that rumor got started. I did find some strange porn on Dave's computer, pictures of women in bondage getup but I can promise you that I've never been involved in any kind of group sex," said Myrosia.

The waitress came over pushing the pastry cart. "Can I interest you in something for dessert?" she asked.

"Come on girls, order dessert. I've got some more stuff to tell you," said Myrosia.

When the dessert was served, Myrosia continued. "I decided to meet with the two of you because I wanted to know what you'd heard about my problems, and also because I think the allegations against Dave are about to spill over and sink the entire firm. If Dave goes down for any of this, your husbands' careers are over too, and you know where that leaves both of you."

"So you're trying to put the blame on the other partners for something you and your husband have cooked up," said Jeannie.

"No, I'm not blaming anyone yet, but the more I think about this whole mess the more I'm beginning to suspect that something else is going on. Dave is a jerk, but I'm not sure he's guilty of all the rest of the stuff. I'm just giving you a heads up," said Myrosia.

She paused for a moment and then went on. "I debated with myself about whether I would tell you the rest of this. I wasn't sure if it was something that you wanted to hear from me. It's not my intention to hurt either of you, but there is a lot that has been going on in the office that your husbands' haven't told you."

"That's impossible. Peter and I discuss everything," said Penny haughtily.

"Oh cut the crap Myrosia. Get on with it. What kind of bullshit is this? You're just trying to cause trouble," said Jeannie.

"Well Jeannie, the news from the office is that Keith has been having an affair with the receptionist Cori, and that he's taken her to Tampa with him for the weekend. And Penny, the story is that Peter's been screwing Stella the clerk who handles the trust accounts. Apparently she left the office sobbing this morning because Peter had taken his new bimbo to Tampa with him. So if anybody is into group sex, it's more likely to be those guys."

"That's just malicious Myrosia, really evil. Unlike Dave, Peter has always been completely faithful to me," said Penny tears welling up in her eyes.

"Yeah well, you can go ahead and believe that if it makes you feel better," said Myrosia.

"I never expected this from you, you've always been a pompous self-righteous bitch Myrosia, thinking you were so much better than the other wives, but this is the first time I've ever seen you be deliberately cruel. I'm not going to sit here and listen to any more of your lies," said Jeannie.

"Oh sit down, both of you. Finish your meal and go ahead and have another bottle of wine on Dave. I knew that this wasn't going to turn into some kind of 'First Wives Club' thing where we all join together to get revenge on our cheating husbands. Let's face it, we've never really liked each other all that much, and the only thing we had in common was that our husbands have been friends since college and they went into partnership together. I'm not trying to be cruel. I just thought that you needed a little more warning than I got when Dave dumped me. So sit here and talk it over. This has been fun, but I'm leaving now. My recommendation is that you both go home and make sure that you've got some money set aside because you're going to need it. Oh, and consider getting yourself checked out for sexually transmitted diseases. Apparently there's a lot of it going around."

With that she got up and walked out.

Out in the parking lot she looked at her watch. Damn it's only 2:30. This waiting is unbearable. I can't take it any more, and called the clinic.

"Hello, my name is Janice and the code number is 4891-5866-4742. I know I'm calling a little early, but are my test results ready?" she asked.

"Just a moment while I look that up for you," said the voice on the other end.

After what seemed like an eternity the receptionist came back on the phone.

"Yes, the results are in but there is a request on the file for you to come in and speak to the nurse practitioner," said the receptionist.

"Oh my god!" cried Myrosia. "Can't you just tell me over the phone? Do I have AIDS?"

"I don't have that information on the file. I just have a note that you need to come back in. I know how upsetting this is, but really, there's no point in getting all worked up. It's probably nothing. Just come back in and we'll get this all straightened out," said the receptionist kindly.

Chapter 11

The drive back to the clinic was torture. Myrosia tried to tell herself that it was probably just a mistake, but the fear of AIDS and the media images of emaciated gay men dying in agony, covered in sores, kept flooding through her mind.

"How could I have been so stupid to trust Dave all these years? That bastard is going to pay for this." shouted Myrosia, alone in the Jeep, tears streaming down her face. "I'm going to kill him!"

By the time she parked the tears had stopped and she had composed herself enough to walk into the reception area.

"I just called and someone told me that there was a problem with my test and that I needed to come back in," said Myrosia and the tears began flowing again.

"I'm sure everything's going to be fine dear," said the receptionist coming out from her desk and putting her arm around Myrosia's shoulder. "I'll take you right into Cynthia's office."

"Cynthia, this is Janice. There is a note on her file that she needs to have a consultation with you," explained the receptionist.

"Hi Janice, I've been waiting for you, I've got your file right here," said the nurse practitioner.

"Oh fuck it! My name isn't Janice, it's Myrosia. Just tell me what I've got. Am I going to die of AIDS?" sobbed Myrosia.

"No you're not dying of AIDS. But your tests did turn up positive for another sexually transmitted disease. You have Chlamydia. Fortunately Chlamydia is easily treated, and doesn't have to cause any long term effects as long as it is caught early and treated properly. You definitely did the right thing in getting tested," said the nurse practitioner.

"What is it?" asked Myrosia.

"Chlamydia is sometimes referred to as the 'Silent Epidemic' because it doesn't cause any symptoms in 75% of infected women, but approximately half of the women who get it will develop pelvic inflammatory disease which can cause a lot of other serious problems. It can cause a whole bunch of problems for infected men as well, so all of your sexual partners have to be informed and treated," she explained.

"I've only had one partner, my husband. Well, back in college there were a couple of men but that doesn't count does it? I got tested back about fifteen years ago and nothing showed up then."

The nurse practitioner smiled. "I'm sure that you probably got infected much more recently than college."

"I've never even heard of it before," said Myrosia.

"Well we're certainly seeing a lot of it here in the clinic. The Center for Disease Control estimates that there are close to 3 million new cases of Chlamydia in the United States each year. It can be transmitted during vaginal, anal, or oral sex. It can also be passed from an infected mother to her baby during childbirth. Although it's a serious disease it's easily treated, but your sexual partners will have to be informed and treated."

"Honestly, the only one is my husband. I just found out that he's been cheating on me," said Myrosia.

"We see that a lot unfortunately. People don't seem to think of the consequences of their actions when they find themselves in sexual situations," she replied.

"What's the treatment?" asked Myrosia.

"Antibiotics. We have two treatment options. There is a one time pill or a seven day treatment. Both are equally effective. I prefer to prescribe the one time dose because many people forget to take the pill at the same time every day for seven days," she explained.

"Definitely give me the one time dose. I want to get this over with. This is going to be so embarrassing getting this prescription filled. Will the pharmacist know what the prescription is for?"

"We can fill the prescription here at the clinic, but I can't stress enough how important it is that your sexual partner be treated as well. If he isn't treated you just end up passing the infection back and forth between you. You should also abstain from sex for 7 days after the treatment. If abstaining isn't possible, make certain to use condoms for all sexual encounters and that includes oral sex," she explained.

"Oh I think I can safely say that I will not be having sex with my husband ever again," said Myrosia.

"Well you feel that way right now, but you never know how you're going to feel in the future. But regardless, he has to be informed and treated, and his other sexual partners need to be treated as well," said the nurse.

"Oh believe me, he'll be informed. Just wait till I get my hands on him," said Myrosia vehemently.

The nurse just smiled.

"An option for treating your partner is something called patient-delivered partner therapy, what that means is that I give you a prescription to give to him so that he doesn't need to go in for treatment," explained the nurse.

"No don't bother. I don't even know where he is and I'm not likely to be seeing him, except hopefully in divorce court. Let him go and get humiliated in person at the doctor," said Myrosia.

"Myrosia, you're lucky this time. It could have been much worse. Now I know that you thought you were in a committed monogamous relationship and he cheated on you and you are very hurt at the moment. But we are all sexual beings and you are an attractive woman so believe me when I say that there will be another man in your future so I am also going to give you some literature about safe sex and some condoms for you to take home with you," said the nurse.

The snow was starting again as she drove back to Bob's apartment.

I guess Jeff will get to find out how his new Mega Cruiser works in the snow, thought Myrosia.

Back in the apartment Myrosia made herself a cup of hot tea and sat down with her laptop to hunt through the county tax department records. Jeannie's comments about Dave being responsible for the swingers club on Nottingham Terrace was bothering her, but she didn't know the address of the house so she began a methodical search of every property on the street.

I couldn't possibly be lucky enough to find it registered in his own name. Something like that would likely be owned by a corporation, she thought.

When Joanna arrived about an hour later Myrosia had compiled a list of possible properties. Her plan was to drive by the houses and see if any of them looked like possible swingers' clubs, although she had no idea what something like that would even look like. She had no idea what she would do if she found the right house but it seemed like somewhere to start.

"Oh my god my feet are killing me, my whole body hurts," moaned Joanna flopping down in the overstuffed chair beside Myrosia. "I should have been an accountant. My mother tried to warn me about being a hairdresser. When I told her I wanted to go to hairdressing school she said to me 'Are you sure you want to do this? You never see any old hairdressers.' But did I listen to her? Nope. Do you think it's too late for me to change careers?"

"What did you have in mind? I'm not sure working with numbers is your forte. Maybe you could find something a little more in keeping with your skill set," said Myrosia thinking of her friend's constant inability to keep her checkbook balanced.

"I'm pretty good in bed. At least that's what I've been told on occasion. Maybe a career in prostitution would work for me. At least I'd get to lie down part of the time," said Joanna putting her feet up on an ottoman.

Myrosia laughed. "I hear that's hard on the knees, and then there's all that time standing out on street corners wearing high heels. Nope, I can't see that working for you."

"Duh, of course I'd want to be a high class hooker. No standing on street corners in Buffalo in the middle of winter for me. Maybe I could be a dominatrix? Well maybe not, I bet they have a lot of rotator cuff issues from whipping clients all day," said Joanna.

"Why the sudden interest in working in the sex trade?"

"You know I'm just kidding, but I had a bitch of a day, and I didn't even make all that much money. Business is always slow in January and February because nobody has any money after Christmas.

But I did hear some interesting gossip. Do you want to hear it?"

"Of course I want to hear it. But wait, let's order some dinner and then we can sit and exchange stories. I've had quite a day myself," said Myrosia.

When the food arrived they took it into the kitchen nook to eat. "I prefer eating in here. That formal dining room is just too big and cold," said Myrosia.

"Yeah I know, but it would be great for having a big Thanksgiving dinner with the whole family. You could get the whole herd in there," said Joanna opening the take out containers.

"So tell me about your day. Did you go to the clinic to get tested?" asked Joanna.

"Yeah, it was a good thing that you nagged me to do it because it turns out that I've got something called Chlamydia. But fortunately it's easily treated. One pill and that's it. I can't have sex for seven days but I don't think that's going to be a problem," said Myrosia wryly.

"Well then, under the circumstances I guess it's also a good thing that you weren't successful the other night when you tried to jump Bob. How embarrassing would that have been if you had to tell him to go and get treated," said Joanna.

"I hadn't even thought of that. Oh my god, I'd have been mortified. That bastard Dave. I spent most of the day while I was waiting for the test results terrified that they were going to tell me I had AIDS. I never ever want to go through that again. I hope his dick falls off!" exclaimed Myrosia.

"That must have been awful for you. I wish I'd had the day off to go with you and keep you company," said Joanna.

"Well I'm just glad it's over. But I gotta tell you Joanna, it was like something snapped in me today. It was so humiliating. The people at the clinic were really kind, but when I was lying there with my feet in the stirrups all I could think about was revenge. And then when she was talking to me about safe sex I just wanted to scream. It seemed so unfair. I've never been unfaithful to him. I went through this fifteen years ago, but it seemed different that time, Dave claimed to be sorry for what he called his 'mistake.' The kids were little and I agreed to stay with him, and everything seemed okay for years.

Obviously it really wasn't okay, and I guess I just ignored the signs, but something changed in me today, not just about Dave, but about everything," Myrosia explained.

"But enough about that. There's way more that I have to tell you," said Myrosia and she told Joanna about the rest of the days events, the $10,000 loan from Bob, the conversation with Jeff, and her lunch with the other partners' wives.

"Does anybody at that office do any work? I should've been a lawyer. Do you think women lawyers get as much action as those guys do with those young women?" asked Joanna.

"Who knew that law could be such an aphrodisiac. There must be something in the water cooler. But that reminds me, when I spoke to that kid Jeff today it felt like he was coming on to me. It was kind of creepy. I mean, I doubt that he's any older than my son. How gross is that," said Myrosia.

"He's not that young Myrosia. I bet he wouldn't like it if he heard you referring to him as a 'kid.' Besides, you see it all the time, old guys with younger women. Why not older women with young men? It's supposed to be pretty good. They've got great bodies and a strong sex drive. I wish some young guy would come on to me. Maybe you should give it a try. You could be a cougar like Demi Moore or Madonna," said Joanna.

"I don't know. It just felt creepy," said Myrosia.

"Well your day beats mine. The only perk of my job is the constant gossip and I did hear some juicy stuff today. Remember I told you about Brenda's client who's a seamstress? Well she was in today and she was telling us about how she was starting to get a lot of business making custom leather products and other stuff and she let slip that one of the people she was making something for was a city planning official, maybe the one that Dave has been trying to bribe. Apparently this guy gets his kicks from being beaten and peed on, and likes to do housework. I don't know about the beating and the peeing part, but it sure would be handy to find a guy that likes to do housework. Anyway, this guy has a weekly standing appointment with this chick who's a dominatrix and works out of that place on Nottingham Terrace. Damn, I remember the good old days when all the old ladies had weekly standing appointments to get their hair done. Hardly anyone does that anymore. Blow dryers have killed the business. Anyway, apparently this guy was ordering a custom made French maid outfit. It had to be custom made because he's a big guy and over 6 feet tall and I guess it's pretty tough getting French maid outfits in his size. She made us all promise not to say anything because she doesn't want to lose such a good customer since his 'play clothes' get wrecked really easily from all the whipping…"

Joanna's story was interrupted by Myrosia's cell phone ringing.

"Oh shit. That's Dave calling again. I'm sick of hearing him scream about his car, but I can't wait to tell him about the Chlamydia," said Myrosia.

She put it on speaker phone so Joanna could hear both sides of the conversation.

"Where is my car Myrosia? I want it back," he shouted when she answered the phone.

"Well I want to turn back the clock twenty-five years and make you disappear from my life, but that's not about to happen. I told you I'd give you the stupid car back when you return all the money that you stole out of our bank accounts and investments," she said.

"I haven't stolen anything. All I took was what was rightfully mine, but obviously you're too stupid to understand finances."

"Yeah, yeah. Tell that to the judge at your fraud trial. I've been hearing stories about your new business venture. I guess you're not planning on practicing law much longer. It's a good thing you've diversified because they're gonna disbar you."

"What the hell are you talking about?" he shouted.

"Oh come on, you know what I'm talking about. But I don't want to talk about that. I've got some much bigger news. You're infected with a sexually transmitted disease. I went and got tested today and it's serious. You'd better get to a doctor right away. I wonder how your new slut is going to like hearing the news, but she probably already knows. I can't believe I trusted you all these years and now you've given me this."

"You've got a lot of nerve calling someone a slut. If anyone's a slut it's you. If you've picked up something you must've gotten it from

Bob. That's what I get for giving you that pity fuck at Christmas."

"Pity fuck? How dare you! The last twenty-five years has been one long pity fuck on my part. I've been faking orgasms with you for years. I had to with a dick like yours. I don't know why I bothered. I should have dumped you for a real man like Bob years ago. You're an idiot," said Myrosia.

"I'm an idiot am I? Yeah, I guess I am because I didn't see what was going on right in front of my eyes. I heard all about how you moved in with Bob and the two of you have been out looking at wedding rings. You two have been sneaking around all these years, ever since college, and I didn't realize what was going on. I wonder which one of us is the father of the kids? I guess we'll need to get some DNA testing," he shouted and hung up the phone.

"Well that was fun. Now he's gonna wonder if I really was faking it all this time, and he'll stew all night worrying about AIDS, and whether his dick is going to fall off," said Myrosia.

"Have you really been faking orgasms? Does he really have a small penis? You and I talk about everything and you've never said anything about that before," said Joanna.

"No, I just said all that to piss him off," said Myrosia.

"Wow Myrosia, it worked. You really knew how to push his buttons. I'd loved to be a fly on the wall when he tells the new girlfriend, 'Oops baby I guess we need to go to the doctor, it seems we've caught something,'" Joanna laughed and then grew somber. "But seriously Myrosia, watch yourself. I don't know what you're trying to do, but you don't want to get him too mad. Taking his Porsche was one thing, but telling him that you've been faking orgasms, and making derogatory comments about his manhood, well men are really touchy about that. That's the kind of stuff that can get you killed."

"He's a bully. I've been letting him boss me and bully me ever since we met. I don't know why I put up with it for so long. I'm tired of it. I've had enough. The only way to deal with bullies is to stand up to them," said Myrosia trying to sound tough, but inside she was wondering if she really had gone too far.

"What the hell, let's forget about him for tonight and pull out the Tarot cards. Let's see if there's a career change and a young lover in the near future for you," said Myrosia.

"I think we need the heavy artillery after all that negativity with Dave. I wish we had something to smudge with," said Joanna as she went into the dining room and brought back 2 new white tapered candles in crystal candle holders. "Bob told us to make ourselves at home. I'll pick up a couple of new ones after work tomorrow to replace these."

Joanna lit the candles and dimmed the lights.

Myrosia got her Tarot cards out of her purse and sat back down at the table. She carefully laid out her purple silk cloth and closed her eyes and centered herself. When she was ready she carefully shuffled the cards.

"Okay Joanna while I shuffle these cards you think about your questions, are you going to change careers and are you going to find a new lover," said Myrosia.

She placed the deck down on the table.

"Okay, cut the deck into five piles," said Myrosia.

Joanna did as Myrosia requested. Then Myrosia took the top card from each pile and laid them out in a line from left to right in front of her.

"The first card is the Empress, Venus the goddess of love. She signifies physical attraction and abundance. In this position it represents your desire, which in this case is for money and a physical relationship, so I think we are on the right track with this spread," said Myrosia.

Then Myrosia turned over the second card in the spread.

"The second card is the Ace of Cups representing new beginnings, love and spring time. A new love coming in the spring time perhaps?" said Myrosia

"The third card is the Knight of Cups representing a new passion. This looks like your new man to me. Not old, not young, probably about our age, so I don't see you becoming a cougar," said Myrosia looking up at her friend and smiling.

"Oh I was just joking about wanting a young guy. I wouldn't mind a boy toy to play with, but not for a real relationship. I mean what would you talk about? Video games and comic books? No thanks," said Joanna.

"The fourth card is the Knight of Wands representing a journey or a change of residence. Or could this be a second man? Someone a little more impetuous than the Knight of Cups perhaps? It looks like you might have a choice of men," said Myrosia looking up and smiling.

"The fifth card is the 4 of Wands representing happiness and contentment. This is the outcome card of this spread and I think this indicates that the answer is yes, at least where a new lover is concerned because the Wands can also represent male energy," said Myrosia.

"You've got Cups and Wands, love and penises. But the Knights could also mean new ventures, so I'm not quite sure. What do you think Joanna, do you read it the way I do?" asked Myrosia.

"The spread seems a little confused. It's probably because we asked two major questions in the same spread. Either that or it's because I'm confused about what I want," said Joanna.

"Well I see lots of indications of happiness and a new love, but I don't know about a career change in your immediate future. I'm not sure that you're about to hang up your scissors yet," said Myrosia.

"Oh well, as long as the new man is good at giving foot massages," said Joanna.

"That's it for me. Let's go watch a movie. I'll grab us some snacks and you go and pick out a movie, pick something fun and happy. I could use a few laughs this evening. But before we settle in I'm gonna try and call Nicki one more time. I've been trying to reach her since Tuesday to warn her not to use her credit cards, but I swear that the only time that girl ever answers my calls is if she wants something. I've been dreading talking to her about it. It's inevitable, she's gonna scream bloody hell, but I just want to get it over with," said Myrosia picking up her cell phone.

"That's odd, it's not dialing. I'm not getting any dial tone. I'm gonna call your cell phone and see if it works. Maybe a cell phone tower is down with all the snow we've been having," said Myrosia.

"Nothing's happening. Is your phone on?" asked Myrosia.

"My phone is fine. Let me try and call you," said Joanna. "It says 'there is no service for the number you have dialed.'"

"That son of a bitch has cut off my cell phone! Shit, he got me again. I can't believe I never thought of that. We were on a family plan and that bastard has just cancelled me," shrieked Myrosia.

Chapter 12

It was Saturday morning and, as usual, the maintenance truck was on the beach at first light long before the sun worshippers were due to arrive to stake out the prime spots. The weather forecast was calling for another hot and sunny day in the 80's. Unseasonably warm for the first weekend of February in Tampa Bay, but a perfect beach day nonetheless, and the crowds at Madeira Beach would be taking advantage of it. It was the city maintenance worker's job to roust any drunks or homeless people who might have spent the night on the beach, and to look for garbage or anything unpleasant that might have washed up on shore at high tide.

When the maintenance worker spotted the woman laying in the tall grass at the edge of the sand his initial thought was that she had passed out drunk. It certainly wouldn't be the first time this had happened in his more than ten years on the job. Things weren't always as idyllic as they first appeared on this stretch of beach, with its luxurious condos overlooking the white sand beaches of the Gulf of Mexico. When he saw the impeccably dressed blonde woman with the empty wine bottle beside her he assumed that she was a resident of one of the nearby multi-million dollar condos who had been down on the beach drowning her sorrows during the night and had simply passed out.

Just goes to show that money doesn't buy happiness, he thought. But I'd sure like to know what these rich people who live here have to feel so sorry for themselves about.

He would wake her up and she would be embarrassed, hung over, and bitten up by sand fleas, he would give her a lecture about how dangerous it is to be out here alone at night and she would creep back up to her condo hoping that no one else had seen her. Maybe the embarrassment would be enough to send her off in search of an

Alcoholics Anonymous meeting.

But when he stopped his truck and stepped out to take a closer look he knew instantly that this was something far more serious. He could tell by her color and the awkward way she was lying that she was beyond help. But, just in case, he stepped over to the woman and felt her wrist to see if he could detect a pulse. He stood up, pulled his cell phone from his belt and dialed 911.

Within minutes two cars from the Pinellas County Sheriff's Department were on the scene followed shortly by a Fire and Rescue truck and an ambulance.

The sight of all these vehicles congregating on the beach began to draw the attention of the few early risers in the nearby condos. People having their first coffee of the day, who normally would have been sitting on their breakfast balconies watching the sun rise over the intracoastal waterway, or gazing out at the Gulf of Mexico looking for dolphins, were instead standing looking down over their balcony railings watching the events unfolding on the beach.

The beach would soon be coming to life. Joggers and couples taking early morning strolls along the beach would be arriving shortly, so the workers at the scene had to work fast. The EMT's examined the woman but it was obvious that any further attempts to resuscitate her would be futile, and she was declared dead at the scene.

Two more Pinellas County Sheriff's cars arrived, followed by two unmarked police cars driven by detectives from the homicide department.

As the detectives began their work, the deputies surrounded a large circular area with yellow crime scene tape.

"So what have we got?" one of the detectives asked.

"Maintenance worker found the victim when he was doing his rounds at first light. She was declared dead at the scene. Looks like she's been dead for a while," replied the deputy.

After scanning the entire scene from a few feet away the two detectives moved in closer to examine the body more carefully.

"Uh oh, this looks like trouble! What do you see?" asked the first detective.

"Well I see what used to be a glamorous blonde, somewhere in her 30's. It's hard to say for sure, but she's definitely got a problem with her neck. Looks like strangulation to me, what do you think? Might be a robbery, but that doesn't feel right, she's still wearing some pretty expensive looking jewelry. Maybe a lover's quarrel that got out of hand," replied the second detective.

"Don't you recognize the victim?"

"No, should I?"

"She's a television celebrity. This is Shelly Hammett. She's on that reality show about the wives of rich men. My wife loves that show. That's Trey Hammett's wife. You know, the football player. He plays for Buffalo," said the first detective.

"Geez, if you're right this does look like big trouble. Shit, so much for my weekend plans, there'll be no Superbowl for me and probably none for Trey Hammett either. Damn, I had money on that game. One thing's for sure, we're gonna need a lot more manpower on this one," said the second detective.

"But what's she doing here? Don't they have a place over in Palm Beach?" asked the first detective.

"I'm guessing that she was here for the Superbowl, staying in one of these luxury condos, but I don't see any clear footprints in the sand. Those EMT's must have messed things up trying to resuscitate her, either that or the wind has blown the sand around. We'd better get the dogs out here," said the second detective.

"If she's here, Trey must be around here somewhere too. We'd better start looking for him. I know we've gotta start with the husband in these cases, but geez I sure hope he's got a good alibi. He's a great player."

"But the case would be a lot easier to close if it turns out to be the husband rather than a stranger. I'll call it in and we'll get an APB out on him."

"Well, let's just hope we don't have another OJ Simpson kind of case, that one killed that LA detective's career and I've got too many years in to lose my pension now. We'd better be real careful with this one. I agree with you this situation justifies calling in the dogs to see if we can get an idea of which direction she came from and what direction the perpetrator went."

"One thing's for sure, we've got to get the Medical Examiner over here right now and get this crime scene sealed up and cleared up before the press gets wind of this. Otherwise this whole thing is gonna be a nightmare to keep under control."

But it was already too late. Somehow the word had leaked out about the identity of the body on the beach. News helicopters were hovering overhead, and speed boats began pulling up in the shallow water near shore. Additional officers were hastily called in to keep curious bystanders from contaminating the crime scene.

Radios crackled and more police and emergency personnel arrived. The two-person forensic imaging team arrived and began scanning the entire crime scene from every conceivable angle. Shortly thereafter, two police service tracking dogs arrived with their handlers.

A Sheriff's Department van arrived and the forensic team donned their white protective clothing and began collecting evidence. By now the number of spectators on the balconies had increased substantially and the deputies' job of keeping bystanders away was made more difficult by the fact that the crime scene was relatively close to the public beach access, so by 10 am the parking lot was filled not just with beach goers, but by paparazzi as well. Screens were set up in a futile attempt to shield the crime scene from curious onlookers with telephoto lenses.

The sun was getting higher in the sky by the time the Medical Examiner had completed her work at the site and the body was on its way to the Medical Examiner's Office on Ulmerton Road in Largo for an autopsy. At this point several of the Sheriff's Deputies had been assigned to interview the occupants of the nearby condos which overlooked the beach.

Myrosia was standing at the kitchen counter in Bob's apartment pouring another coffee and thinking about her plans for the day when the apartment phone rang. She wasn't expecting any calls since her cell phone service had been cut off the previous evening, and she really didn't feel like talking to anyone, but could see from the call display that it was her best friend Joanna calling from the beauty salon so she picked it up.

"Myrosia, oh my god, did you hear the news?"

"What news? I haven't spoken to anyone since you left. I'm still in my robe having coffee," replied Myrosia.

"Shelly Hammett is dead," Joanna shouted into the phone. The normal Saturday commotion of the beauty salon was even louder than usual, and Myrosia could hear the sound of a television blaring in the background.

"You mean Trey's wife Shelly? What happened?"

Although the Hammett's were part of their social circle, Myrosia had never been particularly close to Shelly.

"Quick, turn on the television. It's on all the stations. It's the top news on the internet too. We're all here watching it on the television in the shop," Joanna said excitedly into the telephone. "They found her body in Madeira Beach, on the Gulf Coast of Florida near Tampa. It looks like murder. We're all watching it here in the salon. This is big news for Buffalo, especially with the Superbowl on this weekend."

"Poor Trey, I wonder how he's handling all this. Oh my god, I hope he didn't have anything to do with her death," said Myrosia. "I know it's not right to speak ill of the dead, but I never particularly liked that woman. There was always something about her that just didn't feel right."

"You were probably just allergic to all that silicone and botox," Joanna replied.

Myrosia laughed and then said more seriously, "Did you know that she and Trey were getting a divorce?"

"No kidding! I never really knew her. Unlike you and Dave, I wasn't part of the 'in' crowd. She was way too snooty to associate with a lowly hairdresser like me. I'm not even glamorous enough to do her hair. How did you hear about the divorce?" asked Joanna.

"I found her file among the divorce clients in Dave's computer. There wasn't much in the file, just a copy of their pre-nup and a list of family assets. It didn't look like he'd gotten very far with it. He never mentioned it to me, and I never saw her in the office, but apparently he was handling her divorce," replied Myrosia.

"Oh my god! Myrosia quick, turn on channel 42. Dave's in Florida being interviewed about her death."

Myrosia slopped some of her coffee on the kitchen counter as she reached to turn on the television mounted under the kitchen cupboards.

"That god damn son of a bitch! Well that figures, look at the tan on that bastard, no wonder I couldn't find him. I'm freezing my ass off here in Buffalo trying to deal with the fallout from his treachery, and all this time he's been sitting on the beach in Florida with that bimbo," Myrosia said.

Hanging up the phone she turned up the volume on the television so she could hear what Dave was saying in response to the reporters' questions.

"…well yes, I was representing her in her divorce. It's a terrible tragedy. No, I haven't spoken to Trey. No, I have no idea what happened. I'm sorry but that's all I'm prepared to say at the moment," he said as he was whisked off into one of the waiting patrol cars.

Chapter 13

Myrosia took her coffee into Bob's study and turned on the television. She spent the next hour flicking back and forth among the channels looking at the various news reports of Shelly Hammett's death. When they began showing pictures of Shelly as a teenaged cheerleader in California and excerpts from her reality television show it became obvious that they had nothing new to report about the murder.

She decided to spend the day doing what she had originally intended to do. She got a new cell phone and then drove up and down Nottingham Terrace looking at the corporately owned properties on her list trying to find the home that housed the swingers' club that Dave supposedly owned.

I don't have a clue what I'm looking for, but hopefully I'll know it when I see it, thought Myrosia.

One of the properties caught her attention. It was a stately brick Victorian home set back off the road and partially obscured by mature trees. The driveway went alongside the house and disappeared into the back yard. If there was parking back there it was not visible from the road. The properties on either side housed professional offices, but this house had no apparent signage indicating that it was anything other than a private residence.

If I was looking for a place to house a 'social club' for wealthy individuals and 'office space' for sex trade workers this would work, she thought.

She parked next door in the almost empty parking lot shared by a couple of dentists and a CPA and sat and watched the neighboring house for any signs of activity. After a few minutes with nothing happening she called her friend Joanna.

"Hi Joanna, can you talk for a minute?" said Myrosia.

"You bet. It's 3 o'clock and I'm done for the rest of the weekend, hurray! I'm just cleaning up and then I'm ready to get out of here. What are you doing?" asked Joanna.

"I'm staking out a house on Nottingham Terrace, but it's pretty boring, nothing's happening. It looks like nobody's there right now. I think maybe I should come back later tonight and see if anything happens in the evening. Right now I want to go over to pick up my SUV from John. Now that we know that Dave's in Florida I don't see any reason not to drive my own vehicle. He's going to be too busy dealing with Shelly's murder to worry about getting back at me. I think I'm pretty safe from him for the time being. Then I'm planning to go see my mother for dinner to keep her informed of what's going on. Do you want to come with me? She'd like to see you, she's always asking about you," said Myrosia.

"Sure, I'll come with you, that'd be fun. I love your mother. She's hilarious, kind of a cross between Machiavelli and Don Corleone. Meet me back at Bob's condo in about 15 minutes."

Myrosia got to the condo first and while she waited she began packing up the clothes and things she had brought with her.

"What are you doing?" asked Joanna when she arrived.

"I'm packing up to go home. Now that we know that Dave's in Florida I don't see any reason to stay here. I'm not in any danger from him any more," Myrosia explained.

"Maybe not, but why don't we stay, just for tonight? Bob won't be back till tomorrow and you're a lot more comfortable here than at home with half the furniture missing, and it's a lot more convenient being downtown here if we're going to stake out that Nottingham Terrace house. Besides, I really love Bob's theatre room. Come on, let me have one more night of luxury," said Joanna.

Back at the Pinellas County Sheriff's Department the two detectives were reviewing what they had learned so far.

"The Medical Examiner won't have anything official for us until she completes the autopsy and the toxicology next week, but so far it looks like strangulation. She's given me a tentative time of death somewhere between midnight and 3 am but she won't swear to it," said Detective Ricci studying his notes.

Phil Ricci had been with the force fifteen years since leaving the military. He'd spent a couple of years working undercover but for the last eight years he had worked homicide. Twice divorced but currently single, he was a short muscular man who worked out at the gym religiously.

"That means that the body was lying there for between 3 to 5 hours and nobody noticed it," said Detective Osborne.

Stan Osborne, the senior detective assigned to the case, had close to thirty years on the force and was starting to look forward to retirement.

"If it happened closer to 3 am, I can see it. It was a cloudy night, not much moonlight, and the high tide mark was pretty low. Anybody taking a moonlit stroll along the beach would have been down closer to the water and she was lying further up on shore partially obscured by the grass. The kids that go out there to drink and make out tend to stay a little further south on the beach because of the security guards at those expensive condos," said Ricci.

"So far we've got nothing from the security guards on duty but we still haven't had a chance to look at the security camera footage. Maybe something will show up on that," said Osborne.

"We know that the victim was forty-one years old. She claimed to be thirty-six but her birth certificate says otherwise. I don't get why she'd bother fudging her age by five years but I guess she didn't want it to appear that she was that much older than her husband. This was her third marriage. The first one was to a kid she met in high school. It was a shotgun thing when they were both sixteen and they split up just after her son was born, but get this, the teen father got custody," said Ricci.

"Not exactly the maternal type. What kind of woman walks away from a new baby? You don't see that too often."

"No kidding. It's been a major battle for me over the years just to get my kids on weekends. My ex's were both like mother bears when it came to the kids. Mind you, for the kids' sake I'm not sure

I'd want it any other way. They might be bitches to me, but they were both good mothers," said Ricci.

"We don't know anything about the son, seems she never kept in touch. According to what I got when I talked to the husband, or maybe I should say the widower, she's got another kid, a daughter who's at a boarding school in Connecticut. Apparently doesn't see much of her either," said Osborne.

"Is the daughter Hammett's?" asked Ricci.

"No, they didn't have any kids together. The daughter was from her second marriage, she's a teenager now. Husband number two was a wealthy art dealer who was about thirty years older than her. When the second husband died he left her a bundle. It seems he died of a heart attack, nothing suspicious," said Osborne.

"Are you sure there wasn't anything funny about his death? It always gets my radar up when a rich guy dies and leaves his young wife a lot of money. Maybe we should get somebody to take a quick peak into his death. Also, there seems to be a gap of several years between when she left the first guy and when she married the art dealer. It's probably not relevant, but we should get somebody to check it out anyway," said Ricci.

"No privacy for the victim, that's for sure. She married Hammett eight years ago out in LA, shortly after the death of her second husband. He got traded to Buffalo and they moved up there, at least during football season but they still have places in LA, Palm Beach, and Aspen, Colorado," said Osborne.

"Must be nice. I should have married for money," said Ricci.

"Phil, no woman with money would put up with you."

"No, they'd love me. I'm a real charmer. I just never get the chance to meet any unless they're dead," said Ricci. "So what's she been doing lately?"

"Well according to Margie, who's an avid fan, she was on a reality TV show called 'Married with Money.' Also, apparently she was an art dealer, a business she inherited from her second husband, and she has galleries in Los Angeles, New York City, Miami and Buffalo, New York," said Osborne.

"Buffalo? Who knew that Buffalo was the center of the art

world," said Ricci.

"I doubt that it is, but it gave her something to keep her busy when she wasn't lunching with the other rich women on the show. Anyway that's just what I got from Margie so we need to confirm it," said Osborne. "Let's review what we know about this lawyer boyfriend of hers."

"His name's David Walker and he's a divorce lawyer from Buffalo, apparently him and his wife have known the victim socially for about seven years since Trey got traded to Buffalo," said Ricci.

"We still have to check out the jilted wife. I wonder if she's another one of the rich men's wives on the TV show? We've gotta check out her alibi. You know what they say, there's nothing worse than a woman scorned. If the ME finds fingernail scratches we go straight for the other woman," laughed Osborne.

"This lawyer boyfriend claims he started screwing the victim about three months ago after she came to him to discuss getting a divorce. He claims that the victim and her husband were already talking about splitting before he started sleeping with her. According to him it was true love. His story is that the last he saw her she was sitting on the balcony having a glass of wine and that he went to bed without her because he had an early tee-off time," said Ricci raising one eyebrow.

"Does that sound right to you? I mean if you were in the honeymoon stage of a relationship with a woman that looked like her would you leave her sitting up drinking alone on the balcony watching the ocean while you go to bed to get your beauty sleep? He claims he was in bed alone at 11:30, and the excuse is he had an early tee-off time? The missus and me after thirty years of marriage, yeah I can see it, but after less than one week of shacking up together, that dog don't hunt."

"That boy must really like his golf. We need to check with the golf course to confirm the tee-off time," said Ricci making an entry in his notebook.

"The victim and this lawyer fellow have got this condo rented for the winter. They took a six month rental that started Dec. 1 to the end of May. He claims they flew down a couple of times, once to rent the place and once more in December to move a few things in, but that they just left their respective spouses this week. If that's the case we've probably got two very pissed-off jilted spouses. So let's talk about the husband," said Osborne.

"As we know, the victim's husband is Trey Hammett who's a quarterback for Buffalo and they just happen to be down here for the Superbowl this weekend. He's thirty-two which means he must be getting pretty close to the end of his career. He seems to have a pretty good alibi, but I think we need to check that out a little more closely just to be sure. He claims to have been drinking at a bar in St. Pete Beach with a couple of teammates. Now, even in traffic, that's less than half an hour down the beach so what's to stop him from leaving his buddies, driving down the road, throttling the wife and rejoining his buddies an hour later?" asked Ricci.

"He claims he didn't know the missus was here and that he hasn't seen her since last Sunday. But just to be careful we should get the clothes he was wearing last night at the bar to check them against any fibers that might show up on the victim's body," said Osborne.

"Let's go talk to his teammates again this evening, see if we can shake their stories. They should be at the hotel resting up tonight, and you know the team management is not going to let us near them tomorrow before the game. Later on we should go talk to the staff at the bar to see if they remember seeing him the whole time. You never know, there might even be some regulars who'll remember something," said Ricci.

"I know we've got a really short window on this, with all the people coming and going this weekend for the Superbowl, but jeez I'm getting too old for these hours. We've got to get some more help on this. I know we can get Detective Sanson and the new guy she's working with. They're just finishing up that stabbing case they were working on," said Osborne.

"No, not Deborah, it's just too awkward working with her ever since we broke up," said Ricci.

"Hey Phil, I warned you it wasn't a good idea to date a co-worker. That's why we've got policies about that. How many times have I told you, 'you don't shit where you eat.' Now you've got to deal with it," said Osborne.

"Yeah, yeah, you sound like my father," said Ricci.

"Did you listen to him any better than you listen to me?" said Osborne.

"Maybe you can ask her to do the background stuff on the victim, the husband, the boyfriend, and the boyfriend's wife back in Buffalo. We're gonna need all that anyway and I'll only have to face Deborah when we get together for briefings," said Ricci.

The three women were seated at a quiet corner table in the dining room of the Hazelton Manor. The conversation switched seamlessly back and forth between English and Polish.

"It's good to see you Joanna. You haven't come see me so much since I moved out of the house," said Myrosia's mother.

"I'm so sorry about that Mama Dabrowski. I've got no excuse, except that I'm just so tired after working all day that I just go home and crash in front of the television most nights," said Joanna.

"You got yourself a new man yet Joanna?" asked the older woman.

"No, I'm afraid I'm not having much success in the romance department," said Joanna.

"It's time you got a new one. A good one this time that will take care of you, not like that palant you married. Maybe this year is your lucky year. I always say you should have married Feliks Matyjakowksi. You should have listened to your mother. Both of you girls should have listened, that's what you got mothers for," said the older woman.

"I know Mama D. I know I should have listened, and now my daughter doesn't listen to me either," said Joanna.

The older woman just shrugged as if to say 'What can you do.'

"Well I'm listening now Mama. That's why we're here this evening. To tell you what's been happening and see if you have any ideas what I should do next," said Myrosia. She proceeded to tell her mother everything that she had learned since they last spoke, omitting the part about the STD. She was still too embarrassed to talk to her mother about that.

Her mother listened thoughtfully to Myrosia's story.

"So, who killed this woman? You think Dawid did it?" her mother asked.

"Maybe, they might have had a fight and he got carried away. Or maybe her husband did it, or maybe there was something else that she was involved in that got her killed. I'm not sure," said Myrosia.

There was silence at the table for a few moments and finally the older woman spoke.

"To mi smierdzi, I smell a rat, something is not right. Dawid is greedy, and a crook, that I always know. And he can't be trusted to keep his penis in his pants where other women are concerned. So what, most men are like that if they get a chance." She shrugged again. "And he was a fool to treat you bad, but I always thought he was too smart to get caught stealing money. This trust fund business doesn't feel right to me. It's too obvious, too easy to trace to him. Dawid is too smart for that. He'll steal other ways if he thinks he can get away with it, but nothing so easy to trace. I gotta think some more about this."

After another pause Mrs. Dabrowski continued. "Maybe he killed this woman, maybe not. Anyone can kill if they pushed hard enough. But you say you found these dirty pictures on Dawid's computer? Hmm, I never thought him a pervert, but then again, who really knows about these things."

Myrosia cut in. "One thing we know for sure is who the girlfriend was. That gives me some clues about the money. I'm pretty sure I know what he did with all the art he took out of the house. I'd bet that it's in her art gallery. I'm sure that the intention was for her to sell it. But this might turn out to be a problem getting it back now that she's dead. I hope he's got good documentation, but even if he does, it's going to be tied up in her estate for ages now until things get settled. That sneaky bastard, he never cared about art until we started socializing with the Hammett's. Then suddenly he decides that buying art is a good investment. I bet this thing with Shelly was going on for years, since he first started buying art from her gallery."

"She was married to Trey, now that man is hot, so what on

earth did she see in Dave? What woman in her right mind would choose Dave over Trey? Oops, sorry Myrosia, I didn't mean that the way it sounded," said Joanna.

Myrosia ignored Joanna's last comment and continued. "What I still don't get is why he took the furniture? What was he going to do with it? I mean, if he was going to live with Shelly do you think for a minute that she'd want my furniture? Not a chance. I wouldn't want to put up with another woman's things. Besides, from what I've seen her taste is all modern, but my furniture, the furniture Dave took out of the house was all classic. The only thing I can think is that he did it to cause me the most pain possible and use it as a bargaining chip in the divorce settlement."

"We've been staying together at Bob's condo, but now Myrosia thinks it's safe for her to go home now. What do you think Mama D?" said Joanna.

"We can stay one more night, but I think we should be out of there tomorrow morning before he gets home tomorrow. I don't want to overstay my welcome," said Myrosia.

"I think you should stay with him a little longer. I don't think you in any danger, now that we know Dawid's in Florida, but I don't know, something is funny at the law office. Bob can help you find out. He's a lawyer, but in spite of this maybe he turns out to be a good man. Besides, you save money if you stay with him. When he comes home tomorrow you make him happy, but not too happy, you know what I mean, but you gotta make him think he's got a chance with you," said her mother.

"Oh Mama that's not right, that's so manipulative."

"Oh prosie, men are so stupid about some things, go ahead and use that to your advantage. It makes him feel good to look after you, go ahead and let him feel good. And call me tomorrow after I have a chance to sleep on this," she said.

On the drive across town to look at the Nottingham Terrace house the two women talked.

"I just love your mother, and her pet name for you is so funny. I can't believe she still calls you prosie, piglet, after all these years," said Joanna.

"I know she says it lovingly, she's not trying to be insulting. To her it's sort of a compliment. She's always called me that, both me and Szymon. You know, back in Poland during the war years and even after you never saw any fat babies, almost everyone was starving. But by the time she had me they were here and they had some money and she made sure that both of us kids were the fattest babies anyone had ever seen. I think that's why it's so hard for me to lose weight now. At least that's my excuse," said Myrosia laughing.

"Myrosia, how many times do I have to tell you, you aren't fat. You're gorgeous. And your mother is really something. She's a great ally, but she'd be a scary enemy. All through dinner I kept expecting to hear her say 'we gonna make him an offer he don't refuse.' Almost makes me feel sorry for Dave. Almost."

Chapter 14

Lights were on in the Nottingham Terrace house when they drove by.

"Okay, so what now? Somebody's home, what are we going to do, walk up to the door and ask if they have sex parties going on?" asked Joanna.

"Obviously not. I don't really have a plan. I thought something might come to mind once we got here. I guess I just wanted to see if it looked busier in the evening. Maybe we can just drive by a couple of times and see if we see any cars driving in."

They drove a few blocks further down the street and turned around and drove by again in the other direction.

"This isn't working. We can't really see anything from here. I'm going to pull into the parking lot next door and see if we can see anything from there," said Myrosia.

"Look, there's a car pulling into the driveway now. Damn, it's dark and the car's got tinted windows, I can't make out who's in it. Quick, pull up and park, maybe we'll be able to see them when they get out of the car," said Joanna.

They watched as a well dressed couple got out of the car and walked toward the side door.

"Do you recognize them?" asked Joanna.

"No, I really can't see them that well from here but they don't look familiar to me," said Myrosia.

"Here comes another car. I wish we had binoculars. We really aren't very well prepared for doing a stake-out," said Joanna.

"I don't recognize these ones either; they just look to me like another couple attending a dinner party. Nothing suspicious looking."

"I wish we could get closer and have a look in the window," said Joanna.

"Oh yeah, I can just picture it, a scene from 'I Love Lucy,' where Lucy stands on Ethel's shoulders to climb up and look in the window and Lucy falls through the window into the middle of someone's dinner party," says Myrosia.

"So which one are you, Lucy or Ethel?" asked Joanna.

"Forget it. That's just what I need right now is to get caught trespassing and get charged as a peeping tom."

"Well we're already trespassing and this gold Mercedes SUV isn't exactly designed for stealth. We're pretty obvious sitting here in the dark," said Joanna.

They sat there silently for a few more minutes and watched a couple more cars arriving.

"Myrosia, we aren't accomplishing anything here, I'm freezing and I've got to pee. Let's go back to Bob's place," said Joanna.

"Well I guess we can rule out police work as your next career. It's obvious you don't have the patience to do surveillance," said Myrosia as she started up the ignition.

When Myrosia pulled her SUV into the parking spot in front of the private elevator, Bob's Hummer was parked in its usual spot.

"Shit, there's Bob's Hummer. Obviously he's back. This is going to be awkward. I knew we should have packed up and gotten out of here earlier today. I don't care what my mother said; I don't want him to think I'm a freeloader. There's no reason for me to be here now that I know that Dave's in Florida."

"It'll be fine. Remember what your mother said, 'he likes looking after you, so let him,'" said Joanna.

Bob could hear the pinging of the elevator so when the elevator door opened and the two women walked into the foyer he was there to greet them.

"Hi Bob. I thought you weren't coming back until tomorrow," said Myrosia.

"I decided to come back early. I've been trying to reach you all day, but your cell phone was out of service. I was starting to get worried about you when I couldn't reach you, so I came back. Did you two hear the news about Shelly Hammett?"

"Oh yeah, all of Buffalo is talking about it. It's impossible to avoid hearing about it," said Joanna.

"I'm so sorry about my cell phone. I meant to call you and give you the new number but with the excitement about Shelly's murder I completely forgot. I had to get a new phone because Dave cancelled my old one. I'm so sorry that you had to come back early, I didn't mean to spoil your trip. You must've had a long day, you look so tired," said Myrosia.

"I'm okay. You didn't spoil my trip. I got everything done that needed to get done. I guess I was just looking for an excuse to come back early so I could spend time with you two ladies. I'm just glad you're back. I was sitting alone here watching the news reports and it's nice to have company," said Bob.

"Have there been any new developments?" asked Myrosia.

"Nothing official, but the reporters were interviewing some of the neighbors in the condo where they were living and they claimed that they could hear a lot of yelling," said Bob.

"That sounds like it was a pretty short honeymoon," said Joanna.

"The network is really taking advantage of all the attention. They're really plugging the new season of the show. The last I'd heard was that they were talking about cancelling the show, but with all this publicity they've got another shot at it. I guess the show will just go on without Shelly. In the meantime, both tonight and tomorrow night, they're showing back to back reruns of the first two seasons," said Bob.

"Oh that would be great! I've hardly ever seen the show since it's on Monday nights and our Tarot class is on Monday nights. Let's go watch it in the theatre room. A rich bitch marathon!" said Joanna.

Myrosia winced when she saw the pained expression on Bob's face.

"Joanna, I don't think Bob wants to spend his time watching that," said Myrosia.

"Oh Bob I'm sorry, how thoughtless was that. I completely forgot that Janice is in that show too. I can totally understand you not wanting to watch that," said Joanna.

"No, that's okay. Actually I'm kind of curious to see them now too. I've only ever watched a couple of episodes. I always thought they were just frivolous and petty. Janice and I had numerous fights over that. She claimed I wasn't being supportive of her 'art,' but I just thought it was so pointless watching a bunch of spoiled, pampered women complaining about how tough their lives are. So, a 'rich bitch marathon' it is. Come to think of it that's a pretty good name for the show, maybe the producers should consider changing it," he said smiling at Joanna.

"But I'm gonna need something stronger than this cola to drink. That is, as long as Myrosia doesn't mind watching Shelly. Is that going to be too painful for you Myrosia?" he asked.

"No, not at all. I'm actually really curious too. But I think I'd better stick to ginger ale because if I get loaded I might just start throwing things at your screen," said Myrosia.

"Come on then. We've got about five minutes before the next episode starts," he said getting up and walking out of the room.

The popular restaurant in St. Pete Beach was packed at 10 pm when the two detectives squeezed their way up to the bar.

"Do you mind if we ask you a couple of questions?" Ricci said to the bartender.

The bartender understood that this was a demand, not really a question. Regardless of how she felt about police, or about answering their questions, she knew that she really didn't have a choice, so best to just get it over with. She'd had plenty of experience with police in her life but she thought that was all behind her. She just prayed that they weren't here about anything her teenage kids might have gotten into. So she flashed him her best smile and said, "No problem, officers. What would you like to know?"

"Were you working last night at this time?" he asked.

"Yes," she replied.

"Do you remember seeing a group of guys in here last night, football players? We want to know about this one guy in particular," he said pulling out a publicity photo of Trey Hammett.

She relaxed. Obviously they were here about the murder of the football player's wife.

"Yes, the bunch of them were here right up to closing, sitting outside. They were having a good time. They weren't in no big hurry to leave," she said.

"But do you remember if this guy was here the whole time?" he asked pointing to the picture.

"I think so, but I can't be sure, I'm in here and as you can see it's pretty busy. You should talk to Sonja. She was waiting on them part of the night. That's her over there, the one with the curly red hair," the bartender said pointing to one of the waitresses.

"Hey Sonja, come here," the bartender waved the waitress over.

"These gentlemen want to ask you some questions about that table of guys you were waiting on last night," the bartender explained.

"I've got several tables going. Is this going to take long?" the waitress asked.

"No, we'll make it as fast as we can," replied Osborne.

"Just give me a second to tell the boss what I'm doing. I'll be right back," she said.

She was back in a moment.

"Okay, I'm gonna take my break right now, come on outside so I can have a smoke," she said and led the two detectives outside to a bench where one of the kitchen staff was already sitting. He got up and went back inside when she plopped down on the bench and lit up.

"Ah, that feels good to sit down," she said, taking a long drag on her cigarette. "So, what is it you want to know?"

"Do you remember waiting on a table of football players last night?" Ricci asked.

"Yes I served them most of the night. A couple of the other girls were helping me part of the time."

"What were the guys doing?" asked Osborne.

"The usual, they were sitting there talking, laughing, having a good time. They had a couple of women with them, and they were dancing a bit," she said.

"What about this guy, was he here the entire evening?"

"Yeah, as far as I know. I know that he left at the end of the evening with the other guys," she said.

"Did he seem alright? Was there anything unusual about him?" asked Ricci.

"Like I said he was having a good time with the rest of them. This is the guy whose wife was found murdered in Madeira Beach, right?" she asked.

"Yes, we're just verifying a statement he gave to us earlier," explained Osborne. "Is there anything else you can tell us about him?"

"Well, let's just say he was having a real good time. A lot of women were coming on to him and he was enjoying every minute of it. His wife didn't seem to be on his mind at all."

"What do you mean? How do you know what he was thinking?" asked Ricci.

"I guess I don't really know what he was thinking, but he was up dancing with a couple of different women, and this one waitress, a new kid name Sandi was coming on to him. Here I am running my ass off juggling trays of drinks and this chick Sandi is sitting on his lap. I was pissed. I mean, this is a real nice place, not a strip club. We don't do lap dancing here. I told her to get back to work. Anyway, next thing I know both him and Sandi disappear..."

"What do you mean 'disappear?' Do you mean they left the premises?" asked Ricci.

"Well no, not exactly. I'm rushing around trying to handle all the orders and suddenly Sandi is nowhere to be seen. I get really annoyed and tell Russ to go look for her because I can't handle it by myself. These guys weren't my only table, you know. It was packed in here last night. So Russ goes out to the parking lot and he sees Sandi giving this guy a blow job in the back seat of his Escalade. Stupid kid," said Sonja.

"What happened then?" asked Osborne.

"Well from what Russ told me, they didn't know anyone had seen them so he just kind of backed away and let them finish their business. The two of them came back in separately a few minutes later and Russ told her to go home. Stupid kid lost a good job to give some married guy a blow job. What an idiot. That's what I meant when I said that his wife didn't seem to be on his mind," she said.

"I guess we need to speak to Sandi and Russ," said Ricci.

Midway through the first episode of the show Bob got a text message and left the room to make a phone call.

While Bob was out of the room Joanna said quietly to Myrosia, "Bob is really chugging back that booze. Don't you think we should try and slow him down?"

"I don't see how we can. It's his place and his liquor. It's not like he's going to go out and get in his car," responded Myrosia.

"One other thing I wanted to say to you before he comes back is that I never noticed until now how much of a resemblance there is among all the women on this show. They're all tall, blonde and slim. I guess that's the look that these rich guys go for, which probably explains why I always end up with guys that are broke. But Myrosia, you could be on this show. You're a prettier, more natural looking version of both Janice and Shelly. Don't you find it kind of creepy that Dave picked a woman that kind of looks like you? Obviously tall blondes are his type," said Joanna.

"Jeez, thanks a lot Joanna, comparing me to either of those botoxed skanks. They spend all their time getting manicures and spending money. Besides I'm not that thin," said Myrosia.

"Oh please, give me a break…" said Joanna.

They sat through two complete episodes and were into a third when Bob got up during a commercial break to get another bottle out of the liquor cabinet. He stumbled slightly and nearly fell on Joanna but caught himself on the arm of her chair.

"Whoa Bob, you're really packing away that Scotch. I've never seen you drink this much before. Maybe you should slow it down a bit, maybe add a little mix…" said Joanna.

"You don't add mix to Glenfiddich, that's a sacrilege. You drink it straight like God intended, at least that's what the Scots always say and they should know."

He shakily poured himself another shot and took a sip. "Ah, the golden nectar of the gods, the ambrosia of the angels." His words were beginning to slur.

"You keep it up and you're going to regret it in the morning. I'm just saying," said Joanna.

"Hey Bob, have you eaten? Do you want me to make you a sandwich or something?" Myrosia asked.

"No, no, I'm fine. I just need another drink, another wee dram…" he began to hum.

"I'm going to get myself something, and I'll get you something too," said Myrosia.

"That's sweet of you Myrosia, my sweetie, but you don't have to do that, really I'm fine," he said, stumbling back to his seat.

Myrosia was back in a few moments with leftover Chinese food that had been in the fridge from the previous evening.

"Here Bob, look what I found. Have a spring roll. I don't think you've had enough to eat to sop up all that booze you've been drinking," said Myrosia taking his glass from his hand and replacing it with a glass of ginger ale.

"Okay Myrosia, if that's what you want, anything you want, if that's what you want, come and sit with me honey, there's lots of room," he slapped his hand on the seat beside him.

"No thanks Bob, I'm pretty comfortable right where I am."

"Okay Myrosia, if that's what you want, anything you want…" his words faded off as he continued to stare at the image of his ex-wife looking back at them from the gigantic HD screen. It was a scene in the show where the four women were in a tattoo parlor getting tattoos.

"I remember the day she came home with that tattoo. I should have changed the locks that day, no I should have…" his words faded off again and the scene changed to one where another one of the wives was taking a home pregnancy test and wondering how her husband was going to react because she didn't think he wanted a baby.

"I feel sick," he moaned.

The two woman dove into action. Joanna jumped from her

seat and grabbed the garbage can from the kitchenette while Myrosia grabbed the glass out of his hand and helped him to lean forward slightly.

"Here Bob, if you're going to be sick throw up in here," said Joanna. "Go ahead, you'll feel better."

"I'll hold the bucket. You go get me a cold wet towel out of the bathroom," Myrosia instructed Joanna.

"I didn't mean it, I didn't mean it…" he started to sob.

"Oh great, here we go, he's on a crying jag," said Joanna.

"Myrosia, Myrosia, I didn't mean to hurt her, I didn't mean to hurt her, I'm so sorry, I'm so sorry," he moaned just before he passed out.

"Come on Bob, I think it's time for you to go to bed. Joanna give me a hand with him. He weighs a ton."

Myrosia managed to haul him to a standing position and leaned him on her shoulder. Joanna took the other side and together the two women half carried, half dragged him through to his bedroom.

"Do you think we should undress him?" asked Joanna once they had heaved him onto the bed.

"No, just take his shoes and his belt off. I'm gonna roll him onto his side and prop him up with some pillows so he doesn't choke if he starts to vomit," said Myrosia.

Bob began to stir again.

"Myrosia, Myrosia, stay here with me, I'm so sorry…" he said and he passed out again.

Myrosia covered Bob with a blanket and the two women stood looking down at him passed out on the bed.

"That brings back memories. Thank god it's been ages since I had to put a drunk to bed. Have you ever seen him like this before?" asked Joanna.

"Only once, and that was way back in college. Obviously it was a mistake having him watch that show with us. I guess he's still hurting from the breakup with Janice."

"Well at least he's not a mean drunk. He didn't try to take a swing at either of us," said Joanna. "I wonder who he was talking about? What he's sorry for?"

"I don't know. It must be something to do with Janice and the divorce. People can say and do some pretty terrible things when they're hurting," said Myrosia.

The women stood silently for a few moments watching him stir and moan in his sleep.

"Myrosia, stay here with me, I'm so sorry..." he kept saying.

"It's alright Bob, I'm right here," she said stroking his cheek gently.

"Do you think he'll be alright if we leave him like this?"

"He's gonna feel it in the morning, but I think he'll be fine. You go ahead and go to bed. I'll just pull up a chair beside him and stay here for a little while. I'll go to bed once he settles down," said Myrosia.

Chapter 15

On Sunday morning Joanna and Myrosia were in the kitchen frying up bacon and eggs when a very rough looking Bob surfaced from the bedroom looking for coffee.

"Good morning sunshine," said Joanna. "You're looking a little under the weather this morning."

"No worse than I deserve. That was really stupid of me to drink like that," said Bob.

"Here try some of this. You're probably a little dehydrated," said Myrosia pouring him a glass of water and another glass of flat ginger ale.

"Are you ready for some breakfast Bob?" asked Joanna.

"Oh god no. This is plenty," he said, swallowing some Tylenol.

"What I want to know is how much of a fool I made of myself last night. The last thing I remember clearly is sitting down to watch that awful show and then I vaguely remember someone telling me to slow down my drinking and after that it's all a blur. I don't even know how I got to bed. I haven't done anything that stupid since college. I think I was talking to you sometime in the middle of the night Myrosia. Was I dreaming that?" he asked.

"Well to fill in the missing sections in your memory, you passed out watching the show and Joanna and I put you to bed," said Myrosia.

"Thanks for doing that, but you probably should have just left me where I dropped. Waking up in a heap somewhere might have taught me a lesson. I'm really embarrassed about this."

"Just returning the favor Bob. Remember, it's been twice this week that you've had to hold my hair out of the toilet. It's been a tough week for both of us," said Myrosia. "At the rate we're going the pair of us might want to start looking up AA meetings."

"In your abridged version of events, did I do or say anything that you neglected to tell me?" he asked.

"Nope, nothing I can think of. You were a perfect gentleman," Myrosia replied.

"I think you're lying to spare my pride, but I appreciate it."

Joanna began setting out the plates on the breakfast table.

"Are you sure I can't interest you in any of this? I hate to eat your food in front of you," said Joanna.

"I might be able to tolerate a slice of toast, but that's about it."

"Bob I really appreciate everything you've done for me this week, and it's been great being able to stay here in your apartment. But now that I know that Dave's in Florida it doesn't make sense for me to stay here. I think it's time for me to go back to my own house today," said Myrosia.

"Whatever you think Myrosia, but remember that you're always welcome to stay," he replied. "Do either of you mind if I turn on the TV to see if there are any new updates on the case?"

"Are you sure you want to do that? Watching that show seemed to be painful for you last night," said Myrosia.

"No, my behavior last night had nothing to do with Shelly's murder. I guess I really haven't completely resolved things regarding Janice. It's probably a good thing I watched that show. It sort of brought things to a head. Too bad I anesthetized myself."

"Go ahead, turn it on then. Let's see if there's anything new," said Joanna.

He turned on the television and all three of them were startled to see images of television news trucks parked at Myrosia's lake house.

"Quick, turn up the volume, what are they saying about my house?" asked Myrosia.

"… at the stately lake front home of Buffalo lawyer Dave Walker who is at the center of the criminal investigation into the Florida death of reality TV star Shelly Hammett. Unconfirmed reports indicate that not only is Walker a murder suspect, but he is also under investigation with regards to a failed waterfront development project here in the Buffalo area. Now back to Florida for updates from our correspondent..." said the reporter standing bundled up for the cold.

"Oh no, how can I possibly go home now?" cried Myrosia.

At the Pinellas County Sheriff's Department offices in Largo, Florida, the members of the law enforcement team assigned to the case sat in a meeting to analyze the information they had collected so far.

"The husband's alibi seems to check out. We have numerous witnesses that place him at a bar in St. Pete Beach from approximately 11 pm until around 3 am. After that he left in a vehicle with three other teammates to go back to his hotel in Tampa. The front desk clerk at the hotel confirmed that they arrived back there about 3:30. This doesn't rule out him having hired someone to do the job, but assuming the ME's time of death is anywhere near accurate, I can't see how he could have done it himself," said Detective Ricci.

"I think it's unlikely that he hired someone. If he wanted her killed he wouldn't arrange to have it done on Superbowl weekend. There's even some question about whether the team management is going to put him in the line-up today as a result of this, and no player would jeopardize his team's shot at Superbowl glory. Besides, if he wanted her dead he could've had it done anytime. It doesn't make sense for him to pick a time when they were both in the same town," said Detective Osborne.

"This doesn't feel like a hired hit to me. This seems more like a crime of passion. Like a fight that got out of control," said Detective Sanson, the only woman detective in the room.

"Yeah, that's what Phil and I are thinking too. But just in case, Deborah, can you do a little more looking into their marriage and the family finances, insurance policies, that sort of thing. He had an intimate encounter with that waitress at the bar, so it doesn't exactly look like he was distraught over his wife leaving him, but who knows. See if you can find out if he's been seeing anyone else. See if we're missing any other reasons why he might have wanted her dead. But assuming nothing else turns up we can probably rule out the husband," said Osborne.

"Something else that seems to clear him are the surveillance videos from the condo. Paul and I just finished reviewing them and there are several spots where the garage camera catches the victim and the boyfriend entering and exiting the building. Let me play it for you," she said picking up the remote control and turning on the monitor on the wall.

"See now here's the victim and the boyfriend exiting the building, and here they are two hours later when they come back. In my opinion they don't look happy. Look at the body language. They aren't touching, none of the little gestures and glances you normally expect to see between lovers. Now here we see them going out again. According to the boyfriend this is when they went out for dinner. When they return at 11 pm we can clearly see them arguing. It looks really heated. There's no sound, just the picture, so we don't know what they're arguing about, but it looks serious. At 12:20 we see her exiting the building alone for what seems to be the last time. No sign of the boyfriend. She's wearing the same clothing as when her body was discovered..." said Detective Sanson.

"Wait, stop, back that up. Right there, we've got a clear view of both of her hands. See she's not carrying anything. When the body was discovered there was an empty bottle of wine lying beside her. Where did the wine bottle come from if she didn't bring it with her? Are there any more shots of her in the garage? Did she go to her car?" asked Ricci.

"This is the last time we see her leaving the building and she definitely does not go toward her car. She goes out the side exit past the pool area and out toward the beach and she's definitely alone. However, less than two minutes later the camera on the south side of the building catches a glimpse of a man who seems to be following her to the beach. It's in shadows, the light on that side of the building is out, so it's impossible to clearly identify the man, but he doesn't appear to have the same build as the husband. It's not exactly a high traffic area, and according to the camera, no one else passes along the south side of the building again between this time and the time the body is discovered. We haven't been able to determine the exact height of the man in the shadows. We'll have the techies look at that tomorrow when they come in, but so far we are estimating him to be between 5'10" and 6'2, with a slim build. The husband is 6'2" and very muscular, weighing somewhere between 220 and 240 pounds," said Sanson passing around a picture of Trey Hammett.

"Now here's a picture of the boyfriend. Who happens to be 5'11" tall and 175 pounds," she said passing around a picture of Dave Walker.

"It isn't conclusive. We don't see them together, and we don't see the actual crime taking place, but if this is the murderer, I think we can rule out the husband," Sanson concluded.

"If that's the boyfriend, how did he get out of the building without showing up on the garage camera?" asked Ricci.

"There are a couple of possibilities. He could have come down one of the stairwells. There's one on both the north and south sides of the building. Unfortunately there are no cameras in either of the stairwells which is a big flaw in this building's security system. Another possibility is that he could have gone out across the tennis court and down the exterior stairway on the south side of the tennis court."

"The only reason someone would go to that much trouble is if they wanted to make sure that they weren't seen. In which case it was pre-meditated rather than a crime of passion," said Ricci.

"The other possibility is that the murderer didn't come out of the building at all, but was outside waiting for her and walked along the south side of the building and caught up with her on the beach," said Sanson.

"No, there's still another possibility, that this isn't the murderer at all, but simply someone taking a short-cut from Gulf Boulevard out to the beach, and the real murderer came from the public beach access," said Osborne.

"Well I suppose another possibility is that the murderer waded in from a boat anchored off shore. But before we suggest that the murderer dropped out of the sky parasailing, what do the dogs say?" asked Ricci.

"We'll probably get the official report in a couple of days, but from what the handlers told me it seems that both the victim and the killer came from the direction of the condo, but then the killer left walking south down the beach. The scent disappeared into the water less than a quarter mile down, but I don't think that means that the killer swam away, probably just walked into the water knowing that it would throw off the dogs," said Osborne.

"Any luck talking to the boyfriend's wife?" asked Ricci.

"No, the only phone number we have for her is the house phone and I've left messages for her to call me, but so far I haven't heard from her. The cell phone number we have for her has been disconnected. I called the Erie County Sheriff's department and they sent a car out to her house but there doesn't seem to be anyone at home. She's probably staying with friends to avoid the publicity. Walker's law office will be open tomorrow and I'll try there. They might know how to reach her."

"Maybe she's in Florida tracking down hubby and the girlfriend," said Ricci.

"I did manage to get a little background information on the victim. I called the LA County Sheriff's department and spoke to a records clerk. Seems the victim was picked up for solicitation a couple of times in the years before she married hubby #2. She was using the name Denise Connors back then. Apparently she was doing a little modeling and trying to get into the movie business like all the young girls in Hollywood and she supplemented her income with prostitution. That's all I've been able to find out about that period of her life so far. But I think it's worth digging a little more. We also know that she's on that reality TV show. I've put some calls out trying to reach the other women on the show to see what their thoughts are, but so far I haven't been able to reach anyone. I don't know how valuable it'll prove to be, but my mother has a big collection of National Enquirer's so I've got her going through them and digging out all the stories they've done on the victim and the other women on the show. But don't worry, I'm not talking to my mother about the case. I wouldn't jeopardize things by discussing this with anyone outside of the investigation."

"Great work Deborah. The tabloids probably have more resources than we do when it comes to digging up dirt about someone," said Osborne. "Now let's talk about this Walker fellow."

"We brought him in for questioning yesterday. He strikes me as a cocky, pompous jerk. You know the type. Thinks he's smarter than us dumb cops. He claims he was in bed by 11:30 on Friday night because he had an early tee-off time booked with a couple of business associates and doesn't know anything about what happened. I checked his story and there was no tee-off time booked, so we know he's lying about that. So what else is he lying about? Apparently he's also under investigation in New York State regarding allegations of bribing government officials and misappropriation of funds. He's a real sleaze, but there's no apparent history of physical violence, no police calls, but the neighbors in the condo were complaining about hearing him doing a lot of shouting over the past couple of days. We need to keep a real close eye on this guy, he's our number one suspect right now and I think he's a flight risk," said Ricci.

"We don't have enough to charge him yet, but it sure would be a black eye for all of us if he managed to slip away, so I've got deputies keeping an eye on him around the clock. We've got the victim's condo sealed off and guarded so Walker had to move into a hotel. He's been warned not to leave the county, maybe we'll get lucky and he'll do something stupid and give us an excuse to pick him up. Does anyone have anything else they want to talk about?" asked Osborne.

He paused, but no one in the group responded.

"Okay, if there's nothing else then let's get back to work and see if we can catch this killer. Remember, Pinellas County has a 95% solve rate for homicides and we don't want to mess up our stats," said Osborne.

"Phil, do you mind waiting for a moment? I'd like to have a word with you," said Detective Sanson.

When they were alone Detective Sanson spoke.

"Phil, I really appreciate getting the chance to participate in this investigation. I was a little surprised to be chosen because you seem to have been avoiding me," she said.

"Deborah, why wouldn't you be chosen? You're one of the best investigators we've got. But I guess it's true that I've been avoiding you. It's just that I'm sorry about the way we ended things between us, and I was afraid you'd be angry," he said.

She laughed. "Oh Phil, no need to worry. I'm sorry things didn't work out between us, but I'm seeing someone new. So no hard feelings right?"

"Bob, are you sure you don't mind if I stay a few more days till all this dies down? I really wanted to get home and be alone to go through all of Dave's financial transactions, but I just can't deal with those reporters," said Myrosia.

"No, I really want you to stay here. You wouldn't be able to hold them off out at the lake house. They'd be harassing you continually, but they can't get to you here. I don't think you have a choice really. You have to stay. You can work in my office, or if you'd prefer you can take over the dining room. I've done that before when I've been working on something and I really needed to spread out."

"Well I don't have any excuse for taking advantage of your hospitality any longer. Nobody's looking for me so I think I should go home today," said Joanna.

"You're welcome to stay too Joanna. But if you don't sleep over at least stay and watch the game," said Bob.

"Gee, that's a really tempting offer, but I've got plans to watch the game with some friends over at Riley's pub, so I've got to go home and get tarted up," Joanna replied.

"Oooh, you meeting anyone special over there?" asked Myrosia playfully.

"Maybe..." replied Joanna with a sly smile.

When they were done cleaning up after breakfast Joanna left to go home and get ready for her date, and Myrosia sat down to check the voice mail messages on her home phone. She filled an entire page of calls that needed to be returned.

"Well I've certainly become popular. The voice mail is full. Reporters are calling. I think everyone I've ever met is trying to talk to me. There's even a call from a police department in Florida. They want me to call them back. Why on earth would they want to talk to me?" she said.

"They're probably just looking for background information

about Shelly. I'm sure it's nothing to be concerned about," said Bob.

"I might as well call and get it over with then."

"It might be a good idea if I sat in on the conversation just in case you need some legal advice," he said.

"Do you really think I need a lawyer for this?" she asked.

"No, not really. I'm sure it'll just be some routine questions about how well you knew Shelly, but still, if you put it on speaker phone then I can hear what's going on. I won't get involved unless they ask you something that I don't think you should answer."

"Hello Detective Sanson? My name is Myrosia Walker. There was a message on my voice mail asking me to return your call."

"Thank you for calling. I'd like to ask you a few questions about Shelly Hammett and Dave Walker."

"Sure, what would you like to know?" Myrosia asked.

"Just some routine questions. Are you aware that Mrs. Hammett's body was discovered on Saturday morning?" asked Detective Sanson.

"Yes, how sad. I saw the news reports."

"How well did you know the deceased?" asked the detective.

"We weren't close friends, I knew her casually. My husband and I had numerous friends in common with the Hammett's and so we often saw them at social events. I've been to their home on a number of occasions and they've been guests at our home. Shelly and I knew each other, but we weren't close."

"What about your husband, what do you know about his relationship with the deceased?" asked Detective Sanson.

"If you're asking me if I knew he was having an affair with her, the answer is no. I found that out yesterday morning when I turned on the television. I discovered it at the same time that the rest of the world did. I got home late in the evening last Monday to discover that my husband had left me, but I didn't know where he had gone or who he was with," said Myrosia.

"What can you tell me about the Hammett's marriage?" asked Detective Sanson.

"Obviously they were having marital problems, otherwise why would she run off with Dave, but nothing that I was aware of. On the surface everything looked fine, but like I said we weren't that close," said Myrosia.

"When was the last time you spoke to Mr. Walker?" asked Detective Sanson.

"He called me on Friday evening about 6 pm."

"Can you tell me what you were doing on Friday night and Saturday morning?" asked Detective Sanson.

"What? Are you asking me if I was in Florida murdering Shelly? No, I was here in Buffalo. I had dinner with a friend and we sat in and watched a movie. I went to bed and Saturday morning while I was having breakfast I turned on the television and heard the news about Shelly," said Myrosia.

"Can anyone confirm this?" asked Detective Sanson.

"Yes, the friend who was with me for the evening, the delivery man who delivered our dinner, and the security guard in the lobby who must have seen me entering the building and parking my car," said Myrosia.

"Representatives of the Erie County Sheriff's Department have been trying to locate you but you haven't been at your residence," said Detective Sanson.

"No, I've been staying with a friend, in a high security building in the city. Originally Dave had been threatening me and so I was hiding from him, but now I guess I'm hiding from the media."

"You said that Mr. Walker was threatening you. What was he threatening to do to you?" asked Detective Sanson.

"We were fighting over the division of assets and he was just very angry and made vague threats, nothing specific, but I didn't know at that time that he had left the state. I assumed he was somewhere in the Buffalo area and I felt vulnerable being alone at our house on the lake," said Myrosia.

"Is there any history of violence in your marriage? Has Mr. Walker been physically threatening in the past?" asked the detective.

"No, he has a bad temper and he's been verbally abusive plenty of times, but no, he's never hit me," said Myrosia.

"Do you think it's possible that Mr. Walker killed Shelly Hammett?" asked Detective Sanson.

"I've been wondering that myself. I suppose anyone could kill if they were pushed hard enough, but I've never seen him lose control before and get violent, so I'd be really surprised if he did it."

"I've been trying to reach Janice Williams. I understand that you're friends. Do you know how I can reach her?" asked Detective Sanson.

"No, I have no idea how to reach Janice. We aren't close friends. Dave and I have been very close friends with her husband Bob since college, but since Janice and Bob split up I haven't spoken to her," said Myrosia.

"When was the last time you spoke to Janice Williams?" Detective Sanson asked.

"Oh I don't know, probably the last time I saw her which would have been last August at a barbecue at our home. Why are you asking me about Janice? What does she have to do with Shelly's death?" replied Myrosia.

"Oh we're just trying to reach her for questioning and we can't seem to find anyone who has spoken to her in months," explained the detective.

"Well Dave is the best one I can think of for you to ask. I know he was representing Bob Williams in their divorce settlement so I'm sure he's spoken to Janice more recently than I have," said Myrosia.

"Well thank you for your time. If I have any more questions can I reach you at this number?" asked Detective Sanson.

"Yes certainly," replied Myrosia.

Hanging up the phone she turned and looked at Bob. "Did you hear that? I can't believe she questioned me about my whereabouts on Friday night, like they think I murdered Shelly. How absurd is that. And why on earth were they asking me about Janice?"

"I have no idea," said Bob.

Chapter 16

Myrosia retreated to her room to return some of the other calls. She tried her daughter Nicki again with no luck, she still wasn't answering.

She looked at the time, 2 pm. An excellent time to call her son Dylan over in England, she thought. She got on her computer and called his cell phone.

"Hi Mom, it's great to hear from you," he said.

"Are you near your computer?" she asked.

"No, I'm with some friends at the local watering hole. I'm just stepping outside so I can hear you better," he said.

"Well I won't keep you. I just wanted to let you know what's been going on over here," she said and proceeded to give him an abbreviated version of the week's events including a warning not to attempt to use his credit card.

"Oh Mom, how awful for you! Do you want me to come home? I can probably be there tomorrow some time if I run home, grab my passport and get to the airport. It won't cost too much if I can get the student standby rate. I don't need a credit card. I've got enough money to cover it," he said.

"No, no. You stay over there and focus on your studies. Have a good time with your friends this evening and don't worry about us over here. There's nothing you can do for me here at the moment anyway. Bob Williams is being very kind and letting me stay in his condo, so for the time being the reporters can't get to me in here. I just wanted to call you and give you my new cell phone number and tell you what was going on so that you wouldn't be concerned if you saw something about it on the news."

"We don't get a lot of that sort of US news over here. The English have plenty of their own murders and scandals to read about. But I'll keep my eye out on the internet for any news. Call me if you change your mind and want me to come home. I love you Mom, and say hi to Uncle Bob for me," he said.

"I love you too Dylan. Now you get back inside and have a good time with your friends and don't worry about me. Bye, bye," she said and hung up.

Her next call was to Jeff, the network administrator from the office. He had left at least a dozen messages on her home phone.

"Myrosia I've been trying to reach you. I heard the news about Shelly Hammett and Dave so I turned around and came right back from Chicago last night in case you needed some help. I tried to call you but your cell phone was disconnected," he said.

"That's sweet of you for doing that, but everything's fine. I'm really sorry that you shortened your trip because of me. I had to get a new cell phone because Dave cancelled the old one. The number I'm calling you on now is my new cell phone number. I'm sorry, it just never occurred to me to call you with the new number. I guess I just figured we'd talk this week when you got back. But really, I'm fine, I'm staying in town with friends," she said.

"Yeah, I figured that out. I drove out to your house to check on you but it was obvious that you weren't home. The place was crawling with news trucks," he said.

"I didn't realize that you even knew where I lived."

"Everybody knows that you live out on the lake, and the actual address is in the firm's human resources files. I was going through those files looking for the information you wanted me to find out about that girl Christine," he said.

"Oh, of course, did you find out anything?" she asked.

"Well I found her last address here in Buffalo, but I think you already know that. So I tried to find out where her folks live to see if she might have moved back with them. But no luck. I think I found her Facebook page, but there doesn't seem to have been any action on that for a couple of months. So then I decided to take a drive over to her old address and talk to the neighbors, but no luck there either. No one seems to know where she went," he said.

164

"Wow, you really have put a lot of time into this. I really appreciate it," she said.

"No trouble, happy to help. Besides it's like a puzzle. I enjoy the challenge. You've probably already noticed that I'm a little obsessive compulsive when I get into something," he said.

"Well I admire your focus," she said.

"I have a few more ideas. I was thinking I might try and hack the DMV records and see if she's changed her address on her driver's license…" he began but Myrosia cut him off.

"Oh no, please don't do that. Don't do anything illegal. It's not important enough to get into trouble for. Besides, now that I know where Dave went and who he went with I probably don't even need to talk to her. But if you have any ideas where he hid the money, I'd appreciate hearing them."

"I can give you money if you need some. Like I said, I've got plenty."

"Thanks Jeff, but no, I'm okay for money at the moment. I've gotta go. We'll talk this week," she said and hung up.

Her next call was to her mother. She told her about the events of the previous evening, and what Bob had told her in his drunken state.

"Prosie, you go see him now and keep him company. He's probably worried that he said too much. We talk later."

Myrosia wandered back down the hall to look for Bob. If he's in his room I'm not going to bother him, she thought. But then she noticed that his study door was slightly ajar.

"Hey Bob, you want some company?" Myrosia asked as she poked her head into the room and saw him lying on the sofa.

"Absolutely, come in and sit down. I'm just lying here enjoying the fire and wondering why I choose to live in a place with such brutal winters," he said.

"Those flames are hypnotic," said Myrosia as she curled up under a blanket in one of the overstuffed chairs where she could watch the flames of the gas fireplace. "I really like this room. It feels homey and comfortable."

"Yeah, this is my favorite room. Janice decorated the rest of the place, but this is my refuge. I'm like a kid in my tree house in here.

I've got all my favorite stuff," he said.

"How's your headache, are you feeling any better?"

"I'm fine now. I've pretty much recovered from last night's debacle. Just a little embarrassed. You've seen behind my tough guy façade." He paused for a moment. "You know, I think I more or less remember what we talked about last night in the bedroom."

"I've always seen through your façade. The cracks in it are part of what I love most about you."

"Well now you know my deep dark secret. I was a little surprised to see that you were still here this morning when I got up."

"I know that you blame yourself for Rhyanna's suicide, but really Bob that wasn't your fault," she said.

"No, you know part of it but you don't know the whole story. I was too drunk last night to explain it properly. Of course you know that Dave had been sleeping with Rhyanna. When Dave found out she was pregnant he panicked and confessed to you because he knew you'd be bound to find out and he didn't want to lose you. You've known that part all along, but what you don't know is that I was also sleeping with her, and a few of the other guys had been too. None of us know for sure who the father was, but it was probably me. I was such a jerk back then. Arrogant, self-involved, thought I was the center of the universe, everything revolved around me, and like the idiot I was, I refused to use condoms." He paused for a moment.

"Rhyanna was a little naïve. She really believed the things the guys told her to get her into bed. We all took advantage of that naivety. I don't know what the other guys were telling her, but I'd been letting her think we were going to get married. The night she died I was over at her place. I had sex with her again. I figured, what the hell, she was already pregnant. Afterward she brought up the subject of marriage. I laughed at her and told her there was no way I'd ever marry a slut like her. She was crying, saying how much she loved me. I just brushed her off, told her it wasn't my problem, that she couldn't even be sure it was my kid, that she was a gold digger just after my money. I called her a bunch of names and threw some money at her and told her to deal with the problem. She threatened to kill herself, she showed me a bottle of pills and I told her to go ahead. The next day when I found out that she'd actually done it I felt terrible. The police questioned me because she'd left a suicide note saying that I was the father of her baby and blaming me for her death." His voice was cracking.

"When my mother found out she was furious with me. She paid for the funeral anonymously and arranged to put some money in a trust that would give Rhyanna's mother a small annuity. Remember, we had a little fundraiser to pay for the funeral? Well we raised a little bit of money but nobody else knew that the bulk of it had actually come from my mother out of my trust fund. I told everybody that my mother had cut off my money because she wasn't happy that I wasn't going to work in the family business, but that wasn't the truth. She told me that she was cutting off my money so that I wouldn't turn out to be an arrogant shit like my father. She said I wouldn't have to worry about people liking me for my money. I was so mad at her I wanted to show her that I didn't need the money. But it turns out that she did me a big favor."

"But Bob, regardless of what you did that night you weren't the only one who has to take responsibility in Rhyanna's death. Dave admitted treating her badly and I know that I was terribly cruel to her when I found out that she had been sleeping with Dave. I convinced all the girls in my crowd to ostracize her. We tortured that poor girl. We made her life hell. So for all these years you've been beating yourself up over something that we were all partly responsible for."

"No, I know what I did. I deserve to feel guilty about it. But last night in my drunken state, crying my heart out in your arms, I told you that I was responsible for Rhyanna's death, and I told you that I was responsible for the failure of my marriage, and that I loved you. And in spite of seeing me behaving like a blubbering fool you stayed with me and told me that you loved me too. So how about coming over here and lying on the couch with me and letting me feel your body next to mine?"

"Not so fast Bob. I admitted how I feel about you, but I really think we need to take this a little more slowly," said Myrosia.

"Slowly? It's been twenty-five years, how much slower can we go? I'm sober, you're sober. You know how I feel about you. I know how you feel about me. Dave left you, and Janice left me, we never cheated on our spouses with each other, but now here we are, we're both single at the same time. I feel like I've been waiting all this time for the planets to align, for everything to come together between you and I, so what's the issue?" he asked.

"There are several issues. First, it's pretty obvious that you still need some more time to get over Janice leaving you. Let's face it. You must have loved her at one time. Otherwise why did you marry her?"

"I don't need to get over the fact that she left me. We should have split up years ago. I shouldn't even have married her. What I need to understand is what's wrong with me, why I didn't end it sooner."

He continued. "The truth is that I married her because I was tired of waiting for you to leave Bob. When you didn't kick him out when you caught him cheating on you with his assistant at the office, I figured there was no point hanging around waiting. I was attracted to Janice because of her resemblance to you. Well physical resemblance at least. I was blinded by that. I didn't find out until after we were married that she was nothing like you." He paused and after a moment he continued.

"I know I'm not blameless in all this. I should never have married her. It wasn't fair to do that to her. She knew that I didn't love her. She knew that I loved you. Maybe she thought that I'd get over you and grow to love her. I don't know. I didn't think she cared as long as the jewelry kept coming and she could spend as much as she pleased on clothes and furniture. But the event that changed everything happened a few years into our marriage. She was still a pretty decent person back then, not the angry vindictive shrew that she turned into later. I'd had a few drinks one night, we'd just come home after spending the day with you and Dave and the kids out on your boat. Janice and I were making love and I called her Myrosia. That really hurt her. Let's face it, what woman wants it rubbed in her face that her husband fantasizes about another woman when they're making love. Well, as you can imagine, we had a wicked fight that night. I made some really unkind comments comparing the two of you and she stabbed me with the first thing she could lay her hands on. Fortunately for me it was just a small pair of manicure scissors. If she could have found something longer I wouldn't be alive today. I wrestled her to the floor and we both got pretty bruised up. I felt terrible afterward but she seemed exhilarated. After that she got more and more interested in S&M. She'd try and get me to slap her around, but I just couldn't get into it, not even just playing around. From that point on she'd do everything she could to get me mad. It got to the point where the only time we'd have sex is after we'd had a big screaming fight, otherwise she just wasn't interested."

"Bob, I'm not sure you should be telling me all this..." Myrosia began.

"No, I know it seems like I'm violating some sort of sacred trust between a married couple, but there are some other things you really need to understand. She started with the cosmetic surgery after that. Liposuction, botox, tummy tuck, face lift, nose job, dental veneers, you name it she got it. The only thing she didn't get was breast implants. She was always comparing herself to you. She started picking up men, flaunting it in my face, trying to get me angry. That's what her 'studio' downstairs was all about. She'd bring them back there and the next day the housekeeper would have to go down and clean up the mess. Sometimes there would even be blood, sometimes broken furniture. The neighbors complained about the noise and Janice got special soundproofing installed. The last couple of years have been hell. She even tried numerous times to pick up Dave but he didn't take her up on it. I think he knew what Janice was doing. She was trying to get revenge on you for something that you weren't even aware of. Dave is a jerk in a lot of ways, but he wasn't about to get involved with his best friend's wife. And yet, here I was in love with you all this time. What kind of friend am I, hanging around waiting for the marriage of my two best friends' to come to an end? I'm sure Dave knew, but he also knew that I wasn't about to act on my feelings. There's a lot of things about myself that I'm ashamed of, but I wasn't about to break up your family," he said.

"So why did you stay with her for so long?"

"I'm not completely sure. Whenever she'd come home with some bruises, and I'd tell her I wanted a divorce, she threatened to go to the police and say that I'd been beating her. But that's not the only reason. I guess I felt guilty for hurting her. Like I had turned her into the person she had become. I know you always wondered why I was willing to give her such a big settlement. It was because by the time she finally agreed to go I'd have given her anything just to get her out of my life. Believe me it was worth every penny I gave her," he explained.

"Bob, there's another reason why I'm hesitating. I don't want another man that likes to play around, and I know that you haven't exactly been celibate in the months since Janice left you. And I'm pretty sure that your meeting in Rochester wasn't business either. I couldn't help but notice that you didn't take your briefcase with you," she said.

"I'm that transparent am I? Yes, of course I've been seeing other women since Janice left, before that too. I'll admit it. I'm not cut out to be a monk, and I kept hoping that I'd find someone to take my mind off of you, but it just hasn't happened. I knew exactly what you were talking about when you asked me what I did with all the jewelry that I bought from Goldstein."

"Yes, but I want a man that thinks I'm special enough to want only me. Maybe I'm being unrealistic," she said.

"Myrosia, you are the only woman I've ever really wanted since the day we met, and I am definitely not seeing anyone now," he said.

"I'm sorry to sound so suspicious, but I can't begin to explain what Dave has done to me. It'll probably be a long time before I can trust anyone again," she said.

"I don't know how to prove how I feel about you. I guess you could ask Janice if you want confirmation." He shrugged.

"Where is Janice anyway? That woman police detective from Florida wanted to speak to her."

"I have no idea. She just took the money and walked away. She said she had found someone else and she didn't need me any more. I was so thrilled I didn't ask any questions. I didn't even care what she took out of the apartment. She could have cleaned it out like Dave did to you, and I wouldn't have cared. Funny thing though, she hardly took anything, not even her paintings."

"Well, I've got to admit that there's another reason why I'm not all over you on that sofa," she said.

"Are you telling me that you've been considering asking me to make some space for you?" he asked looking hopeful.

"Oh yeah, that thought crosses my mind every time I look at you," she said.

"Well what's stopping you?" he asked.

"I went to the clinic to get tested on Friday. Dave gave me a little present to remember him by. I've got Chlamydia. It's a sexually transmitted disease," she said.

"Oh shit Myrosia, you scared me there. I thought you were going to tell me you were HIV positive. Hell, Chlamydia's treatable. Did you get the antibiotics?" he asked.

"Yes," she said.

"I've waited twenty-five years, I can wait another few days," he said smiling.

"How come you know so much about Chlamydia? I'd never even heard of it until Friday," she said.

"Oh hell, you don't want to hear about everything Janice put me through on that score. Come on, let's go watch the game. What do you want on your pizza?" he said, jumping up from the couch and reaching out his hand to her.

The game had just finished and Bob was just about to hit the remote to turn off the television when a news flash came on. The banner headline read: Charges filed in connection with murder of television celebrity Shelly Hammett.

"All you Buffalo football fans will be interested to know that the Pinellas County Sheriff's Department has made an arrest in the murder of Buffalo quarterback Trey Hammett's wife, television celebrity Shelly Hammett..." the reporter began, and the next scene was a man in handcuffs being loaded into a police car.

"Here we see Shelly Hammett's lover, Buffalo, New York lawyer David Walker being taken into custody. We'll bring you further updates as they become available."

Chapter 17

"Myrosia, I need your help." Dave pleaded over the phone.

"You've got a lot of nerve asking me for help. After everything you've done why should I help you? I'm the last person in the world that you should be asking for help. Why don't you call one of your girlfriends for help? Maybe if you returned the money you stole from me, then just maybe we could talk," Myrosia replied.

"I wish I could return the money, but I don't have as much money as you think. That whole waterfront deal is turning into a nightmare, and unless I can get out of here a free man I can't access any of the money that I do have. It's all in offshore accounts in various corporate names, but I need to go in person to access it," said Dave.

"How stupid do you think I am? I know you better than to believe that you would put yourself in a position where you couldn't access your money at a moment's notice, from anywhere in the world. Don't try and con me again. I've already been taken once," she replied

"Look Myrosia, this is serious. They're charging me with murder. The District Attorney down here says he's going for the death penalty."

"Good, I hope they fry you. You're such an arrogant jerk, there's probably no shortage of people willing to flip the switch," she replied.

"How can you say that? I know you're mad at me right now, but come on, after all the years we've been together, you of all people should know that I'm innocent. You know I'd never kill anyone," he said.

"I don't know anything of the kind. I don't know anything about you. I never dreamed that the man I was married to would have done any of the things you've done. It still astounds me the kind of sick sex games you're into. You're disgusting," she said.

"Look I'm sorry about the other women over the years. I know

now just how foolish I've been to do that to you. I don't know what made me do it. I think it might have been a mid life crisis thing. But you've got to admit that you've been neglecting me for years. I've got needs. I had to go somewhere to get them met," he said trying to turn the blame on her.

"Oh bullshit, I've always been a good wife to you. You're just a pervert who can't keep your pecker in your pants. And now you've given me a sexually transmitted disease that you caught from one of your tramps. I guess you didn't have a chance to get to a doctor before you got arrested, so you'd better be sure and warn your new boyfriends in jail. Otherwise you're really gonna be in trouble when the good old boys down there find out you've infected them."

"For god's sake Myrosia, you're enjoying this. Why are you being so malicious?" he asked.

"Enjoying this? How can you say that? I'm humiliated. You've taken everything from me. You've taken my self esteem, my good reputation, all of our money, and you've even taken all the money that my parents worked so hard to accumulate, and now here I am scrambling to keep the bank from taking the house and putting me out in the street. But I don't know why I'm even bothering, since I can't even go home. The media is camped out at the lake house, and you can be sure they're going to go wild when word about your little sideline gets out. Oh, and by the way, Bob just called to tell me that the shit has hit the fan regarding the money missing from your trust accounts, so you can be sure that your buddies at the office are going to be reluctant to help you."

"Myrosia honey, this is all a big misunderstanding. I'm being set up. I never touched that trust account money, and I certainly didn't kill Shelly. Just help me get out of here and I'll get all of this straightened out. I'll get all of our money back, and I'll get all of your mother's money back too, but I can't do it when I'm stuck in here."

"Well big shot, why don't you just use some of that money that you've stolen from everyone to bail yourself out?"

"What's with you? Obviously you don't get it. This is serious. I'm innocent and I'm in jail for murder. Down here there's no bail for anyone charged with murder. I couldn't get myself bailed out even if I could lay my hands on the money. They're holding me in the violent felons section of the Pinellas County Jail." He lowered his voice to a whisper. "You wouldn't believe the kind of people they've got me in here with. These guys are crazy. I'm seriously afraid for my life. Any one of these guys could kill me long before I ever come up for trial. Please baby, you've got to help me."

"Cut it out Dave. First of all, I'm definitely not your baby, and if you've got yourself in a bad situation there, too bad. Obviously when you took off with Shelly you didn't care about the situation you left me in here," she said.

"I know I made a huge mistake when I got involved with Shelly. I admit it. But I realize now how much I love you, and how much I need you. I'd give you all the money back right now if I could, but I can't access anything. I put some of my money into Shelly's bank account to keep you from getting at it, and now that she's dead I can't even access that money," he said.

"Well I guess you should have thought about that before you killed her. I guess it's too late for me to take out a big life insurance policy on you. Even if I could afford to make the payments on the policy, if it's as dangerous as you say, there's no insurance company that would take you on. I hope you get the death penalty and I hope they fry you," she said.

"Very funny. Actually it's done by lethal injection. Although death row at Starke does have an old electric chair, but they don't use it any more. They claim that lethal injection is more humane." His voice began to crack with emotion.

"Oh cut out the crocodile tears Dave. You don't deserve humane treatment. It didn't sound like you were very humane to Shelly. Not that she was one of my favorite people, but no one deserves that. I don't suppose the court would let me push in the plunger on you, but there's no shortage of people that would be happy to do that. You've made so many enemies that people will be fighting to get to the front of the line to be the one to execute you."

"But Myrosia, how can you say that? I'm telling you I'm innocent. After all these years together surely you know me well enough to know that I couldn't do something like that. Please, I'm begging you. I need you to help me prove my innocence. I know that I've done a lot of really sleazy things in my life, but I'm not guilty of murder, and I'm not guilty of taking that trust account money. You're the best investigator I know, and the only one that I can trust that's smart enough to get at the truth. I should have been more supportive of you over the years. I should have encouraged you to finish your CPA exams," he said.

"You seem to have forgotten that I was too busy working to pay your way through law school and having your children to complete the CPA requirements too. Not only that, wasn't it just the other night that you were telling me how stupid I was and that I don't understand finances? So if I'm the only one you can trust to get you off, then all I can say is you're in real trouble. Besides, if you really are innocent, your attorney should be able to get you off," said Myrosia.

"My defense attorney? This public defender I've got is a joke. I don't think this kid is capable of doing it. Besides, I'm not sure I can trust him to look out for my best interests. I'd like to get Keith to defend me, but I haven't been able to reach him. I think he's avoiding my calls." He lowered his voice again. "You know Myrosia, there are a lot of people who'd like to see me convicted."

"Duh, that's what I've been saying, and I'm one of them."

"Well if you don't want to help me get out of here, could you at least put some money on my account here so I can make some phone calls and buy some snacks from the commissary? The food here is awful."

"You've got to be kidding," she said slamming down the phone.

On Monday afternoon Myrosia's cell phone rang. Her forehead creased and she frowned slightly as she looked at the call display. It's about time, she thought.

"Mom, what's going on? My credit card got declined. I tried to use it to pay for lunch at the Brick Room and it got declined. It was only about $60 and it was rejected. Did you forget to pay the bill? You've gotta fix it right now, how can I be expected to manage without a credit card. It was so embarrassing, I got Alice to pay for it, but now she wants me to pay her back. And oh yeah, how come you've got a new cell phone number?" asked Nicki.

"Nicki I've been trying to reach you for days to warn you not to use your credit cards," said Myrosia.

"Well I've been busy. This is the first chance I've had to return your calls," Nicki replied petulantly.

"I wouldn't have kept calling you if it wasn't important."

"Okay, so what's up? You've been calling me repeatedly. It was getting really annoying. I finally had to turn off the ringer. Brian and I flew down to his parents place in Cabo for the weekend and I was having way too much fun to call you back and listen to you complain about Daddy. So what's so urgent that you had to keep bugging me all weekend?" asked Nicki.

Myrosia clenched her jaw and wondered for the millionth time how she managed to create a daughter that was so self centered.

"With everything I've been hearing on the news about drug wars in Mexico I'm not sure that you wandering off to Mexico like that was such a good idea. I wish you had called me and told me where you were going," said Myrosia.

"Oh puhleees Mother, you're overreacting. Flying in a private plane to a home in a gated community is hardly 'wandering off.' So what's the deal with my credit card?" asked Nicki.

"The bank has frozen it," said Myrosia.

"Well get it unfrozen. I need it now," said Nicki.

"I can't Nicki. Your father cleaned out all of the money in our bank accounts and our investments. I've got no money," said Myrosia. Choosing not to tell Nicki about the money she borrowed from Bob.

Myrosia continued. "And the reason I've got a new phone number is because your father was being mean and cancelled my cell phone service."

"Mother, I told you I really don't want to listen to you bitch about Daddy," said Nicki.

Myrosia chose to ignore the last comment.

"I guess you haven't seen the news yet. I'm really surprised because it's big news here. I thought by now you would have already heard. The other reason I was calling you was because I wanted you to hear it from me before you saw it on television. Your father's new girlfriend was murdered in Florida sometime early Saturday morning."

"What new girlfriend?" asked Nicki.

"Shelly Hammett, Trey Hammett's wife."

"I heard something about that, but I didn't know that Daddy was dating her. How cool is that! That's big news. Do you think the paparazzi are going to be chasing me around now? Too bad she's dead. I could have been the stepdaughter of a celebrity," exclaimed Nicki.

"What's cool about it? How can you say something like that? The poor woman is dead and the police think your father killed her."

"That's ridiculous. He couldn't have killed her. It's just a mistake. He'll get it all straightened out," said Nicki

"Don't count on it. Your father is in really big trouble. They've arrested him and charged him with murder. If he's convicted he could get the death penalty. Besides that, he's being investigated here in New York State for fraud. He's stolen money from the trust accounts. He's remortgaged the house and cleaned out all of our bank accounts as well as your Bubcha's money and he's gone and hidden everything away in some secret offshore banks."

"Speaking of money, I need you to transfer more money to my bank account. I need to order some more stuff for the reception."

"Nicki, you're obviously not listening to me. I just told you that I don't have any money to send you. I don't have any money, period. I don't have a job any more so I don't even have any money coming in. I've had to borrow some money from a friend or I wouldn't even be able to put gas in the car. Your father cleaned out everything. I don't have any money to make the house payments, and if I can't come up with the money, the bank is going to start legal action to seize the house." explained Myrosia.

"Can the bank do that? Can they seize the house? What about my wedding plans? Surely you can hold them off until after the wedding. All the arrangements have already been made and the invitations are set to go out in the mail. We can't change the location now. You know I planned to have the ceremony on the lawn overlooking the lake. I've even ordered the flowers to float in the pool." Nicki's voice rose in pitch as she began to understand how these events would affect her.

"Well you'd better cancel those orders right now because I don't have the money to pay for any of it. I told you that your father has taken it all and hidden it. You're just gonna have to forget about that wedding extravaganza that you've been planning. In fact, you should probably think about postponing the wedding for a while. I can't imagine Brian's parents being too thrilled about having you for a daughter-in-law when all the details of your father's crimes come out," said Myrosia.

"Don't be ridiculous. Brian's parents love me, and I can't change my wedding plans now. How embarrassing would that be. Besides, it's too late to cancel the orders. You just have to get the money. Get Bubby to pay for it, or get Daddy to give it back," replied Nicki.

"Nicki, I already told you that your father stole your grandmother's money as well. I'm still trying to figure out how to keep her in the seniors' apartment, so for once could you please think about someone else. I've got way bigger problems than trying to pay for your wedding," said Myrosia.

"Mother, you don't have to get so snippy with me. I am thinking about someone else. I'm thinking of poor Daddy in jail. What are you going to do to get him out of there?" asked Nicki.

"What me? I'm not going to do anything to get him out. He can rot in there as far as I am concerned. He called me this morning to beg me to help him, but forget it, I'm not getting involved."

"But you've got to help him. He can't stay in jail. What about my wedding? Daddy's got to give me away," Nicki said.

"I think you can forget about having your father give you away unless you plan on holding the ceremony on death row in prison in Florida," said Myrosia.

Nicki began sobbing.

"Forget it Nicki. Don't try and manipulate me, I'm not willing to help him after what he's done. Besides I'm pretty sure he's guilty."

Sensing that crying wasn't going to get the desired result she changed tactics.

"But Mother, don't you see that getting Daddy out of jail and cleared of all this is the only way you are going to get your hands on any of that money?" said Nicki.

"No. I'm absolutely adamant that I'm not going to help him."

"Well call Uncle Bob, or one of the other partners. Surely they can do something," replied Nicki.

"No, I doubt that any of them will be willing to help after what he's done to the firm's reputation, and unless he's willing to replace the money he stole from me I'm not going to help him either."

"Well if you won't do something, obviously I'm going to have to. Where are they holding him?" asked Nicki.

"He's in the Pinellas County jail in Largo, Florida, but I can't see what you can do…" Myrosia was in mid sentence when the phone line went dead. She looked at the phone in her hand and shook her head. "I can't believe she just hung up on me."

Myrosia went back to work going through all of Dave's financial transactions for the previous year. She had commandeered Bob's formal dining room as her work area. The long dining room table was neatly stacked with print-outs of bank statements. She had taken down one of Janice's paintings and a big whiteboard hung on the wall in its place. About an hour later her cell phone rang again.

"Okay, I've got everything worked out," Nicki said breathlessly. "I couldn't talk to Daddy on the phone, but I did talk to Uncle Keith. I convinced him to help us. He says that he's really sorry about kicking you out the office last week, but that if you agree to go down to Florida and help Daddy and convince him to cooperate and get him to give back the money that they say he stole from the firm, then the firm will give you some money for your expenses."

"I don't see how I can convince your father to do anything. I'm not certain that he's even in a position to give back that money…" Myrosia began.

"Don't argue with me Mother. Just do it. Can't you see that this is the only solution?" Nicki replied coldly.

Chapter 18

Two hours after Nicki's call Myrosia's cell phone rang again. She was not terribly surprised to see that the call was from Keith MacKenzie.

"Okay Myrosia, I spoke to Nicki a little while ago and she's very worried about her father, so I've agreed to assist in Dave's defense. Since I'm not licensed to practice in Florida I'm doing this on a pro hac vice basis, just for this one case, and I'm going to be working with another lawyer I know in St. Petersburg. But although Dave and I have been friends for many years, I've got to admit that I was reluctant to get involved in this for several reasons. The bad publicity for the firm about this missing trust account money for one thing, the allegations of bribery involving Dave's real estate deals for another, and quite frankly your conversation with Jeannie on Friday has put me in an awkward situation at home..." he began when Myrosia cut him off.

"Look Keith, don't try and blame that on me. It wasn't my conversation with Jeannie that caused your problems at home, it was the fact that you've been cheating on your wife that's caused your problems," said Myrosia.

"Obviously Bob's been somewhat less than discrete regarding my personal business. He shouldn't be discussing these things with you, but I guess given your relationship with him it was inevitable..." he said when Myrosia cut him off again.

"What are you talking about? Bob hasn't told me anything about you and Cori. If anyone has been less than discrete it's you. You really have to get a grip on the pillow talk there Keith, because your little chickie Cori is blabbing about all of the firm's business. It was just a matter of time before Jeannie heard it from someone," said Myrosia.

"Where do you get off lecturing me about infidelity when you've been cheating on Dave for years? So how long has this thing with Bob been going on?" he asked.

"So obviously you've been talking to Dave. Well there is nothing going on between me and Bob, but I wouldn't expect either you or Dave to believe that," said Myrosia.

"Well if it isn't Bob then you've obviously got someone else in the office keeping you informed," said Keith.

"So did you call me for a reason, or were you just looking to vent about your marital problems?" she asked.

"I was calling to offer you a deal. Peter and I have discussed this. We know that Dave has left you in a precarious financial position, and we want to help you out, so if you're willing to go down to Florida and help us out with Dave's defense, then we'd be willing to forward you some money for your expenses," said Keith.

"I think you mean that Dave will give me back some of my own money," she said.

"Well it'll be coming out of my own pocket initially, but yes, ultimately Dave is going to be the one paying for it," he admitted.

"So will Cori be the one arranging my flight down? Be sure and tell her I want business class, and a non-stop flight. Otherwise, that bitch'll send me the most indirect route she can find. I could be stuck in airports for days," said Myrosia.

"We were thinking that you could drive down. That way you wouldn't need a car down there. Dave says for you to have fun, make a vacation out of it, drive the Porsche down," said Keith.

"My, my, how generous of him. How am I supposed to pay for all this? All my credit cards have been cancelled. How am I supposed to pay for hotels, and where do you expect me to stay while I'm down there?" asked Myrosia.

"Come over to the office and I'll give you a check and a prepaid credit card that you can use. No wait, don't bother coming over here. The media are camped out around the block. When we flew back this morning it was insanity, both at the airport and here at the office. You'd never get through them. I'll give it to Bob to give you," said Keith.

"How long do you expect this to take? Are you planning to put me up in a hotel for a couple of months? And who's going to look after my house while I'm gone?" asked Myrosia.

"Don't worry about the house, I'll get someone to take care of it. You'll probably have to stay in a hotel for a few days. The condo that Dave and Shelly had rented is currently sealed by the police during their investigation, but when they release it you can move in there. I'll arrange it for you to get a key. It's really nice. You'll be very comfortable there. I've seen it, three bedrooms, three bathrooms, a huge terrace and a big wrap around balcony. You're going to love it. It's right on the beach. Dave says the rent is paid until the beginning of June," he said.

"Oh lovely, so you expect me to drive down there, and live in a crime scene that my husband paid for with money he stole from me, and where he was honeymooning with his new girlfriend. Do you expect me to go in there, put away the sex toys and change the sheets too?" asked Myrosia.

"Of course not. Once the police release it I'll have the cleaners go in and go over everything. I'll get them to pack up all of Dave and Shelly's things and put them in storage so you won't even have to look at them if that's what you want. But you might want to consider going in there first before the cleaners go in and taking a look at everything yourself, just to get a feel for what it looked like the night that Shelly died," he suggested.

Myrosia thought about this for a moment.

"What exactly do you want me to do?" asked Myrosia.

"Go down there and look at the prosecution's evidence, find the flaws in their case and get us some reasonable doubt. Dave says he didn't kill her, so go see if you can figure out who did. Help me get him off. And convince Dave to give us back the trust account money. He's claiming that he didn't touch it."

"How much time have we got?" she asked.

"Under Florida law if the accused agrees to waive their right to a speedy trial it can take up to two years to go to trial. However, the accused can refuse to waive that right in which case trial must take place within 180 days. I spoke to Dave about this, and since there's no bail in this case, he wants a fast trial date. He's going to be in jail right up till the trial. And of course Nicki wants her dad out of jail in time for her wedding, so the clock's ticking. We've got to get right on this," Keith explained.

"What if he's guilty?" she asked.

"Well you'd better hope he isn't, and you'd better hope we can prove it, because otherwise everything he's got is going to be tied up in wrongful death litigation for years and you'll never see a dime of it."

Chapter 19

Monday evening after dinner, Bob and Myrosia were on the sofa in Bob's study. Her feet were on his lap and he was giving her a foot massage.

"I wish I didn't have to go and leave you here," she said.

"I hate this. After all these years of waiting we finally have the chance to really be together and now this. I want to go with you, but I've got a lot of things going on right now that I have to finish up first, so I can't leave until at least Friday night. Why don't you wait and we can go together then?" asked Bob.

"No, I can't. I already explained to you that we're under time pressure on this. We don't have much time to put together a defense," said Myrosia.

"Yes, but if we fly down together on Friday and get a rental car you won't have lost much time. It's going to take you a few days to drive down there anyway. It's got to be at least 20 hours of driving time."

"I know, but I already talked it over with Joanna and she's gonna drive down with me. February is always slow at the beauty salon and she wants a free vacation in Florida. She's never had a chance to take a winter vacation and she really wants to come," explained Myrosia.

"When are you leaving?" he asked.

"We're gonna leave first thing in the morning. I've got nothing much to pack. I don't want to go out to my house to pick up any summer clothes with all the media lurking around so I'll just have to buy a few things when I get down there," she said.

"Well, if I can't change your mind and convince you to stay up here in the frozen north with me, I guess I'll just have to fly down there and come to you. In the meantime, come here and keep me warm. We've got one last night together. I feel like a condemned man about to eat his last meal," he said, moving her feet off his lap and pulling her close to him.

"Bob, we can't…" she started to speak but he cut her off.

"Myrosia, you can't catch anything cuddling. I promise to control myself. Come on, lets go to bed."

Early the following morning Myrosia and Joanna were in the Porsche on their way to Florida.

"This is so exciting! I'm in a Porsche and I'm driving to Florida. It doesn't get much better than this. Well, that's not exactly true. No offense Myrosia, but a good looking man sitting where you are would make it absolutely perfect," said Joanna.

"Yeah, I know what you mean. I hated getting out of that bed this morning. It was tough leaving Bob, but it sure is nice not to have to worry about what people are thinking and saying about me. On the road I can be anonymous. I don't think any reporters are going to bother following us to Florida. I'm sure I'll probably have to face them at some point when we get down there, but for the next couple of days I can relax," said Myrosia.

"That sad puppy dog look on Bob's face when he saw us off was priceless. I think it was a good idea leaving my car in Bob's underground parking. If I left it sitting in my parking lot for a month it probably wouldn't be there when I got back. Either that or the snow would be so deep over it that'd be July before I could find it." Joanna paused. "I hope you managed to get enough sleep to drive. Let me know if you get tired and I'll take over."

"I got plenty of sleep. That bed of his is heavenly."

"So you're saying you spent the night in his bed and all you're going to tell me about is the linen?" said Joanna.

"Nothing else to tell. Honest, we just slept."

"Well you've got more self control than I do. Oh look there's a Cracker Barrel coming up, let's stop for breakfast," said Joanna.

"Honestly Joanna, if we stop at every Cracker Barrel from here to Florida we're never going to get there. I really want to put a push on and see if we can get there tomorrow," said Myrosia

---

Jeff was really starting to get on Myrosia's nerves with his constant phone calls. As they drove further and further south, every hour or so the phone would ring and it would be him with some new information.

"Hey Myrosia, it's me Jeff. I've got some information that you wanted about that Christine girl. She grew up in Rochester, and went to Monroe Community College. She took the two year Office Administration program..."

"Hey Myrosia, it's me Jeff. I've got some more information about that Christine girl. It seems she moved to Buffalo after her folks died in a house fire..."

"Hey Myrosia, it's me Jeff. I've got some more information about that Christine girl. Apparently she was seeing some guy, but no one seems to know who the guy was or where she moved to..."

"Hey Myrosia, it's me Jeff. I wanted to tell you the latest news from the office. Penny Donovan was in here this morning and everyone could hear her crying in Peter's office. No one could hear what they were saying, but she was crying when she left and Peter hasn't come out of his office since..."

"Hey Myrosia, it's me Jeff. I've got some background information on Shelly Hammett. It turns out that she's actually five years older than she claimed she was..."

"Hey Myrosia, it's me Jeff. All the office is buzzing about you going down to Florida to help Dave. Is there anything I can do to help? I can go out and check on your house for you while you're gone..."

"Hey Myrosia, it's me Jeff. I was thinking, do you want me to come down there and help you? I could take a few vacation days, or I bet if you asked Keith he'd send me down there to help you..."

When she hung up the last time she pulled off the bluetooth ear piece.

"This guy is a really sweet kid and I know he means well, and it's really handy having him spying for me in the office. I know more about what is going on now than I ever did when I worked there, but he's starting to drive me crazy. I think I'm going to have to put him on ignore for awhile. I'll just tell him the cell phone reception wasn't good going through the mountains," said Myrosia.

Myrosia and Joanna completed two long days of driving and made it to the Don Cesar hotel in St. Pete Beach on Wednesday afternoon just before 3 pm. Myrosia drove the Porsche under the covered entrance way and the two women walked into the hotel.

"Wow, I can see why the guide books call it Florida's Pink Palace. This place is amazing. I've never stayed anywhere like this before," said Joanna glancing around the lobby.

"Yes, it is lovely. Dave and I stayed here a few times. Let's get checked in and then we can run out and buy ourselves some beach wear," said Myrosia.

"Ah yes Mrs. Walker, we have you booked into one of our Superior rooms," said the desk clerk.

"Really? A Superior room? I think there must be a mistake. We're supposed to be in a Gulf front one bedroom suite with two full sized beds," said Myrosia.

"I'm sorry for the confusion but someone from your office specifically requested this particular room," he said apologetically.

"Really? Do your records show who made the reservation?"

"Why yes, it says here that the reservation was made on your behalf by a woman from your office by the name of Cori Jackman and she specifically requested this room."

"In that case I think I'd like to see the room before we check in," she replied.

"Certainly madam. I can escort you up there myself."

One quick look into the room was enough. They were back down at the front desk in moments.

"I need to call my office and get this straightened out," she told the clerk.

"Keith, what's going on? I'm at the Don Cesar but Cori has booked me into the worst room in the place. I didn't even think they had rooms this small. Don't mess with me on this. Tell the front desk to change it right now. I want a one bedroom Gulf front suite with two beds." She handed the telephone over to the desk clerk.

The desk clerk listened for a moment. "Yes sir, I can take care of that for you."

He turned to Myrosia. "Mr. MacKenzie would like to speak to you again." He handed her the phone.

"Okay Myrosia, it's all fixed. I've got you booked in for two nights. We can extend if necessary but I don't think we'll need to. I spoke to a Detective Osborne and he indicated that they might be finished with the condo tomorrow. Maybe you could try and meet him and see if you can sweet talk him into telling you what they've got. He probably won't reveal much but it couldn't hurt to give it a try," said Keith.

"Okay, e-mail me his contact information and I'll see what I can find out. But honestly Keith, I can't believe you've still got Cori working at the office. What does Jeannie have to say about that?" asked Myrosia.

"Jeannie is making my life hell, thank you very much, and so is Cori too for that matter. I'm ready to get rid of both of them," he said.

"Well Keith, the moral of the story is to stick to one woman at a time from now on, and I'm warning you it'll be a lot cheaper to get rid of Cori than Jeannie," said Myrosia hanging up the phone.

After getting settled in to one of the most luxurious suites in the hotel the two women headed out to go shopping. Driving along Gulf Boulevard Joanna was enthralled with everything.

"This is fantastic. I love the palm trees, the sunshine, and that water. Look at the pelicans. I love it here. I can hardly believe that it was just yesterday morning that we were driving through all that snow. I'm so glad you talked me into getting straight down here fast instead of taking the extra day. Imagine, driving with the top down in February. This is paradise. I don't ever want to go back," said Joanna.

"Since it's your first sunset on the beach do you want to go back to the hotel and watch it from the balcony or there's a little restaurant up here where we can watch it while we eat dinner? It's up to you," said Myrosia.

"Let's go back to the hotel so we can put on some of these new clothes. Sandals in February, I love it!" squealed Joanna.

That evening after dinner they decided to drive over and look at the crime scene.

"We can take a short walk along the beach. We probably won't see much in the dark, but at least we'll know exactly where the building is," said Myrosia.

When they got to the beach access they parked the car and walked over to the water's edge and looked north toward the line of luxury condos.

"From what we saw on the news I think it's that building there, that corner Penthouse unit. I've got the exact address in my bag," Myrosia said pointing to one of the buildings.

"The lights are on in that apartment. Somebody must be in there," said Joanna.

"Probably crime scene techs still working the scene. Let's go over and see if anyone will talk to us," said Myrosia.

They got back in the Porsche and drove over to the condo building and parked in the visitors parking.

"Yep, this is the place. There's a Pinellas County squad car in the parking lot. They must be guarding the scene," said Myrosia.

They walked into the sumptuous lobby and found a uniformed deputy sitting reading a magazine. Myrosia pulled out a business card, walked over to the deputy and extended her hand.

"Hello my name is Myrosia Walker. I don't suppose Detective Osborne is around?" she asked with a smile.

"Yes ma'am he is. He's upstairs. He just got here a few minutes ago," he replied.

"Great, would it be possible for me to speak to him?"

"I can't let you go up, but I'll call him and see if he's available to come down and speak to you," the deputy said.

A few moments later the elevator door opened and two men wearing polo shirts with Pinellas County Sheriff's Department stars stepped out.

The older of the two men introduced himself. "Hello I'm

Detective Stan Osborne, and this is Detective Phil Ricci."

"Hello, I'm Myrosia Walker," she said shaking detective Osborne's hand and handing him a business card. "This is my friend Joanna Lubinski."

"Are you David Walker's wife?" asked Osborne remembering her name from the case notes.

"Well yes, but I'm not here in that capacity. We're estranged. I work for the law firm. I'm here on behalf of Dave's lawyer Keith MacKenzie and the defense team," Myrosia explained.

"If I was in his situation I'm not sure I'd want my 'estranged' wife working as part of the defense team. You should be working for us," said Ricci.

Myrosia laughed. "Yes it is a ridiculous situation when you put it that way."

"What did you want to speak to me about?" asked Detective Osborne.

"Keith MacKenzie asked me to contact you to see if you had any idea when you'd be releasing the apartment. I was driving along Gulf Boulevard getting a feel for the neighborhood and the location on the beach where the body was discovered and I noticed that the lights were on in the unit. I thought I'd check to see if you were here," she said.

"The crime scene techs are finished and Detective Ricci and I were just taking one last look around. It'll be released tomorrow morning," Osborne replied.

"Do you mind taking me up and letting me have a look?" Myrosia asked.

"I'm sorry I can't help you ma'am. I'm not authorized to let you in. You'll have to wait until it's officially released before you can get in there, and even then, there's a bunch of paperwork that'll need filled out before you can pick up the keys. The best thing to do is get your boss to talk to my boss in the morning," Osborne replied.

"Okay, I'll do that. Is there anything you can tell me about the evidence you discovered?"

"Ma'am, I'm afraid that I'm not authorized to release any information about an ongoing investigation. But I will say this, obviously my superiors feel that there is enough evidence in this case to justify having made an arrest," said Osborne.

Back in the suite at the Don Cesar the two women stood looking out over the balcony railing at the moonlight on the waves.

"This is so beautiful. Thank you so much for letting me tag along Myrosia," said Joanna.

"It's nice having you with me. It wouldn't be the same if I was here alone. Hopefully I'll be able to pick up the keys to the condo tomorrow. We're booked in here until Saturday morning, but if the condo is ready maybe we'll be able to move in there tomorrow evening," said Myrosia.

"What's the rush? I'm in no hurry to leave here. Let Keith put us up here as long as possible. I've never stayed in a hotel like this before," said Joanna.

"Oh don't worry, unless I'm very mistaken, I'm sure that condo is even more luxurious than this hotel suite. And I keep feeling that the sooner I get in there, the closer I'll be to finding out what happened to the money," said Myrosia.

"I keep forgetting that this is work for you," said Joanna.

"It's work all right. I've got to meet with Dave tomorrow morning. What a treat that's going to be," said Myrosia.

"I guess there's no point in me tagging along with you when you do that. So maybe I'll just spend the day lying on the beach, soaking up some sun, reading a book. See if I can meet any rich, single men. Give me a call after you've spoken to Dave. Try not to kill him. Leave that for the State of Florida," said Joanna.

Chapter 20

It was now February, and so far neither the police nor the Medical Examiner's staff had been successful in identifying the body of the woman that had washed up on the shore of Lake Erie the previous October. They had put a lot of hours into her identification without much luck, but they had not given up trying, and the remains of this Jane Doe were being held in the freezer at the morgue on Kensington Avenue in Buffalo.

Although they estimated that the body had been in the water a couple of weeks, and was no longer recognizable when it was discovered, they knew a lot about her. They knew that she was a Caucasian female between 30 and 50 years old, 5'9" tall, approximately 125 lbs., with bleached blonde hair. She had never given birth to a child, and her body showed signs of having had cosmetic surgery, but unfortunately for them she did not have breast implants. The serial numbers on breast implants would have made the identification process so much simpler.

Although the skin had begun separating from the body and decomposing, and some of the fingers were missing, the medical examiner was able to deglove what was remaining of the hands and retrieve some identifiable fingerprints but they did not match anything on file. Whoever Jane Doe was she had never had her fingerprints entered into the system.

Technicians had taken the skull and using computer facial reconstruction had been able to come up with some approximate pictures of what she might have looked like in life. The Sheriff's Department had circulated the pictures, with no luck. This may have been partly due to her having had cosmetic surgery. It is possible that people simply did not remember what she looked like naturally, before the cosmetic enhancements. But another part of the problem with the pictures was that a large section of the scalp and hair was missing, and the remaining hair had been cut short, not shaved, but clumsily hacked off, so that in the computer generated images they were only able to make guesses regarding what her normal hairstyle might have been.

The victim had beautiful and very expensive teeth. She had a full set of porcelain veneers which in life would have given her a movie star smile. So dental records could certainly be useful in identifying the deceased but it was impractical to send the records out to every dentist in the state in hopes of finding the right one. She might not even be from New York State. She might not even be an American. They had checked with Canadian authorities to see if they had any missing persons matching her description, but nothing came of it. They had even sent the information to Interpol, and were wading through international possibilities with no luck. It was becoming more and more obvious that they would have to get a lead on the right missing person if they were ever going to be able to identify her and solve the case.

They also knew something else about the victim that had not yet been released to the public. They knew that she had been beaten on more than one occasion prior to her death. There was bruising with varying rates of healing on her back, her buttocks, and her breasts. There were ligature marks of varying ages on her wrists, ankles, and neck. Was she a long-time victim of domestic abuse, or had she been abducted and held hostage for weeks or even months prior to her death?

There were no clothes or jewelry on the body, but the medical examiner was able to find a small tattoo of a dollar sign on her right buttock. The tattoo was not visible to the naked eye due to the decomposition of the skin, but since tattoos usually go beyond the epidermis layer the medical examiner had discovered it through a meticulous examination of the entire body under ultraviolet light. While dollar sign tattoos were not particularly rare, it probably indicated that she was not European.

They knew that the cause of death had been strangulation, and that she had been dead for several hours before being dumped in the water. They knew from the water currents which direction the body had probably floated before washing up on the shore. They knew what kind of rope had been used to tie her up and sink the body, but it was a common brand of yellow nylon rope available for sale all over the area so that was no help. Divers had been sent out to look for a block or other weight that might have been used to hold the body down, but, given the amount of debris lying on the bottom of the lake, that was like looking for the proverbial needle in a haystack. The rope had simply let go. It was not cut or frayed. The killer had simply done a poor job of tying a knot around the weight, so there was no object lying on the lake bed with a convenient length of rope waving in the current like a beacon.

They were fairly certain that the killer had not simply waded out from shore to dump the body, but had probably transported her out to deeper water by boat.

No one could say that the authorities had not been giving it their best effort. The primary problem was that no one matching the victim's description had been reported missing. Detectives were stumped. Why was no one worried about this woman? Christmas had come and gone and still no one had reported her missing. It was starting to look like it would take a lucky break for them to be able to solve this case.

The break they needed came as a result of the murder of Shelly Hammett in Florida.

First, one of the associate medical examiners happened to be watching the same program that Myrosia, Joanna and Bob had been watching the night Bob had gotten drunk. He saw the tattoo segment of the show and remembered the tattoo on the Jane Doe that had been hauled out of the lake. First thing Monday morning he was in the office comparing the ultra-violet images of the tattoo on Jane Doe with those that the women on the show were getting. He could not be absolutely certain, but they looked similar. Since the body of Shelly Hammett was lying in the morgue in Florida she obviously was not their floater. That left the three other women on the show. He went back and looked at the show's web site. He immediately ruled out two of the women, they were too short. He could not prove it yet but he knew in his gut that the remains were those of Janice Williams.

The next break came when the Detective Deborah Sanson of the Pinellas County Sheriff's Department called the Erie County Sheriff's Department asking for help in locating Janice Williams since she had not been able to find anyone who had seen Williams since the previous September when the show had finished production.

Representatives from the District Attorney's Office, the Sheriff's Department, and the Medical Examiner's Office met at the DA's office to discuss the case.

"We've had a real challenge finding Janice Williams' close relatives. Her mother is deceased and her father, Gerald Lawrey, is in a nursing home. He's not playing with a full deck but he claims that he isn't her father, says that Janice's mother was running around on him and he's refusing to give us a DNA sample. We could get a court order and force him but what's the point if it turns out that he's right and he isn't the biological father. We managed to track down her half brother. He lives in Syracuse. He's given us a DNA sample that we can use to compare with our floater, but we've been holding off on the testing since we're not sure how conclusive the results would be since he's Lawrey's son. I sure hope we don't have to exhume her mother's body to get DNA evidence. There are some distant relatives on the mother's side. Obviously they're not a very close family which is one of the reasons no one reported her missing at Christmas time," said Detective Nate Spitzer from the Erie County Sheriff's Department.

"Well let's go ahead and do the test on the half-brother's DNA, even if it doesn't turn up a match. We've put so much money and manpower into this case already why not add a sibling DNA test," said Dr. Lesley Howard from the Medical Examiner's Office.

"Okay, so let's just assume that our floater is Janice Williams. We can't prove it yet and we certainly don't have enough evidence to charge anybody yet, so I don't want our suspicions getting out. Let's find out everything we can about her, and let's keep a real close eye on the husband. If it is Janice Williams, we have to find out why no one reported her missing," said Len Pritchard from the District Attorney's Office.

"If we want to keep this secret a little longer, then we'd better not send the requests to her dentist and her cosmetic surgeon yet. We can tell them to keep it confidential but with a story this big the office staff will be talking to reporters even before they send us the results back," said Dr. Howard.

"According to her bio this Williams woman was an artist, and some of her paintings are in Shelly Hammett's gallery. Maybe we can get a fingerprint off one of the paintings that we can match to the prints that you got off the corpse," said Detective Spitzer.

"What do we know about David Walker? Is it possible that he killed both these women? I've met him socially a number of times. I've even golfed with him. I've met all of the partners at his firm, but I don't really know them. What about this Bob Williams? He seems like a real nice guy, but who really knows. I think we should dig up everything we can about all four of those lawyers in that office. There's something funny going on there. If we make out like we're just investigating Walker with regards to the allegations of bribery, we can probably keep the whole mess here quiet a little longer. The other three partners will probably happily throw Walker to the wolves if they think it'll save their own asses," said Len Pritchard.

"Lesley, your report said that the victim had been beaten a number of times in the days and months prior to her murder. Have you seen any other bodies landing on your autopsy table showing the same kinds of injuries? The reason I'm asking is that I've been hearing rumors about some sort of exclusive S&M club running in Buffalo, apparently catering to wealthy influential people. I'm just wondering if our victim might be a member," said Detective Spitzer.

"Nothing I can recall, but I'll have someone do a search of our records. How far back do you want me to go Nate?" asked Dr. Howard.

"Oh, just a year or two. Don't spend too much time on it, it's just a hunch." said Detective Spitzer.

"Well Nate, you've got a pretty good track record with those hunches of yours. I think I should also have a talk with the ME in Pinellas County and see if their victim had any old bruises," said Dr. Howard.

"Oh shit, an S&M club here in Buffalo? Nate, you've got to get some manpower on that to look into those rumors even if it doesn't turn out to tie in to this case. We don't want to have it look like we ignored something like this just because it catered to rich folk when we've been putting such a big push on cracking down on street prostitutes," said Pritchard.

"Just rumors so far, but I'll look into it." said Spitzer.

"So far it looks like we've got two wealthy local women dead, both by strangulation, both stars on a reality TV show. I'm wondering about the safety of the other women on that show. Besides the show, and a certain physical resemblance, what else do these dead women have in common? What are the odds that we've got two different killers? Do we have a serial killer on our hands?" asked Pritchard.

"I don't know about a serial killer, but right off the bat I can tell you something these women have in common. A game of musical beds. We've got Janice Williams apparently leaving her hubby to run off with some unknown new lover. We've got Shelly Hammett leaving Trey to shack up with Dave Walker, and the story around town now is that we've got Walker's wife Myrosia being consoled in the arms of Bob Williams. How's that for a triangle. And tell me, have either of you gotten a look at Walker's wife? That guy was a fool to trade her for Shelly Hammett," said Spitzer.

"Yes, I've met her. Now that you mention it, I know what you mean. She is a looker, a tall slim blonde just like the other two, but way too classy to appear on that stupid show. She comes from a hard working family of Polish immigrants. I knew her father Caspar Dabrowski. She didn't have to marry Walker for money. If anything it was probably the other way around. If Walker's our man, great, he's already in custody, but if he's not the killer, then someone very dangerous is still wandering around out there. Keep a close eye on Bob Williams but don't let him or anyone else know that we think the dead woman is his wife. This is a really touchy situation we've got here. I don't need to tell either of you how bad this is going to be if someone else winds up dead and we haven't warned the public."

Chapter 21

Shortly before 9 am on Thursday morning Myrosia arrived at the reception desk at the Pinellas County Jail for her meeting with Dave.

"Hello. My name is Myrosia Walker. I'm here to meet with prisoner number 55897734, David Walker. I have a 9 o'clock appointment."

The receptionist looked the prisoner number up on her computer.

"I'm sorry ma'am, we've got you booked for a video conference. Meetings with family members are only available via video conferencing. You will have to go over to the office on 49th St.," explained the receptionist.

"No, there must be some mistake. I'm here on behalf of the law firm that is representing him," she replied.

"Are you his lawyer?" asked the receptionist.

"No, but I am here on behalf of his lawyer who is not able to attend today," explained Myrosia.

"I can't help you. You'll have to go to the 49th St. office and discuss the arrangements with them. Even if I could let you in here, the lawyer/client interview rooms are fully booked this morning," explained the receptionist.

Forty minutes later Myrosia was seated at a video conferencing terminal looking at Dave on the computer screen.

"Dave, before you say anything, I want to remind you that with this video conferencing you can have no expectation of privacy. This is not like the lawyer/client interview room. Don't say anything pertaining to the crime that you've been charged with or any other potential crimes," said Myrosia.

"How can I say anything about Shelly's murder? I don't know

anything about it," said Dave.

"That's enough Dave! I've just spoken to Keith, he's looking into arranging for us to meet in an interview room to discuss the strategy for your defense, but it'll probably be sometime next week before that happens, so for now let's just stick to discussing personal family matters," said Myrosia.

"Okay, you're right. I want you to know how happy I am that you agreed to come down here and help me. I know now how stupid I was to get involved with Shelly..." he began but she cut him off.

"We're not here to talk about Shelly today. Just stick to family matters. I want to know what you did with the money you took out of our bank accounts," she said.

He hesitated. "I think that's something we should probably discuss in the interview room."

"Okay then, where is the furniture that you took out of the house?" asked Myrosia.

"It's in a storage unit in Buffalo. You can have it all back. The key to the storage unit is in the top drawer in my dresser at the condo. At least that's where I think I left it. But the furniture thing was just a mistake. I never meant to clean out the house like that. It was just a misunderstanding," he said.

"A misunderstanding? What are you talking about? You hired movers. How could that have been a misunderstanding?" asked Myrosia incredulously.

"Yes, I hired some movers, but they were just supposed to take the art, the wine, my clothes, my filing cabinets, stuff like that. I never told them to take the furniture. I told them to take the expensive stuff but they must have misunderstood me. I left Shelly at the house to supervise them and I guess they just got carried away. By the time I found out what they had taken, the stuff was already packed away in the storage unit," explained Dave.

Myrosia clenched her jaw to keep from screaming. The idea of her husband's new girlfriend rummaging through her house choosing which of her belongings to take was almost more than she could stand. She decided that it probably was a good thing that their first meeting was by video conference.

"So, are you trying to tell me that you cleaned out the safe by accident too?" asked Myrosia.

"Well, uh, no. I did that deliberately. I guess maybe that was wrong of me to do that. I know those things belonged to your mother, but you've got to understand that getting settled here in Florida for the winter was really expensive and I was running a bit short of cash…"

It was close to noon by the time Myrosia finished her video visit with Dave and had picked up the keys to the condo. She called Joanna.

"Hi Joanna, are you sunburned yet? I'm finished at the jail and I've got the keys to the condo and I wondered if you wanted me to come and pick you up before I go over there? I could use an extra set of eyes," said Myrosia.

"Sure, come and get me. Maybe we could stop for a bite to eat. I'm getting hungry," said Joanna.

It was after 1:30 when Myrosia and Joanna arrived at the condo.

"Wow, you were right Myrosia. This place is incredible! It's almost as nice as Bob's condo in Buffalo. Smaller than his place obviously, but this view is even better than his. I was expecting there to be finger print powder everywhere and the place to be turned upside down from the police search, but you can barely even tell that the police were ever in here," said Joanna.

Myrosia was about to reply when her cell phone rang. It was Keith calling from the office.

"Did you get the keys to the condo?" he asked.

"Yes, I'm in the condo right now. I just got here and I'm taking a quick peek around. So far there doesn't look like there's any evidence of anything, but do you want to get a crew in here to go over things before it gets cleaned just in case?" asked Myrosia.

"No, I don't think that's necessary. The murder didn't take place there, so I doubt that there'd be anything relevant to the case. Besides, if there was anything important lying around the police would already have seized it. I'll get an itemized list from the DA of everything that they took and I'll e-mail it to you for you to look at. The reason I called you is to let you know that I've got some cleaners scheduled to meet you there at 2 o'clock so there really isn't any time to get a crew in there first. It's crazy here at the office today. I just don't have time to worry about anything else today. You're there, you look around. Do what you can before the cleaners arrive," said Keith impatiently.

"Okay, but I'd hate to miss something because we're in too much of a rush. I'll take some pictures myself before the cleaners get here," said Myrosia hanging up the phone.

Myrosia and Joanna were working their way through the apartment taking pictures with their cell phones when the cleaners arrived with packing boxes for Dave and Shelly's personal items.

"Oh I see you've brought some packing boxes. Good. Just leave those here in the hall closet. There's been a slight change of plans. Just go ahead and clean the apartment but leave everything in place. I'll take care of packing it up later," said Myrosia to the cleaners.

"Why did you do that? I thought you didn't want to have to deal with looking at their stuff," said Joanna.

"Dave told me this morning that he left Shelly in our house supervising the movers the day he moved everything out. Obviously that bitch went through all of my stuff deciding what she wanted to take. I'm just returning the favor. I know that sounds so stupid and petty, especially since it's impossible to get revenge on a dead woman. In my case though I'm not taking anything, all her things will get packed up and the trustee of the estate will get them. There might be something here that her daughter would want. But revenge against a dead women isn't the real reason. I think that if I go through all of the things she brought here, actually touch them, I'll get a better idea of who she was and what she was really like. Maybe that'll give me some ideas about who killed her. As for Dave's stuff, well, you don't suppose they allow bonfires on the beach here…"

"Honest officer we were just having a barbecue..." Joanna laughed.

The two women finished snapping pictures and went out to sit on the terrace while the cleaners continued their work.

"Oh my god Myrosia! Look at those fins sticking out of the water. Are those sharks?" asked Joanna.

"No, those are dolphins. See how they go up and down," explained Myrosia.

"That is so cool. I really could get used to this. I've got to send a picture to the girls back at the salon. They're gonna be so jealous," said Joanna snapping a picture.

"I'm going to call my mother and give her an update."

"Hi Mama, I'm calling you from paradise. I'm sitting on the balcony of Dave's love nest here watching dolphins swimming out in the Gulf of Mexico," said Myrosia.

"I'm sitting here staring at snow that never seems to stop falling. I been thinking it's time for me to take a vacation to Florida. You got room for your old mother in that apartment?" asked Mrs. Dabrowski.

"Of course Mama, there's always room for you, but how would you get here?" asked Myrosia.

"How you think? I'm not planning to walk. I gonna fly down. I gonna call and get a flight and then I call you back and tell you when to pick me up at the Tampa airport."

"But Mama do you think you can travel all this way by yourself?" asked Myrosia.

"Of course I can travel myself. Taxi takes me to airport, plane flies me to Florida, you pick me up at the airport. What's so hard about that?" said her mother.

"Okay Mama, but before you book your flight, first let me see what I can arrange from here," said Myrosia.

Her next call was to Bob's cell phone.

"Hi Bob, it's Myrosia. Is this a good time to talk?"

"Absolutely, give me one second to close my office door."

In the background she could hear him speaking to someone in his office. "Okay, so we're done here? I've got an important call I've got to take, so let's deal with this tomorrow."

He came back on the phone. "Okay, my office is empty, the door is closed. I'm all yours Myrosia."

"Oh Bob, you didn't have to do that. I didn't mean to interrupt your meeting. It's really not that important. You could have just called me back," said Myrosia.

"No Myrosia, nothing else is as important to me as you are. This place is an insane asylum. I'm really starting to hate my job, and this snow is really getting to me. I don't know what I'm doing here. Believe me when I tell you that hearing your voice on the phone has been the highlight of my day. I loved waking up to your phone call this morning. It wasn't as good as waking up and finding you in my bed, but still, it was pretty nice."

"Are you still planning to come down here to visit me?"

"I'm counting the minutes. I'm booked on a flight late tomorrow afternoon. Unfortunately it's got two stops so I won't get there until almost midnight. All the more direct flights were full. The rental car places will be closed by the time I get in, so can you pick me up, or do you want me to take a cab?"

"I can pick you up, but I was wondering if you could do me a big favor?" asked Myrosia.

"Sure, what do you want?" he asked.

"My mother wants to come down too, but I'm really hesitant about letting her fly alone. I was wondering if you could possibly pick her up at her apartment and bring her with you?" asked Myrosia.

"Sure I can do that, but in that case I'd better wait and come on Saturday. I'll see if I can find a non-stop flight. It'd be that much longer before I get to see you, but it'd be a lot more comfortable for your mother."

"Oh Bob, that would be so kind if you would do that."

"Let me see what I can arrange and I'll call you right back."

Less than 15 minutes later he called back.

"Okay, it's settled. I've got two seats booked on a flight at noon on Saturday. I've arranged for a wheelchair and an attendant for her at the airport. I'll be at your mother's residence at 9:30 in the morning to pick her up. Can you make sure she's ready?" he asked.

"She'll be ready and waiting. I don't know how she's going to feel about the wheelchair though, you know how she likes to be independent," said Myrosia.

"Don't worry about that. Don't even mention it to her. When

I pick her up I'll explain that it's just so that we get special treatment on the flight and advanced boarding. She'll be fine with it. We arrive in Tampa at 3 pm and I've arranged for a rental car because there's no way you can pick both of us up in the Porsche. We should be at the beach between 4 and 4:30 and I'll take all three of you ladies out for dinner," said Bob.

"Oh that's perfect. I'll call her and tell her," said Myrosia.

"Only one more little detail. Do you want me to book a hotel for myself or is there room in the condo for me?"

"Plenty of room. I'll put my mother in the master bedroom and Joanna and I can share the second bedroom and you can have the third bedroom. I can't put Mama in with either Joanna or me because she snores like a chain saw."

"That wasn't exactly the sleeping arrangement I was hoping for," Bob sighed.

That evening Myrosia and Joanna were eating dinner at a little waterfront restaurant in St. Pete Beach watching the sun set over the Gulf when three men walked in and sat at a nearby table.

"Myrosia, look. Isn't that one of the detectives that was at the condo last night," asked Joanna.

"It could be, I suppose. It kind of looks a bit like him, but I didn't really pay that much attention. I was mainly talking to the other detective," said Myrosia.

"Well I did take a good look at him. I thought he was really hot. I'm sure this is the same guy, and I don't see a wedding ring."

"He sure looks like your type alright, shaved head, big muscles, a bit of an edge to him. If there's a motorcycle out there you'll be all over him in no time. He won't even know what hit him," laughed Myrosia.

"What was his name? Do you remember what the other cop called him?" asked Joanna.

"Sorry, I don't remember," said Myrosia.

"How am I gonna meet this guy?" asked Joanna.

"Why are you asking me? I've been married forever. I have no idea how to go about picking up strange men."

"I've got an idea. We can go over and play some pool on that pool table over there. Hurry up and finish eating so we can get that particular table. There's a direct line of sight from where he's sitting to that pool table Tits and ass leaning over a pool table always gets their attention," said Joanna.

"You ever wonder why you always wind up with the kind of guys you do?" asked Myrosia shaking her head. But she got up and followed her friend over to the pool table.

Joanna's strategy worked. They had barely racked up the balls when the men at the nearby table first noticed them.

"Okay, 8-ball, we'll flip to see who breaks, you call."

"Heads,' said Myrosia.

It landed on tails.

"Oh well, I might as well take a seat and get comfortable because when you break I usually don't even get a chance to play," said Myrosia.

Sure enough, when Joanna broke she sunk one of the striped balls and her game took off from there. Seven shots later and she had won the game without Myrosia even getting up from her seat.

All the men in the place were watching her now. One of the men edged closer and spoke to her.

"That was impressive. Are you a pro?" he asked.

"I hope you're asking me if I play pool for a living? If so, the answer is no, I'm a hairdresser," said Joanna.

He laughed. "I guess that didn't come out right. Let me try that again. My name is Phil, and you're a really impressive pool player. How'd you get so good?"

"Just practice. Obviously too much time spent hanging out in pool halls I guess. My name's Joanna," she said.

"Well Joanna, can I buy you a beer in exchange for a lesson? That is, if your friend doesn't mind," he asked.

"Go ahead, Rick and I are busy here discussing theoretical physics," said Myrosia pointing to the bartender. "Hey Rick, can you give me another ginger ale. It looks like I'll be keeping you company for a while."

Joanna and Phil played and laughed for close to two hours. Myrosia could see that Joanna occasionally flubbed a few shots to keep him interested. She had considered going back to the hotel and letting Joanna take a cab home, but she was fascinated watching the interaction and the chemistry between the two of them. It was like some sort of elaborate mating ritual you might see on a nature program. Watching Joanna in her element was like watching an artist at work.

The bartender was friendly and attentive and Myrosia actually did enjoy their conversation, but finally she decided that she had stayed long enough.

"That's it for me Joanna. Rick and I have solved all of the world's problems. I'm beat. I'm going back to the hotel. Do you want to come with me, or are you going to take a cab?"

"No, I'll come with you," said Joanna.

"That's too bad. I was just starting to get into my stride. I figure if we played right through to closing I might actually be able to win a game. If you want to stick around and give me a chance, I'd be happy to give you a ride back to your hotel."

"That would be fun, but no, it's late, I'd better go, but maybe we could exchange phone numbers and get together another time. That is if you want another lesson," Joanna smiled.

"I bet there's lots of things you could teach me," said Phil, writing down his phone number on the back of a coaster and handing it to her.

"Well call me and maybe you'll find out," said Joanna smiling as she handed him the coaster with her cell phone number.

Back in the car on the way to the hotel Joanna spoke.

"I'm sorry Myrosia. I was having a great time. He was so hot. But that must have been so boring for you."

"No actually I was having a good time. It was fascinating watching you play him the way you did. But I just don't get it, how come we go out together to a bar and the guys are drawn to you like a magnet. And me, I sit there and talk to the bartender all night. What is it about me? Am I that repulsive?"

"God no, you're gorgeous. If anything you're almost too perfect.

You intimidate most guys. You've got to understand that men are just little boys inside and very few of them have enough self confidence to hit on the most beautiful woman in the room, unless they're alpha male types. Regular guys are all afraid to bomb out in front of their buddies. But in my case I'm kind of like one of the boys, sort of second prize. They aren't afraid of me. Besides, you've been married so long you give off a kind of 'get lost' vibe while me, it's almost like I'm wearing a cologne called 'Bitch in Heat,'" explained Joanna.

"Well one guy that isn't getting my 'get lost' vibe is Jeff. He's still calling me about ten times a day. I've been ignoring most of his calls but I'm gonna have to call him back before I go to bed and see what news he's got for me now," said Myrosia as she pulled up to the valet parking at the hotel.

Chapter 22

Back at the hotel Joanna was watching television in the living room so Myrosia made herself a cup of hot chamomile tea and took it into the bedroom to make her phone calls. She piled up the pillows and settled onto her bed. Her first call was to Jeff.

"Hi Jeff. Sorry I couldn't take your calls today. I've been really busy. I know you've been trying to reach me. Did you find Christine yet?" asked Myrosia.

"No, no luck with her, but I went out and checked on your house twice today. Everything looked fine and the news trucks were gone. I guess they finally figured out that you weren't there."

"You didn't have to do that but thanks. Is that it?"

"No, I have something else to tell you. It doesn't have anything to do with what you're looking for, but it sure caused a stir around here today," he said.

"So what is it?" she asked.

"Penny Donovan marched into the office today and started having a screaming match with Stella. A real cat fight. It was awesome, everybody could hear it. I bet they could even hear it over at the dentist office across the hall," he said.

"What were they fighting about?" she asked.

"I guess they were fighting over Peter, although I don't know why anyone would fight over him. He's such a knob," he replied.

"Yes, but what were they saying about him?" she asked. He was driving her crazy. She wished he would hurry up and get to the point. She was tired and she wanted to call Bob before she went to bed.

"Penny was screaming that Stella was trying to steal Peter but that Peter would never leave her for an idiot like Stella. But then Stella said that she knew stuff that Penny didn't know. Then Peter came tearing out of his office and separated the two women and dragged Penny back into his office. Then the two of them had a big fight but we couldn't hear what they were saying to each other. Then you could hear her screaming and Peter hit her and then Bob ran in and broke it up and when Penny came out with Bob she had a split lip. So Bob took her down to Dr. Jansen's office and got her patched up and then took her home. I heard a couple of the girls saying that she needed stitches in her lip," said Jeff.

"Wow. Nothing like that has ever happened at the office before. What time did all this take place?" asked Myrosia.

"Must have been about noon," said Jeff.

"Oh really?" said Myrosia, wondering why neither Keith nor Bob had not mentioned it when they spoke on the phone that afternoon.

"I've been thinking of taking some time off so I can come down to Florida and help you from there. Anything the office needs from me I can do remotely, and I can work on my online business from anywhere. I can do more to help you if I'm down there with you. I could take care of you," said Jeff.

"That's kind of you, but really it's not necessary. What kind of online business is it that you have Jeff?" asked Myrosia, feeling uncomfortable and attempting to change the subject.

"I do online research, pretty much what I'm doing for you. It pays really well," said Jeff.

"Oh, I didn't realize that you do this as a business. I'm sorry. I guess I should have offered to pay you for your help. But the thing is I'm really not in a position to pay anybody anything right now. Maybe if I can get some money back from Dave, but I don't know if that's ever going to happen, so I honestly can't commit to paying you anything," said Myrosia.

"No, I'm not doing this for the money. I just really like the challenge. It's kind of like being a voyeur looking into someone else's life. And besides, I like you. You've always been nice to me. I can give you some money if you want," said Jeff.

"I appreciate that Jeff, but no I don't want you to give me any money. But there is something else I'd like you to do for me if you don't mind. But do it on work time though, because it's actual office business. If you need to bill any extra time bill it to Keith as part of Dave's defense," said Myrosia.

"Sure, what do you want?" he asked.

"Could you find out everything you can about Shelly Hammett. Background information, go right back to her childhood if you can, everything about her life before she married Trey. She's been in the news a lot over the years. Dig up all the news articles about her that you can find. Do the same for Trey. Whatever you find just e-mail them to me. I'm going to be busy tomorrow, but it would be great if you had something for me that I could start reading through tomorrow evening," said Myrosia.

Her next call was to Bob.

"Hi Bob, it's Myrosia. I hope I'm not calling too late."

"I knew it was you even before the phone rang. I was lying here thinking about you and somehow I just knew that you were about to call. And no, it is definitely not too late for you to call me. Call me anytime. Wake me up in the middle of the night if you want to talk. I've got so much on my mind anyway and I can't sleep without you beside me. I miss you so much," he said.

"I miss you too. How come you can't sleep, what's on your mind?" she asked.

"Well frankly, I want you so badly I can't think straight. It's like being a teenager again. Don't get me wrong, it feels pretty good, but it sure is making it difficult to focus on work. This morning I was in Judge Evan's chambers with Ken Greene. We were trying to negotiate a settlement and I was talking and suddenly I completely lost my chain of thought. I looked like an absolute idiot, so of course Greene moved in for the kill. Fortunately Evans is a pretty reasonable guy and we managed to come to an agreement that didn't completely screw my client but still it was obvious that I was off my game. I'm just trying to hold everything together until Saturday. Believe me I'd walk to Florida right now if that was the only way I could be with you," said Bob.

"I want to be with you too Bob. Every time I think about you my heart races and I've got blood rushing to all sorts of places, and when we're together, well I don't even want to tell you the thoughts that go through my mind. But I'm also really scared and confused. It's scary going from being best friends to lovers. If it doesn't work out with us we won't be able to go back to the way it was and then I'll have lost you as my friend. I feel so good when we're together. I know I can talk to you honestly about everything because we've been friends for so long, but what if this thing you're feeling is just lust, and you get tired of me once you get me in bed? What if we try it and it just doesn't click between us? Let's face it, I really haven't been with very many men. I've been married to Dave for so long and before that there were a couple of times with a couple of boys in college but that's it. I'm not exactly all that experienced, and sex with me wasn't enough to keep Dave faithful. So frankly I'm scared. What if it's not that great for you? My self esteem has taken a beating with Dave dumping me, and then this evening I sat and watched Joanna pick up a guy in a bar. I'd be devastated if we tried it and it wasn't that good for you," said Myrosia.

"Hold on, first of all, Dave being unfaithful to you had nothing to do with you. It's his problem. It wasn't even about sex. It was the thrill of the chase. I see it with guys all the time. It's the thrill of the deal, the thrill of the game, outsmarting another lawyer and winning a case. Sometimes it's the rush of a new woman. It's all about conquest for these guys. Dave would have lost interest in Shelly in no time. She wasn't his intellectual equal, but you kept his attention all these years," he said.

"His intellectual equal? What are you talking about? He's been telling me for years how stupid I am. Sometimes when we had a fight he'd say that he was forced to marry me because I was pregnant. He said I trapped him into marrying me, but sometimes I think back to that time and I wonder if he deliberately tried to get me pregnant. I think he was just looking for someone to support him through law school, that and I think he wanted my parents' money and connections. He stuck around because it suited him, and I was too stupid to realize that he was cheating on me all these years so he was able to get away with it. He had it all. He got to have the image of the family man, and he had all the women he wanted too. I feel so stupid because I didn't see it. If you assumed that I knew, then everyone else must have thought so too. How humiliating is that. I'm glad I'm not home in Buffalo right now because I'm too embarrassed to even look people in the face knowing that they either think I am a fool for not knowing or a fool for putting up with it," said Myrosia.

"You're not a fool Myrosia. You're just an honest person and you assumed that the person you married was honest with you as well," said Bob.

"Maybe, but it's gonna be very hard for me to be trusting of anyone in the future. This whole thing has really changed something inside of me. I can feel it. It's like … I don't know, I can't even describe it, but I can feel it," said Myrosia.

"He's the one who should be embarrassed for having done that to you," said Bob.

"But you know, he didn't always behave like a jerk. At least I'd like to think that I'm not weak enough to stay with a man that was emotionally abusive to me all the time. Every time we had a fight and he'd say those terrible things afterwards he'd be all remorseful and say how sorry he was and how much he loved me and like a moron I believed him. I feel so stupid. I don't trust my own judgment any more," said Myrosia.

"No, you aren't stupid. He really did love you and he knew what a catch you were. The problem is that you were, and still are, way too good for him and he knows it. He just said those things because he was afraid that one day you'd figure him out and leave him," said Bob.

"How do I know these feelings you say you have for me aren't just the thrill of the chase? How do I know that you won't lose interest once you catch me?" asked Myrosia.

"I don't know what to say to convince you Myrosia. There are no guarantees in life. But I understand how you feel. I've bared my soul to you. What happens to me if you decide that I'm not what you want? What if I don't perform to your satisfaction? What if after all this I suddenly can't get it up. Do you have any idea how frightening that thought is for me? What if after all these years of longing to be with you, of waiting for you, you decide you don't want me? I'd be devastated," he said.

"Probably not for long. I'm sure there'd be another woman waiting in the wings ready to console you. Let's face it Bob, your dry spells between women have never been very long. In all the years I've known you I don't recall a time when you didn't have a woman falling all over you," said Myrosia.

"I don't want any other women. I want you. I've always wanted you. Yes, I am a heterosexual male and I like women. I like having sex. I'm not apologizing for that. Wouldn't it be kind of weird if I didn't? Do you honestly think you'd want to be with a man that didn't like having sex?" he asked.

"Well okay, you've got a point there," she replied.

"I've loved you since the day we met, but Dave got to you first. You can't expect that I'd stay celibate pining away waiting for you to notice me and dump Dave. I admit that I've always had an easy time getting dates, and yes, I've enjoyed the company of a lot of women. I've never pretended otherwise. And yes I even cheated on Janice a couple of times. You already know all that about me. But the truth is that most of the time these women aren't interested in me, not the real me, not the real boring guy behind the public image, the veneer. They don't want the guy who likes to sit in his study and read novels. They're interested in the money, the name, the perceived status of being married to a hot shot lawyer, as if. Some of them are even interested in my body. Okay, I admit that those ones have been fun, but what would happen if I got fat and my dick fell off? Would they stick around for me? If I suddenly didn't have any money would they still put up with my moodiness? I want someone who enjoys doing the same things I do, not someone who pretends to share my interests just to try and reel me in. Sometimes I think that my fucking trust fund is a curse."

"Oh you poor whiny baby, give me a break. You know perfectly well that your trust fund is a very convenient thing to have. Being broke sucks and you know it," said Myrosia impatiently.

"Yeah, I'm sorry, you're right. That's something else I love about you, the fact that you aren't afraid to tune me up when I need it.

People have been kissing my ass my entire life, but not you."

"Well let's get back to the subject of other women. Is there anyone else at the moment?" Myrosia asked.

"No, absolutely not. I was seeing someone casually a few weeks ago, but I broke it off right after Dave left you. I can't guarantee that there'll never be any voice mail messages on my phone from other women, but I could change my phone number if that'd make you feel more secure. I'll go to the doctor and get tested for everything under the sun so you'll know for sure I'm not infectious," said Bob.

"You're sure this isn't just about sex? I know I was the one that jumped on you first, and that wasn't fair of me. And I know I slept in your bed and wouldn't make love to you, that wasn't fair of me either, but I just don't want to feel obligated to have sex until I'm ready."

"For god's sake Myrosia, I thought we hashed all this out already. What do I have to say to you to convince you? Yes I've already told you how much I want you. You know perfectly well what my physical response is when you touch me. So yes I admit that I badly want to make love to you, but this isn't just about sex. If it was I could have taken advantage of you the night that you got drunk and came on to me. I can wait until you're ready, even if it means taking a lot of cold showers. But don't expect me to go back to pretending that we've got some sort of brother/sister thing going on because we don't. I love you, and you love me, and we've known each other long enough to know what we're getting into. I know all about you and I love you. I have seen what you're like when you're angry. I've seen you when you're scared. I've seen you tired. I've seen you sick. I've seen you when you're under incredible stress. I've seen you grieving when your brother and your father died. I've seen how you are with your children. I've seen how you are with your mother. I've worked in the same office with you for fifteen years, and I love everything about you. Hell, I even really like your best friend Joanna," said Bob.

"I love you too, and yes I really want to make love to you. That didn't just happen because I was drunk. I'm sorry I'm being so weird tonight. I think maybe I'm just tired and I'm missing you, and talking to Dave today was so awful," admitted Myrosia.

"Good, so we agree that there are no guarantees. Maybe we'll try it and it won't work out. Maybe I'll find out that you've got some sort of weird kinky sex fetish that I just can't get into. Maybe you'll decide that I'm just too boring and moody for you. Maybe you'll be able to get Dave out of this mess he's in and you'll decide to take him back. Who knows what might happen, but I want to give it a try. I don't want to get to the end of my life and wonder what might have been," said Bob.

"Okay, I agree, there are no guarantees in life. Enough about that, let's talk about something else. Tell me about what's going on at the office. I heard about the dust up between Peter and Penny. I hear that you actually had to take her to get stitches and then drive her home. How come you didn't mention it to me when we spoke on the phone earlier?" asked Myrosia.

"I don't know, I guess I was just so happy to hear your voice that I forgot. Besides, what is there to say? I'm watching another friend's marriage come apart. It's so sad really."

"Keith didn't say anything about it when I spoke to him this afternoon either," said Myrosia.

"Keith's got his own marital problems to deal with. Besides, that wasn't the only thing that happened today. It was such a crappy day all around. I already told you about my fiasco in Judge Evan's chambers, well when I got back to the office I found a couple of police investigators there wanting to question us about the bribery allegations and the missing trust account money. Then when they left Penny showed up and all hell broke loose. We've all been under a lot of strain but I'm amazed that Peter actually did that to her right in the office. I've known these guys since we were kids, I don't know what is going on."

"How is Penny doing?" asked Myrosia.

"Well she's sore and swollen, and Hugh had to put in three stitches. He gave her some Valium so she wasn't in any shape to drive home. I called her sister Judy and she met us over at the house. I didn't want Penny to be there alone. As you can imagine, she's devastated. She says that in addition to his affair with Stella they've got money problems, but that he's never hit her before. I don't know what to think. I tried to talk to him about it when I got back to the office and he just told me to butt out. When you called, the three of us had been having a discussion in my office about replacing the trust account money personally. We're gonna take care of that tomorrow morning. Maybe if we can suck it back out of Dave later the rest of us can get reimbursed. But Dave still insists that he never touched that money. I don't know what to believe. I feel like running away. How about you and I running away together?" asked Bob.

"Sure, let's go. Where do you want to run away to?"

"Anywhere that they don't have lawyers," he replied.

"Now you sound like my mother. She's always complaining that there are too many lawyers," she said.

"I'm starting to think that maybe she's right. Or it could be that I'm having a mid-life crisis or something. I'm really questioning my career choice. I'm so sick of the adversarial nature of practicing law, especially the civil litigation shit that I do. I don't know. I see the other guys in the office and they're like gladiators, they live for the battle. You know what Dave is like. It's like he's addicted to the rush of winning. I'm not like them, I just don't care that much. Now with all this other crap going on in the office I'm seriously ready to just end the partnership and pack it in. But I'm trapped until everything settles down and I can close off the cases I'm currently working on."

"What would you do instead? Would you stay in Buffalo?" asked Myrosia.

"I don't know. I guess that depends on you. I'd have probably left years ago if it wasn't for you. Buffalo has been great for me, and the partnership with the other guys worked well for years, but being close to you was the main reason I stayed. Janice was always nagging me to pack it in and move to Palm Beach. As you know, I've got seasonal affective disorder, it's no big deal but I do need lots of sunshine and warm weather so I go south every chance I get. These gray snowy days this time of year are driving me nuts. I'd go anywhere sunny and warm except Palm Beach. My dad had a place there. I've got cousins that have houses there. Janice just loved the Palm Beach social scene when we went down there to visit, but I can't stand it. It's so phony, so pompous. Besides I'm not rich enough to live there. I don't have anywhere near as much money as people think I do, especially after the divorce settlement and the downturn in the stock market. I'm okay and I'll never starve, but I don't have that kind of money. What about you? Where do you want to run away to?" asked Bob.

"I'm not sure I can run away. I've got my mother to look after. But it's a nice fantasy. I wish I could run away where no one knows me or this mess that Dave's dragged me into. I just want to be anonymous. But I'm trapped too, at least until all this gets settled. But maybe then we can hop onto a sailboat and sail off into the sunset," said Myrosia.

"That sounds perfect. I'm going to dream about that tonight. Speaking of dreams, what exactly were those thoughts that you mentioned earlier, the ones that go through your mind when you look at me, you know the ones you didn't want to tell me about…"

Chapter 23

On Friday morning Myrosia and Joanna packed up their things, checked out of the Don Cesar Hotel, and moved into Dave's condo in Madeira Beach.

Looking through the kitchen cupboards it soon became apparent that they needed to go grocery shopping.

"It doesn't look like they were planning to eat at home much. I guess Shelly wasn't really the domestic type," said Myrosia.

"I can relate to that. I haven't used my stove at home since the kids moved out, but still, you've gotta have some food in the house even if it's just Ramon noodles, peanut butter and jam, and a loaf of bread. All they've got in here is coffee and booze. There isn't even any creamer. I guess that's how she stayed so skinny," said Joanna.

"Well let's make a grocery list and go over to Publix."

"We've got three bathrooms in this apartment and only two rolls of toilet paper. I wonder what she was planning to wipe her ass with," Joanna yelled from the master bathroom.

Three hours later they were back from the grocery store, the groceries were put away and they were sitting out at the marble dining table on the terrace eating lunch.

"I hope you don't mind me going out for dinner tonight with Phil. I knew he'd call, but I was really surprised that he called so fast. We'd barely gotten back to the hotel when he texted me the first time. It was a good thing I called him back on the hotel phone or I'd have used up all my cell phone minutes. We talked so long you were already asleep by the time I came through to bed," said Joanna.

"No I don't mind at all, go out and have fun, you're on vacation. But don't get him to pick you up, take the Porsche and meet him somewhere. You don't know this guy and I feel uncomfortable about you going out in his car with him. Besides, if you're driving you can't have anything to drink, and if you don't have anything to drink there's less chance that you'll get yourself into an awkward situation."

"Yes Mom. What time is my curfew?" asked Joanna sarcastically.

"I don't mean it like that. I know you can take care of yourself and I know I'm probably overreacting, but I just feel like something bad is going to happen. Maybe it's the vibe in this apartment, I don't know. Just be careful around this guy," said Myrosia.

"Honestly Myrosia, everything is fine. I've got a really good feeling about Phil, but yes I'll take the car and I won't have anything to drink. But look around, we're in paradise. The sun is shining, the weather is perfect, and we are in a luxurious new apartment on a heavenly stretch of beach looking out at the Gulf of Mexico. Nothing bad is going to happen," said Joanna.

"That's probably what Shelly thought too, but look right down there, that's where Shelly was murdered," said Myrosia.

"Okay, I see your point. It is kind of creepy when you put it that way. But she must have attracted it to herself. So here's what we'll do, we'll light some of these candles we bought, we'll put on some happy music, and I'll call around and see if I can buy some sage or something to smudge this place to clear the energy. But if you are feeling creeped out are you really sure that you want to stay here alone while I go out this evening? You could come along with us."

"Oh yeah, that'd be fun. I'd be stuck sitting there watching the two of you play footsie and gaze into each other's eyes. No thanks, I'll be fine here by myself. I just want to stay in and start packing up Shelly's and Dave's things to get the master bedroom ready for my mother. So you go and have a good time and don't worry about me. Maybe Phil is the guy that the Tarot cards predicted," said Myrosia with a smile.

"If I'm not mistaken the cards said I might have two men to choose from. Yum, if they are both as tasty as Phil I'm going to have a tough time choosing. But speaking of tasty, what are you going to do about dinner?" said Joanna.

"Don't worry about me. We've got enough food in here now to last out a nuclear attack. I'll just make myself a sandwich or something and get to work. There doesn't seem to be much of their stuff in the other bedrooms, so once Mom's room is ready I'm gonna start reading up on Shelly's background. It looks like I'm going to have plenty to keep me busy. Jeff's been sending me emails and text messages since 4 am," said Myrosia.

"When does that guy sleep?" asked Joanna.

"I don't know, I've seen other times when it looked like he just worked all night. It would be nice to be young like that again. I just don't have that kind of stamina anymore," said Myrosia.

"No kidding. I remember back when I was younger I could work all day, pick the kids up from daycare, go home, make supper, clean the house, do the laundry, get the kids into bed, the sitter would come over, and I'd go out dancing half the night and then start the whole thing again the next day. Now all I want to do when I get home from work is lie on the couch with my feet up. I remember when I was dating Phil Tannus we'd bump uglies half the night and bounce right out of bed and... Oh my god, I just realized that Phil is the same name as the first guy I starting seeing back when Jack and I broke up. What a coincidence. Do you think that's significant?"

"Honestly Joanna, you date enough guys the names are bound to start repeating," said Myrosia.

"Yeah, you're right. Duh, you'd think I was the blonde one instead of you. So much for stereotypes," said Joanna.

"So much for the old saying that 'blondes have more fun.' I've been living vicariously through you for most of my life," said Myrosia.

"I wonder what a psychologist would say about that?"

"I don't know, I'm no psychologist but I'm starting to wonder if there's something wrong with that Jeff kid, like maybe he's got Asperger's Syndrome or something. He's a really nice guy and very smart, but he just doesn't seem to pick up on social signals. It's like he's coming on to me or something, but I'm not sure. He might just be trying to be nice and he doesn't know how. It's awkward. I've been trying to let him know that I'm not interested but I don't think he's getting it. I don't know what to do. I've tried to keep everything very professional between us, and I've been trying to ignore it when he says something inappropriate. Like last night he told me he 'could take care of me.' It was weird," said Myrosia.

"Well, I wish somebody would offer to take care of me. But I know what you mean, you're not interested and he's not taking the hint. I guess you're gonna have to be more blunt with him. I swear, some guys are just thick and need a whack on the head to get the message," said Joanna.

"I don't know. I don't want to hurt his feelings. I'm torn. I'm a little sorry I asked him for help in the first place, but he's been a big help, especially with the computer stuff. I don't know how I'd be able to dig up all this information so fast without his help. It would take me forever," said Myrosia.

"Let me pull out my Tarot cards and see if we can understand what the situation with Jeff is all about. Maybe the cards can also show you how to solve the question of who killed Shelly," said Joanna getting up and going inside to get her Tarot cards.

Coming back out with her pack of Tarot cards in her hand Joanna's foot caught on the lower frame of the sliding glass door and she began to lose her balance. She managed to catch herself but in the process the box containing the cards opened up and two cards slid out of the box and landed side by side on the marble table.

"What the hell? How did that happen? How could the box open up like that and two cards jump out and land like that? That was so weird, I'd never have believed it if I hadn't seen it with my own eyes," exclaimed Joanna.

"Let's analyze which cards jumped out. Maybe they have a message for us?' suggested Myrosia.

"We've got the five of Cups and the two of Swords," said Joanna sitting down on the chair beside Myrosia and looking down on the cards.

"What exactly were you thinking about when this happened? Were you wondering about Jeff or was it something else?" asked Myrosia.

"Well I was sort of thinking about Jeff, at least I was when I ran into the apartment, but when I was looking for the cards, and on my way back, a whole bunch of different questions were running through my mind. You know what I'm like. It's hard for me to stay focused. You know I've got ADD. I was thinking about Shelly's murder. I was thinking about whether Dave actually was the one that killed her. I was thinking about what you told me about the fight at the office yesterday. I was thinking about whether things with this new guy Phil were going to work out, and I even wondered if Bob is really as perfect as he appears. It was all just a big jumble, so it probably means nothing," said Joanna.

"Okay, but the way it happened was so spectacular that I can't help but think there is an important message for us in those cards. I know that sounds ridiculous, like I'm being superstitious or something, but you know how amazing these Tarot cards can be," said Myrosia.

"Well you're always a lot more focused than I am. What were you thinking while you were sitting here waiting for me?" asked Joanna.

"I was wondering about Shelly's murder and if it was possible for the cards to tell us why it happened and if we knew why would it help prove who did it," said Myrosia.

"So let's look at the cards. We've got two cards that are lying straight up just exactly as if I'd taken the time to lay them out side by side. We've got the five of Cups. Extreme sadness and disappointment and a sense of being let down by someone. Someone has been the victim of betrayal or maybe it's just that things haven't worked out they way they'd hoped. Whatever it is, something has had a really severe effect on someone emotionally," said Joanna.

"The question is, are we talking about the victim or the killer? Let's assume that we're talking about the killer because my question was why it happened. So if that is our assumption then whoever killed her did it because he or she felt betrayed by her, or that they were extremely upset because things weren't turning out the way they had hoped," said Myrosia.

"Then we've got the two of Swords sitting beside it. The two of Swords represents a state of tension, a fragile balance here between opposing energies. Like love and hate, desire and revulsion, happiness and sadness. Wanting to move forward when it just isn't possible, resulting in stagnation and stunted growth," said Joanna.

"Looks like she was killed by someone who both loved her and hated her. Sure sounds like a crime of passion. But I can't see how that gets us any closer to knowing who did it. That could describe Dave, but it could also describe Trey or any other person she had dealings with, like a business partner," said Myrosia.

"I can't see how that was much help," said Joanna.

"Well let's just think about it. It has to mean something."

"Let's lay out a yes/no spread and ask whether Dave killed her."

Joanna shuffled the cards and Myrosia cut the deck into three piles. Joanna then turned over the top card on each pile.

"Three reversed cards. That's pretty clearly a NO. Let's try it one more time and change the question slightly. Is Dave innocent?" said Joanna.

Joanna began shuffling the cards again and they repeated the process. This time all three cards turned up in the upright position.

"Well there we have it. The cards indicate he didn't do it. Hardly something that we can use in court, and I'm sure that's not what Keith had in mind when he sent me down here to investigate this. But it does give me an assumption to start with, that Dave is innocent and that she was killed by someone who both loved and hated her," said Myrosia.

"Well that does narrow it down, though, to people who loved her because most people who had any dealings with her hated her. The number of people who actually loved her had to be pretty small," said Joanna.

"It also means that if Dave is innocent the real killer is still running around out there."

Chapter 24

On Friday evening, after Joanna left to meet Phil for dinner, Myrosia brought some packing boxes into the master bedroom and pulled up a chair in front of the dresser.

"So Shelly, it's payback time. How's it feel to have me going through your things?" said Myrosia to no one in the room.

"Okay, no hard feelings. You did me a favor taking Dave off my hands, but just give me the money back. It's not like you need it now. Talk to me, tell me who did this to you."

Myrosia lifted one item after another out of the drawers and placed them neatly in the boxes. She looked at the labels on the garments and every so often she stopped to take a picture of an item with her cell phone. Sometimes she just sat and held an item in her hand for a few moments trying to get a feel for the woman who had worn it.

In the bottom of the lingerie drawer she found jewelry boxes. These she put in a separate box and set them aside for closer scrutiny later. Before she handed these over to the trustee of Shelly's estate, she wanted to make sure that none of it could possibly be construed as having been gifts from Dave. She would have to talk to Keith later and confirm what the legal position would be regarding any new jewelry.

One thing that struck Myrosia as she went through the clothes was how little was actually here. For a clothes horse like Shelly, it looked more like she had packed for a weekend visit rather than a permanent move to a new home with her new love. Where were all her clothes? Back in Buffalo or over in Palm Beach in the homes she shared with Trey? What was going on?

Myrosia looked around at the bedroom. It certainly was lovely, and the view was spectacular. The condo was worth millions, but it was nothing compared to Shelly and Trey's home in Palm Beach. Myrosia could not envision a woman like Shelly downsizing. On the contrary Shelly was the kind to always be trading up. So what was she doing with Dave? He was not a bad looking man, and many women considered him charming. He had some money. He had done well over the past twenty years, definitely on track toward multi-millionaire status, but really nothing compared to the Palm Beach billionaires that Shelly regularly rubbed shoulders with. Could it be that she actually loved him and was willing to give all that up to be with Dave? It did not seem likely.

Myrosia was not nearly so careful with her packing of Dave's clothes. She picked them up, checked the pockets, and dropped them into the boxes. She found the key to the Buffalo storage unit that Bob had told her about, the place where her furniture was stored, and put that in her purse. She scooped up the cuff-links and tie-pins that she had given him over the years and put those in her purse as well. When she found his wedding ring lying casually in the bottom of a ceramic dish that he used to dump his change out of his pockets every night, she felt a momentary pang of pain. After all their years together he had dumped her as casually as he dumped the coins out of his pocket.

Oh to hell with him. I'm so much better off without that asshole anyway. I might be able to get a few bucks if I pawn this crap, she thought.

"Bingo. So that's were you kept this stuff," she said opening the lower drawer of one of the bedside tables and pulling out a set of fuzzy pink handcuffs. My god, there's stuff in here I've never seen before. I guess I'll have to ask Joanne to take a look. I don't even want to touch this stuff without rubber gloves, she thought.

She dumped the contents of the drawer into a smaller box and carried it through to the dining room table.

She labeled the boxes of Shelly's clothing and personal effects and piled them in the hall closet ready to be turned over to the trustee. She stuck the boxes containing Dave's things into the back of the massive closet in the master bedroom where they would be out of the way until she decided what to do with them.

Then she worked her way through the closets and drawers in

the remainder of the apartment. Not much in any other room, but Dave had set himself up a small office space on the desk in the third bedroom. There was a wireless printer/fax machine, a monitor and a keyboard, but no computer. He must have had it with him when he was arrested. She sat down at the desk, grabbed a piece of paper and began making a list of items of Shelly's that were missing. There was no computer, no cell phone, and no wallet. The police must have seized these items for their investigation. She made a note to talk to Keith about this.

Finally she carried the box of jewelry out to the dining room table. She carefully laid all the individual pieces out on the table and took pictures of them. She'd print these pictures off to show to Dave when she saw him to see if any of these pieces were pieces that he had given Shelly. There were three boxes from Goldstein Jewelers that caught her attention. She took individual pictures of the contents of these boxes planning to e-mail them to the jeweler to see if he could tell her who had bought the pieces.

It was close to 9 pm by this time and there was nothing else that she could think of to do but try and see if she could reach Keith on his cell phone. He picked up right away.

"Hi Keith, it's Myrosia. Sorry to call you in the evening, but do you have a minute to talk? I wanted to talk to you about Shelly's personal effects. I've just finished going through everything," said Myrosia.

"No problem, this is a good time to talk. I meant to call you earlier to tell you about the arrangements I've made for you to meet with Dave, but it was another crazy day at the office again today. I'm home now and Jeannie is giving me the silent treatment so I'm here in my study. I just poured myself a scotch and I'm sitting here trying to take the edge off," said Keith.

"Is Jeannie pissed because you've still got Cori working in the office?" asked Myrosia.

"I don't even want to go there. As if I don't have enough other crap to deal with these days without having two women mad at me. Like Peter always says, I should have been a priest. I've got the celibacy part down pat, and with this bullshit with that waterfront development deal falling apart the vow of poverty shouldn't be a problem either," said Keith.

He took another big gulp of his drink and continued.

"I've made arrangements for you to meet with Dave, in the interview room this time, on Tuesday morning at 10 am. I know that Bob's going to be down there with you so he's agreed to go with you to sign you in. He's got to stay with you through the interview. I don't know, I guess the folks down there are afraid that you'll go for Dave's throat without a chaperone. I just hope that Dave doesn't go after Bob, at any rate, the three of you should make for a cozy little triangle. I'm kind of sorry I have to miss it. How's it going with your investigation?" asked Keith.

Myrosia could hear him pouring himself another glass of scotch.

"I'm settled in at the condo. I went through all of their personal effects and packed them up. I've taken pictures of everything but nothing much is jumping out at me yet. Well maybe there is one thing. I can't help but notice that there isn't much here. Shelly didn't have very many clothes here. It doesn't look like a permanent arrangement for her. There wasn't even any food in the place," said Myrosia.

"Well Shelly never struck me as the domestic type. She probably wasn't used to having to go out and buy groceries. If Dave really didn't kill her, then I think maybe somebody else did him a big favor. That woman was bad news. I've been skimming through some of the background stuff you asked Jeff to compile. It seems she's been leaving a trail of broken hearts and empty wallets behind her for years. Dave was just her most recent victim. They're having a memorial for the dearly beloved over in Palm Beach on Monday. You might want to attend, see how the grieving widower is taking things. I wouldn't be surprised to see him do his famous touch down happy dance right there at the church," said Keith.

"Okay, I'll ask Jeff to get me the time and location of the service. I imagine the reception should be pretty impressive. Are you sure they'll even let me in? I mean I am the wife of the guy who's been charged with murdering her," said Myrosia.

"Oh they'll let you in, everyone knows Shelly. I wouldn't be

Irene McGarvie

too surprised to hear that people are petitioning the Pope to nominate Dave for sainthood as we speak. Besides, if Bob wasn't already busy consoling you I'm sure that Trey'd be happy to handle that duty," said Keith.

Myrosia decided to ignore that comment.

"I guess I'll bring my mother and Joanna along too. I imagine they'd enjoy a tour of Palm Beach," said Myrosia.

"That would be entertaining, Mama Dabrowski and your dear friend Ms. Lubinski at a Palm Beach funeral. The Beverly Hillbillies go to Palm Beach," said Keith.

"Fuck you Keith, that's my mother and my best friend you're talking about," said Myrosia.

"Yeah, you're right, I'm sorry. I shouldn't have said that. I really like your mother. What else do we need to talk about before I slide into a booze induced coma?" asked Keith.

"Did you manage to get the list of things that the police seized for their investigation?" she asked.

"No, sorry, I'll get that on Monday. Anything else?" he asked.

"I've got a bunch of Shelly's jewelry here and I was wondering if any of it could be construed as belonging to Dave. I mean if there were any pieces that he'd bought for her recently, perhaps they could be liquidated to cover some of his legal bills and my expenses. I've taken pictures of everything. I thought I'd print them out and see if Dave recalls having bought any of them," said Myrosia.

"Let me think about that. Show the pictures to Dave and see what he says. You've got two hours in the interview room on Tuesday and I don't know when we can get you back in so I want to make sure that you're got your questions ready when you get there. But, my head's getting foggy right now, so let's talk about this some more over the weekend when I'm sharper," he said.

Myrosia hung up the phone, looked at her watch and decided to make a bedtime snack before calling Bob. She carried her food and her tea into the living room and got settled down to call Bob.

"Hi baby, I've been waiting for your call. I've been counting the minutes till I see you. Only 18 hours to go," he said as soon as he picked up the phone.

228

"I can't wait. I've been thinking about what I'd like to do to you when you walk through the door, but unfortunately I don't think it's going to work out quite the way I'm envisioning it, with Mama walking through the door beside you," said Myrosia.

"Yeah, but I'm planning to have you spend the rest of your life molesting me so we can probably hold off long enough to get your mother settled into her bedroom," said Bob.

"How was your day? I just got off the phone with Keith and he's sitting in his study busy getting wasted on scotch," said Myrosia.

"Yeah, I bet he is. I'd probably be taking a dive off the rooftop terrace right now if I didn't have you to look forward to," said Bob.

"Why, what's going on?" asked Myrosia.

"Money issues mainly. The three of us each forked over more than $100,000 this morning to cover the missing trust account money," said Bob.

"I didn't know that you had an interest in base jumping? But seriously Bob, $100,000 isn't enough to make you take a dive without a parachute," said Myrosia.

"No, I'm not serious about that. It's just that the police were back again all day questioning everyone in the office. They claim they're after information about the waterfront development, the bribery allegations, the missing trust account money, and Dave's relationship with Shelly. But I don't know, it doesn't feel right, something else is going on. Keith and Peter are both acting weird. Cori's got Keith by the balls and thinks she runs the place, nobody's answering the phone and Peter kept himself holed up in his office when he wasn't being questioned by the police. He cancelled all his appointments today and Stella was in his office with him for a while and when she came out she was looking pretty smug but he wasn't looking any more relaxed, if you get my drift. But seriously, I wish those idiots would stop screwing the staff. The last thing we need right now is for someone to file a sexual harassment suit. I spoke to Penny today to see how she's doing and she said that she was going to charge Peter with assault if he didn't get rid of Stella so it looks to me like he is between a rock and a hard place. To top it all off I had a case in court this morning and the other attorney didn't show up. He had a lame excuse about an emergency so the judge just issued an extension, and all I could think was that I should have been in Florida with you instead of cooling my heels at the courthouse. So that was my day. How was yours?" he asked.

"Not nearly as exciting as yours, Joanna and I got moved out of the hotel and into the condo. We bought groceries and turned the kitchen into a repository for food rather than just booze and coffee. Shelly didn't have any food in here at all. It was weird," said Myrosia.

"Well Shelly was never known for her domestic abilities."

"Funny, that's what Keith said too. I wonder what she was known for?" asked Myrosia.

"Who knows, clothes shopping probably," replied Bob.

"Joanna is out on a date with that guy she picked up last night. Turns out he's one of the detectives working Shelly's murder case. They've been texting each other like teenagers all day," said Myrosia.

"Ah, young love," replied Bob.

"Well Joanna's out with the Porsche tonight. I hope she doesn't go parking and get shot spots all over the seats," said Myrosia.

"Well it probably wouldn't be the first time that's happened in that car," said Bob.

"Awww. I hadn't thought of that," said Myrosia.

"I'm sorry Myrosia. That was insensitive of me, I didn't mean to remind you about all that crap with Dave," said Bob.

"No, it's okay. I already had to inventory Dave and his lover's sex toys this evening. Believe me, nothing reminds you that you've been a blind idiot more than doing something like that," said Myrosia.

"Let's not start about that again. Instead, let's talk about how I plan to make you forget all about this. Give me a little time and I'm going to make you so grateful to Shelly for taking him off your hands," said Bob.

"I'm already grateful. I just wish someone had taken him years ago. Keith told me about the arrangements he made to have you accompany me to my meeting with Dave," said Myrosia.

"Yes, that was the highlight of his day. The only time I've seen him laugh since all this started. He wishes he could be a fly on the wall at that meeting. But enough about that, let's go back to talking about how I plan to make you happy…"

It was almost noon on Saturday when Joanna finally stumbled out of the bedroom in search of coffee.

"Wow you're looking rough this morning. I hope you weren't drinking and driving," said Myrosia.

"Nope, totally sober all night. Just not enough sleep. I didn't get to bed until almost 7 am. First we went out for dinner at this seafood place, they've got a bar right next door and so after dinner we went over there and danced till the bar closed. Then we sat in the car and talked for hours. It was like we couldn't tear ourselves apart. We held hands and walked on the beach and then we drove to a spot where we watched the sun come up over the intracoastal. I haven't had that much fun in years. In fact, I don't think I've ever had that much fun with my clothes on," said Joanna pouring herself another cup of coffee.

"Speaking of fun, I spent the evening going through all of Dave and Shelly's things and look what I found," said Myrosia showing the box of sex toys to Joanna.

"Hmmm, that's creepy. Imagine having a stranger going through your toy box after you're dead. How embarrassing is that," said Joanna.

"I don't think Shelly cares any more," said Myrosia.

"I suppose, but promise me that you'll go through my place and clear out anything embarrassing before my kids go through my stuff," said Joanna.

"Okay, you do the same for me and it's a deal. But that's not why I'm showing you this. It's just that there's some stuff in here that I've never seen before. I don't know what it is. I figured you'd know. There's this electronic gadget here. What's that?" asked Myrosia.

"So what are you saying? That I'm the porn queen, the authority on sex toys? I'm flattered, but it's hardly accurate," said Joanna.

"Well do you know what this is or not?" asked Myrosia.

"Yeah actually I do. It's an electronic stimulator. It gives you an electric shock. All those little gadgets there are attachments for it. You attach them to various real sensitive parts of your anatomy and it gives you shocks. I've never tried one, they're too expensive for me, and I'm not into pain. I don't get it, I have enough pain just standing on my feet all day at work. Why pay for something to give you a shock when you can get a shock from shuffling across the carpet. That's never been a turn on for me. Janet at the shop had a sex toy party one time and you could order one of these. She said they were great, but I don't know…" said Joanna.

"Well if I'd known that this was what Dave wanted I'd have electrocuted him years ago," said Myrosia.

Joanna laughed. "Well obviously Shelly was into pain. Look at all those nipple clamps and stuff. I bet Shelly was one of the women in the porn pictures Dave had on his computer."

"That would make sense," said Myrosia.

"What are you going to do with this stuff? Are you turning this over to the trustee to give to her kids? That's kind of gross don't you think?" said Joanna.

"I don't know what I'm going to do. I better check with Keith on that," replied Myrosia.

"Well I think I'm going to work on my tan, which is a euphemism for sleep on the beach for a while. I hope you don't mind, I invited Phil to go out with us for dinner tonight when Bob and your mother get here," said Joanna.

Myrosia spent Saturday afternoon down at the pool reading through the background files on Shelly that Jeff had emailed to her. She was still engrossed in her reading when Joanna came and sat down next to her.

"Bob and your mom should be here any minute. Their plane landed more than an hour ago," said Joanna.

"Oh shit, I didn't realize what time it was. Come on, let's get upstairs. I want to get cleaned up and looking glamorous before they get here," said Myrosia.

They were just entering the lobby and walking toward the elevators when Bob arrived with Myrosia's mother on his arm.

"Oh hi Mama, hi Bob. I'm sorry, we lost track of time, we were just going up to the apartment to get cleaned up before you got here. I'm so glad you're here," said Myrosia giving her mother a hug.

"I'm not sorry. A few hours ago I was sitting at the airport in Buffalo looking at the snow and now here I am in the sunshine with one beautiful woman on my arm and being greeted at the door by two more beautiful women in bathing suits. It doesn't get much better than this," said Bob, giving both Myrosia and Joanna a peck on the cheek.

"Let's get your mother upstairs and I'll come back and get the luggage," said Bob.

After they had settled in and everyone was dressed for dinner, Myrosia served iced tea and cheese and crackers out on the terrace while they waited for Joanna's date to arrive.

"So tell me about this new man of yours Joanna," said Mrs. Dabrowski.

"He's a Homicide Detective with the County Sheriff's Department. He's divorced like me. He's got three kids that live with their mothers…" Joanna began but was interrupted by the door bell.

"Oh that must be him now," she squealed jumping up to answer the door.

"She looks excited," said Bob.

Mrs. Dabrowski shrugged as if to say 'We've seen her like this before.'

A moment later Joanna was back, pulling Phil by the hand through the doorway to the terrace.

"Okay everybody, this is Phil Ricci. Phil, this is my best friend Myrosia and her mother Mrs. Dabrowski, and this is Bob Williams," said Joanna.

"Nice to meet you all," he said reaching out to shake everyone's hand.

"I'm glad you could join us Phil. We thought we'd just take advantage of the beautiful clear sky and watch the sunset before we head out for dinner. Would you like some ice tea?" asked Myrosia.

"Thanks." he replied.

Mrs. Dabrowski began grilling him.

"So Phil. Ricci what kind of name is that, Italian?" asked Mrs. Dabrowski.

"Yes ma'am. It comes from the word ricco, it means curly.

233

Which is kind of funny under the circumstances," he said running his hand over his shaved bald head.

"So, is it true that Italian men are all mama's boys?" she asked.

Myrosia looked mortified, but Joanna and Phil both laughed.

"So they say." He shrugged. "What you gonna do, you gotta be good to your mama."

"You born in the United States?" she asked.

"Yes ma'am, second generation. But my grandparents were from Sicily."

"You speak Italian?" she asked.

"Yes ma'am," he replied.

"That's good. You gotta be proud of your heritage," she said.

"Oh Mama look. What a beautiful sunset," Myrosia said.

Joanna looked over at Phil and smiled. He had passed the Mama Dabrowski test.

After dinner, with Joanna still off dancing with Phil, Myrosia, her mother and Bob sat on the terrace watching the moonlight on the water.

"That Phil seems like a nice guy, and Joanna sure is smitten," said Bob.

"It looks to me like it's mutual. He can't take his eyes off of her," said Myrosia.

"I hope this one works out for her. Joanna is a good girl. She's had a hard life. She deserves a good man," said Mrs. Dabrowski.

"Can I pour you another glass of wine Mama D?" asked Bob.

"No, I had enough. I gotta go to bed. It's been a long day for me. I'm not as young as you kids. Used to be I could dance all night like Joanna, but not no more. Besides, it's getting too cold for me to sit out here," she said.

"I'm starting to feel the chill too. Let's all go inside," said Myrosia.

They moved inside. While Bob began fiddling with the sound system Myrosia followed her mother into the master bedroom to show her how to operate the remote controls for the electric window blinds and the television.

"Don't fuss over me prosie. I'm not a child. You go out and fuss over that man of yours. I think maybe I like this one," said her mother.

"Mama, he's not my man," said Myrosia unable to make eye contact with her mother.

"Hmmph, you think I'm an idiot? Just get out of here and go keep him company," said her mother in exasperation.

Out in the living room Bob had plugged his mp3 player into the sound system and slow soft romantic music began filling the room.

"Do you think this's too loud? Will it bother your mother?"

"No, she loves this song," said Myrosia as Etta James began to sing 'At Last'.

"At last, your mother's gone to bed and I've got a feeling that Joanna's not gonna be back for a while," he said, pulling her close to him. "Dance with me."

They swayed to the music feeling the heat from each other's bodies. One old romantic song after another, Luther Vandross, Buddy Guy, the Righteous Brothers. When Marvin Gaye began singing 'Let's Get It On' she looked up at him and smiled.

"You're really pulling out the heavy artillery tonight," she said.

"Well Myrosia, it's Saturday night and the antibiotics have finished their job. I think that mean's we're good to go. I want you so bad," he whispered as he kissed her on the neck.

"Mmm, that feels so good. Don't stop. No, wait. Honestly Bob, how can you possibly expect me to have sex with you with my mother in the next room?" she whispered pulling away from him slightly and shaking her head to break the spell.

"She takes her hearing aids out when she goes to bed doesn't she?" he whispered back, pulling her close to him again and nuzzling her ear.

"Yes, I guess so," she said hesitantly.

"Does this feel good? Do you like it when I touch you like this?" he asked as he slid his hand gently up under the back of her t-shirt.

"For god's sake Bob, you're driving me crazy! Forget it, you're sleeping in the guest room and I'm sleeping in the spare bed in Joanna's room," she whispered.

"I guess that's what I get for being a nice guy and bringing your mother down here to be with you," he sighed.

"Well maybe I could sneak out and join you for part of the night," she replied uncertainly.

On Sunday morning Myrosia and Joanna were cleaning up after breakfast and Myrosia's mother was having her coffee out on the terrace overlooking the beach. Phil had joined them for breakfast and now the two men were down on the beach.

"Phil sure seems to like you. You're out half the night with him and then here he is again back here first thing this morning," said Myrosia.

"I sure hope so. I really like this guy. He took me over to see his house last night. He lives in a really nice mobile home over in Largo," said Joanna.

"You went back to his house? You hardly know the guy. How do you know he isn't a serial killer? Did you look in his freezer to see if his last couple of dates were still there?" asked Myrosia.

"Oh come on, he's a cop. You can't get much safer than that."

"Well maybe, but didn't you tell me that you weren't going to hop into bed so fast this time?" asked Myrosia.

"No, it wasn't like that, he just showed me around, showed me his motorcycle, and showed me pictures of his kids, that sort of thing and then we talked and talked and talked. Then he drove me back here. It was really nice," said Joanna.

"Well the two of you must be running on adrenaline because you sure don't look like you were up most of the night," said Myrosia.

"Well Bob sure is looking perky this morning too, but I gotta say you don't look very well rested. I couldn't help but notice that you weren't in bed when I got back last night," said Joanna with a smirk.

"Shut up Joanna. I don't want my mother to hear you,"

whispered Myrosia.

"She can't hear me, she's out there on the terrace and she's deaf. You've got nothing to worry about," replied Joanna.

"Deaf nuh, you think so. I swear she wears those hearing aids for camouflage. No, she hears like a jungle cat when she wants to. She can probably tell you what those women way down there on the beach are gossiping about right now. And trust me, she sees everything. Don't kid yourself," said Myrosia.

"So tell me, was it worth missing out on some sleep?"

"Oh my god, it was so worth it! I can always take a nap on the beach later if I have to. That man is so wonderful. I was starving to death and I didn't even know it. Dave walking out on me was the best thing he's ever done for me. I wish now that he'd left me years ago. I'm so happy right now that I almost don't care about the money he took."

"Well you know what they say, 'the best way to get over one man is to get under another one.' That's always been my motto. But I've never had sex that was so good it would make me not care about losing millions of dollars," said Joanna laughing.

"Hey, I said 'almost.' Let's go take our coffee out onto the terrace," said Myrosia.

The three women watched Bob and Phil throwing a football back and forth on the beach.

"What gorgeous scenery. I could watch those two all day long," sighed Joanna. "Mama Dabrowski, would you look at those muscles. Those are two good looking men. So what do you think of the one that Myrosia has landed herself this time. He sure is a whole lot better than that idiot Dawid, don't you think?"

"Anyone is better than Dawid. I think maybe I like this one. It's impossible not to like him. But maybe he's too perfect, too good to be true. We'll see. All the women like this one. That might be a problem. See." She pointed to two women walking along the beach who had turned their heads to look at Bob.

They sat in silence for a moment and then Mrs. Dabrowski spoke. "So Joanna, tell me what's going on with you and this police detective?"

"I don't know yet. He seems like a really nice guy, and I'm

interested in him, but I don't know how interested he is in me."

"Well he sure looks interested. It's been three nights in a row and now he's back again this morning," said Myrosia.

"Yes, but I've got a nagging little question rolling around in my head that maybe he just figures that if he hangs around me and keeps me talking, maybe I'll spill something about the defense strategy," said Joanna.

"Well he's wasting his time if that's the case because we don't have a defense strategy. I still don't even know what that idiot Dave did to trigger his arrest. Maybe if we're lucky Phil will tell us what they've got on Dave," said Myrosia.

"Well don't be in such a big hurry with this one Joanna. He seems okay, but..." said Mrs. Dabrowski.

"I'm trying to play hard to get, just like you always tell me Mama D, but it's really tough. I mean look at him, he's gorgeous. Big hands, big feet, you know... I've been trying to subtly check out the bulge in his pants without looking like some kind of pervert..." said Joanna.

"Subtly?" Myrosia burst out laughing. "I don't think subtle's a word I've ever heard anyone use to describe you Joanna. I know what your idea of subtle is, 'Hey baby, nice to meet you, do you mind dropping your pants, I've got a tape measure here...'"

"You will never let me forget that will you. That was only that one time, and I only did it because Charlene Riley dared me. I've matured since then." Joanna laughed. "Well maybe subtle isn't exactly the right word. I was trying to be subtle but maybe it wasn't working. He must have noticed me staring at his crotch because he kept checking to make sure his fly was zipped."

"How many times I gotta tell you girls it's not how he fills out his pants it's how he fills out his wallet what counts," said Mrs. Dabrowski.

"Well Mama D at least this one's got a job. That's a big improvement for me," replied Joanna.

Chapter 25

"Hey Myrosia, Phil says there's a really big flea market not too far from here. I talked to your mom and she wants to go. Do you want to come with us? Or do you have too much work to do here?" Joanna asked with a slight nod toward Bob who was sitting beside her on the terrace reading.

"Well actually, I do have a lot of work to do. Jeff's sent me hundreds of documents pertaining to Shelly and I really need some time to read through them," said Myrosia.

"Okay. Phil and I'll take your mom with us and let you have some private time to get your work done. Keep your phone handy. I'll call you when we're on our way back," said Joanna.

Myrosia and Bob waived to them from the balcony overlooking the visitor parking and when Phil's car was out of sight, Bob grabbed Myrosia's hand and began pulling her back into the apartment.

"Come on, we've got the place to ourselves for a little while. Let's go make some noise. I want to see if I can make you scream…"

An hour later they were lying, arms and legs tangled together, in Bob's bed, gasping for breath.

"God Myrosia, I love you so much. That was incredible. I don't ever want to get up. I want to spend the rest of my life right here in this bed with you. But I sure hope this place is well soundproofed or we're gonna be getting complaints from the neighbors," he said with a smile, rolling onto his side and propping himself up on one arm to look at her face.

"My whole body feels like Jello. I don't think I could get up right now if I tried," she said.

"Don't try, stay right here with me. I want to kiss you all over," he said leaning over to kiss her on the stomach.

"Bob, no, don't kiss my stretch marks," said Myrosia wincing.

"Don't be silly, these are beautiful. I just wish we'd gotten together years ago, and these were from you having my children," he said as he ran his free hand across her stomach.

"I'm sorry too, but that's not going to happen now. I mean I'm not sorry I had the kids with Dave. I love them so much I couldn't imagine my life without them, even Nicki, although she drives me crazy some times. But I am sorry that they aren't your children. Maybe Nicki wouldn't be the way she is. But you know I've had my tubes tied, and besides there's our ages to consider. Are you sure you wouldn't rather find someone younger and start a family?"

"No, absolutely not, I want to be with you. Besides, your kids are like my kids anyway. I've been their Uncle Bob their entire lives. I want to be around for the grandchildren some day. But sometimes I do wonder how my life would have been different if Rhyanna'd had that baby. I know it wouldn't have worked out between us though. I wasn't the same person back then..." he said.

"None of us were Bob. You've got to stop beating yourself up about that," said Myrosia stroking his hair as he lay his head on her breast.

"Yeah I know, besides it might not have been my kid anyway. I've never gotten anyone pregnant since then, Janice wanted a baby with me and it just never happened. I don't know if the problem was me or her and by the time we figured out that it wasn't happening I was just relieved that we hadn't brought a child into that mess."

"No more talk about the past. I just want to think about the future," said Myrosia.

"You mean like ten minutes from now when we do this again, or do you mean forty years from now when we're sitting side by side in our rocking chairs?" asked Bob.

"You can't be serious about doing it again are you? I'm still trying to catch my breath," said Myrosia.

"I can't help myself. I feel like a teenager. We've got a lot of years to make up for," said Bob.

"We've got to get up and try and make ourselves look presentable before my mom and Joanna get back. I don't want to be running around scrambling to throw some clothes on when they walk through the door," said Myrosia.

"Relax. Joanna said she'd call you when they're heading back and I'm really enjoying lying here with you. But tell me honestly, what's with all this pretending in front of your mother? Your mother knows exactly what's going on. I think she likes me, well at least she tolerates me better than she ever did Dave. When are you going to tell her that we're a couple?" asked Bob.

"I don't know. It's just so fast. It was only two weeks ago that Dave walked out on me and now here I am tearing up the sheets with you. She keeps telling me to take things slow and I guess I'm embarrassed to let her know that I have absolutely no self control where you're concerned. I just need a little more time," explained Myrosia.

"Okay, I can sneak around with you a little longer until you decide the time is right for you to tell her. Speaking of time, are you still planning to go to Shelly's funeral tomorrow?" asked Bob.

"Damn, I'd almost forgotten about that. The service is at 2 o'clock. I thought the four of us would leave early tomorrow morning and come back tomorrow night. We've got to be back for that meeting with Dave on Tuesday morning," said Myrosia.

"It's at least a four and a half hour drive from here to Palm Beach. That's going to be a long day for your mother. Why don't you and I drive over there this evening? We could stay at the Breakers Hotel, have a nice dinner and a romantic evening alone, and then drive back tomorrow after the service. Joanna and your mother will be fine alone here for one night," suggested Bob.

"That sounds wonderful, but I already told Joanna about it and she really wants to go. She's never been to Palm Beach."

"You can take them to Palm Beach some other time. There just isn't really enough time on this trip. Driving there and back in one day'll be really boring for them. If all four of us go another time I can make it really special for them, set them up with a day at the spa, go to a Polo match, let them go shopping, whatever they'd like. Besides, the press are gonna be out in full force at this event. I don't want to go. I'm just going to be with you. But I don't see what the point of going is. It's not like the murderer is suddenly going to throw himself on her grave and confess. You do realize that Janice is bound to be there. I wouldn't be surprised if they film the whole thing for the TV show. There's no way that Janice would miss being chased by paparazzi at the social event of the Palm Beach season," said Bob.

"Ewww, it hadn't even occurred to me that Janice would show up, but you're right. How awkward would that be. I don't know how I can face her. Everybody's going to think that we've been sneaking around together for years," said Myrosia.

"I don't care what anybody thinks, especially not what she thinks, but I wouldn't put it past Janice to create a scene just for the publicity. Are you sure you want to go and wind up in a cat fight on the front cover of the Enquirer?" asked Bob.

"God no, I don't know what to do. I don't want to go, but it was Keith's idea. I guess he figured it'd be a good chance for me to get a feel for any other possible suspects. So I think I should go."

"You don't need to go to the funeral for that. Every man she's ever had anything to do with is a possible suspect in this case. There must be hundreds that would happily have killed her. I can't see how you'd be able to narrow down the list except geographically. Just figure out who was here that night and take it from there," said Bob.

"You sound like you know what you're talking about. Just exactly how well did you know Shelly?" asked Myrosia.

"Like you and Dave, we knew Trey and Shelly socially. I really like Trey, he's a great guy, but Shelly was more a friend of Janice's. Well, maybe I shouldn't exactly call them friends, but they were on that show together. I've heard the rumors. You know what I'm talking about, you've been reading through the tabloid articles," he said.

"Yeah and Jeff's still dropping a ton more files into my e-mail every day. I don't know how he digs up all this stuff. It's actually kind of invasive. I'd hate to think that my whole life was out there somewhere in cyberspace waiting for somebody to go snooping," said Myrosia.

"Well if you insist on going and taking the whole gang, let me make a couple of phone calls and see if I can book us a private plane. We can probably get one out of St. Petersburg or Clearwater to take us over and back, and I'll get us a car and driver at the other end," said Bob.

"No, that's ridiculous. That's way too expensive. We can drive there and back for less than a hundred dollars. What you're talking about would cost thousands," said Myrosia.

"What's the point of having it if I can't spend it on you? Besides it would be fun to see Joanna's reaction to flying in a private plane and being picked up in a limo. Seeing her experience new things is like watching a kid at Christmas time."

Erie County Homicide Detective Nate Spitzer was called out on Sunday morning to view some human remains found in a wooded area about a hundred feet from an unmaintained private road.

"Damn, I sure wish people disposing of bodies would be good enough to put them somewhere easier for us to get to," said Spitzer to the young deputy who was guarding the crime scene.

"You got that right, but I also wish they'd leave them somewhere warm. I've been freezing my nuts off out here for more than an hour waiting for you. I can't see why I couldn't wait down at the car with the heater running. It's not like the body's gonna run off," said the younger man.

"Here, I brought you a thermos of coffee. Maybe you'll get lucky and the next one'll be at a Starbucks. So what have we got here?" Spitzer asked.

"Some kids from the college were out here snowshoeing and tripped over a body. It's in a black garbage bag and they thought someone had dumped garbage out here. They're environmentalists or something and so they decided they were going to drag it back out with them, but when they tried to roll it onto the sled the bag ripped and they saw that it was a body, so they called it in. It was just freak luck that they found it," he said.

"Where are they now?" asked Spitzer.

"They're the lucky ones. They're back at the cars keeping warm," he said.

"Do we know anything else about the body? Male or female?

243

Cause of death?" asked Spitzer.

"Nope, can't tell anything else without messing up the scene," said the deputy.

"I don't think there's much to see in all this snow, but the crime scene techs and the ME's people are on their way. You go back and warm up in the car, I'll wait here, but you make sure and send the other deputy out here to relieve me," said Spitzer.

Myrosia and Bob were showered, dressed for dinner, and sitting reading on the terrace when the others returned from the flea market.

"You two been sitting here since we left?" asked Joanna.

"Pretty much," said Myrosia trying not to make eye contact with her mother.

"Hmmph," snorted her mother giving her head a slight shake.

"Look what we found. Pink flamingos! They've got oodles and oodles of them at that flea market. I've got to go back again next week and get some more. Your Mama and me are gonna send some to Mrs. Matyjakowski for her lawn. You know how people are always stealing them on her," said Joanna.

"How nice. What do you have in mind for supper? Bob and I are starving. We thought maybe we could all go out again this evening. Or do you want me to make us something?" asked Myrosia.

"Phil was telling me about this barbecue place that sounds really good. Lots of ribs, pulled pork, and draft beer," said Joanna.

"I been eating all afternoon. Lots of food at that Flea Market. I can't eat no more. I'm pooped. I just want to go in my room and watch TV. You kids go out for dinner," said Mrs. Dabrowski.

"No Mama, I don't want to leave you here alone. We'll stay in and I can make us something," said Myrosia.

"No prosie, you go out and have a good time with your friends. I want some time alone. I got my show on TV tonight," Mrs. Dabrowski insisted.

"I can make you something before we go. And you've got my cell number and Joanna's number right on the front of your phone, right?" said Myrosia.

"Enough Myrosia! I am not a child. You behave like I'm niekompetentny. I can take care of myself. I've even got my emergency button on my wrist that you bought me. So get out. You're making me crazy with your fussing," said her mother.

"Okay Mama, I'm sorry I just want to make you comfortable. Kocham ci, I love you," said Myrosia.

"Kocham ci prosie," said her mother and the two couples made a quick exit out the door.

At the restaurant Joanna ordered a jug of draft beer and Myrosia gave her a raised eyebrow.

"What? I'm not driving. Now you're behaving like I'm niekompetentny," said Joanna.

"I think I need to learn Polish. I've picked up a few words over the years but I don't think I know that one," said Bob grinning.

"It's nothing, but let's just hope that Myrosia never has reason to say that you are niekompetentny. Sometimes she's like an old mother hen but we love her anyway," said Joanna blowing a kiss across the table at Myrosia.

"That's fine. You drink all the jugs of beer that you want but don't whine tomorrow that you're hung over," said Myrosia.

"Why, what's tomorrow again? My days are all messed up with being on holiday," asked Joanna.

"Tomorrow is Shelly Hammett's funeral in Palm Beach. Do you still want to go?" asked Myrosia.

"Hell yes. I've never had a chance to see how the rich and famous are laid to rest. And you're right, I don't want to be hung over for that. That's going to be a long drive," said Joanna.

"Slight change of plans, we're going to fly over. I've chartered a plane to take us there and back, it'll be more comfortable," said Bob.

"We have to find some clothes to wear to the funeral. We should have gone shopping on Saturday, but it completely slipped my mind. I don't know what I was thinking," said Myrosia sneaking a glance at Bob who smiled back at her.

"You mean we're actually going to go to the funeral service? I thought we'd be hanging around outside with the rest of the spectators and the press. Maybe doing some sort of undercover stuff sitting in a car with binoculars to see if any murderers show up," said Joanna.

"No, that would be me. I'm going to be the one bored out of my mind sitting in a car, watching the rich and famous walk by," said Phil.

"Oh, are you going to Palm Beach too? You'd be welcome to come with us. I chartered a six-seater, so there's plenty of room," said Bob.

"Jeez I wish, but no thanks. I've got to travel over with a couple of guys from the department," said Phil.

"This is so exciting. But I didn't bring any funeral clothes with me. We've got to go to Wal-Mart," said Joanna excitedly.

"We can't go to a Palm Beach funeral wearing fashions from Wal-Mart," said Myrosia.

"Why not? What's wrong with Wal-Mart? Where else am I going to find an appropriate black dress on a Sunday night?" asked Joanna.

"You're right. If we're auditioning for a spot on the Jerry Springer show, where else would we shop."

On Monday morning Detective Nate Spitzer was at the morgue at the Erie County Medical Examiner's office in Buffalo talking to Dr. Lesley Howard about the remains that had been discovered in the snow the previous day.

"We haven't completed our examination because I've been waiting for her to thaw out. But I can tell you so far that we're looking at a young woman probably in her early to mid twenties. the death appears to be by strangulation," said Dr. Howard.

"Any identification on the body?" asked Spitzer.

"Nothing we've found so far. It would certainly make my life easier with these Jane Doe cases if people would be kind enough to have their name and Social Security Number tattooed on their butt, but I've yet to run across such an accommodating corpse, so we'll just have to wait. I don't want to destroy any possible evidence by heating the body to thaw it out faster," said Dr. Howard.

"How long has she been out there?" asked Spitzer.

"Judging by the snow cover at least a couple of weeks, maybe a month, I can't be certain, but we did have that warm spell right after Christmas and a lot of snow melted, but since then we've been in the deep freeze. So I'd say she was placed out at the scene some time since then," said Dr. Howard.

"So she's been dead somewhere between two and six weeks," said Spitzer.

"No I didn't say that. I'm not sure how long she's been dead. The body was frozen solid when she was placed out there. Look at her. No real decomposition, like she was fast frozen. And no animals were taking chunks out of her. Also, see the shape of the calf? You can see what I'm talking about if you look at her from this angle," said Dr. Howard.

"It's got a square corner," said Spitzer.

"Exactly, just like she was placed in a freezer. I measured her when we first got her here and I'd say she was shoved into that big black garbage bag and stuffed into about an 8 to 10 cubic foot freezer. Judging by the way the blood settled she was placed in there within minutes of being killed," said Dr. Howard.

"So she could've been dead for years?" asked Spitzer.

"Maybe, but I doubt it. The clothes don't look vintage to me. We might be able to give you a better estimate when we look at the labels on the clothes and see what we can come up with from there," said Dr. Howard.

"So, for at least the time being, we've got another Jane Doe. At least this one isn't a blonde reality TV star," said Spitzer.

"No, but it's not like we get a lot of women murdered by strangulation and their bodies dumped. I think we should assume that there's a connection," said Dr. Howard.

"Shit. We'd better call Len Pritchard," sighed Spitzer.

Chapter 26

Myrosia, her mother and Bob were sitting at the kitchen table eating breakfast when Joanna came tearing out of the bedroom in a panic.

"Oh my god, I'm so sorry, I slept in. I heard Myrosia telling me to get up but I must have fallen back to sleep. What time is it? What time do we have to be at the plane? Do I have time for a shower? I just looked in the mirror. I look like shit," cried Joanna.

"Relax, you've got time. The beauty of traveling by private plane is that the pilot will definitely wait for us, so if we're a few minutes late it's no big deal," said Bob reassuringly.

"I was just going to go back in and wake you up again in a minute. I decided to let you sleep a little longer because you looked so tired," said Myrosia.

"Looks like I'm the only one around here getting enough sleep," mumbled Mrs. Dabrowski.

Bob stifled a laugh, but Myrosia pretended not to have heard her mother's comment.

"Here Joanna, have a coffee to wake you up," said Myrosia jumping up and pulling a coffee cup out of the cupboard.

"Great, thanks, I'll be ready in a jiff," said Joanna taking the coffee back with her into the bedroom.

"I don't know, I don't think this is the right look with this dress. What do you think?" said Joanna coming back out ten minutes later with a handful of brightly colored costume jewelry.

"Go with the simplest set. We don't want to draw any more attention to ourselves than we have to," said Myrosia.

"I know, but I didn't really bring anything appropriate for a fancy funeral. Too bad we can't borrow any of Shelly's stuff. You've got to admit that she had good taste in jewelry," said Joanna.

Myrosia thought about the three boxes from Goldstein Jewelers.

"Well, whoever bought it had good taste, and no, we definitely cannot borrow her jewelry," said Myrosia.

"I don't have any proper shoes either. Will my sandals and bare legs be okay?" asked Joanna.

"Relax Joanna. This is Florida. Even in Palm Beach bare legs and sandals are fine, especially with as nice a tan as you've got. Are we ready to go?" asked Bob.

On the drive to the airport Joanna squealed.

"Bob pull over, there's a Goodwill Store! It'll only take a minute."

While Mrs. Dabrowski waited in the car, Joanna ran off into the store with Myrosia and Bob trailing behind her.

"I knew that a trip to Palm Beach with Joanna would be fun, but this wasn't what I was envisioning. I haven't shopped at Goodwill since college," said Bob.

Once inside Bob went off toward the used books and Myrosia attempted to catch up with Joanna.

Ten minutes later they were at the cash with their haul. Joanna had bought a pair of black sandals with stiletto heels and an assortment of jewelry.

"I got these to go with this dress. What do you think? Aren't they hot? Now these are my idea of hooker heels. Don't they just say fuck me? I hope Phil likes them," said Joanna.

Myrosia and Bob both laughed.

"Well, judging by the time you got home last night, I think he likes you regardless of what you're wearing," said Myrosia.

"I also got these awesome black Jackie O sunglasses. Just perfect for warding off the paparazzi don't you think?" said Joanna.

"I didn't find anything that exciting, just some beach reading," said Bob paying for a couple of novels.

They arrived at the airport and parked the car in the private parking area next to the private plane hangar and walked into the office.

"I'm Bob Williams, I have a plane booked for myself and a few friends."

"Certainly Mr. Williams, I have your reservation right here. May I have your identification and your credit card? Would you mind signing right here? Your pilots are waiting. We've got you down to fly from here to Palm Beach and back. The pilots will stay with the plane and bring you back whenever you're ready. But keep in mind that the plane needs to be back here by 10 pm or there will be additional charges," said the young man at the reception desk.

"I hope to be back long before that," replied Bob.

"May I see the identification of the passengers traveling with you today," he asked and one by one Myrosia, her mother, and Joanna all handed over their identification.

"Can I help you with any luggage?" asked the man.

"No thanks, we don't have any. Just the ladies purses," said Bob.

"Excellent, please come with me. Would Mrs. Dabrowski be so kind as to take my arm while we board the plane," said the young man.

The six passenger jet was sitting waiting for them just outside on the pavement. The pilots got out to introduce themselves and help board the passengers.

As they settled in to the luxurious leather seats, Bob had some instructions for the pilots.

"It's a beautiful day out there today, so would it be possible for us to fly straight across the state and then down the coast to Palm Beach? I know that's not the most direct route, but if it's possible, I'd like the ladies to have a chance to see Disney World and as much of the east coast as possible from the air. If you could point out the sights as we go along, that would be great," said Bob.

"Sure we can do that for you. Can we get you something to drink? There's pretty well anything you can think of in the bar, soda, alcohol. Or we can get you a pot of coffee from the terminal building before we take off if you'd prefer," said the pilot.

"Soda is fine. We're going to Palm Beach to attend the funeral of a family friend and I don't know how long this is going to take. I'll call you when we're heading back to the plane, so you can have everything ready to go as soon we get back. I'm sure this won't be the only private plane flying in to Palm Beach today for this event, and I guarantee that there'll be a lot of public figures and therefore a lot of media attention. However, we're not public figures and we're definitely not looking for publicity, so would it be possible for us to deplane inside the hanger and have our car waiting for us in there? I'm depending on your discretion, and so I'm asking that you not give any information about us to the press. Absolutely nothing regarding the names of the passengers or of the flight plan. Do we understand each other?" asked Bob.

"Absolutely, that's no problem. Does anyone need any help with their seat belts?" asked the co-pilot as he proceeded to explain the safety features of the plane.

Within minutes the plane was heading off down the runway.

"This is the way to travel! I could really get used to this. I've gotta take a bunch of pictures to send to the girls at work. It must be great to have money," said Joanna.

"Yes, money definitely makes some things easier," said Bob wistfully.

They flew past Disney World in Orlando then over to Daytona Beach, and down the east coast. When they arrived at Palm Beach the pilot took an extra long swing down the coast past the airport so that they could see the billionaires' mansions before swinging back and landing. The plane rolled gently into the hanger where a limo was waiting for them.

After lunch and a short window shopping excursion along Worth Avenue, the car pulled up in front of the Church where the service was being held.

"Look at these crowds. It's a good thing we've got a driver or we'd be parked up in Daytona and walking from there," said Joanna.

"Oh my god, I'm not sure this was such a good idea. Look at all the photographers. It looks like a movie premier in Hollywood," said Myrosia.

"I've never thought this was a good idea. So if you want us to just keep driving, that's fine with me," said Bob.

"No, we've come all this way we might as well do it. I want to have a chance to speak to Trey and I don't know how else to reach him. The phone numbers I have for him have been disconnected. We'll just have to hold our heads high and walk straight from the car into the church," said Myrosia.

"I'm going to stay in the car," said Mrs. Dabrowski. "I couldn't stand the woman when she was alive. I wanted to thank her for taking out that trash Dawid, but too many crowds for me."

"Okay, Jimmy, could you drive Mrs. Dabrowski around and show her the sights of Palm Beach, maybe take her shopping or out for a snack, whatever she wants? Put it on my bill. Keep her away from the reporters, but don't go too far away because when this carnival is over we're gonna want to make a quick getaway. Whatever you do, don't leave us stranded here. Keep your phone on so I can reach you. Actually, it might be a good idea to pick up a bodyguard before you come back to get us. Get somebody big. Call your company and arrange that for me," Bob said to the chauffeur.

"Do you really think we need a bodyguard?" asked Joanna.

"No, I just want somebody big who can get between us and the photographers. I should have thought of that. I knew it was going to be a freak show but this…" replied Bob.

"I wish I was dressed better," said Myrosia.

"You look stunning. It doesn't matter what you wear, you turn heads. I'm very proud to escort you anywhere, regardless of what you're wearing," said Bob.

"Besides, maybe everyone will be so busy looking at these great shoes of mine to notice anything else. Oh look I think that's Kiki Kendrin in that car. Do you think we'll get to meet her?" asked Joanna.

"Jimmy, pull up two cars behind that car, and we'll get out while the media frenzy is focused on her," said Bob.

The three of them got out of the car and slipped past the crowd and into the vestibule of the church. A security guard began to look for Bob's name on the guest list, but Trey came over to greet them.

"Hey Bob, thanks for coming man, and you too Myrosia, thanks for coming. Shelly would have appreciated it," said Trey Hammett coming up and giving both Bob and Myrosia a big hug. "I gotta admit I'm a little surprised, but it's nice to see you both. What a weird connection the three of us have in this mess. I'm having a few people over to the house afterward. I hope you'll come. Just give your name to my guy here and he'll see you get through security."

"Thanks Trey. This is my friend Joanna Lubinski," said Myrosia.

"Nice to meet you Joanna, hopefully we'll have a chance to talk later. I've gotta go and greet some more people," he said and he moved off toward the next group of mourners entering the church.

Bob gave their names to the security guard and he gave them each a card with Trey Hammett's Palm Beach address and a security code.

"Just give this code to the guy at the gate later on at the house and he'll let you in," explained the security guard.

"Let's go get a seat near the back where we can see everyone as they come in," whispered Myrosia and the trio walked through into the church.

The church was already getting quite full but they were able to find a spot at the back on the right hand side. Myrosia sat between Bob and Joanna.

"That Trey was really nice. I can't believe that he invited me back to his house," whispered Joanna.

"Yes, he's a nice, regular guy. I don't know how he managed to get sucked in by Shelly," said Myrosia.

At that moment one of the clergy stood up to make an announcement.

"Ladies and gentlemen, I would like to remind you that there are to be no photography or any form of recording devices used inside the church."

"Oh shit," said Joanna. "Look at all the celebrities in here. If I can't take any pictures, nobody is ever going to believe that I was actually here. Hell, I can hardly believe that I'm here."

"You know one celebrity that I don't see yet is Janice. I really don't want to have to face her," whispered Myrosia to Joanna.

"No, I don't see her, but look, is that Remy Dalton the movie star?" asked Joanna.

Myrosia leaned closer to Bob and whispered, "Bob, do you see Janice anywhere? I don't see her."

He lifted his arm and placed it around her shoulders and pulled her slightly closer to him. "No, I don't see her either. She's probably going to make a dramatic entrance just before the show starts."

The church was filled with elaborate floral arrangements.

"I completely forgot to send any flowers. That was so rude of me. I guess my mind's been occupied with other things," said Myrosia.

Bob smiled. "Both of us have been preoccupied, so it's a good thing that Ingrid takes care of things like that for me. I don't know what I'm going to do when she retires."

Ingrid was Bob's administrative assistant, a very efficient older woman who had been working for him since the office opened.

"Does Ingrid do everything for you? Does she buy some of the jewelry that you give to your lady friends, especially the ones you've decided to dump?" Myrosia asked.

Bob looked at Myrosia thoughtfully for a moment before he spoke. "Yes, that's been known to happen, not very often, but a couple of times," he acknowledged.

They were silent for a moment and then Bob whispered, "Oh shit, there's Elyse. Janice can't be too far behind."

Elyse Beck, one of Janice and Shelly's co-stars, came sweeping down the aisle on the arm of her billionaire husband Dieter Beck the producer of the show. She saw Bob and Myrosia and her eyes narrowed. She gave the two of them a scathing look but kept walking up to the front of the church.

"What a bitch," whispered Bob.

Anika Neilson, another of Janice and Shelly's co-stars, was the widow of Swedish billionaire Alrik Neilson. She came down the aisle on the arm of her latest fling, tennis star Ole Rasmus.

Once the two co-stars and their escorts reached their seats the plaintive wail of bagpipes began to sound and the entire congregation rose to their feet.

The ornate coffin was carried into the church by six of Trey's teammates led by a bagpiper playing Amazing Grace. Trey, with his stepdaughter on his arm, followed closely behind.

The sermon began and Myrosia found it odd listening to the minister talking about living a good life and spending eternity with Jesus in heaven, given what she had learned about Shelly over the past few days.

"I'm glad that Trey and Ginny seem to have a good relationship. That poor girl is going to need someone. It's terrible to lose your mother in your teens, and to lose her in this manner must be dreadful," said Myrosia.

"I don't see any son. Doesn't she have an older son?" asked Bob.

"That's what the information Jeff dug up said. I didn't know that she even had another child. She never mentioned him. I don't think anyone has ever met him. I don't see any young men sitting with Trey, so I don't know if he's here," said Myrosia.

Two people that Myrosia did not know got up to give a eulogy.

"Are we at the wrong funeral? I don't recognize the woman they're giving the eulogy about, do you?" whispered Bob.

"I wonder what they'll say about us when we go?" Myrosia whispered back.

"So what do you want to do when this is over?" asked Bob.

"I think we should go to the cemetery then over to the reception at the Breakers. Then we'll see what happens. I'd like to go back to Trey's house if we've got time," said Myrosia.

"I'm warning you again. It's going to get ugly, but we can go if you insist. I'd better text the driver and get him back here to pick us up," said Bob, pulling out his cell phone to text instructions to their driver.

A few minutes later he got a response.

"Okay, everything's set. He's putting the car in the line following the hearse, but pretty far back so maybe we won't be noticed. He's going to stay with your mother and the car, but he's going to send the bodyguard in to come and get us. He said he's described us to the body guard. I'd love to know how he described Joanna's shoes. He said the body guard is a 6'4" black guy who is about as wide as he is tall and his name is Lemoyne. We're to stay in the vestibule until Lemoyne comes looking for us." Bob chuckled. "Apparently he's wearing a navy blue suit with a red rose in his lapel to make it easier for us to spot him."

Myrosia tried not to laugh and held a kleenex up to her face to appear to dab her eyes.

Finally the service was over and the procession retreated the same way it came in, followed row after row by the congregation.

Myrosia was able to get a look at the faces of the people as they passed. Nothing jumped out at her, and there was definitely no sign of Janice.

Finally it was time for their row to slip out of the pew and follow the rest of the mourners. Once out into the vestibule they saw Lemoyne immediately. He could have passed for one of the larger of the football players. He came over to them and introduced himself.

"Jimmy tells me that you aren't worried about your physical safety, you just need a shield from the photographers. I think I can handle that for you. I'll just take this lady's arm, and Mr. Williams, you bring your lady friend in real close beside us and we'll slip out of here right now before the crowd thins out too much. I'll get you straight over to the car," said Lemoyne.

"Oooh Lemoyne, you are one big guy. This has been one of the highlights of my day. Are you single?" said Joanna as Lemoyne hustled them out the door. Myrosia could feel Bob shaking with silent laughter beside her.

There were rope lines holding back the spectators and she could hear and see the camera flashes but no one accosted them or got up in their faces and within a few moments they were in the car, and Lemoyne was seated up front beside the driver. With the tinted windows rolled up they could see out but no one could see in.

"Wow, what a rush. I felt just like Madonna leaving a concert," said Joanna.

"How are you doing Mama D? Did Jimmy take good care of you?" asked Bob.

"Oh yeah, he drove me around a little and then we went to pick up the big guy here. We had a good time. They are two nice boys. The big guy looks scary, but you can't go by looks, turns out he's in college, only does this part time. He wants to be a CPA. Thank god he doesn't want to be a lawyer. Now Jimmy here," she reached through the opened partition and gave the driver a light slap on the side of his head with the back of her hand. "Jimmy needs to go back to school unless he wants to get hemorrhoids from spending all day on his ass in this car."

"Ouch, Mama D that hurts," said the chauffeur playfully.

Myrosia raised her eyebrows, and her mother shrugged.

"I told him to call me that. He's a nice boy," her mother replied.

"Well please don't smack him like that when he's driving or we're gonna have an accident," said Myrosia.

The procession of cars began the short drive to the cemetery.

"I feel more comfortable staying in the car here. I don't need to hear what the minister has to say that badly. I can see everyone getting in and out of the cars from here. I just have a strange creepy feeling like someone is watching us," said Myrosia.

"Well you're probably right. Lots of people are watching us. I feel much better in here too," said Bob.

"So Bob, did you run into your wife?" asked Myrosia's mother.

"His ex-wife Mama," Myrosia corrected.

"They not divorced yet. Don't forget that. And neither are you," she said pointedly and Myrosia flushed.

"We're getting definitely getting divorced, Mama D. I can assure you of that. All the paperwork is done and the financial settlement is completed. It's uncontested. She wants the divorce as much as I do, so it's just a matter of waiting the six month legal requirement. Dave was handling it for me, but now I guess I'll have to ask Peter to petition the court for me, or maybe her lawyer will, but one way or another, in another six weeks or so I'll be free. But to answer your question, no, she wasn't there. I'm surprised that she wasn't. I was sure she'd make a huge scene for the cameras," said Bob.

"So Bob, what are we going to do after the cemetery? Are we going to check out the food at the reception at that fancy hotel?" asked Joanna.

"That's up to the boss here," he replied indicating Myrosia.

"Yeah, I think so. When the crowd starts leaving we'll go over to the hotel for a little while," said Myrosia.

"Good, because I've got to pee," said Joanna.

"Me too," said Mrs. Dabrowski.

Myrosia sighed.

"Jimmy, can you manage to get the car out of here and take us over to the Breakers right away?" asked Bob.

At the entrance to the Breakers parking lot there were police directing traffic. The car pulled up to the first officer and the chauffeur rolled down his window.

"We're a bit early, but we're here for the Hammett reception. The name is Williams."

The officer checked his list and directed them to the next driveway at the other end of the building.

"I'll take you right up under that awning and Lemoyne can escort you in. I'll move the car out of the way so you just text me or call me when you're ready to leave," explained the chauffeur.

"Okay big guy, Joanna and me gotta get to the ladies room, so let's go," said Mrs. Dabrowski.

Inside Myrosia and Bob waited for Joanna and Mrs. Dabrowski. Lemoyne stood further down the hall watching everything that was going on around them.

"I'm sorry about my mother's comments about your divorce," said Myrosia.

"That's okay. I'd rather be upfront with her. She's just worried about you. She's afraid I'm going to hurt you," said Bob.

Just then Mrs. Dabrowski and Joanna come out of the restroom and sauntered over to Lemoyne.

"Hey Lemoyne, take your name tag off and pretend to be my date for the evening," said Joanna.

Lemoyne looked questioningly over at Bob. Bob shrugged and grinned as if to say 'It's up to you.' Lemoyne removed his name tag and said, "It would be my pleasure, ma'am."

"Oooh baby, call me Joanna," she replied taking his arm.

With Joanna on one arm and Mrs. Dabrowski on the other, Lemoyne escorted the ladies into the reception hall. Just before they got out of range Myrosia and Bob could hear Joanna say, "Hey Lemoyne, what size shoes do you wear..."

"Poor Phil, I don't know how he's going to compete with this," said Bob as they followed them into the room.

"Hey Myrosia, this sure don't look like any Polish funeral I've ever been to. You ever seen a funeral with food like this? Look at that ice sculpture and that monster pile of shrimp. Where's the egg salad sandwiches in the basement of the church?"

They did not have long to wait long before the rest of the guests began to arrive. Trey was mingling around thanking everyone for coming when Elyse Beck and her husband strode purposefully toward them trailed by a photographer and a videographer.

"Where is Janice? She should be here today," she demanded of Bob in a voice that carried across the room. Everyone turned to look in their direction.

"How should I know where she is? We're separated. I don't keep track of her whereabouts. Tell your crew to turn off the cameras. We're not part of your show," replied Bob.

"Well she probably didn't come because she knew you'd be here," hissed Elyse.

"Nice to see you too, Elyse," Bob replied.

"You've got a lot of nerve bringing your little tramp here. Honestly Bob, what are you doing? Slumming? But really, is this the best you can do? How humiliating for Janice to know that you've gone from her to this," Elyse hissed in Myrosia's direction while the camera clicked away.

"That's more than enough Elyse. You owe Myrosia an apology. If anyone's slumming here, it's Myrosia," said Bob in a calm cold voice.

"Verlassen meine Tochter allein. Ich warne dich," said Mrs. Dabrowski in German to the irate woman.

"You're warning me? No I will not leave your daughter alone.

How do you plan to stop me you old crone? What are you doing here anyway? I don't see any scrap metal lying around," said Elyse.

"Dieter, take your wife away before she makes an even bigger fool of herself," said Bob.

"If anyone should leave, it's his bimbo and her whore hairdresser girlfriend," said Elyse.

"Who you calling a whore?" shouted Joanna.

"Well if the shoes fit…" sneered Elyse.

At that moment Lemoyne stepped between Joanna and Elyse, and Trey and a couple of his teammates rushed over.

"Enough Elyse! This little publicity stunt ends now or you'll be the one leaving," said Trey.

"You have no respect for your wife's memory, befriending the wife of his murderer. Shelly must be turning in her grave," she said haughtily, before turning and strutting away.

"I'm so sorry about that folks. Mrs. Dabrowski, Myrosia, I'm so embarrassed that you were subjected to that. It's all a just a big publicity stunt. Truth is, Elyse and Shelly couldn't stand each other. Now she's just using Shelly's memory to get the show extended. You know what it's like Bob, nothing like a good cat fight to pump up the ratings, you've lived through it. I hope you'll all come over to my house this evening. I'd like to make it up to you for this ugliness. I'm just having a few friends and family over, none of the TV phonies," said Trey.

"Thank you Trey. We'd love to come," said Myrosia.

"Great." He smiled at her and then frowned suddenly as he heard a commotion coming from the other side of the room. "Shit, now what?" he said and moved off in the direction of the disturbance.

"Well that was fun. How did she know I was a hairdresser? I didn't even think she knew who I was," said Joanna.

"They've got researchers for the show. They looked all of you up and scripted the whole thing. Elyse is a bitch, but Dieter is behind it. He put her up to it. Somebody should look into where he was the night Shelly was killed. That barracuda would do anything for the ratings. But don't worry, they won't be able to use much of what they filmed because they haven't got releases," replied Bob.

"Have you seen enough Myrosia? Let's drive around Palm Beach until it's time to go to Trey's place. I'll show you where my cousins live," said Bob, and the group trooped out to the car.

Two hours later they were at Trey and Shelly's beach front mansion. Trey met them at the door.

"Come on in. Tell your driver and your body guard to come in too and get something to eat. We've got tons of food here. This is ridiculous. I'm gonna have to find a homeless shelter or something to give all this to. Let me introduce you to everyone..." said Trey.

While Trey's mother and sister took Joanna and Mrs. Dabrowski on a tour of the palatial home, and the other guests mingled in various parts of the house, Myrosia, Bob, and Trey sat in Trey's study watching the Atlantic waves breaking on the white sand beach.

"You've got a beautiful house here, Trey," said Myrosia.

"Thanks, it's bigger than I really need, but it's nice to have room for company. Actually this house was more Shelly's than mine. This room is mine though, my sanctuary away from all the insanity in the rest of the house," said Trey.

"I understand about that," said Bob.

"I know you do. Your marriage to Janice looks a lot like my marriage to Shelly," he said.

Bob just shrugged and nodded.

"I'm glad you two came over because I wanted to talk to you. I've got some things I want to say but I don't know how much time we've got alone before someone comes in here and tries to drag me out to spend time with the rest of my guests, so let me get straight to the point. We've been friends since I got traded to Buffalo and I'm hoping we can stay friends, but this whole thing is really awkward. Myrosia, I know that you really have nothing to do with any of this. I know this thing with Dave and Shelly was a huge surprise to you. I also know that you have nothing to do with the money that Dave has been defrauding from investors..." he said.

"Money from investors? I know he's stolen my money but..." Myrosia began

"Wait, hear me out. I also know that you're working on Dave's defense. Fine, whatever, I don't know why you'd do that for him but that's up to you. And I hear that Dave's claiming he didn't kill her. Maybe he did, maybe he didn't. The police must have some pretty good evidence to prove that he did or they wouldn't have arrested him. So I figure you're probably here trying to find out if I was the one who killed her," he said.

Myrosia began to protest.

"Look I'm not going to pretend that there weren't a million times that I was ready to strangle her myself. But I didn't do it. I can understand how she could make a guy angry enough though, so if Dave did it, I can understand. But you've got to understand that she had a lot of men over the years, both before we got married and since. We almost broke up regularly. She'd run off with a guy for a couple of weeks, but she always came back, so I wasn't really expecting anything different this time. I don't know why I kept taking her back. It was complicated between us. But I'm no saint either. Women are always throwing themselves at pro ball players and I've never been very good at holding them off. I guess I've never tried very hard. But I've got something to confess to you, Bob. I was with Janice a couple of times. From what I gather, it was me and every other man she met for the last few years that you two were together, including your partners Keith and Peter. I think she was trying to hurt you, at least that's what Shelly thought. Apparently Janice tried to make a move on Dave too, but he didn't go for it. I think that's why Shelly went after Dave, to piss Janice off because Janice wasn't able to land him. It wasn't really about sex with Shelly, and it certainly wasn't about love. It was all about money and power. She had a real hang up about money. All those women on the show do. They just can't get enough," he said with a slight nod to Bob.

"Throughout our entire marriage, Shelly kept her own money to herself. She spent mine as fast as she could, but hers she hoarded. Anytime I tried to get her to cut back on her expenses, she'd find herself another boyfriend, a victim that would spend money on her until his finances ran low and then she'd come running back to me. Frankly I know that a lot of people are saying that Dave did me a big favor by killing her. Well…" He paused. "Like I said, it was complicated between us. A lot of people are under the impression that now that she's dead, that her money goes to me, but that's not true. Shelly's estate goes into trust for her daughter Ginny. This house is mine and so is the one in Buffalo. I'd have been keeping them regardless, but all of her assets belong to her estate. We had a pretty secure pre-nup, she had at least as much money as I did and she made sure that she wouldn't be losing a dime in a divorce. There's a generous trust fund set up for Ginny and the remainder of the money gets turned over to her when she's thirty-two. I'm out of that end of things completely," said Trey.

"But didn't Shelly have an older son from her first marriage?" asked Myrosia.

"Yeah, but she had no idea where he was. She's never been able to find him. She set some money aside for him, but it gets turned over to Ginny if he doesn't surface by the time Ginny gets her money," said Trey.

"Yes, I'm working on Dave's defense team, but like you said, it's an awkward, complicated situation. If Dave really is guilty, I'd be happy to see him convicted, but if he isn't, then in spite of whatever else he's done, I don't want to see an innocent man convicted of murder. So, if it wasn't you and it wasn't Dave, do you have any other ideas who could have done it?" asked Myrosia.

"Every man who ever had the misfortune of falling in love with her could be driven to kill her. But there is one other possibility, Shelly had a stalker. I tried to tell the police but they wouldn't listen to me. They just thought I was trying to turn the blame away from myself. So if Dave really is telling the truth then maybe that's where you should look."

Chapter 27

"Wow, aren't you the glamorous power couple this morning with your business suits and briefcases," said Joanna as she sat slumped in her chair in her bathrobe, sipping her morning coffee.

"Why thank you. I wanted to look particularly good this morning because I'm off to rub salt in Dave's wounds. He'll be the one in the room wearing orange, and that never was his best color. Is my mom still in bed?" asked Myrosia.

"Yep, she's still sleeping off our big day yesterday. I had so much fun. Thanks again Bob," said Joanna.

"I'm glad you had a good time. It turned out to be not nearly as bad as I was expecting," said Bob.

"Well, I had a nice day too. Thanks to Bob. But I had even more fun after we got home. Also thanks to Bob," said Myrosia setting down her briefcase and giving Bob a big kiss.

"I'm very glad that you had a good time. It exceeded my expectations in every way," he replied with a smile.

"But what about you Joanna, how did you manage one night without either Phil or Lemoyne?" asked Myrosia.

"Oh Lemoyne was fun. I had a great time yesterday. I think I could go for being a cougar, but Phil's a real sweetie. We've been texting each other on and off all night. I'm going to see him tonight when he gets off work," said Joanna.

"What about between now and then? What are your plans for today?" asked Myrosia.

"Your mom and I are probably just gonna hang around here, soak up some sun. I want to be well rested for my big date tonight," said Joanna.

"Well go ahead and take the Porsche if you decide to go out," said Myrosia as she and Bob walked out the door.

"I can't believe that you've got enough gall to bring your boyfriend with you," said Dave.

The three of them were seated in the lawyer/client interview room at the Pinellas County Jail. Myrosia and Bob on one side and Dave across from them. The guard had removed Dave's wrist shackles at Bob's request, but the ankle chains remained.

"Shut up Dave. Bob's here to help you. You're lucky anyone's willing to help you after all the crap you've pulled," said Myrosia.

"How's the Porsche? Are you taking good care of it?" asked Dave.

"Yeah it's fine, well except for the passenger side rear quarter panel. Joanna was driving it the other night and backed into something. It's not that big a deal, probably shouldn't cost that much to fix," said Myrosia casually.

"What! You let Joanna drive my Porsche? That thing better be okay when I get out of here," Dave fumed.

"Relax, your car is fine, I just said that to get a rise out of you. But you're an idiot worrying about that car, a car that you'll never see again if we can't prove your innocence. You do remember that you've been charged with murder, don't you? So let's get down to business and start talking about your case. We've got a lot to cover and only a couple of hours today to get through this material. First of all, did you kill her? If you did, then we need to look for legal technicalities and areas of reasonable doubt. I find that repulsive, but you're still entitled to a defense. If you're guilty maybe we can keep you off death row. But if you didn't murder her, then maybe we can find out who did, or at least come up with a plausible list of suspects," said Myrosia.

"No, I did not kill her. I told you that already," said Dave

"Do you know who did?" asked Myrosia.

"No I don't," said Bob.

"Do you have any ideas about who would want her dead?" asked Myrosia.

"Almost everyone who knew her. Certainly every guy that ever managed to get caught in her snare. Why not ask lover boy here. He knew her at least as well as I did, and I do mean knew her in the Biblical sense," said Dave.

"Cut the crap Dave. You're getting off topic again, let's just stick to topics that we can use in your defense," said Bob.

Myrosia looked at Bob for a moment, but then went on with her questions.

"Okay, we'll work from the premise that you really are innocent. If you're not, then you're just shooting yourself in the foot by lying to us," said Myrosia.

"No, I'm telling you I'm innocent," said Dave.

"Okay, so tell me about that Friday and Saturday, when Shelly was killed. Walk me through everything that happened from the time you got up on the Friday morning until the time you found out about her death on Saturday morning," said Myrosia.

"I woke up about six, made some coffee and sat out on the balcony, the side facing the intracoastal, watching the sunrise. Shelly was still sleeping. I just sat out there thinking," said Dave.

"Thinking about what?" asked Myrosia.

"Thinking how beautiful the sunrise was and also thinking how this thing with Shelly wasn't working out the way I had expected. After that I went looking for something to eat, but there was pretty much nothing to eat in the place. I was hungry, so I ate the only thing in the cupboard which was these meal replacement granola bar things that Shelly had. After that I just worked on my computer looking at the stocks, placed a couple of trades on some shit that was tanking and waited for her to wake up. When she woke up I made her some coffee and then when her usual morning hangover subsided enough she wanted one of those bars and she was pissed because I had eaten them. We had a fight about that," said Dave.

"Doesn't sound like much of a honeymoon," said Myrosia.

"You got that right. I'd say that the honeymoon was over the minute I transferred some money into her bank account on Wednesday," said Dave.

"We'll get back to that later, just keep on going with the events of Friday," said Myrosia.

"We argued over the stupid granola bars, then she put some Bailey's in her coffee and that perked her up a bit. I took her out to eat breakfast, so she'd have some food in her stomach, so she wouldn't get loaded quite so early in the day for a change, but of course next thing you know the bulimic bitch is puking in the restroom at the restaurant. We went back to the condo and she wanted to get frisky. Her morning workout she called it, but I wasn't interested. I mean, vomit breath just doesn't do it for me. So she got pissed about that and that caused another argument. The only thing that would shut her up was to take her out shopping. I wanted to go get some groceries, but she wanted to go look at jewelry. She found something she wanted so I bought it, but it needed to be resized. It's still at the jewelers. But knowing that she had a gift coming always made her a lot friendlier so this time when we got back to the condo we did get it on. Things were going great until she tried to electrocute me with that stupid sex toy of hers," said Dave.

"Tried to electrocute you? What do you mean?" asked Myrosia, looking up from her notes.

"This is sick Myrosia. Do you really want me to give you the play by play details? I was trying to spare your feelings," said Dave.

"Just explain the electrocute part," said Myrosia through clenched teeth.

"She has, or I guess I should say had, this sex toy that gives you a shocking sensation. It's an interesting sensation. She was always coming up with different stuff to try which was what kept sex with her so exciting you know," he said.

She knew that he had inserted that last bit just to hurt her, but Myrosia would not give him the satisfaction of knowing it had worked, so she forced herself to maintain an air of indifference. "Go on, just hurry up and get to the electrocute part."

"Everything was going great until she had me blindfolded and tied to the bed with some neckties and she stuck a clamp on my balls and turned on the power full blast," said Dave.

Myrosia could feel Bob wince and suck in air beside her, and she burst out laughing.

"Thank you Shelly! So what happened then?"

"You women are so vindictive," Dave said shaking his head in disbelief. "What do you think I did? I ripped my hands out of the ties and made a dive for the controller mechanism. She was laughing just like you are. I asked her what the hell she did that for and she said that she was just getting back at me for spending so much time on the phone with you trying to get my Porsche back," said Dave.

"So obviously she wasn't trying to kill you, just teach you a lesson. What happened after that?" asked Myrosia, struggling to maintain her composure and keep from laughing.

"I iced my balls and we called a truce. Then we went out for dinner and I got a call from Peter who tells me that all these years it turns out that you were busy banging lover boy here, the guy that I thought was my best friend," said Dave, glaring at Bob.

"That's not true, Dave. Myrosia never cheated on you. Yes I love her, and yes we are together now, but none of this happened until after you left her stranded the way you did," said Bob.

"Don't bother Bob, he can believe whatever he wants." Turning back toward Dave she said, "Go on, what happened after that?"

"I got up from the table at the restaurant and went outside to call you. We had that screaming fight on the phone and then after we hung up I called and cancelled your cell phone service. I went back into the restaurant, finished eating, paid the bill and we left. She was in one of her moods again because I'd left her alone so long in the restaurant and we argued all the way back to the condo. We got up to the apartment and I left her sitting drinking a bottle of wine out on the terrace and I went to bed. I thought I heard the door at one point, and I got up once during the night and saw that she hadn't come back to bed so I looked around the apartment to see where she was and she wasn't there. So I figured she had left and gone back to Trey. I wasn't sorry, I was actually relieved. I got up on Saturday morning and saw the commotion on the beach but it didn't occur to me that it had anything to do with Shelly. It wasn't till the police arrived to question me that I found out what happened," he said.

"What did you tell the police?" asked Myrosia.

"I told them that I went to bed because I had an early golf

game with Peter and Keith. I didn't want to tell them that we had been fighting and I went to bed. I thought the guys would cover for me," said Dave.

"That was stupid. So what was it that caused the police to arrest you?" asked Myrosia.

"They had told me not to leave the county, and I panicked. I was getting short of cash and the money was all in banks in the Caribbean so I booked a private plane from an airport in Sarasota to take me to Grand Bahama to get some of the money. The picked me up on the Skyway Bridge. I was going to come right back," said Dave.

"For god's sake Dave! How could you be that stupid? You're a lawyer, you know better than that. I hope you realize now how difficult that little stunt makes it for us to prepare a defense for you. Flight looks like an admission of guilt to most jurors," said Myrosia.

"But honestly I wasn't trying to flee, I just realized that I had made some really stupid mistakes regarding the money and I knew I had to straighten the banking situation out. I was planning to come right back. I had been so busy devising a strategy to keep you from getting at it that I effectively blocked my own access to the bulk of it as well. I had given about four hundred thousand to Shelly to hold for me, but that was a huge mistake. I didn't realize till after I'd done it that once money goes into Shelly's bank account she considers it a gift and it isn't coming back out again. Now all of her assets are frozen by the trustee, but that money is gone because I don't have any proof that it wasn't a gift," said Dave.

"Well it's official, you're an idiot. But if it's any consolation to you, I gather that she pulled this stunt on a few other men over the years. She has a pattern of latching on to new boyfriends, sucking them dry and then going back to Trey. It was obvious to me when I surveyed that apartment that Shelly had not really moved in. She had no intention of staying with you. You just didn't see it because of your arrogance. You thought she was crazy about you and that you could play her the way you played me all these years," said Myrosia.

"No Myrosia, it wasn't like that, I love you, I wasn't playing you…" Dave began.

"Yeah well if you loved me so much how come you cheated on me with one woman after another all these years? I keep hearing more and more stories about your little escapades. I'm tired of it. Even if we manage to get you out of this mess, I'm not taking you back. I want an honest monogamous relationship," said Myrosia.

"Well then what are you doing with Casanova here? He can't keep his pecker in his pants. Just ask Janice. The stories about his exploits are legendary," said Dave.

"You know that's not true, Dave, you're just trying to stir up trouble," said Bob.

"Oh yeah? Well Shelly told me all about you and her," said Dave.

"Cut the bullshit, both of you. We're running short of time. I need to know where the money is hidden," said Myrosia.

"The bulk of it is in a Panamanian corporation. I've got the number and the name of the Panamanian lawyer memorized. I can give you that. That corporation controls some other corporations. There's a list of banks and account numbers on my computer, but it's all hidden in different files, and the police have seized my computer, my iPad, and my phone, so I can't access any of that. There's also a memory stick in my safety deposit box here in my account at the Bank of America, but I'm the only one that can get at that," said Dave.

"Oh I bet the IRS can probably manage to trace it all, so don't worry about that. What about the trust account money, where did you put that?" asked Myrosia.

"Really, I never touched the trust account money. People keep asking me about that, but honestly I didn't take it," he said.

"Okay, what about these allegations of bribing a public official?" asked Myrosia.

"I've been bribing officials for years. How do you think I managed to make so much money? Do you honestly think I'm the only one doing it? This thing all came to a head when the guy on the planning board I was dealing with got all sanctimonious and wouldn't cooperate. The waterfront development project looked like it was going to fall apart. The investors started wanting their money back.

I got word that I was going to get investigated for fraud and bribery and I figured it was time for me to liquidate what I could and come down here to Florida with Shelly," said Dave.

"Tell me about the mortgage on the lake house," said Myrosia.

"Yeah, I signed your name to the documents and got one of the girls in the office to witness it. The money is in the Caribbean with the rest of it. I mortgaged everything as high as I could because I knew the whole house of cards was about to collapse. I didn't want to tell you that everything was a big fraud. I was ashamed, and I knew you wouldn't approve of my strategy for dealing with it. I knew that you wouldn't run away with me. No, you'd insist on sticking around and paying everyone off even if it meant starting from nothing again. Well I wasn't about to go back to the kind of life I had growing up. It didn't matter what I had to do," said Dave.

Myrosia just shook her head and continued going through her list.

"What about the things you took out of our safe, the stuff my mother gave me for safekeeping?" asked Myrosia.

"I didn't get a chance to sell it. It's all in my safe deposit box here at the Bank of America," said Dave.

"You mentioned some jewelry you bought for Shelly on that last Friday that you left at the store to be resized. What was it, and where's the receipt for that? Could that be returned?" asked Myrosia.

"That was a necklace. It just needed to be shortened a bit to fit her better. The receipt is in my wallet which the police seized when they arrested me. I don't know if the jeweler will take it back. It wasn't a very expensive piece of jewelry. It was less than $1000," said Dave.

"Shelly had three boxes from Goldstein Jewelers in Buffalo. One was a pair of diamond earrings, the second was a pearl necklace, and the third was a Celtic cross pin. Did you buy these for her? Do you have the receipts? I'm wondering if those could be considered to be your property rather than Shelly's?" asked Myrosia.

"I bought her the diamond earrings back when I first started seeing her. I have no idea where the receipt is now, probably in my files for last year's income taxes which are in the storage unit in Buffalo. I don't know where she got the other pieces. Probably some other poor sucker she was stringing along," said Dave.

"What about this kinky sex club on Nottingham Terrace? What made you start that?" asked Myrosia.

"Shelly was a member. She took me over there a couple of times before Christmas. What a bunch of freaks. It was kind of fun the first time but after that, I couldn't really get into it," said Dave.

"So you're saying that you don't have anything to do with the ownership of that club? Or the property where it's housed?" asked Myrosia.

"No, I don't know what you're talking about. I thought you were asking me why I started going there. I'm not involved in the ownership or anything. I just went there a couple of times with Shelly, but that's all," said Dave.

"Well what about the bondage photographs of women that are on your computer? Who are they?" asked Myrosia.

"What are you talking about? I never had any bondage photographs on my computer. Somebody must have put them on there. Did the police tell you I had porn on my computer? They must have planted it," said Dave.

"Come on Dave, I have a hard time believing that anyone would plant porn on your computer to make you look bad. It's not like it's anything illegal, and you've got enough actual illegal business going on to put you away forever, so why would anyone want to do that?" asked Myrosia.

"I don't know, but somebody is trying to frame me for this. I didn't kill Shelly, I didn't touch the trust account money, and I don't know anything about any porn on my computer," said Dave.

"I talked to Trey. He says that Shelly had a stalker. Do you know anything about that?" asked Myrosia.

"That was one of the things we argued about. I caught her on the phone a couple of times talking to some guy. I thought she was cheating on me, setting up her next victim, but she said it was just some guy that was annoying her. She said she was trying to brush him off, but she wouldn't talk to me about it, so I figured that she was lying," said Dave.

"That's pretty much it for my questions. Can you think of anything to tell me that I've forgotten to ask? But frankly Dave, I'm not sure that you're being entirely honest with me. Something feels off about all this, and I can't see what kind of defense we're going to be able to come up with," said Myrosia.

"I'm being completely honest with you, Myrosia. It's been really hard to tell you about all these stupid things I've done, and it's been especially hard being forced to do it in front of him. But I'm telling you the truth about everything. I still love you, and it's killing me that you're with him. He can't be trusted. You think you know him, but you don't, not like I know him," Dave said.

He turned and looked directly at Bob. "I'm warning you, Bob. You and Keith and Peter had better get me out of here or I'm going to spill all your nasty little secrets."

Chapter 28

"What was he talking about Bob? What dirty little secrets?" asked Myrosia as they sat in Bob's rental car in the jail parking lot.

"Myrosia, that was just Dave spouting off. He's just scared and jealous and he's trying to cause trouble," said Bob.

"I don't think so. It's time for you to tell me what's really going on among the partners. Then we need to talk about you and Shelly," said Myrosia coldly.

"I don't know what secrets he thinks he can reveal about the three of us. He's got nothing on me. Maybe there's something about some real estate or development deal that I'm not aware of, but I wouldn't know," said Bob.

"That's bullshit Bob. Something is going on and either you tell me right now or I'm going to find out on my own. Keeping secrets from me is definitely not the right way to start our life together," said Myrosia.

"I'm telling you the truth. I don't know what leverage he thinks he has against the others but he's got nothing on me. He probably thinks that you don't know about my involvement with Rhyanna, but I've told you all about that. He knows about the times I cheated on Janice, and he knows all about Janice's sexual indiscretions. Maybe he thinks I'd be embarrassed to have all that become public knowledge. About the business dealings there's nothing. Sure I've always been in on Dave's real estate deals since the beginning, but I was just an investor. You remember what it was like in the beginning. The deals were small because we couldn't scrape together the kind of money needed to play in the big leagues. We were close friends. I'd give him some money and he always made sure I got a good return, probably a bigger return than was legally possible, but I chose not to look too closely at the details. I knew he was straddling the line as far as legality was concerned. He used to brag to me about that, but the investments were a success and I figured he was just smarter, and more ambitious than the guys he was competing against."

Myrosia remained silent, and Bob spoke again.

"No, I guess that's not completely true. It wasn't just that he was smarter and more ambitious. I knew he was desperate and he'd do anything to move into the world that I had grown up in. He'd cheat anyone, and he'd step on anyone to get ahead. So we used each other. He used me to learn the 'ways of the rich' as he would put it, and to make connections with people in my world, and I used him to help me make money so that I could get back into that world that my mother had cut me off from when she froze my trust fund. I let him do all the things that I didn't have the stomach for. I got the money I wanted without having to do the dirty deeds."

Still Myrosia remained silent, and after a moment Bob continued.

"Okay, that's not the whole story either. I haven't exactly been a choirboy. There have been times when I didn't do my best for my clients. This must be what Dave is referring to. He knows I wouldn't want him to talk about that. Although there's nothing that anyone could prove, nothing that could get me disbarred. I'm not that stupid. It would just be unproven allegations on his part, but it would be enough to kill my practice. I mean, who'd trust me in the future to look out for their interests? He's probably got something like that on Keith and Peter too, but I don't know for sure. What happened in my case was that a couple of times Dave would come to me and ask for a favor. He told me to ease up a little, to not try too hard on a particular case I was working on, just let the settlement come in a little easier on the opposing side, that it would be a big help to him. I knew it was wrong but I rationalized it by telling myself that it was just one big corporation fighting with another big corporation and what they might lose on this one lawsuit they'd make up ten times on something else. Dave must have been using his influence with me to offer as incentives, no bribes, to the opposing parties. But no one could actually prove that I did anything," Bob said, his eyes remaining focused on his hands gripping the steering wheel of the car.

"I'm really surprised at you Bob. How could you participate in something like that?" asked Myrosia.

"I'm surprised at myself too. I told Dave a while back that I wouldn't do it again when he asked me to ease off on a wrongful death case where my client was the family of a man who had died in an industrial accident. Shit, I feel guilty enough when I try my hardest and I don't get a good enough settlement for my clients without throwing a case like that. I struggle with guilt about things that I'm not even responsible for. I couldn't deal with the guilt I'd feel if I actually hadn't done the best I could for that family." He paused and leaned his head onto his hands. "God I hate the life I've created for myself. I really hate my job. It's eating away at me. If I didn't have you in my life I don't know what I'd do," he said raising his head and turning to look at her.

Myrosia remained silent.

"Do I still have you in my life?" he asked.

"Let's talk about you and Shelly. On Sunday afternoon, when I asked you how well you knew Shelly, you told me that you knew Trey and Shelly socially. Why didn't you tell me the truth?" asked Myrosia.

"For god's sake Myrosia, do you remember the context of that conversation? We had just made love and I was practically still lying tangled between your legs. Did you really want me to give you the details about my indiscretion with Shelly right at that moment?" asked Bob.

"I think you're rationalizing again. You lied to me about being involved with Shelly and now you're pretending that you did it to spare my feelings. You know I will not tolerate being lied to," said Myrosia.

"I didn't lie. I just didn't give you all the details. I figured you knew or at least suspected when you asked me yesterday if Ingrid ever bought jewelry for my lady friends," he replied.

"Don't give me that. You know very well that an omission like that is the same as a lie. I started to suspect on Friday night as soon as I saw the three boxes from Goldstein among Shelly's jewelry, and my suspicions were confirmed at the funeral and by the way you behaved when we were with Trey. You didn't say anything then, but I knew that you were feeling uncomfortable. So were the pearls and the Celtic cross jewelry from you?" asked Myrosia.

"I bought her the pearls, but I don't know anything about the Celtic cross pin. I don't understand why you are making such a big deal out of it. It was months ago, before we got together. You know there've been lots of women in my past, but that's the past. I can't change that. I'm with you now and you're the only one."

"Well it is a big deal. Shelly has been murdered and I'm trying to figure out who killed her and you didn't think to mention that you were one of the men she was sleeping with? Honestly, how many other things do I need to know that you aren't telling me?" asked Myrosia.

"It was months ago. I can't see how it's relevant to her murder. If it was bothering you, why didn't you say something? Why didn't you come right out and ask me if I'd been sleeping with Shelly?"

"I was hoping you'd find a way to tell me, and I guess I figured that since it was something that happened before we got together that I could deal with it. You're right, I didn't want to know the details, but I am so sick of being lied to, both by you and by Dave. The thing I want most from you is honesty. All this talk about struggling with guilt is crap. Hasn't it occurred to you that maybe you wouldn't have to struggle so much with guilt if you didn't do anything to feel guilty about in the first place?" said Myrosia.

"You're absolutely right," he replied.

"Well just quit doing stupid things. Do you guys honestly have no control over your brains where sex is concerned?" asked Myrosia.

"I don't think with Shelly it was about sex. It was more about stroking our egos. She made guys feel good. There was just this sweet, vulnerable, quality about Shelly that sucked guys in. She made me feel like she needed me. I think that's probably how Dave got caught too. She must have come to him asking for help with the divorce and she sucked him in. I had sex with her once and realized that she wasn't at all someone I wanted to be involved with so I brushed her off with the pearls. It wasn't until a couple of weeks later, when Janice was moving out and told me that Shelly had told her all about it, that I realized that Shelly had just come on to me to annoy Janice. I felt like an idiot," he said.

"Yeah but what was it about sex with Shelly that was so great that so many otherwise intelligent men could get sucked in? What's she got that other women don't have? What's she do to them that other women don't do? You've had sex with me. Am I really that bad? Why would Dave choose her over me?" asked Myrosia with tears coming to her eyes.

"Oh Myrosia, baby, please don't cry. You are the most special woman in the world to me. You know how much you turn me on. Sex with you is incredible. I can't get enough of you. Trust me when I tell you that there was absolutely nothing special about Shelly. She was just a manipulative, greedy, desperately unhappy woman. I made a mistake, and Dave made a huge mistake. He just explained why he left you. It was because he knew you wouldn't tolerate him defrauding people once you found out. I should have been more upfront about my involvement with her and I'm so sorry. Please come here and let me hold you," he said.

She leaned across the seat and rested her head on his shoulder.

"I guess I'm not really mad at you, Bob. That meeting with Dave and hearing about his sex life with Shelly has just stirred up so many feelings that I don't really understand. I'm so glad you're here with me. Just hold me for a minute," she said.

"I want to hold you like this forever. But for now, how about we go home and get changed and go for a walk on the beach? I've got some ideas about some drastic changes I want to make in my life and I want to tell you about them..."

Mrs. Dabrowski and Joanna were sitting out on the terrace watching dolphins swimming past the condo.

"I love it here," said Joanna.

"Yeah, me too," said Mrs. Dabrowski.

"Mama D, I've been thinking about making some changes in my life and I want your advice. I really like it here and I'm sick of

Buffalo winters. I'm sure I can get another hairdressing job down here. I called the state licensing board and they told me I could just write an exam and I could have my license. Sure, my kids live in Buffalo, but they're grown up and out of the house and they've got their own lives. I've got lots of friends in Buffalo, but I think I can make friends here too. You know that my family isn't very close, so staying around for them isn't that important. The only thing is my friendship with Myrosia. I hate leaving her in Buffalo especially now that she's having these big problems with Dave and the money, but if she ends up marrying Bob then she'll be okay. She won't need me so much. But I've never moved out of Buffalo before, actually I've hardly ever even been out of New York State before so I don't know. I'm scared, but I really want to make a change. I was thinking we could go out for a drive. I want to show you this place where Phil lives. It's a really nice 'age qualified community' not too far from here. He's not really old enough to live there, but with the economy and everything a lot of these places have been letting in some slightly younger people and in his case they were happy to let him in because he's a cop. It makes the other residents feel more secure," said Joanna.

"You're not thinking of moving in with him already are you? You hardly know this man. It's too fast Joanna," said Mrs. Dabrowski.

"No, no, nothing like that, I just wanted to show you the place. There are some other houses for sale in there and some for rent. Let's face it Mama D, I know that if I move down here I won't be living in some fancy condo on the beach like this. I'd have to find somewhere cheap to live. I just thought maybe I'd see how much those places cost and see if there is anything I really like. We can just look," said Joanna.

"Sure let's go look. I been thinking of staying down here too. Life is too short to suffer through winter. Sometimes I'm sorry I sold my house. I hate that place where I live now. It's nice, but too fancy to suit me. The other women in that place are too snooty, not like the old neighborhood. But even the old neighborhood is no good no more. Everything changes. After Caspar died I thought I was going to die too, so I didn't care when Myrosia wanted to move me into the Manor. She was just trying to make sure I was comfortable and safe, but that place is killing me and now I think I want to live some more. Besides, now that Dawid has stolen the money I can't afford to stay at the Manor no more so I got no choice. I gotta find somewhere else to go. I'm 79. I know I'm an old woman, but I'm not dead yet. My problem is Myrosia. Her and the grandchildren are the only family I have left and she still needs me. I'm just not sure she's done with that swinia Dawid yet," said Mrs. Dabrowski.

"What do you mean she's not done with Dawid yet? She'd be a fool to take him back after all this. Besides, Bob is crazy about her and she's in love with Bob. I know you can see that," said Joanna.

"Maybe, but outsiders can never really know what goes on between a husband and a wife. I could never see what she saw in Dawid in the first place, so I'm not sure that it's completely over yet," said Mrs. Dabrowski.

"But Bob is so much better than Dave. He's kind and he's generous. I don't think he'd hurt her," said Joanna.

"Yes, I think maybe Bob might turn out to be a good man. It takes a lifetime to know for sure, but he's got a conscience, something that Dawid don't got. At first I was worried about Bob hurting Myrosia, but now I'm thinking maybe he's the one gonna get hurt..."

Joanna and Mrs. Dabrowski come in from looking at mobile home parks to find Myrosia and Bob in the kitchen making dinner.

"Hi guys, that smells good. I love coming home to find food cooking that I didn't have to make," said Joanna.

"We decided to have a nice family dinner at home tonight. Bob doesn't get enough of those so I'm making him some good Polish food. We've got borscht, pierogies, kielbasa and sauerkraut," said Myrosia.

"You feeding him store bought pierogies and sauerkraut from a can? You should be ashamed. I didn't raise you to serve guests store bought pierogies," said Mrs. Dabrowski.

"Mama D, my heart is broken. You calling me a guest? After all these years when do I get to be considered family?" asked Bob giving the older woman a kiss on the cheek.

"Okay, okay, you're family, but Myrosia really," said Mrs. Dabrowski.

"Aw Mama, give me a break. You wanna eat tonight or a month from now? I didn't have time. Besides, these ones taste pretty good. I found them at a Polish deli. Here try one," said Myrosia.

"Hmmph. Not too bad I guess, but you can do better," said her mother.

"Let's eat here in the kitchen. It feels more homey. I'll set the table," said Joanna.

"But first let's take some vodka out on the terrace and watch the sunset. I got some big news to tell," said Mrs. Dabrowski.

Once they were each seated on the terrace with a shot glass of vodka, Mrs. Dabrowski spoke.

"Here's my big news. I bought a house in Florida. I'm moving down here," said Mrs. Dabrowski.

"What? How could you do something like that on the spur of the moment? I don't think you're being realistic. What about your life in Buffalo, and your friends? Besides, you can't afford to buy a house now. And you Joanna, what the hell are you doing encouraging her," Myrosia exploded.

"I didn't do anything. Your mother knows what she's doing," said Joanna.

"Relax, it's nothing fancy. Joanna and me, we both decided that we going to live here in Florida. I'm sick of winter in Buffalo. So we went out and looked at some of these trailer parks," said Mrs. Dabrowski.

"They call them 'manufactured home communities,' Mama D," said Joanna.

"Yeah, whatever, fancy way of saying trailer park. Anyway some of them are pretty nice. Lots of places for sale. I found one I liked, price was good, I went into the office and made a deal. I can pay for it out of my social security. It's going to be tight but I know how to stretch a dollar. I can move in April, give me time to go back and pack up my things," said Mrs. Dabrowski.

"But Mama how are you going to manage looking after yourself?" asked Myrosia.

"What do you mean how am I gonna look after myself? Don't you talk to me like that. I can look after myself just fine, I been looking after myself and everybody else around me since I was 11 years old. Don't argue with me Myrosia, my mind is made up. Just be happy for me," said Mrs. Dabrowski

"I'm gonna help her get moved and settled in. She said I could stay with her for a little while till I can get a hairdressing job and find my own place," said Joanna.

"It's an old folks park, but they gonna let Joanna stay anyway. That was part of the deal," said Mrs. Dabrowski.

"It's not an 'old folks park.' It's called 'age qualified,'" said Joanna.

"Oh yeah? So tell me what age you gotta be to qualify huh? You gotta be old. So don't be smart with me. It's an old folks trailer park. You can call it any fancy words you want, but it don't change nothing," said Mrs. Dabrowski.

"I'm sorry Mama. I'm happy for you, but how am I going to manage without you?" said Myrosia.

"You gonna manage just fine. You gonna stay here in Florida for a few months, you get the financial mess taken care of and then you decide what you do next. Everything is gonna work out fine. So let's toast," said Mrs. Dabrowski.

"Na zdrowie! To health!" They all toasted.

"Yuck, this stuff tastes like paint thinner. Why do we toast all our important moments like that? We need a new tradition. Come on, let's go in and eat," said Myrosia.

After dinner Joanna left for her big date with Phil, Mrs. Dabrowski went to her room to watch television, Bob settled onto the couch with one of his Goodwill store novels, and Myrosia continued reading through the background material on Shelly Hammett. About twenty minutes later the apartment phone rang.

"Myrosia, you're not going to believe what Phil just told me. Janice Williams is dead, and so is some other woman that used to work in your office," said Joanna excitedly.

"What happened?" asked Myrosia.

"Remember the unidentified body that washed up near that

boat launch last fall? Well that was Janice. People have been trying to call both you and Bob all afternoon, but you aren't answering your phones," said Joanna.

"Oh shit, we turned our phones off this morning when we were at the jai_ with Dave and then we decided to leave them off when we went for a walk on the beach. I guess we forgot to turn them back on," said Myrosia.

"Turn on the news channel," said Joanna.

Myrosia hung up the phone and turned to Bob.

"Bob, I don't know the details, but Joanna just called to tell me that Janice is dead. Turn on the TV," said Myrosia.

He turned on the television and flipped through the channels until he found the news channel. A female reporter was talking.

"...there's been another twist in the murder case that has been gripping the nation regarding television celebrity Shelly Hammett, wife of football star Trey Hammett, whose body was discovered in Madeira Beach, Florida, ten days ago. Today, Buffalo, New York's Erie County Sheriff's Department called a press conference to release the identity of a woman's body that was found washed up on the shore of Lake Erie in October. The woman has been identified as Janice Williams, who was one of Shelly Hammett's co-stars on the reality TV show 'Married with Money.' Williams was the estranged wife of Buffalo lawyer Robert Williams. No one had reported Williams missing until she failed to show up for Shelly Hammett's funeral in Palm Beach, Florida, yesterday."

Myrosia looked at Bob. The color had drained from his face and he was staring at the television screen in shock.

On the television, images of Janice, Shelly, and Trey flashed across the screen, followed by a scene showing the reporter and another woman sitting in a lavishly decorated room.

"I'm speaking with one of the dead women's co-stars, Elyse Beck, at her home in Palm Beach, Florida. Ms. Beck, can you tell me when it was that you became concerned that your friend Janice Williams was missing?" said the reporter.

"Well obviously I was concerned when I hadn't heard from Janice for several months, but we had finished taping for the season and she had just gone through a particularly nasty breakup with her husband and she had told me that she was planning to go to Europe for a few months to deal with the pain. So when I didn't hear from her, I assumed it was because she was travelling. But then when she didn't call when Shelly's murder was announced, I became concerned, and then yesterday when Janice didn't show up at Shelly's funeral I knew something was seriously wrong. Janice and Shelly were very close and I knew that, however much she was suffering over the breakup with her husband, she would not miss Shelly's funeral. At first I thought that perhaps she had stayed away because she couldn't bear to see her husband in the company of the woman that had destroyed their marriage, but then I realized that not even something that painful would keep Janice away from paying her respects to Shelly, so something must be seriously wrong. My husband Dieter and I discussed it and we knew that we just had to report it to the authorities…"

The scene flashed to an image of Bob, with his hand placed protectively on Myrosia's back, entering the church for Shelly's funeral.

The voice of the reporter continued.

"Janice Williams' estranged husband Robert Williams is a partner in the Buffalo, New York, law firm of Walker, Williams, MacKenzie, and Donovan. Another one of the partners, David Walker, has been charged in the murder of Shelly Hammett and is awaiting trial in Florida. In another surprising development the police have announced the discovery of a third body. This third victim has been identified as Christine Bennett who was employed as a clerk at the same Buffalo law firm. Ms. Bennett's body was discovered in a remote wooded area near Buffalo on Sunday. Police are presently trying to determine if the three murders are connected…"

Chapter 29

"I can't believe it. I wanted her out of my life, but I never expected anything like this. Shit, I can't think straight. I don't know what to do. I'd better turn my phone on. The police have probably been trying to reach me all afternoon. Oh my god, I feel sick. I need a drink," said Bob his face still pale with shock.

"Wait Bob, don't turn your phone on yet. Give yourself a few minutes to clear your head. Just relax and get your senses back before you speak to anyone," said Myrosia.

She moved toward her mother's bedroom calling out, "Mama, Mama, I need your help."

"What's the matter prosie?" her mother asked opening the bedroom door.

"It's Bob. He's just had a big shock. We just found out that Janice is dead. She's been murdered. Sit with him and don't let him turn his phone on. Don't let him near the booze. Don't let him speak to anyone until he gets his sense back. Just talk to him. I'm going to the kitchen to get him some hot chocolate," said Myrosia.

Myrosia was back in a minute with a cup of hot chocolate and the portable apartment phone.

"Here drink this. I'm going to call Keith and find out what's going on," said Myrosia already dialing Keith's cell phone.

"Keith it's Myrosia. We just heard about Janice and Christine. What's going on?" said Myrosia.

"Where the hell is Bob? Is he with you? People have been trying to reach him for hours. He needs to call a Detective Nate Spitzer from the Erie County Sheriff's Department. I've got his number right here," said Keith.

"Does Bob need a lawyer?" asked Myrosia.

"Probably a good idea, but it can't be me. I'm already representing Dave so it would be a conflict of interest. I'll give you the home number of someone else who'll represent him."

Myrosia hung up the phone and called the number of the lawyer that Keith had given her.

"Hello, is this Jake Brody? I'm Myrosia Walker. Keith MacKenzie gave me your number and said that you would possibly be willing to represent Bob Williams if it became necessary. Bob's here with me in Florida right now and we just heard the news about his wife Janice's murder. He hasn't spoken to the police yet and I wanted to make sure he had someone to represent him if it became necessary," said Myrosia.

"Sure I'll represent Bob. Is he there with you right now? Can I speak to him?" asked the lawyer.

She put Bob on the phone and walked out onto the terrace to give him privacy to talk. After a few minutes Bob came out looking for her.

"Jake said he's going to call the police and find out what they want me to do. He said to just sit tight until he calls me back on the apartment phone."

They sat holding hands and watching the ripples of moonlight reflecting off the waves on the water.

"I wanted her out of my life so badly, but I never wanted anything like this for her. I just wanted her to be happy somewhere far away from me. I'm so confused. I feel so guilty because I'm so happy here with you, but I don't know why being in love with you feels so wrong. I don't know if what I just said even made any sense," he said.

A few minutes later the apartment phone rang and Bob went back inside to talk.

When she saw him hang up the phone, Myrosia walked back into the apartment.

"I don't need to do anything tonight. I have an appointment in the morning with a Detective Stan Osborne at the Pinellas County Sheriff's Department. They'll take my statement here and that way

I don't have to rush back to Buffalo right away. Jake's arranged for a lawyer from Clearwater to accompany me," he said.

Myrosia's mother was digging around in the fridge pulling out leftovers.

"Bob, come sit down with me and eat," said Mrs. Dabrowski.

"Oh no, Mama D, I feel sick. I can't eat," said Bob.

"Glupi, do as you're told, sit. You've had bad news. You need to eat. I'm going to warm up some food for all three of us. I got some soup here. Myrosia, you warm up that bread, and get the butter and jam out," said Mrs. Dabrowski.

Once they were seated and the food was in front of them, Mrs. Dabrowski spoke.

"Okay Bob, we gonna talk. I been trying to keep my nose out of this business between you and my daughter, but you need to listen to a mother's advice. You're Mama's not here, so you gonna listen to me."

Myrosia raised her eyebrows.

"Don't look at me like that, prosie. You just shut up and listen too," said her mother.

"This is a terrible thing what happened, and you gonna be hurting for a long time. She was your wife and you loved her…"

Bob began to protest.

"No, you don't talk, you just gonna shut up and listen. I know you love my daughter. I know this for years. If you were my son I would've smacked some sense into you years ago. It don't do nobody no good to be in love with somebody else's wife. But you loved your wife too at one time even though you wanted Myrosia. Nobody outside really knows what goes on between a husband and a wife. So, what you gonna do now is you gonna do the right thing. You gonna be a good husband, you make a nice funeral for your wife, settle everything up regarding her estate. You gonna cry for your marriage, you gonna grieve, and then you gonna take some time to decide what you gonna do. You gotta give yourself some time. Then maybe you and Myrosia can be happy together. Myrosia should have left that swinia Dawid years ago. I don't understand why she didn't, but she loves him, she still does, even though she loves you too. But she's gotta grieve too. Neither of you can expect the other one to heal right away. It's gonna be hard for both of you. You're hurting, and Dawid hurt Myrosia with all these other women. He's a fool, that's something we all know, but you…"

She wagged her finger at Bob.

"You got one big problem, the ladies like you too much. It's too easy for you. You already sowed enough wild oats for ten men. It's enough. Time for you to grow up. You know what's good for you? You want to be a good husband to my daughter? You keep your pecker in your pants where other women are concerned. You understand me?"

It was a cool evening and Joanna and Phil had just walked back to his house after soaking in the community hot tub. Joanna had changed out of her wet bathing suit into her dry clothes, but was still feeling cold.

"I can't believe how fast my body's adjusted to the temperature here. A week ago if someone had told me that I'd be feeling cold at 65 degrees in February I'd have never believed them," said Joanna.

"I've got something that'll warm you up," said Phil.

"Oh yeah? What have you got in mind, big guy?" she asked with a grin.

"A blanket," he said reaching into the closet and pulling out a soft comforter.

"Oh, that wasn't exactly what I had in mind, but I guess that'll work." She sighed, feigning disappointment.

"Well, what exactly was it that you had in mind? I could turn the heat up if you want," said Phil pretending not to understand what she was saying.

"Jeez Phil, I know you're not that thick. Would you get over here and warm me up under this blanket," said Joanna.

"Yes ma'am." He saluted and sat down on the couch beside her. She cuddled up under his arm and covered them both with the blanket.

"Actually Joanna, this is a subject that I've been wanting to bring up with you, but I wasn't sure how to approach it," he said.

"What? Are you trying to tell me that you've got some old war injury…" she asked.

He laughed. "No, not exactly. I've been running around with a hard-on since the first time I saw you leaning over that pool table, and I know that you've noticed. That's not the issue."

"Well that's a relief. I'm glad we cleared that up. I was starting to wonder if you were carrying your service revolver in a funny location," said Joanna.

"Joanna, seriously, I really like you. I can't believe we only met five days ago. I'm really rattled by what I'm feeling. I guess I'm afraid of getting my heart broken by you," said Phil.

"Hey buddy, I'm not nearly as tough as I pretend. I do a lot of flirting, but the truth is, I'm more talk than action. You know I like you, so just don't you hurt me. Let's be honest with each other. Is it a deal?" asked Joanna.

"Deal," he replied.

"Suddenly it's feeling a lot warmer in here," said Joanna brushing off the blanket, straddling Phil's lap and kissing him.

The following morning Phil rolled into work with a spring in his step singing the James Brown classic 'I Feel Good.'

"It's that Walker woman's friend isn't it. Damn it Phil! How many times have I told you not to get involved with women at work," said Detective Stan Osborne.

"Her name's Joanna and she's not at work," replied Phil.

"You know what I'm talking about. She's involved in a case. You know better than that. It can jeopardize the case we're building," said the older detective.

"But she's not involved in this case," insisted Phil.

"You met her on the job didn't you? That's close enough," replied Osborne.

"Well it's too late. I'm already involved, and I really like this woman. She's different than any woman I've ever met. I've never laughed so much in my life as I do when I'm with her. I'm not going to end it," said Phil.

"You idiot, you're thinking with the little head. Do you really want to spend the next 20 years as a mall security guard? End it now, or it could end your career."

Bob was depressed and distant as he got ready to leave to go for his interview at the Pinellas County Sheriff's Dept.

"Are you sure you don't want me to come with you?" Myrosia asked.

"No, I can handle this alone. Besides, there might be media there if somebody's tipped them off that I'll be there. You don't want to get caught up in all that," he replied.

"Well at least you look good for the cameras. You look like a model in those khakis and that golf shirt," said Myrosia trying to make him smile.

"Thanks," he said and without another word he walked out the door looking like he was heading off to an execution.

"Wow, that's not the same Bob. I can't believe how cold he was. Not even a peck on the cheek. I know you said that he can be moody, but I've never seen it before," said Joanna.

"Obviously he's really hurting. It's not the same not seeing his smile and the twinkle in his eyes," said Myrosia.

"Give him some time, prosie," said her mother.

"Let's take our coffee in the living room and check the TV to see if they've got any more information about the murders," said Joanna.

It was the top news on all the news channels.

"… authorities are comparing the two murders. Both women had been strangled. Janice Williams body had been tied up and weighted down while Christine Bennett's body was apparently stored in a freezer for an unknown period of time before being dumped in a remote wooded area near Buffalo…"

Images of the area where Christine Bennett's body was discovered flashed on the television screen.

"This doesn't look good for Dave. I think you can forget about getting him off on all these charges," said Joanna

"What makes you think that Dave did this?" asked Myrosia.

"The police obviously think that the same person murdered all three women. For one thing they were all strangled. And Dave has a connection to all of them," said Joanna.

"How do you figure that?" asked Myrosia.

"He was having an affair with both Shelly and Christine, and he must have been involved with Janice because he had sexually explicit pictures of her on his computer," said Joanna.

"Anything else?" asked Myrosia.

"Janice's body was taken out on the lake and dumped. Dave has a boat. That Christine girl was dumped out in a remote area where you'd need a 4-wheel drive to get to it and Dave had his Escalade," said Joanna.

"Well maybe, but lots of people on Lake Erie have boats, and most of the guys I know have got big monster trucks that could get out to where Christine's body was discovered. What would his motive be? Most murders are motivated by either money, or passion, or revenge. Dave denies having killed Shelly and as of yesterday I believed him. Shelly's murder certainly looked like a crime of passion, a spur of the moment thing with no attempt to hide the body. The other two could also have been crimes of passion, but the murderer went to a lot of trouble to hide the bodies.

"About the connection between the women and Dave, let's try and look at this logically. Yes Dave was having an affair with both Shelly and Christine, but he denies any involvement with Janice and if Janice had been involved with Dave she most certainly would have thrown it in Bob's face, but Bob says Janice tried coming on to Dave lots of times, but Dave wasn't interested," said Myrosia.

"Are you sure you're not just hoping Dave is innocent?" asked Joanna pointedly.

"God no! Mama here thinks I'm not over Dave for some reason, but she is so wrong. It's true I'd like to get him off in order to straighten out the money situation, but I'd rather go bankrupt than help him get off if he's a murderer. Besides, do you honestly think that Dave could have stuffed Christine Bennett's body in our freezer at home without me noticing? That alone is enough to make me question Dave's involvement, not to mention that the Tarot cards the other day were unequivocal that he didn't kill Shelly," said Myrosia.

"Let's pull out the Tarot cards again and see if they can tell us any more about the murderer," said Joanna.

Myrosia went to the bedroom and got her Tarot cards and brought them back to the living room and spread her silk cloth over the coffee table in front of them.

"What kind of spread do you think we should try? I was thinking a three card body, mind, and spirit spread might describe the murderer and give us an insight into his motive," asked Myrosia.

"Okay, your cards, you shuffle," said Joanna.

"Our first card, the body card, is the Knight of Wands. In this case we're hoping to get an idea of the physical body or appearance of the murderer. But let's face it, Tarot cards aren't very good at showing physical characteristics of people, so we should take this with a grain of salt. The Knight of Wands could be someone with blond hair and blue eyes, or it could represent one of the astrological fire signs, Leo, Aries, or Sagittarius. Or it could mean someone who is ambitious, motivated and passionate," said Myrosia.

"Or it could represent starting or ending a passionate relationship," said Joanna.

"Hmm, the murders would certainly mean the end of a passionate relationship. But if we go by physical characteristics, then we can rule out Dave because that weasel is a brown haired, brown eyed, Scorpio," said Myrosia.

"We do know one gorgeous, passionate, blond haired, blue eyed, Aries man. This card could be describing the end of his fiery relationship with Janice," said Joanna.

"Well we know that Bob's not the murderer, but I suppose it could represent the end of someone's fiery relationship with Janice," said Myrosia.

"How do we know that Bob didn't do it? I don't think he did it, but how do we know that for sure?" asked Joanna.

Myrosia thought about that for a moment before responding. "I guess we don't know for sure, but let me think about it. In the meantime let's go on with the reading. The second card, the mind card, is the Page of Swords, but in this case it's reversed. This card can represent a devious and vindictive person, someone who pretends to be a friend while seeking out your weaknesses. Someone who will use anything you tell them against you. Someone on the hunt for buried secrets, but who keeps the truth about themselves hidden."

"So the killer is somebody that pretended to be a friend to the victims. That makes sense. These weren't random stranger killings. The victims are connected," said Joanna.

"It would have to be someone from the office. That's where the connection is, so we're back to looking at the partners, Dave, Keith, Peter, and Bob. So, maybe it's Dave. He's certainly devious and kept lots of things about himself hidden. But Peter and Keith are pretty sneaky too, and we know that Peter has a bad temper. Remember what he did hitting Penny like that," said Myrosia.

"Hmmph, they all lawyers, they all prey on people's weaknesses," said Mrs. Dabrowski.

"The third card, the spirit card, is the Page of Cups and it's also reversed. The spirit card is about spiritual lessons or the spiritual issues behind the circumstances. The Page of Cups reversed represents a spoilt person who tries to manipulate people's feelings. This person is not to be trusted. I don't get what spiritual lesson this card is describing. I guess it's just that there are some people who will break your heart if you let them into your life," said Myrosia.

"Obviously the killer is someone that the victims all trusted, but that doesn't get us any closer to knowing who he is," said Joanna.

"I don't know nothing about Tarot cards. When I was a girl we used to drip candle wax into water and look at the shapes, or make tea from dried herbs and look at the leaves in the cup. We had lots of old magic rituals, but I didn't know nobody who had Tarot cards, so I don't know for sure, but I think you're making a mistake the way you're reading them. You know all the meanings by heart but you don't trust your instinct. You analyze everything too much instead of going with your intuition," said Mrs. Dabrowski.

"Yeah, maybe you're right, Mama," said Myrosia packing up her cards.

Just then Myrosia's cell phone vibrated and she looked down at the caller ID.

"Shit, it's Jeff again. I've been ignoring his calls, but I guess I'd better talk to him," said Myrosia walking into the bedroom to take the call.

"Hi Jeff. Sorry I couldn't take your calls yesterday. I've been really busy. I know you've been trying to reach me," said Myrosia.

"I wanted to make sure you got all that stuff I sent you about Shelly Hammett and tell you my news," said Jeff.

"Yeah, I did. Thanks. That's a lot of reading. I'm still working through it all," said Myrosia.

"I guess you heard about Bob's wife Janice, and that girl Christine. That explains why I couldn't find her back when you wanted me to track her down. Do you want me to find out everything I can about Janice?" he asked.

"Yeah, that's a good idea. If there was any way to find out where she was staying after she left Bob, that would be great, and if we could find out who she was seeing, that would be really helpful too. I know you've already looked for information about Christine, but maybe you could give it another try," said Myrosia.

"I did find out something else. I guess that girl Christine liked old guys because not only was she getting it on with Dave, but with Bob too," he said.

"With Bob? Where did you hear that?" asked Myrosia.

"I heard some of the girls in the office talking about it. When the news about her murder came out everyone in the office was talking about it. I guess he was seeing her after Dave dumped her. He was seeing her around the time she disappeared. His new girlfriend should be pretty nervous, or she would be if she had any brains," said Jeff.

"What new girlfriend?" asked Myrosia.

"Didn't you hear? He's been seeing the other bimbo on the TV show, Anika Neilson," said Jeff.

"Are you sure? I thought she was dating that tennis player Ole Rasmus. I saw Anika with Ole at Shelly's funeral," said Myrosia confused.

"What can I say, I guess she gets around and so does Bob. They were seen having dinner together last Wednesday night. But I can't talk long. I'm on my way to the airport. I mainly called to tell you my good news. I'm coming to Florida. I'll be there tonight some time. I'll call you when I get there," said Jeff.

"That's great. I've gotta go," said Myrosia not really hearing what he said.

She hung up the phone and threw herself sobbing down onto the bed.

"That lying bastard. How could I get conned again," she wailed.

Chapter 30

Myrosia cried, screamed, threw a few pillows, and discussed the matter endlessly with Joanna and her mother. But then remembered that she still had to call the jeweler in Buffalo to see if she could get a receipt for the jewelry that Dave had bought Shelly. She had a long talk with the jeweler and by the time she got off the phone she had formulated a new theory about the murders.

Phil arrived at 6:15 to pick up Joanna and she told him about what Myrosia had learned that day.

"I think we should stick around for a little while just in case it gets ugly when he gets back here," said Joanna.

When Bob walked in the door at 6:30 Myrosia practically had steam coming out of her ears.

"Where have you been all afternoon? Phil tells me you left the police station before noon," asked Myrosia coldly.

"Around. I just drove around. I had a shitty morning and I needed to be alone so I went over to the Apollo Beach power station to watch the manatees for a while. Then I just drove to the beach and sat in the car. I guess I should have called. I wasn't thinking," said Bob.

"You had a shitty day did you? You poor thing. Well I've had an enlightening one. You lying son of a bitch. I heard about your latest conquest. I just got off the phone with the jeweler Mr. Goldstein. I called him to discuss some other matters and to find out who bought the Celtic cross pin for Shelly and he let slip that you had been in to his shop to buy some jewelry on Friday. He wondered how I liked the earrings!" Myrosia screamed at him.

"I don't know why you're so upset. Those earrings were for my mother. It's her birthday next week. You can ask Ingrid, she couriered

296

them out to her on Friday afternoon," he said.

"I don't believe you, and I don't give a shit who the earrings were for. You lied to me about Christine and about Anika. I told you I wouldn't tolerate any more of your lies or omissions," Myrosia sobbed.

"What are you talking about? What about Christine and Anika?" asked Bob puzzled.

"Don't give me that puzzled, innocent look. I know all about your affair with Christine and now it seems you're busy romancing Anika. Is that where you were this afternoon, fucking her in some hotel room? Or did you pick up some other tramp for a quickie between the Sheriff's office and here?" screamed Myrosia.

"Whoa, hold on there Myrosia. I definitely did not have anything to do with Christine, and I certainly have not spent the afternoon fucking anyone. I know Dave hurt you, but I haven't done anything. Is this what it's going to be like every time I've been out of your sight for a few hours? If so, I'm not interested. I don't need the drama. I had enough of that with Janice. I thought you were different," said Bob.

"Just get out. I never want to see you again. There's your suitcase and the rest of your stuff's in that garbage bag," screamed Myrosia pointing to where his belongings were piled by the door.

"Wait a minute, this doesn't make any sense. What set this off? What makes you think I had anything to do with Christine?"

"It's the talk of the office," said Myrosia.

"You're kicking me out based on office gossip?" said Bob incredulously.

"So you've got the nerve to deny it? What about you and Anika?" asked Myrosia.

"What about Anika? I always thought she seemed like the nicest of the four women on the show, but I hardly know her. I'm certainly not sleeping with her," said Bob.

"Oh give me a break Bob, you'd screw anything that casts a shadow," said Myrosia.

"We've been through all that before Myrosia. I'm getting really tired of you bringing this up. All that was before we got together. I am not seeing anyone," said Bob through clenched teeth.

"Well what was the business trip to Rochester all about? I know it wasn't any business trip because you didn't take your briefcase. You came down here and killed Shelly. I don't know why I didn't see it before. I can't believe I fell for your lies. I trusted you, and you took advantage of me," said Myrosia.

"I went to Rochester that weekend. I went to see Rhyanna's mother. She's in a nursing home. I go three or four times a year just to check on her, she's got no one else. I don't know why I'm still doing it. She's got Alzheimer's and doesn't even know who I am. I chose that weekend to go because I wanted to give you a chance to stay in my apartment where you'd be safe. I wanted to give you some space, some time to think about us," he said.

"Saint Bob, go ahead and try that on a jury. It just might work. I know that you killed Janice and the others. You are evil. You killed them and then tried to pin it on your best friend Dave. Well I'm going to see that they convict you for this," Myrosia seethed.

"This is nuts. Phil would you tell her…" Bob pleaded.

"Myrosia, there's been some …" Phil began, but Myrosia cut him off.

"Don't try and stick up for him. It's taken me this long to see through his charming façade, but scratch beneath the surface and you'll find out what you're really dealing with. I suppose you stole the trust account money too and tried to pin it on Dave. Well I'm going to find that money and get it back," said Myrosia.

"You're insane. I can't believe it. It's all about the money. I can't believe that you of all people would try and pin this on me just to get Dave off so you can get the money back. You're just as mercenary as every other woman. You don't care about me. It was all an act. It's all about the money. It always is. I'm out of here," said Bob picking up some of his things and tossing them out into the outer hallway.

"Bob, stop. Stay where you are," said Mrs. Dabrowski.

"Mama, stay out of this," said Myrosia.

"Prosie, enough. Time for you to sit down, shut up, and calm yourself," said Mrs. Dabrowski.

"Just get him out of here," shouted Myrosia and she stomped

off into her bedroom.

"I don't need this. I'm out of here," said Bob picking up the last of his things and stomping out the door.

Phil ran out into the hall after Bob the elevator door was just opening.

"I'll talk to her after she calms down…" said Phil.

"Don't bother," said Bob stepping into the elevator. The door closed and he was gone.

Phil went back into the apartment.

"Is Myrosia okay? What should we do?" asked Phil.

"Her mother's in there talking to her. I have never seen her this mad and I've known her my whole life. I think she just needs a little time to calm down. She'll probably sleep for a while and then she'll be better when she wakes up," said Joanna.

"Should we hang around?" asked Phil.

"No, let's go get some dinner and come back," said Joanna.

Mrs. Dabrowski went to get Myrosia a cold, wet cloth for her face, and Joanna and Phil left.

Five minutes later Myrosia was lying on her bed and her mother was sitting on the edge of the bed beside her when the interior doorbell rang.

"Shit, who could that be? Maybe the neighbors called the police to complain about the noise," said Myrosia.

"You stay here prosie. I'll get the door," said her mother.

"No Mama, it's my fault. Whoever it is I'll deal with it," said Myrosia.

Myrosia got up and walked to the door. She peered through the peep hole and was surprised to see Jeff standing there. She opened the door.

"Hi Jeff. What are you doing here?" she asked.

"I know I said I'd call you when I got here but my flight from Buffalo landed a bit early and I got the shuttle over to pick up my rental car and everything was going so smoothly that I just decided to surprise you," he said.

"Oh, it's nice to see you, but, well this is kind of a bad time for me right now. I've got a wicked headache and I was just going to lie down," said Myrosia.

Out of the corner of her eye Myrosia could see her mother duck back into her own bedroom.

"That's okay. I'll stay out of your hair. I'll be working on my computer most of the time anyway. So, where do you want me to put my stuff?" asked Jeff walking into the living room.

"Your stuff?" asked Myrosia perplexed, following him.

"Yeah, where am I going to sleep?" asked Jeff.

"Oh Jeff, I'm sorry but you can't stay here. We really don't have enough room," said Myrosia.

"It's okay. I don't need my own bedroom. I can crash here on the couch," said Jeff setting his suitcase down on the floor and placing his computer bag on the coffee table.

"No, I don't think that's going to work," said Myrosia.

"But Keith sent me down here to help you…" said Jeff.

"Well let's just call Keith and get him to set you up at a nice hotel where you'll be a lot more comfortable," said Myrosia pulling her cell phone out of her pocket.

"Wait Myrosia. Just give me a chance. I love you. You just need to get to know me. I'd treat you way better than Dave ever did. I can give you more than Bob can, and you'd never have to worry about me cheating on you. Just give me a chance," said Jeff reaching for Myrosia's hand. She tried to pull away, but he was too fast. He had a grip on her wrist.

"Sit beside me and talk to me," he said.

They were sitting on the couch with their backs toward her mother's bedroom. Myrosia was leaning as far away from him as she could, her eyes darting around the room as she frantically analyzed her options. Could she break away from him? But where would she run? Would he go after her mother if she got away from him? She couldn't risk it. She'd have to placate him till she thought of something.

"Don't do that Myrosia. Don't pull away from me. Relax, I won't hurt you. We were meant for each other. You're such a good mother. I see how you talk to your kids, even to that bitch Nicki. They don't deserve you. Dave doesn't deserve you. Bob doesn't deserve you. But I'll prove to you that I'm good enough," he said.

"But Jeff, I'm too old for you. I'm old enough to be your mother. You don't want an old woman like me. You want a nice young woman so you can start your own family. I bet you'd be a good father," said Myrosia trying to distract him.

"Yeah, I would. I'd be a good parent, way better than that bitch that gave birth to me. She walked away and abandoned me when I was a baby. I wouldn't do that. I gave her lots of chances to make it up to me, but she wasn't interested. She just used me. Women use me all the time. They ask me to help them and then they just dump me. Janice did that. She wanted help hurting Bob and then once she got her money she didn't need me any more. Christine used me. She wanted my help getting revenge on Dave for dumping her and I did it. He's in jail thanks to me. But she was going to dump me. I could see it in her eyes when she came over to my place. My mother was the worst though. She kept leading me on, pretending that we'd be a family again, but she was lying. Do you want to see where I killed her? It's right over there," he said grabbing Myrosia and dragging her across to the sliding glass door.

"No Jeff, you're hurting me," Myrosia cried.

"Look. Right there, that's where I did it," he said pointing out onto the stretch of beach where Shelly's body had been discovered.

He dragged her back over to the couch and threw her down. She tried to bend her leg to put a knee into his groin, but she missed and hit him in the hip bone instead. He forced himself on top of her and got his hands around her throat.

"You were using me too, weren't you, bitch. You're just like all the others," he hissed into her face.

"No, Jeff, No!" she screamed, and his hands began to tighten around her throat.

Suddenly, miraculously his grip loosened and he went limp. Myrosia gasped for breath and pushed him off of her onto the floor. She looked up and her mother was standing behind the couch with a bronze statue of a heron in her hand.

"Quick Myrosia, I don't think he's dead. We gotta find something to tie him up with." said her mother.

Myrosia jumped to her feet and ran over to the kitchen island

and grabbed an extension cord. Not fast enough though because Jeff was already beginning to stir. Mrs. Dabrowski was attempting to hit him with the bird statue again, but he was too fast for her and he pulled it out of her hand. He stumbled to his feet and Mrs. Dabrowski ran toward the back stairway door. Myrosia chased after him, ready to tackle him to protect her mother. Just then the doors burst open. Phil rushed in through the back stairwell door while two Sheriff's deputies rushed in through the front door.

"Stop! Police! Freeze! Put down your weapon." shouted the deputies with their weapons raised.

The events of the next few seconds seemed to happen in slow motion. Jeff turned and made a leap toward the one deputy, swinging the statue at the officer's head. At that same moment Phil made a lunge and jumped between Jeff and the two women. A shot was fired and Jeff slumped to the floor, a pool of blood beginning to widen on the tile floor underneath him.

Phil helped Mrs. Dabrowski to a chair and the two deputies made a quick sweep of the apartment.

"All clear, get the paramedics in here," the deputy shouted.

The first team of paramedics rushed in and began ministering to Jeff, but it was too late, the deputy's bullet had gotten him directly in the heart. A second team rushed in to attend to Myrosia and her mother.

Bob and Joanna pushed their way in through the pandemonium.

Mrs. Dabrowski was waving away the paramedic. "I'm fine, look after my daughter."

Myrosia was sitting on the floor sobbing uncontrollably. Bob knelt down on the floor beside her and she leaned her head into him.

Chapter 31

By the time the police were done questioning everyone and they were allowed to leave the crime scene it was almost 11 pm. The paramedics suggested that Myrosia and her mother should go to the hospital for observation, but they refused. So Bob booked the four of them into the largest two bedroom suite at the Don Cesar Hotel.

"I didn't think any of us wanted to be alone tonight, and I know it's going to be cozy with the four of us in two bedrooms, but I think we can manage. Joanna, the front desk clerk had a present for you. Here's some earplugs. You and Mama Dabrowski go and sleep in that room with the two beds," Bob said.

He turned to Myrosia.

"You, come with me. We can continue our fight in the morning if you want, after we have a good night sleep, but for now I want to know that you're safe in my bed," he said.

Myrosia hesitated.

"Mama D, would you please tell your daughter what you told me, to smarten up?" said Bob.

"Myrosia, go to bed. We'll talk tomorrow," said her mother.

Bob held out his hand to her and she walked into the room with him and they closed the door. Once alone inside he pulled her close to him.

"I'm so sorry I said what I did to you, and I'm sorry for how it all looked. I don't want to fight with you. I can't imagine how frightening that must have been for you tonight. Come to bed and get some sleep. You can lie in my arms or you can stay far over on the other side of this king sized bed. It's up to you. Tomorrow I'll leave if you want, but for tonight I want to stay with you," he said.

"I'm sorry too, Bob. I got everything all wrong," Myrosia replied.

They got into bed and she lay in his arms. She woke up several times, crying, disoriented and shaking and he soothed her back to sleep.

Late the next morning the four of them were about to sit down at the table to eat breakfast from room service when Phil arrived.

"Hi Phil, my hero, come on in. Sit down and eat with us. We've got lots of food here," said Joanna giving him a big kiss.

Myrosia went and pulled one of the chairs off the balcony and brought it over to the table. When they were all seated Myrosia spoke.

"Mama, thank you so much, you saved my life. I'm so sorry I ever suggested that you couldn't look after yourself. Obviously I was wrong. Kocham ci. I love you."

"Kocham ci, prosie," said her mother.

"But I'm really confused about how everyone got there the way they did? It seemed like one minute he was choking me and the next minute the room was filled with people. How did you know something was off about Jeff? How did you know that we were going to need help?" asked Myrosia.

"That was easy, I saw him outside the church at that Hammett woman's funeral on Monday. He was hanging around watching from near the back of the spectators, but I could see him real clear from where I was sitting in the car. I didn't think nothing of it at the time. I didn't know who he was. You never saw him because you were going into the church, and then when you was coming out you didn't see nothing because the big guy Lemoyne was blocking you. So, when he came into the apartment and told you that he had just come from Buffalo, I knew he was lying. It made me wonder, why he should lie about something like that? That's when I called Joanna and told her to get back here right away and bring her police detective with her.

"Then when I heard him tell you he loved you, I got thinking about the Tarot cards you and Joanna were talking about. You know I don't know nothing about Tarot cards, but I remembered you talking about someone who was devious and pretends to be a friend, but who will manipulate you and break your heart. I never thought that was Bob the cards was talking about, so I called him up and told him that if he really loved you he should smarten up and get back here fast.

"Then when I heard the young man talking so strange about how bad his mother treated him. That's when I called 911 and I left the phone near the bedroom door so that it would record everything. When he grabbed you and you screamed, that's when I pushed my wrist button to summon the ambulance and when he started to choke you, I grabbed the heavy bird statue and came rushing out to clobber him. I wasn't going to let him hurt my baby," explained Mrs. Dabrowski.

"Well, you sure did everything right. I don't know anyone who could connect all those pieces of the puzzle and know what to do so fast. You sure got the cavalry charging over there. Lights and sirens were coming from all directions. And it was pretty smart to put that phone where the 911 operator could hear everything. It's all on tape. There's no question about how it all went down. The deputy who shot him has been thoroughly interrogated, but there's no question that it was justified. He had no other choice. I'm telling you, Mama D, you should be working for us," said Phil.

"When I answered the phone and all you said was to come back right away and bring Phil, I started to protest, but when you told me to shut up and listen for a change, I knew it was serious," said Joanna.

Bob spoke, "I almost didn't come back. I was so angry and hurt about the things you said to me Myrosia that I was just going to drive to the airport and get on the first plane I could back to Buffalo. I know I was being childish. But then when your Mama called and said that if I loved you I'd better smarten up and come back, I figured it might be my last chance to salvage our relationship. When I think how close you came to being killed..." Bob said.

"Not to mention that you'd have been the number one suspect if we'd walked in here and found two bodies right after the fight you and Myrosia had," said Phil.

Phil continued. "I came over this morning because I figured there were some things about all this that you needed to know. It turns out that what Jeff told Myrosia was true. He was Shelly's son from her first marriage when she was a teenager. She left him with his father and took off in search of fame and fortune. His father remarried and he had a stepmother that treated Jeff pretty badly and really warped his feelings about women. I guess that combined with his gift for computer hacking created the perfect storm," Phil explained.

"He was a smart kid and finished college early. After college he tracked down his mother, found out that she was now married to Trey Hammett and moved to Buffalo to get closer to her. He decided to take the job at your law office, Bob, because your wife Janice was one of the co-stars on the TV show with his mother. Jeff was Shelly's stalker. He'd call her and e-mail her and text her. It didn't matter if she changed her phone number or her e-mail address, he'd find it again. She knew who he was, and she must have suspected that he was nuts, but she didn't go to the police or even confide to Trey the truth about it because she didn't want that whole part of her early life to come out in the tabloids. I guess she'd been working as a prostitute for a while back then under a different name.

"Apparently Jeff had inherited his mother's love of money. His online research business that he told Myrosia about was actually computer hacking, bank fraud, and blackmail. I think that part of his twisted thinking was that if he had enough money he'd be able to get his mother back, but she kept brushing him off.

"Jeff befriended Janice during the time that she and Bob were breaking up and he offered to help her get revenge on Bob. In his mind Janice was his replacement for Shelly, but Janice brushed him off too, so then Myrosia became the new mother replacement target.

"The murder of Christine was different. She appears to have been just a naïve young woman who befriended the geeky guy at work, let him into her life and got murdered for her kindness. She had an insurance settlement from her parents, who'd been killed in a house fire, and he saw an opportunity to get the money. Rochester police are taking another look at that house fire just in case, but so far it looks like it was an accident. She had been having an affair with Dave and thought Dave loved her. But Dave was just having a fling and when he ended it she was devastated and turned to her friend Jeff for sympathy. I don't think she really wanted revenge. She probably just wanted a friend to listen to her. Jeff took her up to his apartment and I don't know what triggered it, whether they had a fight, or if she saw something that she shouldn't have pertaining to Janice's murder, or if it was just a convenient opportunity, but he strangled her and popped her into the freezer. Then he arranged for movers to pack up her apartment and move everything into storage in Rochester to make it look like she had moved out of town. He then siphoned off her bank accounts and insurance settlement money and transferred it around to offshore accounts. Forensic accountants will be tracking that money for ages. He just kept the body in the freezer until a couple of weeks ago and then plunked her in his fancy big Toyota truck and dumped her out in the bush when they were expecting a lot of snow. My suspicion is that he was planning on moving on shortly so that even if her body, or parts of it, were found come spring, he'd be long gone.

"When Shelly came down here to Florida with Dave he tried one last time to connect with her. From what we've been able to piece together, we think he texted Shelly, maybe pretending to be Trey, and asked her to meet him down on the beach. We haven't been able to confirm that yet because her phone and computer hard drive had been completely erased, including the online backup service she used, and the cell phone company system, but we've got techs working on trying to recover all that. She'd been fighting with Dave and was ready to go back home to Trey and knew that Trey was in town for the Superbowl, so she went running down to the beach to meet him. Instead she comes face to face with her stalker and he ends up killing her. No one knows for sure what took place during that confrontation because both of the participants are dead. They may have sat on the sand together and talked for a while drinking the bottle of wine that he had brought with him as a gift for her, or maybe he drank the wine before hand and just had the empty bottle with him, or maybe the bottle just happened to be sitting there from a previous beach drinker we don't know, but there were no prints on the bottle, so somebody must have very carefully wiped it clean. If he was the one who brought it, why he didn't just take the empty bottle away with him and dispose of it miles away still has us stumped. But who knows how this guy's twisted thought process worked." He shrugged.

"He messed up on Shelly's money though. Because the body was found immediately, he wasn't able to suck any of her money out of her accounts after she died. There were some offshore transfers done earlier in the week, but we thought Dave had done that. So now we aren't sure whether Shelly herself made the transfers on Dave's behalf, or Dave had done it, or if Jeff had done it in advance. One way or the other, he didn't seem to get much money from Shelly. Maybe he didn't bother stealing it because he knew that according to her will, he'd have been entitled to a share of Shelly's estate anyway. That is, of course, assuming that he was never convicted in her death. And I can't see how we'd have connected him if he hadn't made this move on Myrosia. We think that his half-sister Ginny was going to be his next target based on some crazy stuff the Erie County investigators found in his apartment when they searched it this morning.

"He's been tracking Myrosia's emails, voice mail messages, computer searches, everything. We know that he's been following her and obsessing about her for months because when the Erie County guys went in to his place, they found thousands of surveillance pictures of Myrosia, photos taken from the beach looking into her house, photos of her driving down the road, photos of her grocery shopping. You name it, he had it. He had similar photos of Shelly but those went back for years and he had scrapbooks full of newspaper clippings about her. He had some pictures of Janice, but not nearly as many as he had of Myrosia."

Myrosia cut in. "Did he have any nude photos of me, like in the shower or anything?" she asked, thinking of the nude pictures she had seen on Dave's computer.

"No, not that I'm aware of, just pictures he could get from a distance with a telephoto lens. There were lots of pictures of you in your bathing suit in your pool at home. He had the GPS on your phone set up to tell him exactly where you were at all times. He was doing the same thing with Bob and so when Bob left the condo here in Madeira Beach, Jeff was ready to make his move. We think that when Myrosia moved in with Bob at his condo in Buffalo, instead of taking Jeff up on his offer of help, he felt like he was being rejected again," replied Phil.

They were silent for a moment and then Bob spoke quietly.

"I still don't understand about Janice's murder. How and where did he do it, and how did he dispose of her body?"

"How much detail do you want? This is delicate. It might be something that you'd want to discuss privately," said Phil.

"No, I want Myrosia to know and the others might as well hear it at the same time. But just give us the general idea. None of us need any more material for nightmares," said Bob.

"Well it seems that Janice had been having numerous affairs for some time. I think you already knew that," said Phil.

Bob nodded.

"Apparently she had a short dalliance with your partner Peter, but that ended some time during the summer when she took up with your partner Keith. Apparently she was into S&M, some very rough stuff and it had been getting progressively rougher. When she moved out of your condo she didn't tell you where she was going, but she had moved onto your partner Keith's boat. Apparently they were having sex there and also at some club Keith owned in Buffalo."

"So that's who owned that club. I'd been going under the assumption that it belonged to Dave. Joanna and I even staked the place out one night." said Myrosia.

"Well maybe Dave's a shareholder, I wouldn't know about that, but Keith is the primary owner. I wouldn't be surprised if there are charges laid against Keith in regards to this, but I really don't know. Keith acknowledges that he and Janice had sex on his boat. He roughed her up pretty badly, but he insists that she was alive when he left her. Jeff must have showed up sometime after Keith left. He strangled her, tied her up, hacked off most of her hair, and took the boat out and dumped her. He left some of her clothes and other DNA evidence on the boat. I don't think Keith ever had any idea that she was dead. He just thought that he had gone too far that time and she had walked out.

"Now the interesting thing is that this kid Jeff also took some of her hair and blood and saliva coated clothing and put it on each of the other three partners' boats as well. They found some on your sailboat Bob, on Dave's and Myrosia's sailboat, and on Peter's cruiser. They searched each of your boats last Friday once they had tentatively identified the body. I guess Jeff's idea was to plant evidence on each of the boats, maybe to try and implicate each of you, but who knows for sure what this nut case was thinking," said Phil.

"So they already knew that she was dead and suspected that one of us had murdered her last Friday, the day they kept us busy at the office answering questions about the waterfront development deal? I wonder how they got a warrant for the search? I'm surprised that nobody from the marina let that slip," said Bob.

"I don't know how they managed the search warrant, extenuating circumstances I guess. The marina's pretty quiet these days with the boats sitting in storage, just the manager and a night time security guard and it was a real fast search. Only the manager knew anything. He had no idea what they were looking for and he'd been warned to keep quiet. Initially they searched Dave's boat and your boat, Bob, and they found her hair and clothes on both of them, which was confusing enough, but besides that, the scenes didn't look right. The stuff looked like it had been planted. That's when they searched the other two boats. On Tuesday they concluded that the actual crime scene was Keith's boat," said Phil.

"I'm surprised they let me get on the plane on Saturday."

"Well I guess originally they were looking at Dave for it since he was already charged with Shelly's murder, and besides they were thinking that if you were going to kill her, you'd have done it before you gave her all that money. But believe me they were keeping a tab on you," said Phil.

"I think you mean that you were keeping a tab on me."

"At first, sort of, but then…" Phil began, but Joanna cut in.

"Wait a minute, what are you saying? That you were just hanging around to spy on Bob? I thought you really liked me and here you were just using me. You asshole! Was fucking me a part of your assignment too or just a little perk of the job? I can't believe I fell for your bullshit," screamed Joanna, tears streaming from her eyes. "I don't need to hear any more. I'm going through to the bedroom before I kill you."

"No Joanna, you've got it all wrong. We don't work that way. I'm no undercover agent. I was warned to stay away from you if I wanted to keep my job, but I couldn't do it. I fell for you the first night I met you, that night we played pool. That was before I ever heard Bob's name. I've been with you every minute that I wasn't at work because I couldn't tear myself away. I've been risking my job to be with you. You can't even begin to imagine how much explaining I had to do about how come I was with you last night when all this went down," said Phil.

"I don't believe you, asshole," she cried and ran out of the room.

"Wait Joanna…" said Phil starting to rise from his chair to follow her.

"No Phil, stay where you are. She wasn't kidding. She's angry enough to kill. I know what that's like," Myrosia said glancing sheepishly at Bob. "Give her a little time to calm down. Let me get you another coffee. You must be exhausted. Did you get any sleep last night?"

"No I haven't slept yet, but I'm fine. I'm supposed to be sleeping right now, but I figured you needed to know what was going on, so I told my boss that I'd come down and fill you in," said Phil.

"You don't have to keep going. We can hear the rest of the details later," said Myrosia.

"No I'm fine," he said, putting on his cop face, but the cracking in his voice belied his words.

Muffled cries and the sound of something being thrown could be heard from the bedroom.

"Joanna just needs a little time to cry. She'll be fine, she's pretty tough. Right now she's just really upset. That was probably just her purse or a shoe that she threw. She's hurt, she really fell for you too, and now she's feeling like an idiot. I know what that's like. You can talk to her after she's calmed down."

Phil cleared his throat and continued.

"The Erie County guys found some hair in Jeff's apartment that they haven't confirmed yet, but they're pretty sure it belonged to Janice. I guess he was keeping a trophy. He really seemed to like blondes. Like I said the murder of that girl Christine was different. But I don't think his interest in Janice was sexual. She reminded him of Shelly, but mainly, I think he wanted her money. He knew that she was negotiating a settlement with Bob and he waited until it had been transferred to her before he killed her. Once she was dead he transferred her money around and made it look like she was diversifying into different investments, paid her bills, parked her Jaguar at the long term parking at the airport, sent off emails to a few of her friends for a while to make it look like she was travelling, so nobody noticed she was gone. Not that she had that many real friends," said Phil.

"Would she still be alive if I hadn't given her that money?" asked Bob.

"No, I don't think so. He was about to kill Myrosia and that wasn't for money. His issues regarding women were a lot more complicated than that," said Phil.

"If she had moved onto Keith's boat, I can see why she didn't take everything out of the apartment. I guess she figured I'd let her come and get the rest of her things later, when she decided where she was going to be living. What was the date that she was killed?" asked Bob.

Phil looked down at his note pad.

"Late on the evening of October 13 or sometime in the early hours of October 14. October 13 was the last day that Keith claims he was with her, and it coincides with the bruising on her body," said Phil.

"The papers were signed and the money transferred on October 8. On the thirteenth I was in New York City. I had tickets to see Phantom, and then I flew down to see my mother in Barbados," said Bob in a low voice.

"Yeah, we know. They checked." said Phil.

"Did they also check where I was the night Shelly was killed?" asked Bob. "Myrosia thinks I was down here in Florida that Friday night."

"Yes, we checked. You weren't in Florida. Your Rochester alibi holds up," said Phil.

"I'm sorry, Bob. I didn't really think you had murdered anyone. I didn't know what to think. I was just so confused," said Myrosia.

Bob did not say anything. He just put his hand over Myrosia's.

"So it was Jeff who lied about where he went that weekend. He told me he went to Chicago to a comic convention," said Myrosia.

"It seems that the Chicago Comic Con is held in July, not February, but how would you be expected to know that," said Phil.

"Jeff had offered to stay with me that weekend. Maybe if I had taken him up on his offer, Shelly would still be alive," said Myrosia.

"But you would almost certainly be dead. That kid was a fruitcake. And he would have gotten to Shelly eventually, if not that weekend then some other time. He'd already gotten away with killing two women by that point, and maybe more. They're going through cold case files everywhere looking for others," said Phil.

Phil continued. "For the record, he made up that stuff he told you about Bob and the Bennett girl, and Bob and the other television celebrity Anika Neilson, just to get you suspicious of Bob. The Neilson woman was in Sweden with her tennis star boyfriend on Wednesday when Jeff claimed she was having dinner with Bob."

"I'm so embarrassed by my behavior yesterday. I'm so sorry I didn't believe Bob. I guess I was just…" Myrosia faltered.

"It's okay honey, I understand," said Bob.

Myrosia continued. "I think I understand why I couldn't figure it out before. I was assuming that they were crimes of passion. I figured that if all three of the killings were done by the same person, then they would have the same motive, but they didn't. Although we didn't know it at the time, Janice and Christine were killed for money. The motive for Shelly's murder was a combination of passion and revenge. I would have ended up being the fourth one and it would have been passion. Not passion in the sense of love, but anger. He was projecting onto me the mother figure that Shelly never was to him," said Myrosia.

"Now that I'm seeing things a little more clearly today than I was yesterday, I think I know what happened to the trust account money. Dave's been saying all along that he didn't touch it, and I think he's telling the truth about that," said Myrosia.

"What's your theory?" asked Bob.

"All of the partners were desperate for money because they knew that the house of cards was about to come crashing down with the waterfront development fiasco. Well maybe desperate isn't exactly the right word in your case, Bob, but you've got to admit that even you're feeling the pinch what with giving all that money to Janice, and knowing that the partnership was about to fold. But I don't think that $300,000 would be incentive enough to make you risk criminal charges," said Myrosia.

Bob shrugged. "Go on."

"We know that Dave committed mortgage fraud to scrape together money and then he took off. He came down here to Florida initially, but I think his plan was to run off to the Caribbean, change his name again and disappear with as much money as he could lay his hands on. He was running when he got arrested, but it wasn't because he had committed murder. He was running to get to the money because he was arrogant and stupid enough to think that he could get away," said Myrosia.

"That Dawid is an idiot," said her mother.

"I'm following you so far," said Bob.

"Keith got into the sex club business partly because it was his hobby, his fetish, and partly because he needed the money. I can't prove it, and I don't care enough to look into it, but I suspect that Keith has a number of other sex related businesses. I'm pretty sure that the porn pictures of Janice and Shelly and a couple of other women actually came from Keith's computer. I suspect that Keith's little sidelines are probably earning him enough to withstand the losses from the waterfront thing.

"Peter is the only one left. He's a little weasel. I caught him going through Dave's files that first day after Dave left me. He claimed he was looking for something regarding a divorce case that Dave had asked him to handle, but that isn't what he was doing. He was planting evidence to make it look like Dave had stolen the money.

"Peter stole the trust account money because he saw an

opportunity. He knew what Dave was doing in the days leading up to that Monday when Dave left and he took advantage of the situation to steal the money and try and pin it on him. We know that he was having an affair with Stella in the office and he used her to steal the money. Stella isn't the sharpest pencil in the box and she didn't know initially that she was doing anything wrong, but eventually she figured it out and started putting pressure on Peter. He couldn't fire her because she knew too much and she was pressuring him to divorce Penny and marry her. That's what caused him to snap and hit Penny that day. By the way, it's not important, but Peter was the one who gave Shelly the Celtic cross pin. Apparently he's awfully proud of his Irish heritage," said Myrosia.

"So what's happening with that swinia Dawid?" asked Mrs. Dabrowski.

"They're making arrangements to cut him loose. They've already moved him out of the general population and into an individual holding cell, but before they let him go, they wanted to check with the FBI and the IRS just in case they want a crack at him," said Phil.

"Let's hope he rots in there," said Mrs. Dabrowski.

Epilogue

The house looked beautiful. Everything was exactly as the bride had envisioned. Even the weather had cooperated on this beautiful Saturday in early June. It was spectacular. When the guests drove up the circular driveway to the massive front doors, uniformed valets were waiting to take the cars away to be parked in the parking lot. There was a coat check for the guests just inside the front door where the office had once been located.

The party tent looked like a fairytale castle, gleaming white against the green of the lawn, the turquoise water of Lake Erie, and the azure blue of the sky. Aside from some early morning hysterics from the bride over minor changes in the seating plan for dinner, the wedding went off without a hitch. The guest list turned out to be much smaller than was originally planned. It seemed that after the sordid events of the winter many of their former friends had found that they were unable to attend the festivities. But, in spite of everything that had transpired, the bride had gotten her wish, her father was there to walk her down the aisle.

The photographer and his assistants had finished taking the formal photographs and were snapping casual shots as the orchestra played in the background and uniformed waiters moved carefully among the assembled guests, serving champagne. In a few moments everyone would be seated for dinner.

But it's all a beautiful façade. Just like most of my adult life has been up until now. Glamorous on the outside, but covering up a foundation of lies and deceit, thought Myrosia.

Everything was rented from the wedding suppliers. Even this house, that had once been their dream home, was no longer theirs. It was sold, and the closing would be in a few days. Then what? The Tower card had been accurate. Her old life was gone. She was starting over, and she had no idea what would happen next. There had been so many things to settle between her and Dave, and the preparation for this wedding had taken up a lot of her time and energy. They really couldn't afford this grandiose spectacle, but she still wasn't able to say no to her soon to be ex-husband or her daughter. She worried about her daughter, and worried more for her new son-in-law. How would he ever be able to stand up to Nicki's demands? But, as she kept reminding herself, that was her new son-in-law's problem now.

She liked to think that their son Dylan was more like her, competent and practical. He was having no trouble taking this whole shift in fortune in stride. Money and prestige had never been as important to him as it was to Nicki. Completing graduate school would have to wait for a while, but he was fine with that, it seems that he had never really cared about getting a Ph.D. He was only doing it to appease his father. He would be leaving shortly to work with some friends he had met at school in England, running a start-up technology firm in India, creating affordable solar electrical power generators and water treatment systems. So for him, all of these changes might actually turn out to be a good thing.

She still could not understand her daughter Nicki. She was so much like her father, so demanding and always putting on a big show. It had been so humiliating going to the new in-laws to ask for help in paying for all this. Nicki still behaved like a princess with a trust fund, but the truth was that once today's charade was over and everything that was left was sold, there would be just barely enough to satisfy the creditors.

All the investment properties in the various corporate names had either been seized by the lenders or sold at bargain basement prices to vulture investors. Myrosia might still be left with a few small debts but, as long as she could find a way to support herself, she would be able to avoid bankruptcy.

Dave would not be quite so lucky. He was being sued by everyone involved in the waterfront development scandal. Myrosia's mother was suing Dave and the banks to try and get her investments back. Bob was handling that for her pro bono. The murder charges against Dave had been dropped, and somehow he had managed to slide out from under the attempted bribery charges. Knowing Dave the way she did, she suspected that he would probably be able to make a deal and get off with limited jail time and some community service for the fraud charges. But still, he was facing censure from the New York State Bar Association and would probably be disbarred. What would he do if he couldn't practice law? This was also not her problem. Why should she even care after all this?

Not surprisingly, neither Peter nor Keith, nor their wives, came to the wedding. The partnership among the four lawyers had been dissolved and Peter and Keith were mired in their own legal, financial, and marital problems. Bob was left with the task of selling off everything in order to wind up the partnership affairs. He still had a few outstanding cases to be settled, but other than Myrosia's mother's lawsuit, he was not accepting any new ones. Dave was furious that Bob had been invited to the wedding, but Mrs. Dabrowski had insisted. Bob was family as far as she was concerned.

It had not exactly been a fairytale ending. After that terrible night, none of them had wanted to go back to stay at the Madeira Beach condo, so when the Pinellas County police told them they were no longer needed they returned to Buffalo. Myrosia had spent the weeks since returning from Florida on Craigslist selling off everything that she and her mother could live without. Joanna had cleaned out her apartment, quit her job and gotten in her tin can of a car and headed straight back to Florida as fast as her wheels would take her.

Myrosia and Bob were still dealing with their own issues. Coming so close to death that awful night, Myrosia still had nightmares and moments of panic and felt unable to trust her own judgment about people. If she was not able to see the truth about Jeff, and did not see the truth about Dave for so long, how could she really be sure about Bob? She still questioned whether it was possible for him to be monogamous, and she knew that she was not interested in a relationship with a man that she could not trust. But Bob decided that he had waited this long, he could wait a little longer. He knew that Mrs. Dabrowski was right, that Myrosia just needed a little more time before she could really commit to a new relationship. Bob knew that he needed some time to recover from the emotional scars left by his failed marriage, the demise of the business partnership, and his wife's murder. As Myrosia had predicted, there was no shortage of women offering to console him, but he just was not interested. For him the months since that night in Florida had been taken up with dealing with Janice's funeral and settling her estate. He was in the process of selling his condo and deciding what to do and where to go once everything was finally settled. The weather had turned nice, and he and Myrosia were spending a lot of time together on his sailboat. But she still had not officially moved in with him, and their future together was uncertain.

While Bob and Myrosia's relationship was still tentative, another relationship was going strong. Myrosia glanced across the lawn and smiled when she saw Joanna, in a new pair of 'hooker heels,' introducing Phil to all the old Polish ladies seated at her mother's table. Mrs. Dabrowski and Joanna were now settled in Florida, but had come back for the wedding. Joanna had a job in a beauty salon and was building up her clientele. The passion between Joanna and Phil was still blazing.

At dinner Myrosia was seated between Dave and the parish priest Father Gorski. She made small talk with both of them, forcing herself to ignore Dave's leg pressed against hers. When he put his hand on her thigh, she glared at him and attempted to brush it away without drawing the attention of the other guests at the table.

After the interminable speeches, during which time both Dave and the parish priest had drunk far too much, it was time for the part of the ritual that she had been dreading most. Nicki expected her to have at least one dance with Dave, as though the events of the past months had never happened, so that the photographer could have a shot of the parents dancing to include in the wedding book. For the sake of appearances, she was expected put on a happy face and pretend to be a loving couple.

By the time they got up on the dance floor, the sun was setting over the lake and the lights on the canopy were twinkling like stars. The romantic setting combined with all of the alcohol Dave had consumed was having an effect.

"Oh Myrosia, honey. It feels so good to hold you like this. We belong together. I haven't had a chance to thank you for everything you did to help me. I know that I owe you my life. If it wasn't for you, I'd probably be sitting on death row right now," he said as the music started and they began to dance.

"It's not like I had a choice. It wasn't like I solved the crime. I just barely managed to keep from being murdered myself. Besides, I didn't do it for you, I did it for Nicki so she could have her fairytale wedding," she replied.

"I love you Myrosia, I've always loved you. Please don't go through with the divorce. I've changed. I think I was just having a mid-life crisis. I'm begging you, give me another chance. I'll make it all up to you. I'll get all of this back for you and more. I've got big plans," he pleaded as he held her tight.

"Look, I've got something here for you, something to show you how serious I am about us," he said loosening his grasp on her for a moment. He reached into his pocket and pulled out the jewelry case containing the wedding rings that she had sold to the jeweler Goldstein way back when all this had started. She had never expected to see them again.

"I managed to buy these back for you from the jeweler. It cost me a bundle, but I got them back. Please, let's start over," he begged.

Tears began to flow from her eyes as he placed them on her finger.

He was such a great dancer. It felt so good to be back in his arms, and he still looked so good in his tuxedo. As their bodies swayed together she found herself wondering if maybe he really had learned something from everything that had transpired. Should she give their marriage another chance? After all, they had been together almost twenty-five years. But then, as she looked up to answer him, she saw that he was looking over her shoulder, smiling at a woman on the other side of the room, and she realized that nothing had really changed. He was still the same old Dave.

"Oh give me a break Dave. You don't love me, and you don't really want me. I don't have enough money any more to satisfy you. You'll find yourself another woman with money to set you up again in no time. But thanks for the rings. I think I'll keep them. You never know when they might come in handy," she hissed as she pushed him away and stomped off.

Suddenly she knew that everything was finally resolved between her and Dave. A huge weight had lifted and she was ready to move on. The confusion, fear, and uncertainty that had plagued her the last few months had cleared. She knew exactly who, and what she wanted, and where she wanted to be. She saw him standing with his back to her at the bar and walked toward him. As if sensing her approach he turned, smiled, and reached out his hand to her. To hell with keeping up appearances, she thought, and ran into his arms and gave him a very un-sisterly kiss.

"I'm ready to run away with you."

If you enjoyed **The Tower** you'll love these upcoming
books in the **Gulf Coast Tarot Mystery Series**

THE LOVERS

Love can be lethal.

When the Lovers card turns up there
are some serious choices to be made.
Something, or someone, will have to
be sacrificed for something else to
be gained. Whatever the decision, it
should not be made lightly, because
the consequences could be fatal.

ISBN: 978-1-926826-36-3

THE EMPRESS

Being a mother can be murder.

The Empress is the giver of earthly
gifts, the fertile mother goddess. This
is the fertile womb where anything can
grow and thrive, including jealousy,
possessiveness, and deceit. Things can
get deadly when someone tries to take
away her "baby."

ISBN: 978-1-926826-37-0

About the author

Irene McGarvie is the author of numerous non-fiction books. This is her first novel.

She loves the sunny beaches of the Gulf Coast of Florida, where she wastes far too much precious beach time sitting indoors at her computer writing.